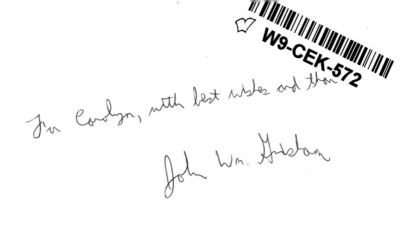

For Carolyn, with best wishes and than[...]

John Wm. Grisham

University

By John William Grisham

University

Published by Aloha Lounge Press
Middletown, Rhode Island

http://www.alohaloungepress.com

This novel is a work of fiction. Names, characters, places, businesses, organizations and incidents are either products of the author's imagination or are used fictitiously. Any resemblance to actual events or locales or to actual persons, living or dead, is entirely coincidental.

10 9 8 7 6 5 4 3 2

ISBN: 978-0-9889604-0-4 (pbk)
ISBN: 978-09889604-2-8 (hbk)
ISBN: 978-0-9889604-1-1 (ebook)

Printed in the United States of America

ACKNOWLEDGMENTS

Thanks to my brother Jerry, for his valuable insights and technical assistance. I am also indebted to Barbara and Erin, my first readers, for their candid comments and suggestions; and to A.J. for the freshman welcoming letter which appears in this volume.

Prologue

[1]

Her audience was a study in contrasts: sober, middle-aged men in dark suits, joined today by two undergraduates in torn jeans and tie-dyed shirts. Professor Julia Horvath, head of Metropolitan University's Classics department, paused as she stood to address the Board of Overseers on behalf of her faculty colleagues. To state the case against the university president, Dr. Fortin Shenford.

Only weeks before—early in the Spring 1970 term—the Faculty Assembly by a four-to-one margin had voted no-confidence in the administration. Previously, the Student Union Senate had taken a similar stand, citing "crimes against free speech." On this March morning, as the board convened to decide Shenford's fate, nearly a thousand had come to bury him, lining the sidewalks of Franklin Street in spite of the frosty New England weather.

WE'LL HELP YOU PACK, read one sign in the crowd. While on a neighboring lawn, a trio of sweatshirted Parker Hall residents sang *Na Na Hey, Kiss Him Goodbye*.

"Miss Horvath, you may proceed." The voice of Chairman Elias Wrentham broke the boardroom's tense silence, four floors above. The window curtains in the background were drawn, concealing a splendid view of the Monadnock River to the north.

"Thank you, Mr. Chairman." Ignoring his omission of her academic rank, she turned to acknowledge her fellow guests—Willard Ferris, her

1

Faculty Assembly co-chair; then the two Student Union representatives. (One male, one female, identically dressed, each with unkempt shoulder-length dark hair.) Then she began her prepared remarks.

"Madam and gentlemen, we are here today because we have serious concerns about the path this university has taken. The history of the present administration is one of constant strife and antagonism toward faculty, students and staff, marked by intimidation, censorship, and ongoing violations of academic freedom. While Dr. Shenford remains president, we have no faith that conditions will improve.

"This administration has intervened personally in tenure decisions, even setting aside unanimous departmental recommendations in order to punish its critics. It has withdrawn support for student publications, including Metropolitan's widely praised campus newspaper, on grounds of editorial content. Of particular concern is its response to the student sit-in last spring, when campus police were called to remove protesters from these offices. There are reports of students being kicked and beaten with billy clubs, and dragged from the building by their hair during this skirmish." The professor turned and glanced about the room, her expression outraged. "This action typifies perfectly the administration's approach toward dissent—to disagree with this administration is to become the target of its vindictive wrath—"

As she spoke, the door to the boardroom opened and the president entered, taking his usual place at the conference table. The familiar gray eyes brimmed with defiance, none fully meeting his gaze in the sudden, heavy silence. Wrentham looked bemused, but seemed loath to interrupt his guest.

Bravely, Horvath forged on. "As employees of the university, we find that there are repercussions—in terms of promotions and salaries—for failure to toe the party line. We are harassed and spied upon, and made the subject of secret dossiers. As tenure candidates, we are questioned at length about our personal beliefs, even subjected to psychiatric inquisition by this man. As if we were his private patients in Boston—"

"Stop!" The iron voice filled the room, with the unmistakable ring of authority. Horvath retreated a step, as all eyes turned in the president's direction. The former Harvard neuropsychiatrist glared at his accusers with unvarnished contempt, his expression unyielding.

"I am not going to sit here and listen to these lies. These allegations have been made time and again, and have as repeatedly been proven false." Shenford permitted himself the faint semblance of a smile. "In truth, I haven't practiced psychiatry in nearly a decade—much as some of our colleagues could use it."

Abruptly, the president stood and walked to the far end of the table, where student spokesman Matt Grubb leaned back heedlessly in his chair, his worn sandals resting on the polished mahogany surface.

"Son, get your feet off that table. Didn't they ever teach you manners?"

Grubb's reply was an insolent smirk. Like his female counterpart, he wore a silver peace medallion around his neck, his unwashed hair in a ponytail. "Lighten up, man..." he chortled under his breath.

Responding with alacrity, Shenford stepped forward and kicked over the chair. Grubb gave a startled squawk, his feet tumbling awkwardly from the table as he fell to the floor in a heap.

In the boardroom, there was stunned silence. The others at the table sat transfixed, seemingly doubting their senses. Grubb made no effort to stand, but stared up at Shenford open-mouthed, eyes wide with shock.

My god, Wrentham thought, he's gone out of his head.

Shenford walked briskly to the door. Opening it, he gestured to the University policeman stationed outside. "Get these troublemakers out of here!" he snapped.

Wrentham was on his feet at once. "Fortin, have you lost your mind—"

"Sit down, Eli!" the president said, as if Wrentham were five years old. "This is a university boardroom—their kind has no business here." He again indicated the outsiders, angered by this breach of the *sanctum sanctorum*. The chairman stood taken aback, his face flushed, unable to respond.

The officer hesitated a split second before entering. He turned to the disinvited guests, waved them from their seats with a sullen "Awright, let's go." The protesters, astonished, remained silent as they were escorted from the room.

From there, Shenford's masterful personality dominated. The president was a fiercely articulate and determined man, aware that his future hung in the balance. Questioned about Met's faculty turnover rate ("the highest of any major university in America," according to former Glanbury City Councilor Nancy Fagan, the sole woman on the board), Shenford replied that his one goal for Metropolitan was excellence, requiring development of a first-rate faculty.

"Although we're not there yet," he conceded, "we have come a long way from the educational backwater I found eight years ago. The quality of our faculty is far superior, in turn attracting a better class of students. With few exceptions, every personnel decision I've made—concerning faculty recruitment or otherwise—has marked a step forward. An improvement over the status quo. And to favor job security at the price of institutional stagnation would defeat that purpose."

Throughout the meeting, Shenford cited his accomplishments—a 50 percent increase in enrollment, with College Board scores for entering freshmen rising an average of 35 points; the tripling of the school's endowment fund; the elimination of operating deficits. Faculty critics were dismissed as "undistinguished charlatans," their credentials disparaged at length. "Why should we tolerate incompetence at any level?" he replied to complaints about his abusive behavior toward subordinates: Deans and administrative assistants reduced to tears;

berating his Vice President for Development for an hour over a shortage of plastic forks at an alumni event.

"Fortin, it seems clear to me that you have a problem with human relations." Walter Abernathy, the chairman of Huddleston Mining, leaned forward in his place. "While not all of these accounts may be true, we've witnessed it firsthand, in the way you dealt with that young man earlier." Several colleagues nodded vigorously, endorsing his stand.

"'That young man' is a prime example of what's gone wrong in this country," Shenford rejoined. "Had they been properly punished for misbehavior as young children, these kids would have learned that actions carry consequences. They would have learned manners, respect for authority, law and order. Instead, it falls to us—and to the courts, and to our legislative bodies—to fill the vacuum left by their doting parents. A vacuum that grows steadily larger each day."

From his briefcase Shenford produced two slightly yellowed copies of the former student newspaper, the University *Press*. Holding them aloft, he proclaimed, "These children run editorials advocating defiance of the draft and legalization of hard drugs, then cry 'free speech' when we refuse to fund this subversion. They trespass on university property, break into private offices, and react with outrage when lawfully removed, demanding amnesty for their illegal actions. Moreover, these extreme positions are not confined to the student body.

"What they are doing—with the encouragement and support of certain elements among the faculty—is seeking sanction for their misdeeds. 'We act, therefore it cannot be wrong.' That is the whole of this generation's moral code!

"Shall these radicals determine university policy? Are we willing to undo eight years of progress on their behalf? To forgo the opportunity of building Metropolitan into the elite learning institution it can become?"

The president paused before quietly adding, "In our own time, we have answered the bugle call. From fighting the Axis forces as young men to containing the expansion-minded Soviets, we have faced down every threat to the American way of life. How can you now think of surrendering to these coffeehouse revolutionists?"

From his supporters, there were nods of assent. "Hear, hear," Edward Poole, one of the city's leading financiers and the president's staunchest ally on the board, seconded.

Forgoing lunch, the board began an hour of heated deliberation, with Shenford and his partisans often shouting down opponents. Finally, Woody Glenn moved the question of the president's discharge.

"Second, Mr. Chairman!" Jacob Klein shouted.

Shenford remained motionless in his chair, his stomach knotted with tension as the roll-call progressed. At forty-eight he was still comparatively young, and would not lack for options. Yet far more than his position was at stake.

From his earliest years, Fortin Shenford had known that he was destined for greatness. His stewardship of Metropolitan, even the Nobel Prize he'd nearly won at Harvard—to his mind only the beginning, the prelude to greater glory. Though now everything hinged on this ballot.

"There is before the Board a motion that Dr. Fortin Shenford be dismissed as University president," Wrentham somberly intoned. "The Secretary reports nineteen votes in favor of the motion—that is, in favor of dismissal—with fourteen opposed..."

A thin smile of triumph formed on Shenford's lips.

Wrentham's voice quavered. "The vote falls short of the two-thirds majority required under our by-laws for removal of an officer. The motion fails."

Against the odds, Shenford had won. And now he was here to stay.

The news conference was marked by terse exchanges. Wrentham, appearing shell-shocked, spoke vaguely of the need "to put this unpleasantness behind ourselves, and move forward." The president thanked his employers for their vote of confidence, again disclaiming any intention to resign.

"I'll know when I'm no longer wanted here," Shenford said tartly.

In his School of Journalism office overlooking Alston Boulevard, Willard Ferris sat behind the plain metal desk, across from Channel 8's Ed Graddick. Like other local newsmen, Graddick was acquainted with Ferris, until recently a successful colleague. And who alone among the dissidents would appear on camera.

"An overwhelming majority of the faculty here had earlier called on Dr. Shenford to step down," Graddick said by way of introduction. "The students apparently feel the same way. And today, a plurality of Met's governing board turned thumbs down on his leadership. How can he refuse to step aside gracefully, given this lack of support?"

"Ed, you do not know this man." The professor's voice, like his rumpled features, seemed old and tired. "He is utterly without shame."

Within days, Elias Wrentham announced his resignation from the board. By mid-April four other Shenford critics had departed, setting the stage for Edward Poole's election to the chairmanship. From there the president's forces succeeded in packing the board with loyalists, as opponents left in frustration.

For Shenford, the hour of crisis had passed. Though the lesson had been taken to heart. His foes would get no second chance.

[2]

The dean's letter was classic, Mike Hall thought, seated on the narrow bed as he scanned its message for the fiftieth time. Due to their behavior at a recent party on campus, it advised, Mike and his guests had been placed on disciplinary probation for the fall semester.

The indictment duly listed their transgressions. Throwing beer bottles from a fifth-floor window in Parker Hall; violating Met's drinking policies; and—out of mistaken identity—mooning members of the dorm's senior staff who'd come up to investigate. ("Lewd and inappropriate conduct," the actual wording read.) At that point, the affair was summarily shut down, and the perpetrators summoned before Met's Dean of Students.

Grinning, the lanky young freshman put the letter aside. And then stood to resume his last-minute packing. It was Tuesday, September 4, 1979, Mike's personal Independence Day—the morning of his departure from home for Metropolitan.

On probation before the year even starts. Gotta love that, he mused. The eventful gathering had occurred weeks prior, during Met's summer orientation weekend for transfer students.

And there's more where that came from, he vowed, his brain still fuzzy from last night's farewell bash with his friends. After drinks at the A-1 Pub, they had all gone to Brian Scott's apartment across town. Mike could vaguely recall dancing on the couch while blitzed out of his mind, a final rendition of *Summer Nights* playing in the background.

Since high-school graduation, in June of 1978, Mike had foundered. Between summers counseling in Outward Bound upstate, he'd passed two semesters at Sherman Adams State College in Nashua, his major yet undecided. During this time, he'd continued to live at home. Adams was only a short drive from Laconia, New Hampshire, his residence since birth.

But the commuter lifestyle simply wasn't his scene. He had never felt a part of the school, and sensed vaguely that he was missing out on the college experience. Then there were the hassles with his parents over coming in at 2 A.M., while having to sneak girls into his upstairs room.

By midyear, he'd begun looking into transfer prospects. Metropolitan, he'd sensed from the beginning, was the antithesis of Adams: urban, residential, cosmopolitan. And incidentally, a decent school.

At his memorable orientation weekend, the flip side had begun to emerge. Met U., he'd been told, was a monolithic, impersonal bureaucracy. The students were totally apathetic, their spirits crushed by an administration that regarded them as peons. The faculty was likewise disengaged, the school itself a giant red-tape factory.

Sounds pretty much like Adams, Mike had noted. Except this way, I'll be getting out of the house.

His room assignment had arrived in mid-August. A green-lined slip of computer paper from the Housing Office, pairing him with someone named Peter Garrett in Sterling Hall. According to the literature, over 400 students lived in the cinderblock high-rise—thrown together, Mike suspected, in more or less random fashion.

Outside, a horn beeped twice. The sound of Ted Stroudsberg's cream-colored '67 GTO, announcing his friend's arrival. Ted, the organizer of last night's hail and farewell, his chum since sixth grade, hero of many a "9:59 run" before the package stores closed.

Smoothing his thick brown mustache, Mike walked over to the window and pushed it open.

"Just the man I want to see," he called down. "Come on, you can help me get my stuff in the car." The GTO's power top was down as Ted sat parked at the curb, the interior littered with empty Rheingold cans.

"Doing fine, thank you," Ted warbled. And marched obediently through the front door and into the living room, still half-stoned. Like Mike he was dressed in T-shirt and shorts, despite the approaching autumn.

"Dude, I can't believe you made it home last night. You were so obliterated..." Ted stopped himself, then glanced curiously about. He was a tall, skinny kid with long reddish-brown curls and a vacant expression.

"So like, where's your folks?"

"Both working as usual—just another day around here. Guess the second time's not such a charm." Mike's older brother Jared (a.k.a. The Sensible One) had graduated from Bowdoin last year, and worked in the travel industry abroad. Amsterdam, to be precise.

"What the hell. They expect I'll flunk out anyway." Shrugging, Mike went into the kitchen and took two Carling Black Labels from his parents' fridge.

Between sips, the boys loaded Mike's gear into his aging yellow Karmann Ghia convertible. The Ghia had no back seat, and Mike's well-worn camp footlocker filled the trunk, his black trumpet case resting on the passenger side.

"Hey man, I'd love to stick around." Ted's voice was apologetic. "But I've got the day shift at the Chicken Coop, and I'm late already."

"It's cool. I'll call you over the weekend." Both beers were finished, the empties appropriately discarded. Mike paused momentarily before adding: "I guess that's it, then."

"Have a good one." Ted extended his hand. Near the base of the thumb, a pattern of purplish-red scars formed the name LISA. The name had been burned into the flesh with hot wax, a testament to his sophomore-year romance.

"Right back atcha." Mike seized the proffered hand.

"Hey, have a few bong hits for me sometime."

"You got it, bro."

The two friends embraced.

"Wax Museum!" Mike suddenly roared. And waited thirty seconds as they stood motionless, locked in each other's arms.

"Okay," Mike said, after a curious glance from a passing Honda Accord. The boys broke their clinch, again free to move.

"Where did that come from again?" Ted asked, bemused.

"These kids in my group last summer. It's always good for laughs."

After the usual promises to stay in touch, Ted went to don his fast-food uniform, the Pontiac's stereo system regaling Oak Drive with Eric Clapton's *Cocaine*. Mike watched until the car vanished from sight, its pipes spewing dark exhaust.

Scarcely five minutes later, Mike pulled out of the driveway, the Ghia's top neatly folded down. He paused for a last look at the plain white-frame house, then headed east toward the highway, his long dark hair fluttering in the wind.

Before turning onto Ashleigh Road, Mike checked his map again. Ashleigh Road would take him onto Route 4, then onto I-93 South via Exit 7. From there, the city was three hours away.

Idly he flipped on the radio, where the network news was in progress. The administration continued to look into reports of Soviet activity in Cuba, while Ted Kennedy prepared to challenge President Carter for the next year's Democratic nomination.

We'll see who whips whose ass, Mike thought absently.

The newsbreak ended and Michael Jackson's wailing voice came on, urging *Don't Stop 'Til You Get Enough.*

Words to live by, Mike thought, as he cranked up the volume and drove on toward the interstate.

I

Aboard the Starship *Fantasy*

FRESHMAN I

At six in the morning, the campus was quiet. The sky was cloudless, the sun's pink orb emerging in the east, beyond the spires and sandstone turrets of the university enclave.

Beginning today—Saturday, September 5, 1981—thousands of the world's best and brightest students would converge on campus from around the globe. Yet even now, in the waning moments of summer, there were stirrings beneath the surface, the year's activities under way.

On the turbid waters of the Monadnock River, which separated the main campus from its northern annex, the University crew team entered its second hour of rowing practice. The exertions of the shorts-clad oarsmen kept them indifferent to the morning chill as they again stroked past the boathouse, east toward neighboring Reigate College.

Slightly further north, on the artificial turf of Brentwood Stadium, three Titan football players hurled themselves into tackling dummies with savage violence. Their assault was marked by roars and grunts, each silently cursing these hated morning practice sessions. Yet Coach Tom Pickney was relentless. The squad's season opener, against crosstown rival Meldon, was but one week away.

"Come on, Taylor!" The coach's powerful voice carried across the turf, ringed by 15,000 vacant seats. "What do you think this is, some fancy tea party? You gotta *hit* 'im!"

On Alston Boulevard, a University Police cruiser moved slowly past the College of Arts and Sciences, with its white-domed planetarium.

Noting nothing unusual, the officer turned left onto Hilton Way before disappearing behind a queue of brick-fronted rowhouses on Franklin.

Outside Whitmarsh House, a solitary Chrysler LeBaron stood parked at the curb, its trunk laden with baggage. The residence halls wouldn't open until nine, yet the vehicle's occupants—Louis Goren and his eighteen-year-old son Raymond, of Port Chester, New York— complimented themselves on beating the rush.

"It's like I've always told you—planning ahead, that's the secret." The beetle-browed insurance executive smiled at his freshman progeny, a fistful of quarters for the meter in hand. "You remember that, kid, and you'll go far in life."

Dutifully, young Raymond acknowledged this sage advice, bleary-eyed from the five-hour journey. He took in the seven-story brick building at a glance, then looked toward the neighboring School of Journalism, where the morning's first beam glinted off the WMTU-AM transmission tower.

Raymond Goren would then join his father in an early breakfast before checking into the dorm. The first of eighteen thousand arrivals expected on campus that weekend.

The orientation counselor paused at the window of Sterling Hall's fourth-floor lounge, a lit cigarette in one hand, his gray canvas laundry cart parked outside the door. His watch read exactly 11:00 A.M., time for a short respite from his duties.

The counselor was Mike Hall, now a junior Engineering major beginning his third year in the dorm.

Since transferring to Metropolitan, he had changed visibly. The mustache was gone, his once-long dark hair cut shorter. (His neighbors on Four had nicknamed him Wally, after the Beaver's elder sibling—a likeness, he stressed, that was purely skin-deep.)

The street below was bustling with activity. His fellow counselors, with their carts and their red STERLING ORIENTATION '81 T-shirts, shuttled between the 14-story building and the line of parked vehicles outside—cars, vans, orange U-Hauls, yellow Ryder trucks—guiding freshmen through the move-in process. Unlike the Boulevard, Franklin Street was a narrow tree-lined path, with columns of 19th-century rowhouses on either side. He looked across the road to the administration building, whose modern five-story glass exterior seemed aloof and out of place.

Resting his cigarette on the windowsill, Mike placed his left hand in the crook of his right elbow and brought his arm upward in a one-finger salute. And, retrieving the half-finished butt, seated himself at one of the lounge's three card tables.

The incoming first-years would receive the standard orientation packet from housing. But for those assigned to Sterling 4, Mike and his floormates had prepared a special welcome, addressed to each of the newcomers. Mike practically knew its message by heart:

September, 1981

Dear New Sterling 4 Resident,

Welcome to what we sincerely believe to be the best floor on campus. Within these sacred tequila-stained halls, you will discover a proud tradition and a sense of camaraderie found nowhere else at Metropolitan. Right now, we realize that you are just getting settled into your new home, and are in a state of confusion as to just about everything. Should you have any questions, be advised that there are many returning floor residents willing and able to assist you. This fall, there are at last count 14 returning students on Four, along with another half-dozen transplants belatedly come to their senses. You will find that these neighbors can help you through many problems, as well as cause a great deal more.

Unlike other floors, Sterling 4 is unique in that it has taken on a unifying spirit of its own, a spirit that has endured even as old people move off and new people move on. It has a rich history, and an atmosphere of closeness based on respect for the individuality of its members. In the past, we have also been labeled one of the rowdier and more troublesome floors in the dorm—a noteworthy achievement, considering Four's co-ed status and its official designation as a quiet floor. (Yes, really.) At this point, a brief history is in order.

It all started two years ago on Sterling 12. That fall, our revered "Founding Fathers"—guys like Pete Garrett, Bob Spencer and Mike "Wally" Hall—moved into the dorm, among approximately 25 new residents on Twelve. The floor's members grew into a tight-knit group—so tight, in fact, that when the next year's room selection came around, almost all wanted to stay together. The floor itself, Sterling 12, was being converted to specialty housing for pre-med students.

Because so many insisted on staying, Hall Director Norm Godwin made an exception to the twelve-freshman-spaces-per-floor rule and sent them down to Four, where 23 returning students took up residence. Since Garrett and Spencer were among them, Four could not officially be labeled a quiet floor. It was <u>in transition.</u> The unity of these people was extraordinary in that they refused to be broken up, rule or no rule.

The next year, an extremely tight group of nine freshmen moved in. At room selection, eight of them managed to return to the floor, as did six upperclassmen. Garrett and Spencer moved off, and Four became an official quiet floor. We had tried to move to a different location, but then weren't assured of staying together, and so opted to live with the more restrictive noise rules. (Seriously.)

Our sense of community manifests itself in other ways. We take pride in our floor and our dorm, which leads us to become involved in a wide range of activities, from orientation counseling to student politics. For the past three years, the president of Sterling Student Government has hailed from our ranks—first Tim Lazar, then Angus Cole, and now George Hunter. (This year, Kirsten Shea is also Secretary of SSG.) This is the area in which we assert our greatest influence, and in which past floor residents have left their mark.

We hope that your stay on Four will be enjoyable, and that you feel welcome and comfortable here. Our advice: Get involved and join in the fun, you won't regret it. Besides, you have to...IT'S BEEN CALLED!

Sincerely,

The Mutants of Sterling 4

His cigarette finished, Hall stubbed the butt out in a tinfoil ashtray before checking his watch. Eleven-fifteen. Time to get back to work, he mused.

Rising from his chair, he turned and left the lounge. Then dragged his empty cart over to the elevators and pressed the down button.

Marcus Pullman fidgeted nervously on the bed, his brown vinyl suitcase resting at his feet. The mattress was bare, the suitcase untouched since his father's awkward, emotionless exit from the dorm.

You're a college man now, son, the elder Pullman had jested in valediction minutes earlier. You don't want your old man hanging around.

Marcus was alone. His roommate, whom the index card on the door of Sterling 405 named as Robert Moreland, had not yet arrived, leaving Marcus by himself, forty minutes from his home in suburban Westmont, a stranger in New England's third-largest city.

Living on your own will be good for you, his mother had repeatedly emphasized. You will learn to be a man, to stand on your own two feet. And who knows? With luck, you might even grow a few inches this year.

Until now, he'd existed within a protective cocoon. An only child, he'd rarely been allowed out after dark, save for school functions, and had no social life to speak of. His mother's overweening caution had kept him from riding a bicycle until age eleven, and from playing most sports. In consequence, his athletic development had become hopelessly stunted, with Phys. Ed. a continuing ordeal.

Inwardly, Marcus knew this coddling had damaged him. And the worst part was knowing he'd been helpless to resist. He had simply lacked the willingness to stand up for himself, a fact known to his parents as well as the Cro-Magnons who once held him upside-down over a toilet at Westmont High…

He gave a start as the room door opened and an orientation counselor shuffled in, dragging an olive-green footlocker before him. While a gray canvas laundry cart, filled with boxes of various sizes, appeared in the doorway.

"Heyyy, Marcus the Wildman! What's the buzz?" Wally Hall grinned, setting the trunk down in the middle of the room. And looked back at the pale freshman, whom he'd moved in a short while ago. "How's Met treating you so far?"

Marcus shrugged tepidly in response. "No complaints yet," he managed.

"I'll tell you, you really lucked out landing on Four, m'man. You're gonna have a blast! Like I said, I'm in 408—it's the room right down at the end of the hall. If you ever need anything, or want to stop by for a beer, feel free."

Politely, Marcus answered, "Thank you."

The laundry cart had stalled in the doorway. From outside, a second orientation counselor cleared her throat.

"All right, let's get this baby in here." Wally helped steer the cart inside, and a short-haired brunette entered the room. Followed by an athletic-looking boy in a New England Patriots sweatshirt and red gym shorts.

His female colleague waiting in silence, Wally performed the introductions. "Marcus, your roommate, Rob Moreland. Rob, Marcus Pullman."

"How're you doin'?" Rob said absently. He was tall and broad-shouldered, with blonde hair and hazel eyes. The muscles of his upper body rippled beneath the sweatshirt, his features tanned from a summer job with a state road crew.

Rob gave the room a quick glance, noting the stark symmetry within its walls. On each side an iron-frame bed, a wooden desk and chair, a dresser with a mirror. He nodded slightly, as if to convey acceptance. And then looked back at Marcus.

His roommate was small and thin, with limp ash-blonde hair and wire-framed glasses magnifying intelligent brown eyes. He was at least sixty pounds lighter than Rob, his arms like pipestems in loose-fitting shirtsleeves. Rob remained thoughtfully silent, his expression unchanged.

"You Jewish?" he finally asked.

"No...Episcopalian." Marcus remained seated on the bed, bemused. A brief pause, then: "How about you?"

"I really don't know what I am." Rob blandly shook his head. And with sublime indifference added: "I don't give two shits."

"Come on—help me unload this stuff." Marcus immediately stood, obedience having become deeply ingrained. Later, the boxes scattered about Rob's side of the room, Wally and his partner eased the empty cart out the door.

"Later on!" Hall waved briefly in parting. Leaving the freshmen to become further acquainted.

He was nearly eighteen, primed for his first taste of independence. Bright and engaging, he had graduated in the top tier of his high school class, and was a whiz at computer science.

He had also been wheelchair-bound since the age of twelve.

Dwight Manning had been born with muscular dystrophy. Diagnosed at age two, he could not remember being able to walk steadily, and unlike his younger brother Roger had never been able to run. The knee-jerk reflex disappeared in early childhood, and by the time Dwight was ten he could no longer climb stairs without crawling.

But the illness had not limited his aspirations. ("A little thing like a crippling disease shouldn't get in the way," he'd told his high-school guidance counselor in Park Lane, Connecticut during a discussion of his college plans.) He hoped eventually to find work as a systems analyst.

Simply coming to Met had been a miracle in itself. Enabled only through a grant from the Glanbury Institute for Independent Living, a charitable foundation for the disabled. (Like all Met freshmen, Dwight was required to live on campus, his parents paying the standard rate for room and board.) The Institute would fund a maximum of forty personal-care attendant hours per week, plus seven dollars nightly for an attendant to sleep in the room. Dwight would have the double room to himself, the other bed reserved for the attendant on duty.

"Megan, tell me the truth. Were you scared when you first left

23

home?" The eighty-nine-pound freshman looked at the blank screen of his desktop computer. Aware that he was hours from Park Lane, dependent on virtual strangers for his basic needs.

"Trust me, I'm as scared as you are." Megan Brunelle smiled gently, alluding to her own freshman status. Megan was one of four PCA's hired through the Institute, and had helped Dwight's counselors and his parents (*sans* eight-year-old Roger) move his things into Sterling 403.

"But God willing, we'll get through this together." The attendant reached out and patted his hand. Short and slight, with brown curly hair and metal-framed glasses, she appeared almost frail. Her wardrobe consisted mainly of loose-fitting skirts and sweaters, a legacy of her parochial school background. Yet beneath the prim exterior he sensed a beneficent spirit, a simple kindness that allayed his fears.

With an effort he smiled back, grateful for her assurances. Though inwardly his anxieties remained.

The president enjoyed Freshman Convocations.

Followed onstage by Dean of Students Casper Grayling and two University Police bodyguards, his gaze swept Whitehall Theater, where two thousand members of the first-year class had assembled. The event, as always, sparked a sense of renewal. A reminder of the eager intelligence that had characterized his younger self.

From an early age, Fortin Charles Shenford's brilliance had been apparent. At nineteen he'd been the youngest student at Harvard Medical; at twenty-two, his studies sidelined by war, the youngest Major on the European front. Completing his studies afterward, he'd interned in psychiatry at Mass General and begun a dual practice, consulting with patients in Brookline while directing Harvard's Neurological Research Center.

During the summer of 1960—months after his brain-wave studies had garnered a nomination for the Nobel Prize in Physiology—a delegation of search-committee members from Metropolitan had come to personally offer the deanship of their medical school. Like the university itself, the school possessed no significant reputation, its outlook uncertain at best. To the surprise of his colleagues, Shenford accepted the dean's post, assuming his duties in January, 1961.

In July of that year, University President Benedict St. John, plagued by eroding confidence in his stewardship, abruptly resigned. St. John, who had left a small women's college in Delaware for New England, had lasted but twenty-six months. Chairman of the Overseers Elias Wrentham, having recruited Shenford for the deanship, now floated his name for the top job—a choice he'd later regret.

In a series of interviews, Shenford overcame initial reluctance to choose a "head doctor" for the position. His breadth of learning was vast, his vision for Met's future more farsighted and ambitious then any previously entertained. And on January 5, 1962 a unanimous board named the 39-year-old the fifth president of Metropolitan University.

Under his leadership, Met had become an academic success story. The endowment, a minuscule six million dollars in 1962, now stood at 110 million. The faculty was laden with internationally-esteemed scholars, including four Nobel laureates. Among entering freshmen the median SAT score was at 1240 and rising, despite the national downward trend.

From the beginning, he'd grasped that excellence alone could move the university forward. Standards for tenure were rigorously tightened, those found wanting ruthlessly cast aside. Detractors charged that such personnel moves were often politically motivated.

"You can freely speak your mind," Willard Ferris had told the Glanbury *Wire*, for the newspaper's 1974 investigative report on Shenford's turbulent regime. "But you'd better be damn good."

By the late sixties, tensions with students had similarly escalated. The president had struggled to fathom the sudden, shocking change in America's youth during these years. The new breed shouted obscenities in public, while openly shirking their military obligations. They numbed their minds with hallucinogenic drugs; and most damning of all, knew no purpose beyond self-gratification.

To Vietnam-era protesters who shouted "Make Love, Not War," he replied that none looked fit for either purpose. He quipped to a local newsman that, "If we held a beauty contest on campus, everyone would be disqualified for lack of effort." And he ridiculed demands for student representation on the Board of Overseers, stating pithily that, "Our boardroom is not a day-care center."

On April 17, 1969 some sixty militant students had overrun the administration building, seizing Met's executive offices, to protest the presence of ROTC on campus. Responding immediately, Shenford summoned the campus police, and within minutes the intruders were taken into custody. The university had pressed criminal charges, and subsequently expelled all students involved. Metropolitan, Shenford stressed for the news media, was not Harvard, where Derek Bok supplied such lawbreakers with coffee and doughnuts.

Following the next year's abortive rebellion, student activism had waned, the ensuing faculty purges effectively quelling criticism from that quarter. Yet the rancor persisted, if in muted tones. Critics cited cases of professors dismissed or denied tenure on the basis of their political beliefs. Displaced instructors told of being forcibly removed from their offices, while campus police rifled their papers. The school had acquired such sobriquets as "Totalitarian U." and "the Uganda of higher education." With Shenford himself dubbed the Mad Scientist, the Monster of the Monadnock, and the Fiend of Franklin Street, among less printable appellations.

His freshman audience, unaware of this history, applauded Shenford as he took the podium following Dean Grayling's brief introduction.

"It is my great pleasure to welcome you, the Class of 1985, to Metropolitan University." The luminous gray eyes stilled the auditorium at once. At fifty-nine the president's features reflected the assurance of autarchic rule, his hair iron-gray beneath the black mortarboard. An inch under six feet tall, he gave the impression of greater altitude, his bearing erect, the ceremonial green gown expertly tailored.

For an hour the audience listened as Shenford discoursed on the purpose and methodology of higher education. Learning, he advised, was essentially a self-driven process, quoting St. Thomas Aquinas' dictum that "The way of discovery is the higher, the way of instruction secondary."

"What we seek to impart here," he concluded, "is not rote factual knowledge, but the capacity for critical reason, and independent thought. These, above all else, mark the foundation of wisdom and understanding."

When he finished, Shenford received a lengthy round of applause. The freshmen then left the auditorium, suitably impressed.

"So what did you think?"

"He seems like a pretty cool guy."

"He knows his stuff, that's for sure."

"I hear he's really turned this place around."

"Very intelligent man. Extremely intelligent man."

Though in the end, these first impressions were fleeting. For the honeymoon, as always, would be brief.

Metropolitan University was founded in 1903 by William DeWitt Funk as a business school for working people, and was originally known as Metropolitan College of Commerce and Finance. Led by its first president, Asa Sterling, the school expanded judiciously, adding the Colleges of Theology and Engineering to its campus; and in 1921 received its university charter by act of the state's General Assembly.

For much of its history, Met was considered a working man's institution. Over decades it had assembled itself along the riverfront, literally and figuratively in the shadows of Reigate College.

The transition to a residential campus had begun in the 1950's, during the administration of President Hugh Macallan. Most of the larger residence halls were erected during this period, capped by the 1960 completion of Sterling Hall. Yet through the St. John interregnum and into the present administration, the commuter-school image had persisted.

The main campus centered on the river's south side, bounded on the east by the intersection of Wayland Avenue and Alston Boulevard. Excluding the Three Jokers Pub (Jokers to its mostly-student clientele), Met owned all real estate from this point west to the Dunhill Street Bridge. Between Hilton Way and Walden Chapel, a series of 1920's-vintage sandstone structures housed its core academic plant, abutted by the seven-story quadrangle of Digby Library. The latter was tastefully set back from the road, its lower floors partly obscured by the Student Union building.

The prettiest stretch was on Franklin Street, which ran parallel to Alston on the north, along the river's edge. The street's venerable brick rowhouses had been converted to student housing, with residents dining in Sterling or Parker Hall. And at the west end, an open space known as University Green, where students sunbathed or played Frisbee on warm days.

The northern annex was less clearly defined. Over the bridge, the school's athletic facilities dominated, with Phillips Arena closely adjoining Brentwood Stadium. And looming in the background, the 22-story Vernon Hall, whose 600 denizens included most of Met's student-athletes.

Beyond the silver-gray dome of Edwin Hale Auditorium, Callender Drive dwindled to a series of low-rise apartment buildings, most purchased by Metropolitan in recent years. (President Shenford's lust for property was a campus joke; he was said to have once had designs on Glanbury's tallest skyscraper, the 70-story Mercantile Bank Building.)

Except for the traffic racing along Alston Boulevard, the campus offered a measure of sanctuary from urban stresses. Crime appeared virtually nonexistent, checked by Met's 40-man police force, an elite unit headquartered west of Dunhill Street, on quiet Langston Road. Here people moved at their own pace, untouched by the poverty and violence of the city's slums.

To an outsider the campus seemed a buffer zone, an autonomous enclave. Its knowledge of Glanbury's woes largely secondhand, with a prevailing sense of security rare among modern urbanites.

September 11-12, 1981:
A Day in the Life of the University

At 4:00 A.M., the City of Glanbury is sound asleep. The streets, impassable at all godly hours, are blissfully free of traffic. Per municipal ordinance, the bars have been closed for two hours, the city buses yet to begin their rounds. And of course, most sane folk are comfortably in bed.

The university, by contrast, never wholly slumbers.

With great ceremony, Wally downed the last shot from the bottle of Jack Daniel's, signaling the end of Sterling 4's Day One Quarters Game. The event, staged in honor of the fall's first classes, had been a battle of attrition, with only the floor's staunchest imbibers going the distance.

"Congradulations...you're a heavyweight!" Hall smiled while gallantly helping Beth Brown to her feet. The others, equally toasted, sat on the rug in a semiconscious haze. Dan Kirk, Wally's roommate and co-host, looked deeply absorbed in his Electronic Quarterback game; sophomores Jeff Philbrick and Bill Kaplan closely studying Wally's Rubik's Cube.

"I've had years of practice," Beth replied. The only freshman in the group, she wore an oversized green flannel shirt and multiple layers of dark eye shadow. And attached to the belt loop of her jeans, a small brown vial of liquid Rush.

"Around here, it's a prerequisite." Wally smiled sagely in her direction. And without warning, felt the room start to spin.

31

"Are you all right?" Beth asked, politely interested. But Wally was already out the door, one hand clamped over his mouth.

Without hesitation she followed him into the men's shower room, where he knelt beside the toilet, his face green. Wordlessly she knelt beside him, one hand resting on his shoulder while his stomach shifted into reverse.

When it was over, Wally wiped his mouth with toilet paper (MET DIPLOMA – TAKE ONE, read the graffito above the dispenser) and flushed the commode. Slowly he staggered to the long row of sinks and rinsed his mouth thoroughly, as if to purge the taste of the Jack Daniel's.

"I'm seriously losing it." The upperclassman groaned, his forehead resting against the mirror's surface. "Can't chug all night anymore, like when I was young."

"Sounds pretty beat." She squeezed his left forearm with one hand, the other moving slowly up and down his back.

"Want to go to my room?" Beth said evenly.

Wally turned, but looked unsurprised. At Met the direct approach was nothing new.

"What about your roommate—what's her name?—Megan?"

"You don't have to worry about her. She's sleeping in the crip's room tonight, probably getting some."

Wally's eyes narrowed. "Don't call Dwight that," he frowned. "Dwight's cool. And, he's a legacy. His cousin lived on our floor—"

"So is that a yes or no?" Her voice was husky, with the jaded edge of an older woman.

In spite of himself, Wally looked her over. Beth was a short girl, with a pleasantly round face and upturned nose. Her shoulder-length blonde hair was thick and fluffy, her ample curves soft and inviting. Except...

"I'm kind of seeing someone," he confessed.

The hand strayed to his lower back again. "Is it serious?"

"It's been almost two years," he replied evasively.

Beth seemed to ponder this for a moment. "It's cool," was her noncommittal response, before turning to leave the room.

Wally slumped back heavily against the mirror. Despite having Done the Right Thing, he felt a twinge of regret, and his nausea immediately returned. He wanted only to crawl into bed and sleep for a week.

Slowly he inched toward the door on rubbery legs, leaning against the wall for support. Finding the heavy wooden door, he pushed it open and stumbled into the corridor, where Beth and Dan headed casually toward the back stairwell.

Opening the fire door, Beth turned and whispered something to Dan. Dan made no reply, but followed her into the stairwell, and Wally heard the door open, then close on the women's side.

The others were gone, and Wally had the room to himself. To die in peace.

5:00 A.M.

From his parked cruiser, University patrolman Sam Jennings again scanned the block for any sign of movement. Though at this hour Raleigh Street was calm, serene in the shadows of approaching daybreak.

In years past, the president's mansion had been a Mecca for student protest. During the turbulent sixties and seventies, the white-columned three-story Neoclassical had witnessed countless demonstrations; five years earlier, a smoke bomb had forced the evacuation of the residence. Since then the site had been under twenty-four-hour guard, a wrought-iron fence surrounding the neatly manicured lawn.

Five o'clock and all's well, Jennings thought sourly, looking at his watch. A tall, lean black man in his mid-thirties, he was built for action, and loathed this sedentary assignment. For the past six months he'd sat in the cruiser from eleven to five, four nights a week, smoking Winstons and watching his fingernails grow.

Soon, Jennings realized, The Man would come out of the house for his morning stroll around the neighborhood. Duty compelled Jennings to follow—and afterward, to drive his charge to the president's office on Franklin Street, two miles south of this exclusive residential area.

Speak of the devil, he thought as the president emerged through the front gate. He was, as always, impeccably dressed, the red silk tie perfectly knotted. Shenford wasted no time on pleasantries, but glanced in the cruiser's direction and waved Jennings out of the car as if he were a child.

Stoically, the officer reached under the dashboard and lifted his radio microphone.

"Unit One to Dispatch. Eagle leaving the nest. Over."

"Copy, Unit One. Advise on arrival at Franklin. Ten-four."

Patience, man, Jennings thought. Only two more hours to go. But first, it was time to do some walking.

6:30 A.M.

Like his boss, Executive Vice-President Steve Patrick made productive use of the morning. He appeared in the office punctually at six o'clock, and seldom left it in daylight.

His position notwithstanding, Patrick remained a shadowy figure. Four years into his present job, he had previously served as chief of the University Police and Director of Campus Security. According to rumor, he had secretly wiretapped the offices of several dissident faculty members, while engaging private detectives to keep them under surveillance. Though nothing had been substantiated (despite the efforts of two state attorneys general), his elevation to second-in-command had been shrouded in controversy. To this day, campus radicals sported buttons which screamed SHOOT PATRICK FIRST.

His association with Met dated to his years as a city police detective, paid from the president's contingency fund to do odd investigative work. An expert in electronic surveillance, he had supervised installation of the hidden cameras that videotaped the president's office meetings. And approved plans for the sophisticated telephone system that tracked the origin and destination of every call within the University exchange.

Additionally, Patrick's office maintained jurisdiction over the University Police. Through James Fullerton, his successor as chief, he continued to direct the force's operations, and remained its de facto head. After his boss, the supreme commander.

His actual administrative burdens were not onerous. The boss was known for his personal oversight of the smallest detail. Yet Patrick stayed busy, serving as the man's eyes and ears.

As usual, he was hard at work when his superior came in to wish him good morning.

7:00 A.M.

Precisely on the hour, Rob Moreland's clock-radio alarm went off, and the Steve Miller Band began wailing *Jungle Love*. Rob sighed in protest, heavy-lidded, and with his usual string of curses fumbled for the alarm and shut it off.

This 8 A.M. physics class blows the big wet one, he observed. And making matters more enjoyable, the course's hour exams were scheduled for nine o'clock on *Saturday mornings*...

He rolled over and looked across the room, where Marcus lay beneath the covers. An Aerospace Engineering major, Marcus shared this class with Rob, whose concentration was in Mechanical. It figured, Rob thought. The kid had apparently gone through life with his head stuck in the clouds.

Okay, out of bed, he boldly resolved. And with a heroic effort, brought himself to a standing position.

"Hey Marcus, come on...we'd better get bootin'." Wrapping himself in a white cotton robe, the former All-State halfback from Wetherly High grabbed a towel and hovered over his roommate's bed.

"*Urgfgh,*" Marcus groggily replied. Rob let it go, certain the kid wouldn't dare miss class.

From the dresser, Rob took his boom box and toilet kit before leaving the room. Not long after, the Doors were singing *Riders on the Storm.*

9:15 A.M.

Biology 107 was a daunting experience.

For Megan Brunelle, the coursework itself was not unduly burdensome. Yet the classroom's sheer size dwarfed anything she'd envisioned.

Inside the cavernous lecture hall, on the second floor of the Arts and Sciences building, nearly two hundred students sat, diligently transcribing Professor Corbin's remarks on cellular structure. More people in this class alone, Megan guessed, than the entire student body at Academy.

The eldest of five children, Megan had grown up in Allentown, Pennsylvania, where her father owned the Pie-in-the-Sky Pizzeria. From kindergarten through ninth grade she'd attended St. Hippolytus' School, a weather-ravaged concrete structure abutting the church of the same name. Where students wore Navy-blue uniforms, and handbells were used to signal the end of each period. Where kids joked that the perpetually-strapped school could quintuple its income overnight by charging $91.77 monthly per head instead of per family, and where the student handbook's *in terrorem* provisions included a $25.00 fine for gum chewing.

(Still, despite its quirks, one grew attached to the place over time. At her ninth-grade graduation ceremony the tears had flowed like waterfalls, with lifelong rivals embracing one another, the strains of *To Sir, With Love* filling the church where most of the class's members had been baptized.)

Her high-school years were spent at the Academy of Our Lady of Lehigh Valley, an all-girl institution known to locals as "the Nunnery." There, her piety and solemn demeanor had been the butt of constant scorn. Her classmates dubbed her the Blessed Virgin, while spreading rumors that she was forced to invent sins at confession. Megan rarely deigned to acknowledge her tormentors, instead finding solace in her own faith.

She could not remember a time when she hadn't wanted to be a nurse. Family tradition held that she'd chosen her life's calling at age four, seeing a child-nurse in an ABC picture book. Yet even now, having entered Met's nursing program, she would wait another two years to begin her clinical studies. The freshman and sophomore curriculum consisted mainly of anatomy and biology courses, among other science prerequisites.

Sighing softly, she again scolded herself for her lack of patience. And refocused her attention on the front of the room, and Dr. Corbin's observations on the Golgi apparatus.

11:00 A.M.

Willard Ferris moved silently about the small classroom, handing back the obituaries his Introduction to Newswriting students had crafted during Wednesday's inaugural session. Most were liberally covered in red ink, but no grades were given. The assignment had been a mere trial exercise.

"Being a journalist," he said, "requires not only getting the facts, but using sound judgment and discretion once you have them. That was the main thrust of this exercise. Not everything on the fact sheet I gave you was relevant or of interest; and some things you should have entirely ignored."

Ferris paused, then scanned the room with bloodshot eyes, his white hair matted and unkempt. The tell-tale signs of another solitary drinking binge.

"For instance," he resumed. "About half of you quoted the police officer's statement that suicide hadn't yet been ruled out." Pained, Ferris shook his head. "Go directly to court, do not pass Go. Until you get the word from the medical examiner's office, you will disregard that."

Again he glanced over the room, as if to take the measure of his students. There were twenty-two, all freshmen and sophomores, each with a copy of the text he'd written himself. The fledgling journalists, seemingly awed by his reputation, waited in respectful silence.

At one time, his future had seemed limitless. As a reporter for Channel 11, he'd covered the State House in Bristol, producing an award-winning series of exposés on corruption within the capital. Now, in the twilight of his career, he was known as the university administration's chief critic. A role assumed largely by default, heedless of the personal toll exacted.

"On a less libelous note," he added, "some of you mentioned Mrs. Fisby's fondness for bridge. Unless she had been a world-ranked player, or a recognized authority on the game, you wouldn't add that in. It's just too trivial to be newsworthy. And obituaries are as much news stories as anything on the front page."

A few heads went up and down, nodding in reflexive agreement. Encouraged, he warmed to the task. It was his only Friday class, the weekend an hour away.

"I could tell that most of you debated whether to mention her previous marriage. As a rule, where divorce is concerned the answer is no, with certain exceptions. Mr. Wallis Simpson—either of the first two—would be a case in point. And certainly Jane Wyman, when the time comes…"

12:30 P.M.

Sterling Hall's cafeteria took up most of the building's basement, sharing the space with its boiler room and laundry facilities. The cafeteria had been renovated over the summer, its once-pale interior repainted apple-green and adorned with rows of potted plants.

The quality of the food, however, was unchanged. To the 800 residents of the dorm and its satellite rowhouses who ate here, the food was a target of constant derision, reminding some of meals eaten on airplanes. (FLUSH TWICE – IT'S A LONG WAY TO THE KITCHEN, read one snatch of restroom graffiti.)

Seated at his usual table, Wally Hall took a swig of chocolate milk from his hard-plastic glass. And, while his floormates watched, leaned forward and exhaled, producing twin jets of brown liquid from his nostrils.

"Gross!" Joanne Stewart, to his left, cringed in revulsion. An attractive dark-haired junior, she had no taste for Hall's lunchtime antics.

"Anything interesting in today's *Guardian*?" Dave Logan, less rattled, turned to sophomore classmate Kirsten Shea.

"Just the usual stuff." The petite brunette looked up from the current edition of the twice-weekly underground student newspaper. The *Guardian* had originated as an independent revival of the *Press*, following Met's 1969 withdrawal of funding for student publications. (The administration had since appropriated the *Press'* name and facilities

39

for its own house organ, described by Willard Ferris as "propaganda that would have embarrassed Big Brother.") Though barred from distributing on campus, the *Guardian* was readily available in neighboring food stops and convenience stores. On Tuesdays and Fridays, the caf was littered with discarded copies of the forbidden gazette.

As an afterthought, Kirsten added: "They're saying that Shenford wants to make everyone live on campus through sophomore year, starting next fall."

"Great idea. Shake the kids down for more room and board money, so he can keep buying those apartment houses on Callender Drive."

Innocently, Marcus asked, "Who's Shenford?"

"'Who's Shenford?' Now there's one way to spot a freshman." Kirsten and Dave exchanged amused glances.

Wally cocked a spoonful of peas under his thumb. "Kaplan—think fast!" he said, launching them across the table at Bill.

"That's it—I can't take it anymore!" Disgusted, Joanne picked up her tray and moved to a seat beside Kirsten.

"We've been going out since freshman year," she said, venting her wrath on her neighbors, "and I still hate when he does that shit!"

2:00 P.M.

In the dean's office on the second floor of Kennedy Hall, Elizabeth Kerr hung up the phone, the inquiry from Northwestern tactfully brushed aside. Though her recent guest lecture had been well received, she would not be a candidate for the school's Taft Professorship of Constitutional Law.

Since joining the Met Law faculty, Kerr had drawn countless offers. At forty-three she was among the ranking experts in her field, recognized as one of America's leading constitutional scholars. Tapped for the deanship two years prior, she'd begun to feel rooted in New England, despite Met's lack of job security.

She had arrived in Glanbury in January, 1974, with her dentist husband and their teenaged daughter, after two years at the Department of Justice. Disillusioned by the Archibald Cox affair, she'd resigned from the agency in protest. (A onetime Rhodes Scholar, her prior *curriculum vitae* included two years of Peace Corps service, a law degree from Fordham, and a Supreme Court clerkship with the demanding and eccentric Justice Douglas.) Forewarned of the working conditions at Metropolitan, she'd nonetheless envisioned teaching as a change of pace, removed from the infighting and treachery of Washington.

In time, Kerr had developed a fondness for her domain. Like most law schools, Met was a self-contained unit, separated by the river from the main campus and its constant turmoil. With its hall lockers and fifty-minute periods, the resemblance to a suburban secondary school was comic fodder, Met Law being alternately known to student wits as "Kennedy High."

And while lampooned at times as Dean ConKerr for her reluctance to make waves on campus, the administrator sensed her affection was reciprocated.

Later, she assumed, there would be further steps on the career path. But here, for the moment she felt settled, on the threshold of the elusive comfort zone.

The dean's secretary sat hunched over a typewriter when Kerr appeared in the outer office, carrying a weighty tome. It was two minutes past the hour, her weekly Supreme Court seminar scheduled to begin.

"Vivian, I'll need a thank-you note to Northwestern for their hospitality last week," she said. "You can leave it on my desk; I'll sign it when I get back."

"I'll do that." The young woman answered briskly, looking up from her desk.

Satisfied, Kerr left the office with text in hand. And proceeded downstairs to begin class.

4:00 P.M.

Dwight Manning sat parked in front of the Space Invaders machine in Sterling's lobby, the week's shortened class schedule at an end. While PCA Jack Kendall watched closely, awaiting his turn.

Now comes Miller Time, Dwight thought, his laser cannon veering left after blasting an entire column of invaders.

Arcade games were Dwight's favorite pastime, his skills already legend on campus. Tuesday night at the Union, he'd logged a Pac-Man score of 327,000 for a house record, before attending a single class.

"I didn't know you could get 300 points for those things." Jack frowned as Dwight pumped two quick shots into his left bunker, then dispatched the UFO emerging at the top of the screen.

"Sure you can." Dwight picked off two more foes before cutting sharply to the right. "It's really quite simple, once you know how..."

Alertly tracking the remaining invaders, he continued to pick his shots while hunting mystery saucers. At the end of the screen, he had bagged six of them—each worth 300 points.

"That was incredible! How did you do that?" Jack stared in open amazement.

"It's all based on the number of shots." Dwight began zapping away at the second screen, explaining, "Your twenty-third shot, then every fifteenth one after that, that's when they're worth 300."

"Wait—you actually count shots?"

"It's not as hard as it sounds. Just watch..."

Jack waited a while longer for his turn.

7:00 P.M.

"Hey, Duke! Get a job, you bum!"

Outside Umberto's Pizzeria, the bearded man in the tired denim jacket ignored this imprecation, slouched against the twilight darkness. To the man known as the Duke of Alston Boulevard, the street had been home for most of the eleven years since his return from Cambodia.

His real name was Stanley Boston. Though none had used it in years, save for the Municipal Court judges who periodically sent him away on disguised vagrancy charges. (Sleeping in a doorway, for example, was classed as disorderly conduct.) With his persistence and his flair for showmanship, he'd become a legend on campus, his famous juggling act once captured on film for the *Guardian.*

"I saw this recession coming, and I wanted to be prepared," he would often quip to those who deigned to speak with him.

Despite the efforts of the campus police and university administration, he'd become a fixture in the neighborhood. True, there were hecklers, and teens would occasionally deck him for sport...but like most colleges Met was full of idealistic kids, willing to help a man down on his luck.

Sustenance was seldom a problem. The block was crammed with fast-food restaurants and convenience stores, and he rarely had difficulty cadging enough change for his meals. Far from haughty-cuisine, perhaps—but it could keep a man alive.

And you can't beat the scenery, he thought, eying a pair of passing coeds in their tight sweaters and jeans. It's a shame they'll never look that good again.

Discreetly, he patted the front pocket of his ragged chinos. The afternoon's receipts had come to just under nine dollars, enough for a small pepperoni pizza with fried mushrooms on the side. And afterward, a beer at Jokers.

From his pocket he took a battered Ace comb, and raked at his scraggly black mane until he felt presentable for dinner. He was whistling as he mounted the pizzeria's steps.

9:45 P.M.

Each year, Zeta Pi's Fall Rush attracted scores of hopeful freshmen. Like pilgrims they flocked to the ivy-covered frat house on the Monadnock, in search of a place among its elite brotherhood.

Zeta Pi, Rob discreetly reminded Marcus as they entered the crowded foyer, was *the* Greek organization on campus. The undisputed *crème de la crème,* its membership included the current Student Union president and all of Met's top athletes. Not necessarily in that order of eminence.

Christ, this kid can't hang. No way in hell, Rob privately mused. Though tonight would prove a learning experience for his cloistered roommate.

"Hey, catch you later." Rob scoped a slim brunette seated on the kitchen counter, in halter top and jeans, her soft brown loafers dangling inches from the beer keg. His sights locked on target, Rob waded through the crowd, leaving Marcus without a glance.

"Right." Abandoned, Marcus stood in the living room, surrounded by a faceless mob, the word lost beneath the staccato strains of *Whip It.*

Later that night, he sensed, Rob would be waltzing the brunette back to their room. (For his libidinous roommate, it would be Conquest Number Three thus far.) While Marcus resumed the role of unwilling voyeur, trying to sleep with the two of them going at it seven feet away...

Near the grand staircase, a pretty blonde turned in his direction. Like her companions she wore a yellow Zeta sweatshirt, her complexion smooth and flawless.

"Hi—I'm Karen." She thrust out a hand as he approached.

"My name's Marcus." Again he studied the Zeta sweatshirt, pondering his next move. "So…do you know anybody here?"

"I'm a Little Sister," her voice cut through the din.

"Whose sister?" He leaned in closely.

"No—I'm one of the frat's Little Sisters," Karen laughed. "We do, like, these things for the guys…" she tried to explain.

"Actually, I've heard some cool things about Zeta. My roommate says this is a totally happening house." Marcus nodded like an experienced judge.

She favored him with a half-smile. "Were you thinking of pledging?"

His reply was cut short by the sudden arrival of two boys in Zeta shirts—obviously members. The taller of them, a heavy-set hulk with flowing blonde hair, clapped Marcus on the back, nearly sending him sprawling.

"Yo, guy—what're you doin' empty-handed? Where's your *beer?*"

The fair-haired interloper—whom an upperclassman might have recognized as Titan tailback Pat Winston—looked from Karen to Marcus, and back again. "So are you two like, hooking up?"

"This guy's Studley Do-Right!" His moon-faced companion grinned at Marcus.

"He is—I want him so bad," Karen gushed. The living-room stereo then began playing *Super Freak.*

Laughing, the two Zetas hoisted her aloft and carried her, squealing, to the dance floor. Leaving Marcus befuddled, again on his own.

11:00 P.M.

"So how did you do on Space Invaders today?"

Megan asked this in a perfunctory fashion, straightening the sleeves of Dwight's Porky Pig nightshirt.

"Got to forty-one thousand. I was on the 25th screen." His upper body leaned forward, their noses nearly touching as he sat on the mattress's edge. After changing Dwight and getting him into bed, Megan would spend the night in the room, as the schedule ordained.

"Is that good?" The nightshirt in place, she began fixing his hair. The dull earth-brown hair matched his eyes, as did the tortoiseshell glasses she'd earlier removed.

"You could say that." Dwight smiled chivalrously, having broken a hundred thou once last summer.

The eight-to-eleven shift was the most taxing for Megan. Before putting Dwight to bed, it involved brushing his teeth and taking him to the toilet. The shower room's narrow stalls made the latter task difficult, and sometimes a suppository was needed to move things along, so to speak. As a future nurse, she was not squeamish about this aspect of her duties...but lifting Dwight in and out of the chair was murder. At 104 pounds—a figure she once exaggerated in order to give blood—Megan was not built for strenuous labor.

You're all going to get stronger this semester, Glanbury Institute liaison Glenda Turner had told the attendants last week at their orientation session. Though of course, it wouldn't happen overnight.

Megan began untying Dwight's shoes. Like all of his shoes, they were designed to accommodate the curl of his toes from loss of muscle tone, and removing them was a chore. One down, one to go, she thought idly when the left sneaker came off.

Dwight's first week had been a qualified success. Like other freshmen, he'd felt overwhelmed by the volume of reading his courses required. The people he'd encountered were well-meaning but dense, often discussing him with his attendants as if he were far away. Some wondered aloud if he could speak, while others seemingly thought him retarded. (He was in *college,* for Chrissakes...)

"There!" Megan deeply exhaled as the other shoe at last came free. From here, changing him into his pajama bottom would be a snap.

Her task completed, she turned off the lights and knelt piously at the foot of her bed. At which second Dave Logan's stereo next door began blasting *Highway to Hell*.

Megan remained kneeling until the assault had passed. And after a minute of silence, crossed herself and began saying her prayers.

2:25 A.M.

On campus, Fred's Diner enjoyed a cult following. Since 1971, the cafeteria-style restaurant had remained open through 5 A.M., six days a week, long after its competitors on the Boulevard had shut down.

Behind the long stainless-steel counter, Fred Sheehan tended grill while his customers waited patiently in line. Short and stoop-shouldered, he looked the part of an aging working stiff, in white apron and paper wedge cap, his face brown and leathery.

He had begun business in 1957, during an age of curfews and parietal rules on campus; since then his menu had varied little. Burgers and subs were perennial favorites, with a char-broiled sirloin tip dinner (a house specialty, with your choice of macaroni, rice or mashed potatoes on the side) priced at just $4.85. An innately frugal soul, he'd shrewdly invested his earnings over the years, while leading a monastic existence. Though worth well into six figures, the former Army cook occupied a small rent-controlled room on Howard Lane, with a secondhand Vespa for transport.

Smiling, Sheehan turned back to the waiting mob. It was Friday night, the bars now closed, the line spanning the length of the counter.

"Yes, sir?" He greeted a red-bearded young man in a UNH sweatshirt.

"Steak tips with a side of mac, please."

"You got it, my friend."

"So how's business, Fred?"

The owner answered with a sly grin, "I'll tell you, business here is like sex. Even when it's bad, it's pretty damn good."

"There you go." The kid nodded as Sheehan scooped the macaroni onto a plate.

In a far corner, a trio of Titan football players filled one booth, engaged in a profanity-filled colloquium on new and exciting ways to trash the Vernon Hall cafeteria. The leader, a Bunyanesque blonde, remarked that Vernon's "Kindly Bus Your Own Trays" sign ranked in the same league with "Please Hold Handrail."

"But when I'm in here, I always throw my shit away and wipe the table before I leave," he quietly confessed. "I mean, look at this old man. Busting his hump all his life, slinging hash for a bunch of college kids, and what does he have to show for it?"

His back to the customers, Sheehan resumed working the open-flame grill. And heard the jingle of the register as his cashier tallied another sale.

How sweet the sound, he mutely observed.

4:00 A.M.

The night was winding down. In Sterling 408, only the floor's staunchest revelers remained on hand. Bill Kaplan sat at Dan's desk, absorbed in his host's Electronic Quarterback game; Beth Brown intently focused on Wally's Rubik's Cube.

"Don't forget. Party at The House tomorrow night," Wally reminded his guests. And putting aside his empty shot glass, added, "I want to see everyone there."

Megan had not come tonight of her own volition. College parties, to her mind, were drunken orgies of iniquity and sin. With marked emphasis on "orgies."

Yet Dwight had insisted on attending his cousin's Housewarming bash. Following the Meldon game, they'd left Brentwood Stadium for Leeds Road via the Number 7 bus. (Though they'd used the lightweight folding wheelchair, the aid of two other passengers was needed to put Dwight on board.) The game—an epic 47-41 Titan victory—had gone into double overtime, and it was past eleven-thirty when they arrived.

The House was one half of a Victorian duplex, in a once-quiet neighborhood three miles south of campus. At Number 8 the front door was open, a series of high-pitched, karatelike yells sounding from within.

Entering the foyer, they perceived a swarthy young man destroying a wooden coffee table with his bare hands, his Housemates rooting him on. Megan ducked and moved Dwight out of the way as the lunatic began hurling the wreckage outside.

"What are you people doing?" she screeched. Each word distinctly emphasized, her murmuring voice an octave above normal.

"It's cool—I live here." Bob Spencer, still grasping one table leg, regarded her with amusement. And then belatedly noticed Dwight.

"Well howdy, cousin!" Bob smiled with genuine pleasure. He tossed the table leg aside, gently shook Dwight's hand. "Welcome to our humble commode—how the hell are you?"

Spencer's grin widened, exuding the hospitality of the House he shared with six other Sterling 4 "alumni." "How do you like Met so far?"

With an effort, Dwight shrugged. "Can't complain much. They feed you swill, but other than that it's all right. Lots of fine-looking women, too."

"For sure, there's some prime doke around." Bob chuckled, adding, "Just make sure you leave some for the rest of us."

"No promises." Slowly Dwight lifted his hand. "This is Megan Brunelle; she's one of my PCA's—"

"This boy giving you trouble?" Bob turned back to Megan, who looked flustered.

"What—no! Dwight's been great to work with—"

"I'm just yanking your chain." His gaze swept the living room, where Wally and two others had joined Don MacLean in the last chorus of *American Pie*, the crowd applause building toward the end. "Check this out..." Bob waited until the ovation subsided.

"Wax Museum!" he loudly roared.

Immediately, as if by magic, all movement ceased. All through The House guests stood motionless, poised with drinks in hand as thirty, then forty seconds elapsed, the living-room stereo blaring on in the background.

"Okay." Bob broke the enchantment at last. The festivities then resumed, as if nothing had happened.

"Did you two abide?" He looked to his guests, who affirmed compliance.

With his cousin, Bob compared notes on Met U's female student body. Megan then went into the kitchen for a glass of water, returning as the clock struck midnight. An hour at which she'd seldom been awake in the past...

Abruptly, the stereo shut off. The sudden silence turned heads toward the front of the room, where a short, balding figure with horn-rimmed glasses—plainly another of The House's tenants—stood and called for attention.

"Ladies and jism," he solemnly began. "We have come to the moment you've all been waiting for: The Second Annual Presentation of the Pete Garrett's Liver Memorial Trophy, awarded each fall to Sterling 4's Rookie Drinker of the Year." Amid great applause he hoisted an empty Everclear bottle, marked by two strips of masking tape, honoring each of the award's claimants.

"Now, as you may have guessed, this prestigious award bears the name of its inaugural recipient, to wit your humble host. But the time has come to pass the torch on to a worthy successor. And a worthy one he is: A man who set an all-time floor record by polishing off 32 Schlitzes in one night. A man whose blood hospitals use to sterilize surgical instruments. A man who leaves no bottle undrained—Jeffrey "the Troll" Philbrick. Get up here, you bum!" The crowd burst into applause, then into raucous chants as the honoree—a six-foot-two-inch sophomore with dark hair and primitive features—came forward.

"Troll! Troll! Troll!" the guests roared in celebration.

"Mr. Philbrick," Pete finally resumed. "It appearing to the Rookie Drinker Committee of Sterling 4 that you have been duly elected by your fellow Mutants, I am pleased to present you with this trophy commemorating your selection as Rookie Drinker of the Year for 1981. Congratulations." The junior pre-law student shook his successor's hand, and left the stage as Troll flaunted his award.

"Speech! Speech!" some members of the audience shouted.

"Dokey now!" Troll screamed, happy to oblige.

I don't believe this. You're giving prizes for drinking? But Megan watched, oddly fascinated, as Troll then downed the traditional boilermaker—a quart of beer with two shots of J.D.—in just 11 seconds.

51

Later, the ceremonies concluded, Bob glanced toward the kitchen counter, with its array of glass bottles. "What's your pleasure, cousin?"

"You can't give him alcohol!" Megan warned, aghast.

"Rum and Coke, please," Dwight said.

"It's one drink. And it's not like this is the first time." Dwight reassured his speechless attendant. And when Megan hesitated, added, "In case you've forgotten, I have a mother at home. And I don't need a baby-sitter."

Bob poured a Seagram's 7 for himself, then mixed the rum and Coke into a glass, which Megan faithfully held to Dwight's lips.

Outside of the Eucharist, she'd never touched a sip of alcohol herself. An irony not lost on Megan.

The University Bookstore was a converted warehouse on the Boulevard, a short step from the Lucky Convenience Mart. Its three miles of shelf space housing more than 180,000 volumes, the largest inventory in Southern New England.

In a third-floor aisle, Marcus restocked the latest chemistry-book returns. It was Thursday, the last week of drop-add, the checkout lanes jammed with students waving checkbooks, or their parents' Gold Cards; an infinitesimal minority paid cash.

To earn pocket money, Marcus had applied for work at the bookstore, where he spent fifteen hours a week pricing merchandise and stocking shelves. (And once, for two traumatic hours, operating a register in a pinch.) It was his first paying job; his parents, while welcoming the news, remained faithless as ever. ("So you didn't get fired yet?" his mother had said, only half joshing, in her perky real-estate saleslady's voice last weekend over the phone.)

In truth, Marcus rather liked the bookstore. His experience at the register aside, the work was not so demanding, the pace unhurried. Nor did he object to wearing a nametag, a practice labeled "uncool in the extreme" by a colleague from Van Nuys.

From behind, a familiar voice hailed him in loud tones.

"El-roy!"

Startled, Marcus dropped the textbook in his hand, then turned to see

Wally and Troll flashing identical grins.

"Hey—what are you guys up to?" The freshman relaxed, then picked up the book and reshelved it with feigned casualness.

"That's okay, we don't need help. We're just loitering," Troll said.

"Seriously, we'd always wondered what it looked like in here." Marcus smiled while Wally added: "Elroy—get me psyched!" The elders of Sterling 4 had given him the nickname, after George Jetson's progeny, for reasons unknown.

"We saw you slaving back here, and we didn't want to give you the Rodney." Hall nodded, invoking the floor's argot for a rejection or snub.

"Elroy—high-three!" Troll lifted one hand in the semblance of a Boy Scout sign. Perplexed, Marcus did not respond.

"You're going to have to learn to give high-threes." Troll gripped his right hand and tucked the little finger under the thumb. "Now try it," he said. On Marcus's second effort their fingers came together with a wet slapping sound.

"That's the way." Troll leered at Marcus, who seemed pleased at his initiation in this tribal custom.

He hesitated a moment, then asked, "What are you boys doing this weekend?"

"Everybody we can," Wally joked, before filling Marcus in.

"Actually, we've been planning this trip for weeks." His tone was conversational. "Saturday morning, seven o'clock, a bunch of the guys are taking Spencer's van to New York—as in Central Park, for the Simon and Garfunkel concert. You want to come, there's a seat with your name on it."

Marcus looked down at the floor. "I can't. I have to work Saturday," he replied. "But thanks for asking," he hastened to add.

"They're not going on tour or anything, right?" Marcus frowned.

"Nah, it's a one-time thing." Patiently, Wally shook his head. And, turning back to Troll, repeated: "Get me psyched!—Elroy's our bookstore mole.

"Now get back to work!" he snapped at Marcus. Who flushed, then smiled gracelessly in response.

"Later on..." Wally waved as he and Troll exited stage right.

Marcus's floormates had scarcely gone when a young couple approached, both wearing jeans and sweatshirts, scanning a copy of *The Official Preppy Handbook.*

"Here you are, my good man." His free reading finished, the boy handed the book to Marcus, adding, "This goes in the Humor section, third aisle on the left."

"You're terrible!" The girl giggled to her boyfriend as they walked on; neither looked back at Marcus.

Customer contact, Marcus thought, was highly overrated.

On September 21, Dwight Manning turned eighteen. And like most of his peers, looked to celebrate in the traditional manner.

"I want to go to Jokers," he told Megan, leaning forward in his wheelchair.

They were alone in Sterling's lobby, where Dwight's visiting parents had left him to her care following dinner at Antoine's Seafood Restaurant downtown. The meal had been enjoyed at a leisurely pace, and it was now after eight o'clock.

"Where?" But Megan knew she'd understood correctly. And with foreboding, acceded to her employer's wishes.

Though of course, both ordered Coke. And left, at his urging, to catch the Monday Night kickoff—tonight, the Patriots were hosting the Dallas Cowboys.

"So how does it feel to be a man?" Megan sounded upbeat as they returned to the dorm, satisfied the bar wasn't full of semiconscious derelicts.

For some reason, Dwight appeared to take umbrage. "You'll never know, will you?" he returned.

And neither will I, he added ruefully to himself. Every night, with either you or Cindy Keffler or Moira Perry in the next bed. Seven feet away, and you might as well be on the moon. A man at eighteen? Yeah, right. Soon I won't be able to lift my own fork, or play games with multiple controls. Then I'll become de-potty trained, and finally my lungs'll just pack it in...

Stop, damnit. Remember, it's your birthday—maybe the Pats will win the game.

"Fat chance," he said aloud.

"Pardon?" Megan leaned in closer, while pushing him along.

"Nothing." Dwight was silent as they reentered the lobby, where a guard waved them through without an ID check.

Upstairs, Megan took Dwight's key from the knapsack on his chair...but curiously, the room was unlocked. Puzzled, she swung open the door. The room's lights were on, and she perceived with horror that they were not alone.

"Surprise!" a chorus of male voices shouted at once.

Megan gasped, and Dwight flinched at seeing his neighbors—Wally, Troll and Bill Kaplan, joined by his cousin Bob—sprawled about the room, the tiny black-and-white television perched on the desk. HAPPY B-DAY, DWIGHT, read a yellow posterboard sign on one wall.

"Well, look who's here." Bill drawled slowly, lifting a bottle of Bud from the case at his feet. "Do come in. So good of you to come visit."

"How did you get in here?" Megan's voice, sharp and accusing.

"How *did* you get in here?" Dwight smiled back at his dormmates.

"The locks on this floor are all similar," Wally explained. "My key opens this door, Bill's opens Joanne and Kirsten's...and so on, *et cetera*.

"Isn't that wild?" He looked greatly amused.

You're wild, Megan thought, finally moving the chair inside. The others stood to shake Dwight's hand, welcoming him to the fraternity of men.

Still smiling, he asked, "How long have you all been waiting?"

"An hour or so." Bob shrugged, his absence from the family dinner explained. "But that's okay—we didn't mind."

"Megan—want a beer?" Troll thrust a bottle at the attendant, who curtly declined.

The phone rang, and Wally grabbed it at once. "Speak!" he sang into the receiver. He listened, then turned and put his hand over the mouthpiece.

"It's the pizza-delivery guy," he announced. "He says he's downstairs in the lobby.

"Yes, this is Mustafa Horowitz," he said into the phone. Bringing loud laughter from his cohorts.

"Mustafa Horowitz—classic!" Troll guffawed.

After gathering sufficient funds Hall left the room, then returned with three Domino's Pizza boxes.

"What did you get for toppings?" Dwight edged forward in anticipation.

"Pepperoni, 'shrooms, sausage…Check this out." Wally showed him the address label on one box. MUSTAFA HOROWITZ – 215 FRANKLIN ST. RM. 403, it read. TEL. 881-4241.

"Is that a trip, or is that a trip?" He laughed cheerily.

"LET'S GO, PATRI-O-OTS!" Troll grabbed two slices at once, while Bob adjusted the set's vertical hold.

"You guys better win this game—or you ain't gettin' no doke tonight!" Philbrick shouted at the three-inch screen.

Megan felt an urge to leave the room. She saw the evening ahead as a show of excess drinking, swearing, belching and mindless vulgarity.

In short, a typical gathering of college men.

As if reading her mind Dwight said casually, "Megan, I'm all set for now. Why don't you just come back after the game, say 12:30ish? We'll put down 8 to 11 on the time sheet as always."

"I can help him as far as eating goes. I've done it before," Bob said.

"But that would give me an extra two hours. That wouldn't be honest!" Megan objected.

"You've worked enough unpaid overtime already. Go on. Unless you enjoy watching football and listening to guy-talk."

The attendant had scarcely left the room when Bob asked, "Is she for real?"

"Completely." Dwight nodded without elaboration.

"I say she could be all-right looking if she ditched those glasses. And shed those June Cleaver outfits," Bill said.

"Nah, too skinny." Troll grunted, adding, "I need something I can hang on to. Better cushion for the pushin'."

The game got under way. Both sides traded scores in the first quarter; then midway through the second, the Pats had a go-ahead touchdown nullified by an in-the-grasp call.

"Yes! New rules!" Bill, the floor's resident obnoxious Dallas fan, punched the air with his fist. Troll unleashed a feral scream, then stormed down the hall and flung a half-empty bottle out the rear window, to shatter noisily on the Nursing School's blacktop.

When he returned, he was still fuming. "You make another bullshit call like that, and I'll come over there and kick your ass!" he roared at the screen.

The Pats took a short-lived third quarter lead, before enduring another of the late fades that would mark a dismal 2-14 season. It wound up 35-21, Dallas. Kaplan, magnanimous in victory, stood and waggled a partly-clenched hand in Troll's face.

"Hey, cheer up. You guys'll get first pick in the draft," he said brightly.

Before leaving with his band of merry men, Wally turned back to his host. "See you for L.B. this Friday, Mr. Horowitz?"

"For sure." Dwight was, of course, expected only to make an appearance at the monthly Liquid Breakfast, the floor's infamous ritual of early-morning shots and beers. The event began promptly at 7 A.M., with early classes of secondary importance.

"Awesome!" Wally gave a quick thumbs-up sign. "Remember—

Philbrick's room, precisely on the hour…"

When Megan returned, she was horrified. Despite the boys' good-faith efforts, some pizza crumbs lay on the floor, an acrid pall of smoke lingering behind. The desktops were dotted with cigarette ash, the wastebasket filled with empty brown bottles.

"What did they do to this place?" the attendant nearly screamed. "It looks like a pigsty in here!"

"I know." Dwight smiled, suddenly close to tears. "Is that great or what?"

Marcus woke with a start that early October morning, conscious of the sunlight streaming through the window. Panic-stricken, he sat up and whirled to look at the digital clock on his desk. Last night he and Rob had been up past 3 A.M. cramming for their first physics exam, sleep having come through attrition of consciousness.

The clock's lighted numerals read 8:48 A.M.

Eight forty-eight! Twelve minutes until the exam! Marcus kicked off the sheets, raced frantically to his sleeping roommate's bedside, and began shaking Rob's shoulder.

"Get up—fast!" he implored. Rob eyed him quizzically a moment before checking the time.

"Ho-ly shit!" Rob roared as he leaped out of bed. Hurriedly, the pair dressed in last night's clothes and fled the room, neglecting to lock the door behind themselves. It was Saturday morning; their neighbors slept soundly, indifferent to their frenetic haste.

"Come on, you whore!" Rob banged the elevator with his fist. Then, losing patience, turned and bolted for the stairwell.

Within sixty seconds, the two raced out the front door of Sterling Hall. And, forgoing the sidewalk route, sprinted across the courtyard, to the chain-link fence behind the School of Nursing. Over the fence, across another stretch of grass onto the Boulevard, then through the door of the white-marble Engineering building and up to Room 310. Rob ran well ahead of Marcus, who was further delayed when he slipped going over the fence, and was seated at a desk with the exam before him when his roommate stumbled in, panting audibly.

"You may begin." The proctor eyed Marcus closely as he took his seat.

Within the classroom, a mute shuffling sound as the tests were flipped face-up. For eighty-three anxious freshmen, the first college exam was now a reality.

"I feel like crying." Rob sat on his bed, dejected, after the boys had returned to the dorm. "I'm serious. I really feel like crying."

Marcus nodded sympathetically. "That was tough," he agreed.

"It absolutely blew me away. I wasn't sure of one thing I wrote down."

"What did you get for the one with the—" Marcus ventured.

"Don't start." Rob cut him off with an upraised hand. "I don't even want to think about it. Right now, all I want to do is get supremely wasted."

Dryly, Marcus laughed. "Do you want to get some lunch first?"

"Yeah, might as well," Rob sighed. "*After* we've both had a shower."

The next Thursday morning, with great trepidation, the roommates stood outside Professor Fogel's office, the exam results listed by Social Security number on the bulletin board. Rob had received an 83 and Marcus a 74, compared with a class mean of 51.

Having aced his first exam, Marcus left the building on a cloud. Indifferent to Rob's smugness at having outscored him.

The clock in Sterling's lobby showed 3:20 A.M., its tapered hands unmoving as Mark Walsh waited in silence. Since he'd called his roommate upstairs, aeons ago, time had been at a standstill.

The situation was entirely bogus, he thought, having to be signed in as a guest after paying three grand to live in the dorm. And yet it was funny too, as everything was when he was totally wrecked.

Hours ago he'd begun Columbus Day weekend early, puffing on a bong in his room while Sanjay attended Friday classes. Then a couple of lines at a house party that night before returning to the dorm.

"Come on, man—you know I live here," he'd appealed to the guard at the security desk after searching his pockets for his student ID. The guard was in fact acquainted with Mark, who'd once slept on the lobby's couch after wandering the halls in a similarly confused state...but rules were rules. Politely, he'd directed Mark to the house phone in the entryway.

"Heyyy, there he is!" Mark stood as Sanjay Motwani appeared, dressed in Navy bathrobe and slippers. His roommate was what Mark's mother termed "an India Indian," with coal-black hair and dark sunburnt skin. A freshman premed, Sanjay spent his nights at the library and was in bed by eleven.

"Dude, can you sign me in?" Mark again asked. Eyes vacant, his speech slurred and uneven.

"Where is your card?" Sanjay rounded the four-foot partition separating the lobby from the main hall, obviously displeased.

"Don't know, man. Guess I must've left it in the room."

"You should bring it with you every time." The smaller man's voice dripped with disdain.

Mark gave an impatient hissing sound. "Could you just sign me in?"

The alert brown eyes narrowed. "You are drunk?" Sanjay said with disapprobation.

"No, not drunk." Mark laughed, leaving Sanjay to his own conclusions. "Now are you gonna sign me in or what?"

Approaching the desk, Mark took a pen and began filling out a guest pass for himself. SANJAY MOOTAAANIIA – ROOM 4022, he scrawled in the "Host" space. And, aware of the guest ID requirement, slid the form across the counter with his New Jersey driver's license.

The guard took the information from Sanjay, completing the form himself. "You're all set," he said indifferently.

"All right—the man comes through!" Mark clapped the Indian's shoulder as they moved toward the elevators. Sanjay ignored him and walked on, still resentful at being awakened.

Shit, what's his problem, Mark thought, bemused. But let it pass as they boarded the elevator and rode upstairs in silence.

"Why didn't you shoot that last one?" Puzzled, Marcus frowned, his eyes tracking the lone asteroid onscreen.

"Just watch." Slowly Dwight eased his ship upward, Marcus and PCA Cindy Keffler observing in silence. It was Sunday, 10:30 A.M., the Student Union rec room hushed. Save for the long-haired attendant at the counter, the three were alone in the games area, a windowless L-shaped catacomb in the building's basement.

"Did I show you this before?" Delicately he moved into position, toward the top of the screen. Beyond the Asteroids console an array of pinball and video games twinkled in silence, the pool tables dormant beneath their vinyl coverings.

"I think so." At least twice, the dark-haired attendant thought to herself. Marcus silently shook his head, then perceived Dwight's stratagem almost at once.

Dwight's ship sat parked in the upper left-hand corner, approximately an inch from the edge of the screen. Resting one hand on the button for continuous firepower, he eliminated the flying saucers as they emerged, his shots disappearing behind the screen to blast those on the opposite side.

In theory, as long as one small asteroid remained, one could wait and ambush UFO's indefinitely. Using this tactic, Dwight had twice topped one million points at the Outer Limits Arcade back home. A feat he would replicate by game's end.

To pass the time, the three touched idly on random topics: the curious strike-season baseball playoff format, the grind of midterm exams.

"So who's going to play the Yankees in the World Series?" he asked, zapping another 1000-point saucer.

"Montreal." Marcus hazarded a guess.

"I say L.A. They've got the edge in postseason experience. It sucks, though, the way the Reds didn't even get in. I mean, they had the best record in the game this year..."

"Not that it matters. The Yankees'll take either of them," Cindy said happily.

"*Pthh*—yeah, right." Like most Red Sox fans, Dwight felt a moral obligation to loathe their Bronx archrivals.

"Marcus, slap her for me, will you?" Still firing, he added, "I'd do it myself, but I've got a planet to save."

Two hours later, Dwight's pet asteroid continued to flit across the screen, while he lay in wait for UFO's. His score at 719,000 points, the indicator on its eighth trip around.

Behind him a small crowd had gathered, watching in near-silence. His audience included Rob Moreland (joined by two other pool-playing Zeta pledges); and Megan Brunelle, summoned by pay phone to report to the rec room for her one o'clock shift.

Rob watched as a succession of flying saucers vanished. "Shit, this kid's Captain Eliminator with those UFO's," he said.

Thus, unwittingly, a lasting moniker was born—Dwight becoming known as the Captain to his dormmates from then onward. With the million mark yet an hour away.

"Sir, will there be anything else?"

"What was that?" Fortin Shenford set down his wineglass before dismissing his valet for the evening. "Oh yes, of course Carlos. You may be excused." The valet wished him good night and retired to his quarters, in the servant's wing of the mansion.

The president sat alone at the oak dining-room table, where once he'd hosted the family dinner hour. But the children had since grown and married, and Betsy's passing had left him alone for the first time since his student days at Harvard.

He had begun life as the third of six children, born of working-class parents in a crumbling Cincinnati tenement. His mother a kindly, simple soul, a homebody, devoted to husband and children. Now long deceased, she remained Shenford's model for a proper woman.

His father, by contrast, had been a frightening figure—a leather-lunged die-factory foreman who dominated his workers, and terrorized his brood at home. Until his death from emphysema when Fortin was fifteen, Frank Shenford had slighted the boy's intellectual pursuits, troubled by young Fortin's lack of friends, fearful his son would end up a sissy.

In 1931, the elder Shenford had lost his job and taken to drink. To assist the family young Fortin, then nine years old, began selling newspapers in the streets, often battling bigger boys for turf. ("You lose a fight out there, ain't nothin' compared to what you get when you come home," his father had said, florid-faced.) There was no praise for the unvarying straight-A report cards, and skipping grades brought only paternal chagrin at the thought of Fortin's being the smallest boy in his class.

The president looked to the adjoining living room, where Betsy's reading chair once stood alongside the davenport. The chair, like all of his late wife's possessions, now in storage, forgotten but for moments when memory superseded the senses.

They had met during his first term at Harvard Med School, where she had worked in the cafeteria. To Shenford the young Betsy Carter—a perky blonde naïf—stood in refreshing contrast to Harvard's vacuous snobbery. An unlikely romance blossomed between the studious nineteen-year-old prodigy, nicknamed "King Wonk" by his classmates, and the aspiring singer from rural Pennsylvania before war intervened. The two corresponded faithfully throughout his absence; and in August, 1946 they were wed in Cambridge, Massachusetts.

This place beats the hell out of the Quonset hut we lived in when we were first married, he'd exulted twenty years later, upon moving into the president's mansion.

The 30-room house had been built to his design, financed by his colleagues on the board. Through his ties with Brook Miller, chairman of Colonial Heritage Savings and Loan, he'd similarly obtained a half-million-dollar line of credit at four percent interest, principal payment deferred for eight years. The proceeds invested with a Wall Street brokerage firm, returning twenty-one percent last year.

Still more lucrative were his ventures into real estate. Six years ago, with demographics foreshadowing the market boom, he'd set aside one-fifth of Met's endowment fund to invest in residential properties. Though many opposed his audacious plan, the ensuing windfall had surprised Shenford himself, as prices quintupled in short order.

Unknown to his employers, he had at the same time mortgaged the president's house and an entire block of university-owned apartments, to buy some properties of his own. Riding the market's surge, he'd quickly paid off the unrecorded liens, while the profits continued to roll in. As of this crisp fall evening, Fortin Shenford's net worth approached 13 million dollars, the bulk resting in a numbered account in Liechtenstein.

Taking another sip from his wineglass, he thought of the bullies who'd tormented him in his youth, of the father who once quelled his bedtime protest by dangling his six-year-old son feet-first from their third-floor apartment window. Success, he'd concluded with satisfaction, was the sweetest revenge.

But today, the worst of the conflict was past. In January he would celebrate the twentieth anniversary of his inaugural, with no bar to another two decades if he wished. Charles Eliot had similarly reigned for forty years at Harvard, and Nicholas Murray Butler at Columbia even longer.

He looked again to the living room, where Betsy's portrait hung over the mantelpiece. The painting was ten years old, depicting his wife as she lived in memory: Her smile still girlish, rosy cheeks pleasantly round, hair marked with silver highlights. The fine lines absent from her face; yet a certain wistfulness showed the strain of the busy, tumultuous years in Glanbury.

His gaze lingered over the portrait, upon the face of the woman who'd been his spouse for 33 years. The young wife who worked overtime while he earned his medical degree; and the woman with whom he'd raised three fine, upstanding children, in defiance of a decadent age.

Shenford willed away the lingering bitterness at her untimely decease. And in silent tribute, held aloft his glass.

From his battered living-room easy chair, Willard Ferris stared at the TV while the late news droned on. As usual, saddened by the decline in quality at Channel 11 since his departure.

Pouring another shot of Gilbey's Gin, he sighed as the weatherman predicted an unseasonably cold week ahead, and groaned at the sports anchor's feeble jest about the Celtics "icing" an exhibition opponent. Ferris had no professional objection, *per se*, to so-called "happy talk"…but the vapidity of these exchanges was embarrassing.

"None of that in my day," he muttered aloud. The phrase was one he detested, and used increasingly often.

His day had dawned in the spring of 1960, in an age of fifteen-minute newscasts and no-nonsense reporting. A crack investigative journalist, he'd uncovered the secret-pension scandal that brought down the Pezzullo administration, among other breaches of the public trust. Leaving the newsroom for academia, he'd won a tenured professorship at once, on the strength of his résumé.

Now, fourteen years later, only the past glories remained. Today Willard Ferris was a short, rotund man of fifty-two, his career in shambles. His wife Rhonda had walked out in late 1973, during their daughter's sophomore year at Northeastern. His annual salary, after two arbitrations, stood at $27,000—well below average for a full professor in the department, and less than what many associate profs earned. The only salary guidelines at Met being that Fortin Shenford looked after his friends—and his enemies.

"Why can't you just let go?" Rhonda Ferris had said, months before taking her own advice. "It's obvious there's nothing here for you anymore, and for god's sake you're not getting any younger!"

Yet stubbornly he'd soldiered on. He'd realized belatedly that Shenford wasn't Carmine Pezzullo, an unpolished hack who was said to have rummaged through a restaurant's dumpster for a $10,000 bribe he'd accidentally thrown away after finishing lunch.

From his coffee table, Ferris lifted the November edition of *Forbidden Knowledge*. The bimonthly exposé journal was printed on recycled pulp, and like all student publications circulated underground. He opened it to the lead article, a profile of himself entitled "His Majesty's Opposition." And again reviewed his own sad story.

Both he and Rhonda had served on the Met faculty. An art history instructor, Rhonda had begun teaching the year before her husband, whom the president had personally recruited. In the beginning he'd enjoyed favored status, his prospects golden.

His first clash with the administration had come after addressing a student rally on Walden Plaza, opposing America's involvement in Vietnam. Angered by the news coverage of Ferris's remarks, the president had called the next morning. Respectful at first, Shenford had soon unleashed a torrent of invective impugning Ferris's patriotism, his manhood and his sense of duty. The assault had left Ferris shaken, questioning Shenford's emotional balance.

Following the shutdown of the *Press* in early 1969, Ferris, who had been the paper's faculty advisor, openly condemned the "fascist mentality" of the Shenford administration. Ultimately, he'd led the call for Shenford's ouster, his crushing defeat the first step on the path to oblivion.

In June of 1970, Rhonda Ferris learned her contract would not be extended. Her husband then enduring a succession of salary freezes, his perquisites reft one by one. Ferris's present office was a doorless cubbyhole in the School of Journalism basement, an area reserved for untouchables.

Naturally left unmentioned—and, Ferris assumed, unsuspected—was his advancing alcoholism.

At one time, he'd merely been a social drinker. But as the reverses mounted, and unalterable failure took hold, his craving had intensified. These days Ferris often taught his morning classes hung over, succored by Excedrin and Visine.

The professor poured another shot of gin while Johnny Carson appeared onstage. Then another after the monologue, his seventh of the night.

He passed out shortly after one A.M., with remote clutched in hand. His next class nine hours away.

"Okay guys, we've got two minutes. We can do this." Wally encouraged his teammates in the huddle, his spirits unbowed by another season of abject futility. "We stop them on this drive, get a quick score, then take the onside kick and go for 15 points."

"Alcoa presents...*Fantastic Finishes*." Bill Kaplan, the team's beleaguered quarterback, muttered sourly. Tonight, for the eighth consecutive week, the Mutants were getting trounced, 21-0 by the Budsters of Vernon 16. Through this final game of the intramural season, the football team had failed to dent the scoreboard, running its overall losing streak to 24 outings.

"Maybe everyone should borrow some of N.H.'s stickum." Bill indicated Dan Kirk, whose performance at wide receiver had earned the nickname "No Hands." Dan replied with an obscene invitation.

Despite the November chill, a loyal majority of Sterling 4's residents had trekked to Brentwood Stadium for the finale. Now, with another contest out of reach, the Mutant sideline was indifferent and restless, huddled on the edge of the stadium's maroon track oval.

"De-fense! De-fense!" Wally attempted to rally his floormates as the Budsters racked up another first down. Faced with a first-and-goal from the eight-yard line, the Mutants gathered themselves for a last stand.

With thirty seconds to play, the Budster captain suddenly called time-out. Then nodded toward the official before rejoining his teammates.

Taking the snap from center, the quarterback reversed toward midfield and launched a soft punt in their opponents' direction. Wally fielded the kick cleanly, and the Mutants had the ball with 12 seconds remaining.

"What the hell's going on?" Frowning, Mark Walsh turned to sophomore Dennis Haggerty, whose red hair brushed the shoulders of his denim jacket.

"Just watch—this is classic." Haggerty smiled, giving nothing away.

"Go for it!" the Budster captain yelled. And, with his teammates, assumed a kneeling position on the turf. For the third consecutive year, the Mutants would be allowed their only points of the season in the waning seconds.

Bill took the snap and waved Kirk downfield, his adrenaline flowing. With the Superdome crowd going wild, he planted his feet and prepared to launch. He was Danny White, hurling the Pass of the Cenozoic Era to a wide-open Drew Pearson to return the Cowboys to Super Bowl glory. Seeing his man alone, he reared back, he pump-faked, he fired…and the ball sailed wide of target.

After a long silence the opposing captain stepped forward, exasperated.

"Okay, penalty on the defense," he snapped. "Unsportsmanlike conduct—not trying. The game can't end on a defensive foul, so you guys get another shot. Let's get it right this time!"

Two tries later, the Mutants scored.

No one would subsequently recall how the rumor began, and none on Sterling 4 alluded to it afterward; yet the incident lingered in memory. The tension that gripped the floor that December night, the specter of World War III appearing at hand.

Fresh from his induction ceremony at Zeta House, Rob Moreland stepped off the elevator shortly after 1 A.M. "Yo—what's up?" he acknowledged his dormmates. There were three of them, huddled by the loading area, uncharacteristically grim-faced.

"The Russians just invaded Poland," Wally announced, without preliminaries.

Rob eyed him flatly for a second. "Are you serious?"

"It's true. We heard it on the radio," Dan confirmed. Dave Logan's nod making it unanimous.

"Holy shit," Rob said quietly.

Emerging from their room, Marcus appeared at his elbow, wearing a tattered terrycloth robe. "Hey, what's going on out here?"

"Go back to sleep," Rob said, for no reason he could explain.

"Russia's invaded Poland," Dan told Marcus, who defiantly stayed. The hum of voices attracted others, and before long a small crowd had assembled.

"They're gonna have to wake Reagan up for this," George Hunter quipped to his floormates. The president of Sterling Student

Government was tall and thin, his voice high-pitched.

Somberly, Bill Kaplan said, "He's probably shitting bricks."

"What if this is too much for him to deal with, and he has a heart attack," Dave foolishly prattled. "Then Nancy takes over and orders all the bombers painted pink—"

Presently R.A. Lisa Kornberg appeared and was advised of the situation. The others looked expectantly to the senior premed, whose abbreviation stood unofficially for Rarely Around.

"Oh no," was Lisa's controlled response. Sensing their dissatisfaction, the Resident Assistant counseled her charges not to assume the worst, and withdrew to her private suite.

"What would you do if there really was a nuclear attack, and all of a sudden you only had thirty minutes to live?" Marcus looked thoughtfully at his neighbors.

"Get doked as many times as possible," Troll volunteered.

In time, the session exhausted itself, and the Mutants dispersed to their rooms. Tomorrow was Monday, with final exams upcoming.

In the morning, the headlines would clarify that there had been no invasion, but the Polish government had declared martial law, suspending civil liberties and effectively outlawing the Solidarity trade union. But the daylight would further reveal an unsigned note on Wally and Dan's message board, a reminder of the evening's chaos:

> HAVE A GOOD TIME IN POLAND, GUYS,
> AND DON'T FORGET TO WRITE.
> OUR NEW ADDRESS IS:
>
> PO BOX 4F
> YUKON TERRITORY, CANADA
>
> WE PICK UP THE MAIL EVERY 3 MONTHS.

Marcus sighed when the phone rang, prepared to tell another of Rob's feminine admirers that his roommate had gone home for Christmas break. It was Sunday night, one week after the Poland incident, the Hall nearly deserted after final exams.

To his annoyance, the ringing persisted. Marcus considered letting it ring, while he went for a roast-beef-on-pita-bread sandwich at Cassidy's.

"Hello?" he answered without enthusiasm.

There was no response on the other end. Marcus heard a faint static hum in the background; and underneath, the theme from *Hill Street Blues.*

"Hello?" he repeated more sharply, suddenly tired of being victimized. "Troll, if this is one of your lame gags—" But Philbrick too was gone.

"Hello," a faint male voice said at last. "I just called because I wanted to talk to somebody. I don't think I did very well on my finals..."

"Who is this?"

"...and right now, I feel like I want to kill myself."

Marcus's face paled. Like other Met freshmen he'd heard the rumors, the stories of those who cracked under the competitive strain. Campus folklore held that students whose roommates committed suicide during exams received an automatic 4.0 for the semester, conditioned on psychiatric counseling. ("I'd kill you for a four-point," Rob had once said, poker-faced.) Though Marcus couldn't imagine anyone actually being so worked up, so distraught over a few tests as to...

"Don't do that," he replied, gathering his thoughts in a nanosecond. "You don't want to do that. There's no reason—trust me, it's not worth dying over a few lousy exams."

Keep him talking, Marcus thought. Whatever you do, keep him talking.

Holding the receiver to his ear, he quietly crossed the room and opened the door, glancing around wildly for help. But the hallway was deserted.

"I don't see how I can go home and face my parents," the nameless voice resumed.

"Screw your parents!" Stunned at his own outburst, Marcus paused. "I mean, sure your folks want you to do well, but really, whose life are we dealing with—yours or theirs?

"Where are you now?" Leaving the door open, he eased slowly back inside the room.

The caller then hesitated. "I'd rather not say."

"Okay, then." Marcus tried another approach. "What year are you?"

"Freshman," the caller replied. A slight pause, before adding: "In pre-med."

"So you've got all the more time to make up for this semester," Marcus urged. "If you really did bomb out—I mean, if things really didn't go all that well. No one has a clue in any of these science courses..."

Repeatedly, Marcus assured the unknown caller that his family cared about him, that people were more important than grades. Banal, tired clichés, now seeming the acme of human wisdom.

"Thank you for talking to me," the caller whispered cryptically at length. And then hung up without another word.

"Hello?" Marcus said urgently. "Hello?" In response, there was only a dial tone. He replaced the receiver, and waited thirty seconds before calling the campus police.

"Can you remember anything else he said?" The uniformed officer had appeared within minutes, accompanied by Hall Director Jean Cornell. Yes, the caller had sounded fairly lucid, Marcus told them. No, he didn't seem hysterical. No, he hadn't given his location, nor offered any other clues.

The freshman asked hopefully, "Is there any way you can still trace the call?"

"I'm afraid not," the officer replied, unblinking. As Marcus could help them no further, he and Cornell excused themselves.

Marcus heard nothing more about the incident. Ever after, he wondered what ultimately became of the mystery caller.

A night later Marcus was back in his own living room, in front of the television, a Hostess pie in one hand and a glass of milk on the end table. Upstairs his parents slept; he had the room to himself as the Chargers and Raiders waged the final game of the regular season.

His own exams, he knew, had not been a rousing success. But here, in the familiar comfort of home, it no longer seemed so imperative.

FRESHMAN II

The affair was black-tie, the university's Harvest Moon Ballroom a veritable sea of tuxedos and designer gowns. Within the cavernous space, upstairs from Whitehall Theater, administrators and faculty doyens had joined local luminaries—including Glanbury Mayor Kathleen Steadham and Mercantile Bank Chairman David Gauss—in honoring President Shenford for his twenty years of service.

The president himself had arrived fashionably late, emerging from his long black limousine with his eldest daughter on one arm, trailed by two stone-faced bodyguards. Despite the evening's cold drizzle, he'd been greeted by perhaps thirty student protesters, chanting their displeasure over their tuition bills. During the holiday, parents were advised that tuition for the next year had been set at $8,450, an increase of 12.1 percent.

> *Shenford-hey, Shenford-ho!*
> *Where did all our money go?*
>
> *Shenford-ho, Shenford-hey!*
> *How much did you spend today?*

Yet an equal number of students applauded Shenford as he made his way to the building's front entrance. At thirty-one, Frances Shenford Butler was accustomed to the drama that attended her father's position, and remained equally oblivious.

"Was that his wife or his daughter?" piped one of the curiosity-seekers outside.

"Probably his wife," another responded. "Old guys with money get all the hot young chicks."

"Is he really that rich?"

"That tux ain't rented, that's for sure."

The University *Press* would commemorate the occasion with banner headlines, assorted encomia, and a special pullout section chronicling the advances of the Shenford era. By contrast, the *Guardian* merely touted the president's survival skills, in an editorial simply captioned "The Shenford Score." The less charitable *Forbidden Knowledge* declaimed "Enough is Enough," citing a legacy of conflict and dissension and "erosion of student rights."

Though tonight, Shenford had relished the singing of his praises, a series of guest speakers extolling his leadership. Mayor Steadham hailed the president's vision, putting aside their fierce clashes over the school's expansionism. Edward Poole, chairman of the Overseers, gave an eloquent panegyric calling Shenford's achievements "nothing short of miraculous." Finally the gathering erupted in applause as Shenford himself took the podium, following Poole's introduction.

At length, Shenford raised his hand for silence. The room hushed at once.

"I must say that I am touched by your kind words," he pleasantly began. "Tonight's accolades are something I shall always cherish—even if I did write them myself."

In response, there was a wave of laughter. The audience listened, enraptured, riveted by his powerful presence.

"You have paid me many compliments tonight," he averred. "Until now, I'd never known how enjoyable that could be." More laughter. "However, I must grant that the changes we have witnessed during this administration could not have been the work of one man. Together, we can all take pride in the evolution of Metropolitan University from third-rate commuter college status to international prestige." Thunderous applause.

Buoyed by audience approbation, the president outlined his goals for Met's *next* twenty years. The university would take its place among the world's elite institutions, its student body culled from the top ten percent of applicants. The faculty, already first-rate, would be second to none. A series of ambitious fundraising campaigns providing impetus for further years of unparalleled growth.

At the end, the audience rose to its feet in applause—an ovation that continued as Shenford left the podium and disappeared into the throng.

"Well, hello, Jacob." He greeted a familiar face at the bar. Jacob Klein was one of three Overseers remaining from the anti-Shenford faction of years past. Now reduced to token opposition, his antipathy undimmed.

Shenford clapped his longtime antagonist on the shoulder. "I'm glad you could make it tonight."

"That was quite a speech, Fortin," Klein said guardedly. He paused, and with an effort added, "Congratulations."

"Thank you, Jacob. Can I get you a drink?"

The Overseer shook his head. "No, nothing for me, thanks."

"Well, don't mind if I have one myself. If you'll excuse me…"

Later, surrounded by adoring well-wishers, the president sipped a Manhattan, his expression satisfied. Tonight's celebration having partly atoned for years of internecine strife.

From Shenford's perspective, it was final: The war, at last, was over.

And victory was his.

Despite campuswide promotion, Video Game Night was a bust. By 7 P.M., the tournament had drawn fewer than twenty patrons—roughly the average attendance for a Friday evening—to the Union rec room.

I guess it's true what they say about these kids, game room manager Eddie Halloran thought sourly, prior to opening the event. They don't much give a rip about anything.

But the half-dozen Mutants who accompanied Dwight Manning had come with a purpose—to see their floormate win the Galaga competition.

Galaga was Dwight's current pet project. During Christmas break he'd spent hours honing his skills at the Outer Limits Arcade back home. Since then, he had twice breached the million-point mark, his supremacy on campus unchallenged.

At three minutes past the hour, Halloran and two attendants indifferently explained the competition's rules. (Providing in essence, that the high scorers on each of the four featured games would claim bragging rights, plus a complimentary dinner for two at Yee's Chinese Restaurant.) Then they declared the contest open.

"I think I'd better go last," Dwight told his rivals, who stood clustered about the machine; and then waited his turn.

His four competitors crashed and burned in quick succession. The most able of them tallied 56,000 points.

"Go nuts," the fourth said, his last ship in ruins.

The rec room was suddenly quiet as Megan moved Dwight in front of the machine. Apart from Galaga, Dwight held the house record on Qix and Pac-Man, two of the other tournament games. (The exception was Defender, whose complex controls defied his mastery.)

"Let's go, Captain!" Dan Kirk said, while Megan took a quarter from the roll in Dwight's backpack and fed it into the slot. The machine then played its brief opening theme, and Dwight's ships materialized for Stage 1.

Dwight began cautiously, letting his foes fall into formation as they swarmed onscreen. ("They're worth more points when attacking," someone explained.) At this early stage their movements were slow, their fire easily evaded.

From the top row one of the alien flagships began to descend, emitting its purple tractor beam. In response Dwight cut sharply to the left—directly into the ray's path. The Phoenix sucked up his ship, and returned to the head of the formation with its captive.

The game is 45 seconds old, and Dwight's ship has been captured, the sacrifice seemingly deliberate. Outwardly unconcerned, he moved his second ship to the right and began picking off the red invaders on that side.

The Phoenix began its downward sweep, its captive in tow. Seeing his chance, Dwight blasted it, careful to leave the hostage ship intact. The now-freed spacecraft docked with its twin onscreen, providing double firepower.

"See, that's what he intended all along." Wally relayed this obvious fact to the audience.

"KICK ASS, CAPTAIN!" Troll suddenly roared. Startled, Megan shushed him. Others turned to stare at Troll, Halloran glowering from behind the desk.

Undistracted, Dwight kept shooting. Soon, only two of the yellow bugs remained. Dwight zapped one, then curiously let the other flit by.

Toward the bottom of the screen the bug executed a circular motion, then disappeared and reemerged from the top.

"This is the boring part. You all might want to come back later," he said. But no one moved as Dwight continued to let the yellow bug pass.

"What is he doing?" A freshman in a Hartford Whalers jacket nudged Marcus Pullman.

"I don't know." Marcus shrugged, admitting, "I've never seen this before."

Gradually, the onlookers became restless. Finally one yelled, "Hey, give someone else a turn if you're just gonna sit there!"

Wally turned toward the voice. "Shh. Quiet, buddy." Nonthreateningly, he smiled. "Genius at work. Do not disturb."

"How long is this supposed to take, whatever it is?" another boy persisted.

"Just be patient." Dwight's reply was flat and toneless.

"Will you leave him alone, you'll make him nervous!" Megan sputtered. Still dodging his opponent's fire, Dwight ignored them.

While the crowd watched in silence, the bug's shots became less frequent. And within minutes, ceased altogether.

"See, it's stopped," Dwight said. "When it goes by twice in a row without shooting, that means it's stopped."

The alien ran its fishhook pattern down the screen four more times.

"Now we can shoot this sucker." Dwight erased the lone bug, and Stage 1 at last was history.

A fresh swarm of aliens appeared. Again Dwight let them fall into position before launching his counterassault. Yet something was surely amiss...

"Why don't they try to shoot you?" someone finally asked.

"I just fixed it so they can't," Dwight said without elaboration. And slowly the light dawned.

The second stage was the opposite of the first. His foes defenseless,

Dwight cleared the screen in no time, winning his first bonus ship at 10,000 points. Stage 3 was the first of the game's Challenging Stages, a free target-practice round with aliens traversing the screen in set patterns.

With the advantage of double firepower, Dwight dispatched the incoming swarms almost as they appeared. The display announced that he'd shot a perfect 40-for-40 in the stage, earning a 10,000-point bonus.

During the next three rounds, his foes began dive-bombing aggressively, in an effort to ram Dwight's ships. But he eluded them with ease, in Screen 7 posting another perfect Challenging Stage and winning his second bonus ship at 70,000.

The crowd behind him, having grown steadily since the 50K mark, began buzzing as Dwight hit 100,000 with his full fleet intact. The bugs began swooping down three, then four at a time…and still he routed them as if by magic. The score indicator passed the 200,000 post, then topped 300,000 in short order.

"Oh, my Gowad!" a frizzy-haired brunette said as Stage 33 began. "I've never seen anybody get this far before!"

"I've seen *him* get this far before," replied one of the game-room regulars.

Another perfect Challenging Stage lifted Dwight beyond 400,000. Then at 420,000 another bonus spacecraft—this one stored in memory, with no room left onscreen.

Dwight breezed through Stages 40 and 41, then eclipsed the 500,000 level in 42. His audience reverentially silent, the competition itself forgotten. The other games in the rec room abandoned as patrons came over and watched. Others, alerted by jungle telegraph, wandered in at odd intervals.

"Gonna put another million up there tonight?" Halloran smiled as he passed by on his way to the front counter.

"You know it," Dwight quickly responded.

"Good man." Halloran nodded and resumed his position at the desk.

Reaching under the counter, he took a copy of *Player One*, the amusement-industry trade journal, and sat back in his chair. The wall clock showed a quarter to nine, an hour and fifteen minutes before closing time.

At 610,000 Dwight mistimed a dodge and lost his right ship. A collective moan went up from the crowd.

All right, we got that out of the way, he rationalized. It was the longest he had gone without losing a life. Undaunted, he finished the screen, regaining double firepower for the next Challenging Stage.

As Dwight passed seven, then eight hundred thousand, the crowd began to buzz in anticipation of witnessing a million-point game. "So what do you think—is he gonna do it?" the kid in the Whalers Jacket turned to Marcus.

"Don't say anything; you'll screw him up," another voice admonished. But beyond 900,000 the tension became unbearable.

"Hey, you gotta see this—I think he's gonna break a mill here!" one plaid-shirted patron greeted a newcomer at the door.

In Stage 77 Dwight lost both ships at once, and survived another shaky moment before completing the round. Balls of ice formed in stomachs while the audience held its breath, the magic number within 50,000...

"Stay with it, Captain. You're almost there." Troll's voice was uncharacteristically subdued.

"Let's go, Captain!" Wally encouraged. The crowd then picked up the chant as Dwight eliminated all of the winged scorpions in the next Challenging Stage. Halloran looked up at the sound, bemused, and returned to his *Player One*.

All at once Halloran sat up straight, his attention riveted on an item in the magazine's "Bonus Points" column. The brief squib spotlighted 15-year-old Ryan Luckovich of Wilmington, Delaware, who last month had set the official Galaga world record at 1,637,000.

He looked toward one wall, where the rec room's high scores were displayed on white posterboard. Including Dwight's house mark of 1,482,670, set just days past. The clock's hands showed nine-twenty, forty minutes before closing time.

In the crowd, anticipation hit a fever pitch as Stage 82 opened with Dwight's tally at 994,000. And when the display reset to zero, a roar of ecstasy filled the game room—a primal, exultant sound, giving way to sustained applause.

"Yesss!" Wally and his floormates jubilantly exchanged high-threes. Dwight gave a quick thumbs-up sign, and kept firing. His fingers were slightly numb, the sensation spreading to his arms. His shoulder felt stiff, and he wondered how much longer he could go on.

From the jukebox, Foreigner began performing *Feels Like the First Time.*

"Classic tune." Wally nodded his approbation, while Dwight kept shooting. Spurred by the memory of countless gaming sessions at Park Lanes, his hometown bowling center, during his middle-school years.

Behind the counter Halloran fidgeted nervously, aware that Dwight had again exceeded one million. And then performed a first in fifteen years on the job: leaving his post to view a game in progress.

The audience oohed as Dwight neared, then passed Stage 100. The jukebox played a blend of contemporary and classic: *Waiting for a Girl Like You*; Steve Miller's *Rock 'n Me*; Fleetwood Mac's *Don't Stop.* (This last, Wally remembered, had been the theme at his senior prom, a yesterday forever gone.)

In Stage 114, Dwight surpassed his own house record. Then the million-five mark fell in rapid succession. Behind him, a worshipful crowd stood mesmerized, unaware of his approach to immortality.

"He must be kicking some butt." The voice came from a small, greasy-haired freshman wedged behind Troll, where latecomers struggled to follow the action.

"Damn straight," Troll said. And felt Megan's light swat on his forearm.

"What're you hittin' me for? I was just being sociable." Troll then turned, and used his bulk to draw the freshman in where he could see.

Again in Stage 128, Dwight lost both ships at once. And, within seconds, shot his own captured fighter by mistake. The audience groaned with empathy.

"Damn—that pisses me off!" He slapped the screen in frustration. But Halloran said not a word. The kid was on the brink, with 5,000 points to go.

"That's okay, son. You're just trying to keep it interesting." The manager ran a hand through his close-cropped, silver-white hair. And as the next stage began, determined not to make a sound.

For seconds, Halloran looked straight ahead. Then the dam broke as the stage's three winged scorpions gave Dwight a quick 2,000 points— and vaulted him over the top.

"Hot damn, you done it!" Halloran exulted. Then, oblivious to the stares from the audience: "Kid, you just broke the world record!" He held up the trade journal, as if for verification. "Did you hear me, you *broke the world record—*"

His words were lost in a roar of celebration, as the rec room exploded with joy. Megan darted forward to peck Dwight's cheek, and began jumping up and down in glee as others applauded, then surged forth to hail the new king.

"I'm not finished yet," Dwight reminded his audience. But within, a supreme ecstasy reigned—a triumphant jubilation beyond anything he'd experienced. *Right now*, he was Number One, alone atop Mount Everest, each subsequent stage a new horizon...

"Captain—what do you want to hear?" Wally waved a quarter aloft. He listened, then turned and sidled over to the jukebox, returning as Earth, Wind & Fire began pounding out *Fantasy*.

Dwight Manning was flying. His wheelchair was the starship Fantasy, sailing at warp speed through previously uncharted galaxies. The cosmos lay before him, unbounded, its frontiers marked by increasing stage numbers: One-fifty, 160, 175. His nirvana was such that Dwight barely noticed when he hit his second million, the song's pulsating rhythms echoing in his mind...

The reverie abruptly ended in Stage 194, with the loss of his right ship. Dwight's audience moaned softly, as though awakened from a hypnotic trance.

"Does this game have an end?" Whalers Jacket inquired.

"Let's find out," Dwight said, his ships heeding the clarion call for Stage 200.

The rest of the game was a blur. The same foes in their accustomed formations, even the now-familiar advanced challenging stages...everything seemed to run together. After the atoms came the arrowheads, then the Galaxians...

Stage 255 brought another showdown with the blue centipedes—the last and most difficult bonus stage in the cycle. Dwight eliminated the first four intergalactic arthropods, but missed the last two segments of the fifth as they left the screen in opposite directions. Exhausted, he readied himself for another alien assault.

He fired two shots, then stopped. This time, no enemies appeared on the screen. The screen itself was blank, except for the stage indicator and his four remaining ships.

The indicator read STAGE 0.

Dwight fired two more shots. Again, nothing happened. His ships remained poised, alone in the blackness of interstellar space. The audience, puzzled, gave an uneven chorus of "What happened?"

"I win," Dwight said, quickly grasping the situation. The game had somehow become suspended in limbo—his ships remained battle-ready, but play would not continue. His final score was 3,341,800, more than double the previous record.

"Go ahead and turn it off," he told Halloran. "This game's over."

It was three minutes before midnight.

The show over, the spectators converged on Dwight, patting his wheelchair and yelling homage. Halloran shook Dwight's hand, then quickly shut off the machine and announced that the game room was closed.

(The phenomenon of Stage 0, it was later explained, stemmed from a condition known as "byte overload." Stage 255 in base 10—in binary, 11111111—represented the limit of capacity, the count afterward resetting to zero. A situation unaddressed in the game program, the machine not knowing what to do at this point.)

The Mutants escorted the new titleholder back to Sterling Hall, raucously chanting his name and pumping their fists into the frigid night sky. Even Megan joined in the chant as she steered Dwight along, convinced she could push the Titanic up Alston Boulevard.

For Dwight, the procession mirrored his intergalactic travels, the path boundless and unobstructed. He did not feel handicapped at all. It was that rare, sublime moment of absolute perfection.

Returning to the dorm, the Mutants staged an impromptu celebration, and it was past 2 A.M. when Megan was able to put the Galaga champion of the world to bed. And Dwight had no sooner shut his eyes than he was again on board the good ship Fantasy.

Excerpt from "The Wizard of Park Lane," *People* Magazine, Feb. 5, 1982 (p. 54):

Though confined to a wheelchair by muscular dystrophy, Dwight Manning continues to explore uncharted frontiers. The 18-year-old Metropolitan University freshman, a native of Park Lane, Connecticut, is believed to be the first such severely handicapped student to attend the prestigious institution, where he is working toward a degree in computer science. Aided by a staff of four personal-care attendants, he lives on campus, and recently completed his first semester with a 3.2 grade-point average.

The latest remarkable chapter in the Manning saga, however, unfolded last Friday night at the Met Student Union, where Dwight managed to play Galaga for 3 hours and 47 minutes on one quarter, setting a new world record with a score of 3.3 million points before the game mysteriously shut down after the 255th screen...

From "Aboard the Starship Fantasy," Glanbury *Wire* Sunday Magazine, Feb. 7, 1982 (p. 5):

...Of his adjustment to college life, Dwight admits that, "Like most freshmen, I have to continually remind myself why I'm here. I have to force myself to stay focused, and not party too much."

Like many of today's video-game masters, Dwight began by playing pinball, starting at age twelve. ("I could've paid this semester's tuition with the money I've put into these games," he says matter-of-factly.) By his account, he began "concentrating seriously" on Galaga last November, and within weeks was regularly scoring over 500,000. As for his discovery of the game's admittedly arcane secret, Dwight says, "I don't know, it's really weird…it's like no one person discovered the trick, but a bunch of players sort of put our notes together and came up with it." Wryly, he laughs. "Of course, now that I'm blabbing to the press, it won't be a secret anymore…"

It is a matter of history, though, that Dwight Manning's reign as world Galaga champion lasted just twelve days. On February 10, sixteen-year-old Scott Belzak of Chicago, who'd independently uncovered the game's secret, tallied a score of 3,411,000 to claim the throne. In time, the trick became common knowledge, with subsequent marks obscured as players asymptotically approached the game's theoretical maximum score.

Inwardly, Dwight knew there would be no encore performance. His hour of glory having passed, he returned to playing the game "the honest way," thereby removing himself from contention.

"Hey-y, look who's back from the dead!" Wally Hall grinned as Marcus appeared in his doorway.

"*Good* morning, gentlemen." Marcus beamed at his floormates, as if to flaunt his recovery from last night's binge—the first drunken evening of his life.

"You were pretty trashed last night there, stud," Bill Kaplan said jauntily.

"You were cruising," Dave Logan affirmed. He was wearing a white T-shirt and boxer shorts, showing the thick matted hair that covered his limbs. It was Saturday morning, raw and damp, most of their neighbors still comatose from last night's floor party.

"I'll take your word for it." Marcus smiled, appropriately modest. Already he had showered and dressed—albeit on autopilot—and there was no hangover. Yet the inability to remember was disquieting.

Through the fog, the night appeared as a medley of disjointed images. Some skinny kid from Seven accidentally dropping a bottle of Molson in their room; Rob making the hapless culprit clean up the mess before banishing him from the floor. Sampling fruit-flavored grain alcohol punch ladled from steel garbage cans, garnished with apples and oranges smuggled from the cafeteria in backpacks and coat pockets. Guzzling water ostentatiously from a used Everclear bottle, and fooling no one. (The label on the bottle warned that the contents were 190 proof, and were advisably kept from open flame.)

He'd tried one glass of punch—the first drink he'd ever taken. It tasted a little bitter, but surprisingly he felt nothing. So he'd had another. And another and...well, the stuff had a way of sneaking up on you. Marcus would learn later that he had puked in a shower stall, and that Rob had finally wound up carrying him to bed.

I drowned my sorrows last night, he thought privately. Though this jest held an unsettling grain of truth. He wasn't like Mark Walsh, who roamed the halls all night wired on coke and then slept through his next day's classes; yet Marcus felt himself...drifting. He'd only pulled a 2.4 last term, it was cold and dark outside, the gutters caked with dirty slush...it was becoming harder to get out of bed in the morning. Last week, his first Physics II exam had come back with an accusing red "43" on the cover. He had also dropped Technical Design—a basic Engineering requirement—to be taken again at a later time.

"How does your head feel?" Wally now asked, almost paternally.

"I'm fine." Marcus again smiled, still standing awkwardly in the doorway.

"Hey, if you want to come in, you don't have to wait for an invitation in the mail," Dan Kirk said at last.

Marcus took a stutter-step forward, then froze. By Dan's desk clock it was 10:40 A.M. Meaning he was due at the bookstore in twenty minutes.

Politely the freshman excused himself, then turned and left the room. Conscious of the light laughter that followed.

Although the winter was not excessively harsh, the arrival of spring was obscured by several false starts. The occasional balmy February afternoon offset by the lingering snow squalls that would persist into mid-April.

During a post-President's Day cold snap, Megan chanced to encounter a homeless veteran outside the Lucky Mart. And, appalled by the city's indifference to the Duke's plight, snuck His Grace into the Hall through a fire door, enabling him to sleep in the floor's lounge before being booted by senior staff members the next morning. For this act of charity, Megan was placed on disciplinary probation and threatened with expulsion from the dorm.

"You're wasting your time trying to help someone like that," Rob Moreland chided her at dinner that evening. "He's a bum; he's living out on the street because he wants to. You could give him a thousand dollars, a suit and a job, and six months later you'd find him as he was before."

"Why don't you try it for yourself, and see how you like it?" Megan returned, with such conviction that Rob let it pass.

Later that week, the Housing Office announced that as of September 1983, all freshmen and sophomores would be required to live on campus. The Athletic Department denied reports of the Titans' bid for an Ivy League berth, amid charges of status-seeking. The administration further disavowed any such interest, President Shenford stating that, "Our athletes would gain no advantage, apart from less formidable competition." The president also created a stir with a guest column in the Bristol *Telegraph* which advocated raising the voting age to 25, based on the "precipitous decline in maturity among so-called young adults"; and published a scathing critique of America's eroding educational standards in a *U.S. News & World Report* essay entitled "Shall the Illiterate Inherit the Land?"

Subsequent to these pronouncements, the *Guardian* ran a jeering editorial headlined "Fame and Fortin: The Fruitless Quest for Glory." The piece mocked Shenford's tireless self-promotion, and the noxious egotism that had burned many bridges. According to the author, Shenford once had appeared on Richard Nixon's short list for Budget Director, and had spurned subsequent invitations to head the state's Department of Commercial Affairs.

Then there was Shenford's much-publicized offer to manage the state's finances. That had been in late 1974, with the state hobbled by severe recession, faced with crippling deficits. Under Shenford's proposal, the state's fall elections would be held in abeyance, its "bankrupt" government instead placed into receivership. As receiver, Shenford would assume plenary authority over each aspect of the budget, and over all state employees, including elected officials. (Notwithstanding this selfless gesture, the author noted, the state had clung to the constraints of the democratic process.)

"Hey, listen to this." Dave Logan adjusted his glasses on his hawkish nose, before reading aloud the editorial's closing lines. "'Yet at this stage, any reports of Shenford's imminent departure must be taken with the proverbial grain of salt. The good doctor will in all likelihood remain with us to the end of his career, perhaps the end of his days. For no one else will have him, while we remain powerless to exorcise him.'"

"Harsh, but probably accurate," was Dan Kirk's response. He was seated at his desk with a Michelob in hand, joined by Wally and the half-dozen others assembled for the February L.B. His jacket hung over the back of the chair, still damp from the sleetstorm they'd braved to get their beer and chips from the Lucky Mart.

"And who could afford him anyway?" Bill Kaplan said. "He's making what, like one-eighty grand a year now?"

Dave mutely shook his head. And, turning the page, smiled briefly at a cartoon depicting a cutaway view of St. Peter's Basilica. Within the sanctuary, a group of men in miters and black vestments sat in solemn gathering, one looking inquiringly to his neighbor. The caption read: "Can we vote for ourselves?"

Outside, the sleet fell in steady, gray-white sheets. The sky was dark and murky, with no promise of spring at hand.

From *Forbidden Knowledge*, March 1982 (p. 7):

Metropolitan University: A Capsule Outline

Full name: Shenfordian Real Estate Empire of Metropolitan University.

Area: 76 acres and expanding (presently about two-thirds the size of Vatican City).

Population: Approximately 25,000 (18,000 students; 1,800 faculty members [so we're told]; various pencil-pushers and sycophants.

Motto: *Non es* (You do not exist).

Languages: Bureaucratic doublespeak, the official language; Hindi and Chinese (roughly 80% of science labs); some English.

Form of government: Absolute megalomaniarchy.

Chief of state and head of government: His Majesty Emperor-for-Life Fortin I, Defender of the Military-Industrial Complex, Lord of the Realm, and Conqueror of the Counterculture in New England in General and at Metropolitan University in Particular (since 1962).

Currency: Credit-hour (1 = approx. $250 US [1981-82 exchange rates]); 120 credit-hours = 1 diploma; 1 diploma used to = security.

The world's smallest absolute monarchy, Metropolitan University is located entirely within the

City of Glanbury, in a roughly rectangular area on the northern and southern banks of the Monadnock River.

The original settlers were members of the Working Class, for whom the institution was conceived as a homeland at the time of its founding in 1903. Metropolitan subsequently enjoyed rapid growth, centralizing its campus along the Monadnock during the 1920's, under the administration of President Robert Whitmarsh. Succeeding administrations continued to work toward the development of a residential campus, with the result that today some 70 percent of Met's subjects actually live there.

Following the rise to power of President Fortin Shenford in 1962, the Working Class was systematically driven out by the Exorbitant Tuition Hikes. A few members of the aboriginal tribe, though, are believed to remain, thanks to the financial aid programs which they wouldn't need to begin with if the place weren't so darned expensive.

Since putting down a 1970 insurrection, Shenford has solidified his grip on power, crafting a totalitarian regime marked by press censorship and suppression of civil liberties. The exact date on which Shenford crowned himself Emperor and established the university as a sovereign state independent of the U.S. Constitution (particularly the Bill of Rights, and most especially the First Amendment) has been lost to history. All we know is, that's how it went down in the end. The ruler's expansionist policies have also resulted in frequent clashes with outlying...

Hey—yo! What the hell? Who do you goons think you are, breaking in like this? Where's your warrant? Get away from that press, what do you think you're...

———

Graffiti on a carrel in Digby Library:

Q – How many Met girls does it take to change a light bulb?

A – Five. Four to bitch about it, and one to pout until her boyfriend does it.

"One hundred dollars a year out of *your* pocket for Union fees. One hundred dollars—and you have zero input on how this money is used. If elected Student Union president, I can promise you that's going to change!"

From the throng on Walden Plaza, there were shouts of approval. The other members of Steve Elrod's SO WHAT slate—vice-presidential nominee Karen Mays; secretary candidate Robyn Serino; and treasurer hopeful Nick Kerensky—nodded agreement as they stood behind him on the chapel's steps. It was cold for mid-March, and quite breezy; yet their maiden campaign appearance had drawn a lively crowd. The students seemed to like Elrod, a slight brown-haired sophomore with a thin mustache.

The slate's members knew they had pressed a hot button. Though in recent years they'd quietly forked over their program fees, Met students deeply resented the administration's tight control of Union funds.

Standing toward the rear of the plaza, Wally nudged Dan Kirk in the ribs. "I think we've got a winner here," he advised.

"Yeah, but will they be able to *do* anything?" His roommate seemed unconvinced.

"The university administration," Elrod resumed, "thinks we're incapable of handling *our* money. They don't think we're mature or responsible enough—they have said this, in as many words. But the fact is, we're well ahead of them." Another crescendo of applause, as the candidate added, "This administration may never change its mind...but we will never give up our rights.

"The only viable solution"—he paused for effect—"is to create a new and independent Union."

From the crowd, someone asked, "How are you gonna make that happen?"

"That was my next point." Suavely, the candidate smiled. "What we're proposing, in effect, is an amicable divorce. To make the Union a separate legal entity, apart from Metropolitan. When we move into the Executive Suite, the first thing we'll do is fill out some paperwork from the Secretary of State's office, and incorporate the sucker."

There was a pause while his listeners digested this concept.

"That's the Secretary of this state, by the way," Elrod parenthetically added. "No relation to General I'm-in-Charge-Here." The crowd laughed at his witticism, and again began to applaud.

"When you vote for SO WHAT on April 19th, you will vote to declare your independence from the Met administration. Then your money will truly be yours again. And we will spend *your* money the way *you* want to spend it, not the way President Shenford and Dean Grayling want to spend it!" The students applauded wildly, a prolonged ovation that rocked the Boulevard.

"The administration says we're ignorant..." Elrod paused, building toward his climax. "They say we're immature. And, most of all, apathetic. The faculty and alumni say we're apathetic; I think even *Barron's* says we're apathetic. To which we say..."

"SO WHAT!" his running mates finished.

From a cardboard box, the slate's members took four painter's caps, which were immediately donned. The caps were dyed a bright orange, the slate's name printed in black magic marker above the bill.

"That's right, SO WHAT." Elrod flaunted their new campaign

headwear. "Student Oppression Will Halt, And Today. SO WHAT!"

Energized, the crowd began chanting the name and pumping their fists in the air—an unprecedented occurrence in Union politics.

"Well, they've got my support." Sterling president George Hunter nodded to his dormmates on the way back to the Hall, adding, "At any rate, I'd say this election's been decided."

Dan, walking beside him, remained doubtful. "But will they be able to change anything?"

"Who knows?" George brushed the impertinent query aside. "But they'll make things a helluva lot more interesting, for certain."

As she usually did the night before an exam, Megan had gone to the library following a quick dinner at the Union. Tonight, however, she was scheduled to work the late shift, and at seven-thirty she repacked her books and left for the dorm.

Stepping off the elevator on Four, she trudged down the hall to her room, where the pounding beat of Elvis Costello signaled her roommate's presence. She tried the door, found it locked, and used her key to enter.

"Close the door, you stupid ass!" Beth screamed. The room was dark, and filled with the unmistakable odor of marijuana. Bemused, Megan clicked on the lights—and shrieked loudly when she saw what she had interrupted.

"Go on, get outta here—what are you, retarded?" Her roommate sat up in bed, furious.

Hastily Megan turned and ran from the room, quickly closing the door behind her. She heard the stereo shut off, and Mark Walsh then emerged from the room, shamefaced.

"I'll see you later," he told Beth lamely. Then brushed past her waiting roommate without a glance. He had dressed hurriedly, his Hang Ten shirt on backward, the small feet displayed on the reverse.

"You are so ignorant!" her roommate exploded when Megan walked in. Beth was wearing a red satin robe, her long blonde hair in disarray.

"Why can't you get a life of your own, for a change, instead of screwing it up for everyone else?"

Megan was incredulous. "I don't believe you!" she retorted. "You pull something like this, and then you have the nerve to sit there and scream at *me*? Have you no shame whatsoever?"

"Look, I hate to tell you this, but sex isn't just something they made up in Catholic school to scare you. Yes—people really do have sex. And some of them even enjoy it."

"You shut up—what do you know about Catholic school? The point is, I don't ever want to have to see that again. If you had any idea how disgusting that is—"

"Well, how would you like it if someone walked in on you while *you* were getting laid?" Beth smiled nastily, aware of Megan's views on sex outside marriage.

For several minutes, the two argued fiercely back and forth. Finally, Beth paused and shook her head.

"You know," she said evenly, "you're really getting a rep around here."

"Me?" To Megan's mind, it was girls like Beth who got "reps."

"Yes, you. The other girls on the floor ask me, 'Has your roommate ever had sex?' And I say, 'No—I'm not sure she's ever even kissed a guy.' And they're like, 'Well, I don't want to come in your room.' You know what I mean?"

Megan's face flushed scarlet at the insinuation. Her fists clenched, her eyes rolled heavenward, as if seeking deliverance. Then, outraged beyond words, she stormed from the room.

"Did your parents have premarital sex?"

Rob looked inquisitorially at Cheryl Rudin as they sat on his bed one early April evening; Marcus scanning his sociology text, striving to ignore them.

"No!" the short-haired brunette answered with indignation. But she looked away from him, her soft brown eyes staring at the floor.

"How do you know? You weren't there," Rob persisted. A slight pause, then: "Were you?"

"I just know," Cheryl said in a small voice.

"Then what did your father do, whack off the whole time?"

"Stop...could you please just stop?" Cheryl sounded close to tears.

At his desk, Marcus absorbed the exchange with mounting fury. Rob seemed compelled to play these sadistic head games with his lovers—including Cheryl, a freshman art major he'd seen almost exclusively for the past month.

In the end, Cheryl would likely stay overnight, Rob directing him to "do a one-eighty" so she could "get unchanged." Then Marcus would be subjected to the sounds of their lovemaking, unconstrained by his presence.

Yet if Marcus complained, Rob casually dismissed his roommate's protests.

"You couldn't possibly understand these things. You've never even

106

been with a girl," Rob once flatly stated. Marcus thought fleetingly of his lone sexual experience, in the spring of the tenth grade, when he'd gone to Diane Kelly's house to borrow a record and she'd coyly invited him inside, letting it slip that her parents were away for the weekend. It had been over almost before he realized what was happening; afterward he felt only fear. (For weeks, he'd entertained visions of his bohemian blonde classmate expecting quintuplets.) The record—Samantha Sang's *Emotion*—remained in his PlatterPak at home.

"I'm not saying anything," Marcus had countered, refusing to take the bait.

Though nothing vexed him more than the monstrous injustice of it all—the way guys like Rob treated women like dirt and had them come back for more, while nice guys encountered only rejection.

Cheryl did not end up staying over this time. Yet she'd scarcely gone when Rob again declared that he had her "wrapped," exulting in his dominance of the relationship.

"Dude—if she gave me even one-tenth the grief I give her, she'd be history," he laughed.

Outraged beyond endurance, Marcus suddenly rose to his feet.

"How do you get away with that kind of abuse?" he screamed at Rob. "Why do women take that from you?—My god, if they had any sense, they'd have nothing to do with you, period!"

Horrified at his own outburst, Marcus suddenly stopped, fearful that Rob would walk over and hit him.

Instead, his roommate responded with a look of paternal indulgence.

"Girls get hooked on having orgasms," he said quietly.

Within weeks of their epic showdown, Megan and Beth were separated, on grounds of irreconcilable differences.

"I can put you with Lori Sullivan in 415," R.A. Lisa Kornberg advised Beth. While Ann Carruthers would join Megan in 412.

"Everybody's in agreement; it's all settled."

To the R.A., the move came as no surprise. And while convinced that the roommates deserved one another, she'd acceded in the interest of harmony.

On April 12, Met's Housing Department released its spring lottery numbers. Within class strata, the computer-generated random digits determined students' places—and range of options—in choosing accommodations for next year.

In Sterling Hall, the numbers were posted by SSN on the main floor, outside the cinema room. Where a mix of groans and exultations from residents told the story.

"It feels weird, this going on and us not being involved." Wally flipped a Frisbee at Dan as they passed the crowd downstairs, en route to the Green. Behind them, Troll and Bill Kaplan viewed the mob with condescension. The four were scheduled to move into The House on May 15th, and had given the lottery a miss.

To no one's surprise, Rob Moreland drew an excellent number—4256—and hinted at "connections" aiding his good fortune. Likewise true to form, Marcus took number 6893—just 107 places from dead last. Though Rob agreed to "pull" Marcus back onto Four with him, while he angled for a room at Zeta House. (Where one of his fraternity confreres was slated to graduate next December.)

"Don't say I never did anything for you," he advised, only partly in jest, as the roommates returned from Phillips Gym after making their selection.

Of Sterling 4's nine freshmen, eight would return. ("At least it's convenient to my job," Megan told her mother during their regular Sunday-night phone conversation.) Meanwhile, the flood of departing sophomores helped Beth Brown claim the much-coveted women's single, and Sanjay Motwani the men's.

"It's like everybody's leaving the floor at once. Including the girls." Bob Spencer, the floor's unofficial historian, made this comment over drinks at Jokers that Thursday night. "Kirsten and Joanne are getting an apartment off campus next fall..." He looked back at Wally, who nodded affirmation. "Then you've got at least twelve new freshmen coming in..."

"Looks like a rebuilding year ahead," Hall observed.

From the Metropolitan University *Press*, April 16, 1982 (page 1):

PRESIDENT TO JOIN REAGAN PANEL

By Ian Vorro

University President Fortin C. Shenford disclosed last week that he has been named to the Executive Committee of the President's Private Sector Survey on Cost Control, an advisory panel created by President Reagan to root out waste and inefficiency in the operation of the federal government.

Dr. Shenford, who recently celebrated the twentieth anniversary of his inaugural, is the only academic among approximately 100 members chosen thus far for the Executive Committee, which includes many of the nation's most prominent business leaders. Chaired by New York industrialist J. Peter Grace and known alternately as the Grace Commission, the panel will be subdivided into roughly three dozen task forces, each assigned to investigate a specific agency or arm of operation. A spokesman for Grace said that the commission would have "in the thousands" of members all told.

"In both the public and private sector, efficiency all too often varies inversely with scale," the President stated at a news conference following his appointment. "At the federal level, the enormous amount of waste and duplication directly affects us all, creating a needless burden on the American taxpayer."

Dr. Shenford added that, "Fortunately, most of the problems could readily be solved with a little courage and common sense…"

***

With the coming of spring, the year accelerated rapidly toward its close. Courses wound down, and Commencement preparations were finalized, with Joel Hollenbeck, the state's senior U.S. Senator, confirmed to deliver the keynote address.

Student government elections were held on April 19th. As expected, the SO WHAT slate won a landslide victory, outpolling their nearest rivals by two-to-one. In Sterling Hall, George Hunter was reelected president; Dave Logan tapped for the Student Union Senate. Both ran unopposed.

A week later, with the start of Reading Period, the *Guardian* shut down for the semester, liberating its deadline-fatigued staff. As most were Journalism majors—ergo without finals to speak of—they felt doubly relieved.

On University Green, students availed themselves of the Reading Period to play Frisbee and work on their tans. Binoculars appeared in dorm windows as male residents ogled coeds sunbathing on the lawns below. Rowhouse tenants sat perched on fire escapes along Franklin Street, as though trusting the warm weather for the first time.

With the arrival of exam week, such leisure activities ground to an abrupt halt. Residence halls were suddenly quiet, save for the late-night rants of harried freshmen on the oral proclivities of chemistry and calculus. At the Lucky Mart coffee and caffeinated sodas vanished quickly from shelves, Digby Library remaining open around the clock.

In the end, most would emerge unscathed. Yet for some the final push was too little, too late.

His bluebook empty except for a few elementary equations, Marcus desperately scanned the five problems on the physics exam, searching for clues. Mean angular velocity, harmonic and fundamental frequencies…the exam might have been printed in Hebrew.

Surrounded by two hundred others in Hale Auditorium, he felt more alone and helpless than at any time in his life. Berating himself for the missed classes, for his reluctance to seek tutoring, his complete cluelessness at the moment.

With one of the allotted two hours elapsed, self-reproach yielded to panic. Sweating, he envisioned Met's Health Department informing his parents their son had freaked out during an exam, and recommending a good deal of rest.

Through the final half-hour, Marcus continued his vain efforts. He fancied that he was beginning to understand some of the questions when time was called.

Slowly he walked to the front of the room and dropped his bluebook in the appropriate box. Then, beaten and resigned, turned and left the auditorium.

On May 14, the university staged its annual Commencement exercises, awarding nearly 3,000 graduate and undergraduate degrees in an outdoor ceremony on the Monadnock. The president, again in green robes, imparted his benediction on the senior class and sent them out into the world.

Another year had thus concluded.

Among the freshmen, there had been casualties.

A hapless few had flunked out of school—among them Mark Walsh, who'd put an entire year up his nose and flagged all his courses. ("We're $12,000 poorer, and it's as if you never were there at all!" his parents screamed before consigning their elder son to Army service.)

Six percent would return on probationary status. Including Marcus Pullman, whose F in Physics II capped a semester in which he earned just nine credits and barely attained sophomore standing.

Some left for financial reasons. Others, seeking a better fit, would resume studies elsewhere. Yet they were fortunate compared to the six members of the first-year class who had taken their own lives.

For the survivors, another three years remained. The journey's most treacherous run behind them.

The summer of 1982 passed. The ongoing recession deepened, with unemployment rates nearing 10 percent. Secretary of State Haig resigned. Britain won a swift and crushing victory in the Falkland Islands War, reclaiming the territory from Argentina.

In June, a record 500,000 demonstrators in New York City rallied for a nuclear freeze. Larry Holmes halted Gerry Cooney in the last great fight of either man's career. E.T.-mania swept the country as the megahit film packed theaters nationwide.

While in Glanbury, life similarly went on.

"I like a man who doesn't forget his friends," Wally told Bill Kaplan as they left Yee's Restaurant on Alston Boulevard. It was July second, Bill having treated his Housemates to dinner for the past three nights, after winning seven hundred bucks in the state lottery.

"De nada, Señor." Kaplan smiled, seated on the passenger side of Wally's elderly Karmann Ghia. Draped from the vehicle's rearview mirror were a Rubik's Cube and a Rubik's Revenge, in lieu of the fuzzy dice of the fifties.

Shortly, mail-in ballots for Rookie Drinker of the Year would be tallied. (Rob Moreland—now back at his old job with the State Highway Department— would win a lackluster campaign, Mark Walsh running a distant second.)   While Fortin Shenford, having begun work on the

Grace Commission, lamented "the utter fiscal incompetence" of the federal bureaucracy.

"It's a shame this can't last." Dan Kirk, riding shotgun in Troll's Plymouth Duster, looked to his associates. "I'll take eating out every night—you ask me, it beats dishwashing and shopping for groceries. You always end up at the checkout counter behind some old woman who writes a check and takes all day…"

Behind him Pete Garrett, his senior year upcoming, surveyed the deserted campus. Where a block away, Sterling's maize-colored brick facade towered above Franklin Street.

"No shit." Garrett nodded wistfully before repeating, "It's too bad this can't last."

SOPHOMORE I

She was the archetypal Marine Corps brat, well-traveled but unworldly. The offspring of an itinerant subculture where social change fought for purchase, and some neighbors did not lock their doors.

The daughter of a Master Sergeant, Rosemary Porter had been born in San Diego, arriving on campus by way of Quantico, Virginia, after four years in Okinawa. Though until this warm September Saturday, she had not visited New England.

"Ahhh hates Yankehs," senior classmate Joel Gunderson had mocked gently when Rosemary applied to Metropolitan. Which in the end, was the best school to offer adequate financial aid.

Leaving home for the first time, she felt little anxiety; for Rosemary had never been well acquainted with fear. As a child, she'd been a tomboy who played tackle football and beat up boys who bullied her friends. Would-be toughs fled at her approach, she would skateboard down the steepest hills…and once in the sixth grade at Cherry Point, she and Paul Fink had carefully taken apart a rusted 50-millimeter shell he'd found in a jungle near Subic Bay. They had collected the coarse, bluish-gray powder in an old pickle jar (it filled the jar about one-fourth of the way), then taken it to a clearing in the woods, lit it and run like hell. The whole works had instantly gone up with a terrific *swoosh,* shooting a spectacular inferno several feet into the air. (To this day, Rosemary would have sworn that the flame had cleared some of the nearby treetops.) When the blaze spent itself mere seconds later, the two slowly crept back toward the jar, finding the neck warped by the intense heat.

"Yeah, I've gone straight since then," she demurred regarding her obstreperous past. She remained most comfortable in jeans and sweats; her face, with its large green eyes and light sprinkling of freckles, devoid of makeup.

Outwardly, Rosemary exhibited a complete lack of artifice. A quality that at once set her apart from her peers.

Her dormmates followed Rosemary's progress as she moved toward the elevator ahead of her cart-pushing orientation counselors, her father's old duffel bag over one shoulder. The girls watched with curiosity, the boys savoring the subtle contours of her willowy five-foot-eight frame. Her thick, rust-colored hair was partly tied back with a rubber band, the nape of her neck visible.

"Hey, thanks guys." She nodded to the two counselors as they set her plain black footlocker on the floor of Sterling 414. The room was bare, its Spartan furnishings reminiscent of a military barracks.

"Sure, no sweat," Stu Cabral replied. The shorter of the two, he had a round, dark pleasant face, with a teddy-bear physique.

"All in a day's work, ma'am," Josh McFadden said humorously. He was a tall, spare black freshman, long-limbed, his smile infectious. Despite their first-year standing, her neighbors in 408 had offered to assist when the dorm wound up shorthanded.

"We're getting up a volleyball game later, if you're interested. The net's already set up outside." Stu paused before adding, "Maybe a floor tournament, if we have enough players."

Her features brightened. "Great, I love volleyball. When are we playing?" she asked.

"We get off at four," Stu said, thinking aloud. "So say about fiveish, downstairs on the lawn?" This was three hours away, leaving time to drop off her scholarship check at the Comptroller's Office.

From the doorway, Josh suddenly turned and pointed in her direction.

"Be there—or be a regular equilateral quadrilateral!" he warned.

Rosemary smiled warmly. "I'll be there," she promised.

Physically, they made an odd couple—Stu short and round, with soft features; Josh angular and robust, a star left-handed pitcher in high school.

The son of Philippine parents, Stu hailed from Oregon, his major Electrical Engineering. While Josh, a native of Kenosha, Wisconsin, had chosen Met's third most popular course of study. Meaning that he was Undecided.

But the roommates shared a passion for sports and games, along with an insouciant, happy-go-lucky approach to life. Outgoing and gregarious, they collected friends with ease, and were happiest when entertaining guests.

And while neither would have claimed the distinction for himself, the duo possessed a certain leadership quality. As shown by their service as orientation counselors, and by their successful promotion of the opening-weekend volleyball tournament.

Because of these qualities, their floormates naturally gravitated toward them. From the beginning their room was the social center of the floor, where residents gathered for a beer or a round of poker.

Yet the two shared another common trait that separated them from their neighbors. A trait that had, paradoxically, fallen from favor in recent years.

They lacked direction.

Like most freshmen, Rosemary spent the next day waiting in a series of long lines.

At the College of Arts and Sciences, she completed her registration. (Thus, officially becoming the first of her family to attend college.) Then a brisk hike across the river, to Phillips Gym for her student ID photo. And later, the Union for an orientation meeting at Campus Directory Assistance, where she had a work-study job.

When she returned to the Hall, her door was open and her roommate had arrived. At any rate someone was inside, busily unpacking the four suitcases that had displaced Rosemary's footlocker. Her roommate's closet door was open, and Rosemary thought she had never seen so many bright-colored outfits at once.

Rosemary made the first move. "Hi. Are you Debbie Grafton?"

The other girl turned warily, looking put off by this intrusion. "Yes, that's me." She was exquisitely slender, with long legs and runway-model features: jet-black hair, supercilious hazel eyes, lip curled in a sensuous pout. Debbie gave the other an appraising glance, noting the cheap sneakers worn without socks, the nondesigner jeans, the absence of jewelry or makeup.

"Rosemary Porter. I'm your roommate." She stuck out her hand. Debbie examined the outstretched palm for a beat, and shook it somewhat coldly.

"Where are you from?" Rosemary asked.

"Newton," Debbie replied. "I was president of the Drama Club last year, at West Newton High."

"Oh yeah? What state is that in?"

"That's Newton, Massachusetts." Amazed that any civilized human being would not know this. Then she cut to the chase: "So what business is your father in?"

Business? Rosemary thought. "He's a sergeant in the Marines."

Debbie blinked, then laughed. "You're kidding, right?"

"No..." More puzzled than provoked, Rosemary said, "Why would I kid about something like that?"

"You're not kidding," Debbie realized. "You must be on scholarship," she added, somewhat disparagingly.

Before the newcomer could respond, she began another line of inquiry: "What was your high-school class rank?"

Rosemary shrugged. "Top ten, I think. I don't know exactly."

"Was it a small school?"

Neutrally, Rosemary replied that there had been about two hundred in her graduating class. Seemingly satisfied, Debbie then presented her own *c.v.*: Her father was among Boston's elite plastic surgeons; she was in the School for the Performing Arts, looking to become an actress or return to modeling after graduation; she once had taken an acting class with Brooke Shields in New York.

"She was a snot—I didn't like her." Deb sniffed with transparent envy.

Rosemary changed the subject. "While we're both here, do you want to go downstairs and get a refrigerator?"

"A refrigerator? What for?"

"For food, of course. What do you think?" She guessed there was still time this afternoon to rent a small fridge from one of the agencies whose trucks were parked outside. "It's forty bucks for the whole year;

that's only twenty apiece."

"They give you three meals a day here—that should be enough for anyone." Eying her roommate's trim figure, Debbie added, "Ever hear of the Freshman Fifteen?"

Rosemary felt suddenly tired of this game. They could discuss this later, she thought, another round of volleyball upcoming.

"You'll change your mind once you've eaten in the cafeteria," she said lightly. And, kicking off her shoes, left to join her neighbors in the courtyard.

While the two girls were becoming fast friends, a heated sociopolitical discussion swept the boys' side of the floor.

In truth, "discussion" was perhaps a misnomer. As was often the case when Brandon Clark held court, the exchange was somewhat one-sided.

"Among the core crimes of Western Civilization," Brandon said, "is having kept women in bondage through the centuries." As he talked, he frequently gesticulated with the clipboard in his right hand. The clipboard held a strongly-worded petition for revival of the failed Equal Rights Amendment. ERA YES, read a large button on his green fatigue jacket.

Intractably, the blue-eyed freshman plowed on. "Never once," he argued, "have they known full freedom to develop their talents, or to establish an identity of their own. Thus, the majority remain personally unfulfilled, with society at large deprived of their contributions." His voice was high and strained, the words like blunt instruments.

The others in the hall—Jay Levin, Brandon's roommate in 406; neighbors Warren Allen and Adam Conway; and Marcus Pullman, the only sophomore in the group—listened with varying degrees of interest. Brandon's manic intensity holding a certain curiosity factor.

"And you'd think we'd learn from the mistakes of our parents," he added, unrelenting. "Even one generation ago, few women had any kind of life worth speaking of. Nothing but stay home and have babies." Since the divorce, when he was ten, Brandon had continued to reside with his own mother, an associate professor of history at Iowa State.

Weakly, Adam shrugged. "That was what women did then," he replied. His tone, like his broad flat face, expressionless, unnuanced.

"It's true. That was their accepted role." Jay adjusted the collar of his white T-shirt. He was tall and athletically built, his Philadelphia accent turning *role* to *rule*. "It was what they more or less had to do to fit in."

Brandon looked pained. "Why do people assume they have to fit in?" he asked. "Fitting in with the crowd means nothing. The wise man is an outcast in the land of the fools!"

"You said 'man.' Shouldn't that be 'person'?" Warren smiled at him thinly. Warren had introduced himself to his dormmates as "Chug," a nickname earned in high school for his drinking prowess. ("I'm named after my favorite verb," said the thickset English major from Vermont.)

Miffed by this interruption, Brandon snapped, "You know what I mean" before regaining his rhetorical balance.

"The root of the problem," he said, "is that this enslavement still reflects the values of the ruling class. Girls are still brainwashed into believing their fortune lies in their looks—specifically, the ability to attract the right mate. That's why, in a rich school like this, you seldom hear them talk about anything beyond hair, makeup, and clothes.

"Those SAT scores don't lie." Brandon considered the test to be the discriminatory tool of an elitist white oligarchy, but that was a separate debate. "These girls are not stupid. They just feel they have to act the part in order to gain acceptance."

At this point Rosemary rounded the corner, her interest piqued by the noise level.

"Hi," she greeted her neighbors in a soft cello voice. Then, aware that the hall had grown quiet, added: "Am I interrupting something?"

"Yes. And we're very grateful," Chug said.

Marcus would never forget his first vision of Rosemary Porter.

She was wearing a pair of well-fitting Lee jeans, with a white cotton jersey. The cuffs of her Lees were rolled up to mid-calf, and she had no shoes or socks on. Her hair in a pleasing disarray in spite of the rubber band, her face the most open and unguarded he'd seen. Worlds removed, he thought, from the stereotypical Metropolitan coed—not one of those walking neon signs from Long Island, with their neuroses and their kinky orange hair; nor some pampered nymphet seeking her M.R.S. degree. She evoked an image from one of his father's *Esquire* magazines when he was twelve, of a denim-clad farmgirl lying on the back of a horse, her bare feet in the reins, windblown hair whipping wildly about her face, laughing as though she hadn't a care in the world...

"Earth calling Marcus." Jay held one cupped hand in front of his mouth. "Earth calling Marcus—come in, please."

"Hi—I'm Rosemary Porter!" Repeating herself, she seized his hand and shook it with exaggerated eagerness, gently chiding him for his lapse.

"I'm Marcus Pullman," he remembered. Up close, painfully aware that she was four inches taller.

"You should come outside. We've got a pretty intense volleyball tournament going." She smiled before heading toward the elevators.

Brandon took a half-step forward, then resolved to get her signature later. The others wordlessly admired her exit, all thoughts of the ERA forgotten.

"Sure," Marcus said in a faraway voice. And like a robot turned and went to his room to slip on his gym shorts.

His neighbors recognized the symptoms at once. MARCUS LIKES ROSEMARY, read a message crayoned on the bathroom mirror the next morning, in Close-Up toothpaste letters.

"They can't do this! No—hell no, those bastards can't do this!"

Enraged, Steve Elrod crumpled the letter from the Dean of Students and hurled it against one wall of the sparsely-furnished office in the Union building. "This is *our* money we're talking about—where do those jerks get off impounding student funds?"

"They're saying that since you intend to separate the Union from Met itself, you're on your own, financially speaking." Beth Brown paused, awaiting further comment from the Executive Board. After interning at the *Telegraph* that summer, the onetime premed had switched her major to journalism, and joined the *Guardian* staff.

"I read the letter—they've suspended allocation of Union funds. I know what Grayling says, and he's full of crap...!" Elrod sputtered angrily, unable to finish.

Treasurer Nick Kerensky inserted a bit of gallows humor. "On the plus side, it makes my job rather less demanding."

"Do you still intend to incorporate the Union? And won't that mean having to raise your own funds?" Beth persisted, undaunted by the student leader's wrath.

Peevishly, Elrod said, "Yes, we're still planning to incorporate. I've got the papers right here in this desk. And we're not worried about money, because the administration will have to back down sooner or later." He paused for a beat. "If we can raise it on our own, well and good. If not, and the Union ends up dead in the water, then everyone knows it's the administration's fault."

"Sounds like they really mean business." Vice-president Karen Mays glanced thoughtfully at the others.

"And so do we," Elrod replied.

True to its word, the SO WHAT government was prompt in filing articles of incorporation; and on September 15, 1982 the Union received its corporate charter from the Secretary of State's office in Bristol.

Next day, the Executive Board was notified that henceforth, the Union would be assessed two thousand dollars in monthly rent for its suite of offices on campus. Further, the Union would assume sole responsibility for collection of student fees, as Met no longer would provide this service. Best wishes in your new venture, the dean's letter concluded.

"Welcome to our Law School, Mr. Justice."

Elizabeth Kerr greeted her illustrious guest in the dean's office, joined by fellow Professor of Constitutional Law Eileen Bridge and Gerard Hagen, Assistant Dean for Academic Affairs.

"What have I told you about that 'Mr. Justice' crap?" Thurgood Marshall boomed, in the voice Kerr remembered from her clerkship days.

"Judge." Kerr invoked the title Marshall favored. The others seemed awed by the presence of the living legend—the father of school desegregation, and the nation's first black Supreme Court jurist.

"Beth, it's good to see you again." The mood changed as he affectionately laid a hand on her shoulder. After a private lunch in the faculty dining room, Marshall and his reception committee would proceed to Hale Auditorium, where he was scheduled to deliver this year's Constitution Day address.

"Likewise, sir." The dean had aged in ten years, but Marshall thought privately that she was still a fetching woman. Kerr's blue eyes were deep-set, the once-straight chestnut brown hair now wavy, with the slightest tinge of gray.

Lunch was shortly preceded by the mandatory *Press* photographs. An accomplished raconteur, Marshall favored his hosts with a seamless body of reminiscences: of commuting to Howard Law School from his parents' home in a Baltimore ghetto; of ugly and sometimes harrowing encounters with white supremacist groups while working for the NAACP; of being mistaken for an elevator operator by two tourists during his early years on the High Court.

Dean Kerr, who knew these stories by heart, again politely listened. Her subordinates, who did not, hung on every word.

To no one's surprise, they ran fifteen minutes behind schedule. Riding to the auditorium, Marshall quipped that, "As the condemned man said on his way to the gallows, 'Nothing will happen until I get there.'"

At the podium, Kerr kept her introduction brief, and the Justice received a rousing welcome from the audience. Unlike years past, Hale was filled to capacity this afternoon—the auditorium's 800 seats fully packed, with dozens of standees to the rear.

In his remarks, the Justice praised the Constitution's adaptability, and the foresight of its authors in crafting a document that stood fundamentally unchanged after two centuries. Through the various amendments, he theorized, one could chart the evolution of democracy in America: women's suffrage; the abolition of slavery; even the failed Eighteenth Amendment, a futile exercise in regulating personal behavior.

"On paper right now," Marshall said in his most-applauded line, "the poorest black child, born to the poorest illiterate black woman in a run-down tarpaper shack in Alabama, possesses the same civil rights as a member of the Rockefeller family. The test of our nation's commitment to equal justice lies in making it happen..."

"Judge, it was an honor having you with us." Kerr smiled as the jurist prepared to take his leave. Following the lecture there had been a lengthy ovation, as dozens of students surrounded the podium, approaching the great man with uncharacteristic diffidence.

Marshall wasted no words on gratitude, but complimented his hosts on Met Law's academic progress. And left the dean's office with a final word for his onetime protégée.

"Next time you're in D.C., you call me, hear?"

"I will, Judge," Kerr said faithfully.

"Anybody want some more hot dogs?"

Turning, Stu eyed his floormates as another of Fenway Park's vendors approached.

"I'm all set." Chug courteously declined. "Good stuff, but those prices..." Tonight Fenway Franks, beer and popcorn had served as dinner on the floor's excursion to the fabled Boston ballyard, home to the Red Sox since William Howard Taft.

"That's what happens when a seller has a monopoly and a captive market," Brandon said. The others ignored him and watched the game. Most making their first visit to Fenway, with its old-time nuances. The asymmetry, the hand-operated scoreboard, the towering left field wall nicknamed the Green Monster.

In late September, with evenings cool and the Sox out of contention, good seats were readily available. For this antepenultimate date of the season, the Mutants had scored upper-box seats on the third-base side, across from the home dugout.

Tonight's game, however, had quickly gotten out of hand. The division-leading Milwaukee Brewers led the Sox, 9-3, paced by two of their trademark longballs: a titanic two-run blast by Robin Yount in the first inning; and a three-run job by Ted Simmons in the sixth. Gary Allenson's solo shot in the bottom of the frame then cut the deficit to six runs, accounting for the game's final tally.

"I was hoping we could get to see Don Sutton pitch." Rosemary turned to Josh McFadden at her right. Seemingly ignoring Marcus, who'd sat quietly to her left all evening.

"That's tomorrow night," said Josh. Whose beloved Brewers had arrived in town when he was six years old. "But I got a paper due on Thursday."

Between innings, the message board announced that Carl Yastrzemski would return next spring for a 23rd season with the Sox. The fans gave the veteran a heartfelt ovation.

"How old is this guy, anyway?" Jay Levin looked curiously at his neighbors.

Derisively, Chug said, "He may remember the last time they won the World Series."

"Hey, show some respect for the last man to win the Triple Crown!" Josh interposed.

"Thank you, Josh," Dwight Manning said aloud. Dwight sat next to Megan near the aisle, the folding wheelchair wedged in front of him. Like many in New England, he'd grown up rooting for the man they called Yaz, hoping fervently that the team *would* win just once, for him...

"What's in the cup?" Rosemary gazed past Marcus at Adam, who sat nursing an opaque plastic mug. Adam silently lifted the Skoal tin in his other hand. The floor's only tobacco chewer, Adam was notorious for emptying his spit cups into quart jars and hurling the jars down the stairwell when full. His "chew bombs" leaving dark stains on the concrete landing.

"Yuck." Rosemary turned back to the game.

In the home half of the seventh, Jim Rice hooked a foul off to the left and into the stands. "Heads up!" Stu said as the Mutants perceived with excitement and trepidation that the ball was coming straight at them. Some of their reactions were revealing: Marcus flinched and tried to duck out of the way; Rob Moreland carelessly jostled his neighbors in his efforts to make the grab; Megan shielded herself with one arm while standing in front of Dwight, who protested and made a token stab at the air. The girls, almost as one, squealed and chattered "Omigod!"

As the ball came down, Rob lunged to his left to make the play, but it was just out of reach, and he gave a curse as it caromed off his fingertips. Playing it off the deflection, Rosemary then timed her grab perfectly and made a clean barehanded catch.

"Well, good for her!" Sox announcer Ned Martin clucked to his TV-38 audience, acknowledging the applause from the stands. Smiling self-consciously, Rosemary held the ball aloft for an instant before turning back to her dormmates.

The boys mostly roared their appreciation. But Rob shot her a dirty look, the girls staring in mute disbelief. There were awkward laughs, and she read the haughty disdain behind their amused eyes. She wondered again, as she had upon meeting the redoubtable Debbie Grafton (who finally *had* agreed to chip in for their refrigerator, now stocked with Tab and lowfat yogurt), and on various occasions since: What was the matter with these strange, nervous, sour-faced people whom Joel Gunderson had called Yankehs?

"Ohhhh, a tremendous catch by Porter on the third-base side!" Josh's rich, ringing baritone sounded in her ear, one arm clutching the back of her neck. "Ho-ly cow, I don't believe it—she went six multigajillion rows into the seats to snag that baby! I haven't seen such range since Bugs Bunny took one off the flagpole of the Empire State Building. Is this girl good?" Josh began giving her head-noogies and she responded in kind, holding on to her prize with one hand.

Finally the two broke it up and sat down. Marcus searched for an appropriately witty remark, and offered: "Nice catch."

"Thank you. I played in Little League for two years." She smiled modestly.

"Besbol been bedy, bedy good to you?" Stu leered in her direction. Rosemary flung a popcorn kernel at him.

Two pitches later, Rice grounded out to second. The Mutants, still abuzz over Rosemary's grab, scarcely noticed.

"That was impressive," Karlene Revens said sarcastically behind her. *"Where* did you say you learned to do that?"

"Finishing school," Rosemary replied, poker-faced.

For the SO WHAT government, the collapse was swift and complete.

Bereft of funds, and without any revenue-raising apparatus of its own, the Union found itself powerless to meet expenses. Not least of which included Met's rental demands.

In a front-page editorial, the *Guardian* condemned the university administration's tactics in setting the Union adrift. A spirited rally on Walden Plaza attracted scores of student partisans, urging its leaders to fight on. Though this outward enthusiasm did not translate into financial largesse.

Upon the Union's default, the administration began eviction proceedings. In mid-October, the executive board found that the locks on its office suite had been changed. Within the week the corporation had voluntarily dissolved itself, and the entire slate of officers had resigned.

Of the forty-one Union senators, thirty-five subsequently resigned in protest. Yet at this stage, it no longer mattered. The Union had effectively ceased to exist.

After debating the need for the Union's presence, Dean Grayling announced that the organization would return next fall "on a trial basis," with elections in the spring as before. The Office of Student Affairs meanwhile continuing to fill the void, directly overseeing all student funds.

A dispirited SO WHAT slate sank into oblivion. Briefly celebrated as martyrs, their orange caps becoming the emblem of student protest. But the leaders themselves soon forgotten, fading into obscurity.

For they had committed the one unpardonable sin in contemporary America, perhaps the one recognized sin.

They had failed.

"**N**o!" Chug screamed, outraged, sitting bolt upright in bed. *"Nuke* the asshole who pulled the alarm!"

But the fire alarm's metallic clang persisted, its maddening two-beat a peremptory summons. Resentfully, Chug kicked off his sheets and began to get dressed. The red numbers on his desk clock showed 2:13 A.M.

"That's the third time this week," he growled at Adam, who pulled a dark sweatsuit from the mound at his bedside. His roommate then followed Chug into the corridor, where traffic moved unevenly toward the stairwells.

"Ah, shut up." Rob Moreland clamped one hand over the alarm bell as he passed. Behind him Cheryl emerged, disoriented, from 405, wearing only an oversized sweatshirt.

"Will you put your pants on!" Rob snapped at his girlfriend, who rushed to follow orders.

"Great, now we'll never finish this game." Stu opened the fire door and followed Josh down the dimly-lit back stairwell. Trailed by Wayne King and Jay Levin, their opponents in a marathon round of Spades.

"And whose idea was it to play to five *thousand* points?" Josh tiptoed as they reached the landing, careful to avoid the remains of Adam's last chew bomb.

"Yo, remember that story about Shenford wanting to buy the

Mercantile Bank Building?" Dave Logan's voice wafted up from the third floor. "I mean, can you imagine what an alarm would be like...?"

At street level the emergency exit stood open, alarm braying continuously as the building emptied. DON'T FIRE ALARMS JUST SUCK? mocked the graffito over the doorframe.

You got that right, Chug thought sourly, stepping into the cool October night, his flannel shirt unbuttoned.

"One good thing about fire drills—you can see the girls' real faces." Brandon smirked as he and Marcus joined their neighbors in the front courtyard, where several young women milled about in curlers.

"I think some of them wear makeup to bed." Marcus noted the auricular pendants, large and conspicuous, flaunted by Debbie Grafton.

"Nice earrings." Josh smiled in her direction.

"Thank you," she evenly replied. "You know, *Brandon Clark* was just babbling to me yesterday about how wearing jewelry is morally wrong, because gold and diamonds are South African exports—"

"He's right here," Stu gently admonished.

Deb immediately broke off, refusing to acknowledge Brandon. The Northeast Coast mentality, Brandon fumed, meant never—under any circumstances—saying you were sorry.

The fire engines arrived within minutes—three yellow trucks, sirens wailing as they rolled up to the curb. The black-jacketed firemen, accustomed to Sterling's false alarms, emerged without haste. And then filed wordlessly into the building.

At least thirty more minutes, Chug silently reflected.

Instead an hour slowly crept by, then ninety minutes. Stu played a passable harmonica rendition of "The Star Spangled Banner," to cheers from the throng in the courtyard. The Mutants made off-color jokes, and laughed when Beth repeated her four-year-old nephew's synopsis of a Woody Woodpecker cartoon. ("He was all old? And his pecker got soft? And he couldn't use it any more?")

Adam looked at his watch. Nearly 4 A.M. While the firefighters remained in the building, out of sight.

Quietly he asked, "Anybody psyched for a Fred's run?"

There were a few unenthusiastic grunts, before Jay verbalized his response.

"Whatever," he sighed. "At this rate, I was gonna bag my nine o'clock anyway."

The thirty-second key was history now, and Dwight was halfway home. He was down to his last man, but from here the pattern never varied.

"Megan, what time is it?" His eyes remained fixed on the screen, during the brief pause between boards. His score was at 524,000; the crowd in Umberto's Pizzeria stood focused on the Pac-Man machine, awed by his mastery.

The attendant turned slightly, toward the clock above the flat hardwood counter. "Ten minutes to six," she replied.

"It's been almost two hours. You're really getting your money's worth." Rosemary gave a wry grin. A fellow computer science major, she'd accompanied Dwight to the restaurant from their Friday-afternoon lab. Unlike Megan, she could effortlessly carry Dwight up the pizzeria's steps, while the attendant grappled with the folding chair.

"Hey Captain, you hungry?" Josh held a slice of cheese pizza in front of his face. Dwight then snatched a quick bite before beginning the next round.

With all four ghosts on his tail, Dwight cut through the tunnel and devoured one of the screen's four energizers. The monsters briefly reversed direction, but did not turn blue. They had ceased to turn blue since the ninth key, nearly an hour ago.

Casually, Jay asked, "What's your high score on this?"

"Nine hundred thirty-two thousand. Just last month." By now the game's limits were well documented, several players having topped three million points...but since his near-miss, Dwight's quest for the seven-figure mark had become an obsession.

"He's been in here every night this week," one of the white-clad countermen volunteered. "Just drops in a quarter, and plays all night long. It's unreal..."

Lulled by the repetitious screens, the dozen spectators scarcely made a sound. Dwight passed six, then seven hundred thousand without fanfare; at eight-fifty Stu went over to the jukebox and put on *Pac-Man Fever*.

Four boards later, Dwight surpassed 900,000. His audience, seemingly reinvigorated, began the countdown, buzzing with excitement.

"You're golden!" Rob yelled prematurely as the 69th key ended with just under ten thousand to go. His fingers filled the back pocket of Cheryl Rudin's jeans, a plastic cup of beer in the other hand.

At the start of the next screen, Dwight cleared the bottom of the maze, then darted beneath the monsters' pen to gobble the first of the board's two keys. Just three thousand more to go...

Emerging from the left side of the tunnel, Dwight flicked his man in reverse, as the pattern dictated. But this time his hand slipped from the joystick, forcing him to scramble for his life. Sensing his vulnerability, the monster quartet moved in for the kill, working as a team to head him off.

Somehow Dwight managed to clear the S-channels above the monster pen. Finally, miraculously, the second key appeared. But his pursuers were closing in, and Dwight saw that his only chance was to race for the key.

Without hesitation he circled the monsters' lair, the four converging on him as he reached the target.

The machine gave a long, high-pitched whine, the sound of his man deflating into nothingness. It was over.

Fearfully he glanced at the high-score indicator, which had tracked his progress since the mid-40,000's.

The indicator read: 997660.

"Damn it!" He slapped the screen in frustration. Exhausted, he slumped forward in his chair, overcome with defeat, awaiting the disappointed groans from the audience.

Instead there was loud applause, with shouts of jubilation. The noise of victory, clear and resounding.

"Dwight—all right, you made it!" Stu touched him lightly on one arm, the words filled with unmistakable relief.

Dwight looked slowly to the left of the screen, to the scoring display headed 1UP.

The display read: 002660.

Involuntarily, Dwight exhaled. The high-score indicator, he realized, did not turn over at one million, but held the last total he'd registered before the key put him over the top.

Exultantly, he relished the cheers. But his night's performance was not yet complete.

"One more game," he announced. And then smiled, savoring the reaction to his jest.

News item from the *Guardian*, October 29, 1982 (p. 1):

MAJOR ANTIADMINISTRATION RALLY ON WALDEN PLAZA

By Beth Brown
Staff Writer

An estimated 600 members of the university community gathered on Walden Plaza Thursday afternoon, in what was believed to be the largest protest rally on campus in more than a decade. The event featured remarks by Professor of Journalism Willard Ferris and campus student government leaders, including members of the former Student Union Senate, denouncing the actions of the university administration in crushing the Union's bid for independence from its control.

"This goes way beyond just the Union fiasco," said Whitmarsh Hall president Daniel McMillen. "The real issue is that we (Met students) are being stepped on left and right, our basic freedoms crudely trampled by this administration." In a similar vein, Professor Ferris termed the Union crackdown "further evidence of King Fortin's obsession with complete control," later drawing sustained applause with a call for the University president's ouster.

"It was repression when my colleagues lost their jobs for speaking out against this regime," Ferris said in closing. "Then it was despotism when my now-ex-wife lost her job. And freedom is when Mr. Shenford loses his."

Several of the student speakers advocated entering protest floats in the Nov. 6 Homecoming parade, and staging other demonstrations during Homecoming weekend, to gain the attention of the thousands of parents and alumni expected to turn out for the event.

"All parents and alumni know of what goes on at Met is that propaganda (crap) they read in the *Press*," said ex-Senator Dave Logan of Sterling Hall. "If you ask me, it's time they learned the truth…"

"We want to send a message with this." Dave addressed the other members of Sterling's float-building crew as they reviewed plans for the dorm's entry in the upcoming parade. "We simply have to let the administration know that what they're doing is not acceptable."

George Hunter, sipping root beer from a Styrofoam cup, nodded assent. His floor as usual well represented among the ranks, the crew devouring subs and slices at Umberto's before tackling the all-night job ahead.

"Also, there'll be a lot of parents and alumni here this weekend," George added. Seated nearby were Brandon Clark, who'd added a free Met U. to his agenda; and Chug Allen, Sterling 4's elected SSG representative. "Like Dave said, we want to clue them in on what's happening. The fact is, they're the ones who carry clout with the administration, on account of they're the ones with the money."

"All we do is make it possible for this place to stay in business," Brandon huffed. As usual he wore his tattered green fatigue jacket, with its obtrusive array of buttons. Recent additions included a one-eyed version of the familiar '70's smiling face, which read MUTANTS FOR NUCLEAR ENERGY.

Chug stood and went to the counter for another slice of pizza. And while waiting, leaned over the jukebox and scanned the titles.

"Okay, I'm dedicating this one to Dean Grayling." He held a quarter aloft and smiled. Soon, Alice Cooper was singing *Go to Hell*.

Some hours later—shortly after 4 A.M.—George and his companions left the elevator on Four, their project completed.

"You *are* going to come out and see the parade?" The SSG president glanced at Chug, who had passed on marching with the others.

"Definitely." In fact Chug intended to sleep through the morning. Parades, in his estimation, were boring as hell.

To avoid disturbing Adam, he quietly opened the room door and tiptoed inside. But Adam was gone; his roommate's bed was empty.

Chug crept next door to Stu and Josh's room. And, looking down, saw the light beneath the crack. He heard Adam's voice, among others, debating whether a full house beat a flush.

"Shit," he softly muttered, turning round, "don't those guys *ever* sleep?"

Homecoming Day was a cool, gray Saturday. Rain threatened, but did not fall as the crowds began arriving early on campus, flooding the streets in a sea of green and gold.

The day's festivities began with the traditional parade down Alston Boulevard. The procession this year visibly truncated, several student organizations having withdrawn in protest.

Others expressed their dissent more openly. WE WANT OUR MONEY, the School of Arts and Sciences float screamed. Parker Hall's flaunted outsized posters of Shenford and Dean Grayling, with the legend WANTED FOR ROBBERY AND EXTORTION.

Sterling Hall's display featured a coffin mounted on a black catafalque. The platform moved at a somber pace, attended by six black-clad "pallbearers." The lettering on the platform read R.I.P. STUDENT RIGHTS. DIED 1962. BURIED 1982.

On the Boulevard, demonstrators in SO WHAT caps dotted the sidewalk, among parents and alumni revisiting the ghosts of youthful indiscretions past. Reaction was generally tepid, the visitors by and large weary of this effete generation's constant whining.

At Brentwood Stadium, the Homecoming game produced an easy

Titan victory, with senior tailback Pat Winston leading the hosts to a 37-15 win over New Haven. The alumni went home drunk and contented, the day's protests forgotten.

Her subject's choice of headwear took the interviewer by surprise.

"Never mind; the joke's over." Fortin Shenford removed the orange SO WHAT cap he'd worn, and smoothed his thinning hair while WDDK 11's Karen Grace sat before the president's desk. The anchorwoman, a pretty blonde, in her late twenties, clearly overmatched.

Responding to her queries, Shenford dismissed the students' wrath. Brusque and uncompromising, he stressed that, "The children don't make the decisions in this household."

"Dr. Shenford," the reporter finally asked, "how can someone who pays himself more than $200,000 yearly deny students all funding for independent activities?"

"You want to talk about salary issues? I'm amazed you would broach the subject," he replied. "I'm not ashamed to earn roughly what you take home for clipping on that vacuous smile and reading scripts furnished by your more literate colleagues."

Grace seemed unnerved by this frontal assault. "Getting back to the topic—"

"A ten-year-old of average intelligence could do your job," he overrode her angrily. "Provided, of course, she were sufficiently telegenic. You, young woman, are a hollow vessel. A mere showpiece. And not a true journalist by any means."

Grace left the office as had countless others, limp and shaken. And grateful for the miracle of editing.

The cinema room was in an uproar. Inside a chorus of heated voices raged, the sound of 300 residents from Sterling and its satellite rowhouses buzzing in anticipation. And up front, a vacant wooden podium, where the University president would shortly make an appearance.

The outcry over the Union affair had taken Shenford by surprise. He'd not expected meek indifference—yet the failed revolt had galvanized student opposition to a degree not seen since Vietnam.

To his mind the current crop of students, lacking the vitality of their '60's counterparts, posed no threat. Still, rebellion was best nipped in the bud. He'd decided to take a swing around the circle, engaging them in direct dialogue. The good doctor had recently visited Whitmarsh Hall, with Sterling the next stop on the tour.

As the scheduled hour of 8 P.M. approached, tension mounted. Students glanced expectantly at the door, their voices a steady hum.

"How can he even show up? There's going to be a riot!"

"I'm gonna ask him about that comment he made on TV. And if he still sees our issues as a joke, I'm going to come out and tell him he shouldn't be running this school."

"You watch—there's always someone stupid enough to try to argue with him, and it's not pretty."

"You wonder why they bother. Nobody's ever won an argument with him, maybe in his whole life. Do they think this is going to be the first time?"

"I'm telling you, you don't want to get into it with him," sophomore resident Evan Rovner told Brandon Clark. "The guy's a professional. He'll cut you to pieces. I've seen him make people cry."

Resolutely, Brandon replied, "He's going to hear what I have to say." Rovner let it pass, thinking some had to learn the hard way.

The minutes passed—eight o'clock, then 8:10, 8:15. Anticipation became restlessness, then annoyance. Finally, at twenty past the hour George Hunter walked to the podium and called for attention.

"I know we're running a little late tonight," he said. "But President Shenford had an earlier engagement in town..." A hail of boos and groans cut him off.

George waited for the catcalls to subside. "If everyone would listen up," he resumed. "I'm told that Dr. Shenford has arrived in the building, and will be here shortly—"

As he spoke, the president entered the auditorium, seeming to materialize at George's left. The room hushed, its atmosphere abruptly transformed. As though the air itself had become electrically charged.

"See the way everybody shuts up when *he* walks in," someone whispered in one of the back rows.

Shenford's carriage, as always, was ramrod-straight, his head erect. Maroon silk tie perfectly knotted, dark suit impeccably tailored and pressed. ("It was like you could smell the power," George later recalled.)

Involuntarily Hunter stepped aside, surrendering the podium. When he introduced Shenford there was a thin round of applause, with a smattering of boos.

Following the president into the room, two unsmiling bodyguards in shapeless gray suits. Trailed by Executive Vice-President Steve Patrick, a hulking figure with a sandy crewcut. The former chief appropriated a seat in the front row, his University Police subordinates taking their positions at the door.

"Good evening." Shenford smiled thinly, as though unaware of the tension in the room. "I'd like to thank you all for coming tonight; I'm pleased to see so many of you on hand. I just have a brief opening statement, and then I'll gladly take your questions..."

Unobserved by the audience, Patrick reached into his wool peacoat and turned on a concealed minicassette recorder.

Calmly, Shenford touched on the interdependence between the university administration and student body. The interests of the two, he emphasized, were by no means mutually exclusive, being better served through cooperation than needless antagonism. The president spoke in a reasoned, thoughtful manner, and nodded attentively as the first hand rose.

"Dr. Shenford," Brandon said belligerently. "Your actions in quashing our newly-independent Student Union are in line with your past record—for years, you've sought to destroy all opposition forces on campus. My question is, do you have any moral restraints? Is there no limit to how far you'll go to achieve total control of Metropolitan?"

Shenford's cordial manner departed at once. The gray, cold eyes focused on Brandon, who seemed to shrink within himself.

"Did I encourage the executive board to break with the university? To forgo adult supervision, like a child running from home?" the president countered. "In fact I advised them repeatedly of their incompetence; yet they would not be dissuaded." Ignoring the boos which filled the auditorium, Shenford added, "If I'd wanted to destroy the Union, I could think of no more effective way than to turn it over to the students.

"As for your baseless assault on my character—I will return your insolent letter unopened," he said with imperious finality.

Brandon remained on his feet, but Shenford beat him to the punch.

"No follow-up questions tonight," he said, explaining once Brandon was seated that time constraints made this provision necessary.

Near the front row, a student in an orange SO WHAT cap rose to say his piece. "How can you justify taking *our* money like this?" he shouted, to a rising crescendo of applause. "The way I see it, I should determine how it's used, because it's my money to begin with. And I'm not only the one paying the Union fees and the outrageous tuition, I'm also the one paying your salary!"

"Not true." The president smiled sadly, responding to a child's tantrum. "Unless I'm mistaken, you wouldn't be here without your parents' fully paying your expenses." When the boy remained silent, he added, "We'll discuss your fitness to provide for others once you begin pulling your own weight." The crowd again hissed and booed.

The next questioner tried a more rational approach. "Don't you think it's a bit ridiculous," he asked, "to say on the one hand that at eighteen we're mature enough to vote for President of the United States, and to fight and die for our country—but not to sponsor our own activities, or manage our own funds?"

"When did I say that? I've never taken that position," Shenford replied, unhesitating. "In 1971, I testified before Congress against that travesty I call the 26th Appeasement, which granted suffrage to eighteen-year-olds. For regardless of what the law says, children your age are lacking in maturity of judgment—at the ballot box, and elsewhere. Your parents know this, which is why they entrust the money to our care.

"I'm sorry, sir, but eighteen-year-olds are not adults—and the gulf continues to widen each day."

There were howls of protest, but surprisingly no counterarguments. For the iron conviction in Shenford's voice could not be withstood.

A small blonde girl accused the administration of acting autocratically in withholding Union funds. Shenford then challenged her to define the word "autocracy," and picked apart her efforts until she sat down, on the verge of tears. At last, weary of the subject, he announced that no further discussion of the Union affair would take place.

To a plumpish brunette who questioned the loss of her financial aid, Shenford said offhandedly that, "Maybe your father hit the Pick-Six at Santa Anita" before pledging to look into the facts of her case. Asked about Met's lack of funding for student publications, he cited liability concerns; and dismissed the idea of student-run journals with faculty advisors as "tantamount to censorship."

A second-year student with a "Question Authority" button asked why Met's tuition was comparable with Harvard's, the two schools being so disparate in quality. "You're charging Cadillac prices for a Ford Granada, and not fooling anyone," he said, to light laughter and applause.

Shenford looked almost amused. "Since you're such an authority on higher learning," he replied, "then let me ask you this. Would you favor an undergraduate degree in education from Harvard over one from our own humble institution?"

"Definitely." The kid smirked. Shenford pressed on, inviting him to compare the merits of Harvard's journalism and robotics courses with those at Metropolitan. The answer in each instance was that Harvard's "must be" superior.

"In fact, not one of those programs exists at Harvard." Shenford looked ruefully at his antagonist, while the room exploded in loud laughter. His face flushed, the boy did not sit down, but turned and left the auditorium without a word.

Asked his thoughts on the recently-passed Solomon Amendment, Shenford voiced unequivocal support for the measure. Higher educational assistance, he stated, was not a right but a privilege, those evading their Selective Service obligations properly excluded.

"Only those Americans who are willing to die for their country are fit to live," he said to an angry chorus of boos.

Unfazed, the president added, "I wish I could claim credit for those words. In fact they were spoken by General Douglas MacArthur, more than thirty years ago—to the ringing endorsement of the American public." There then followed a scathing rant on how the Depression generation's well-meaning parental indulgence had bred "a nation of weak and inadequate human beings," unworthy of the sacrifices made by their betters.

"This generation," Shenford concluded, "wants just one thing— complete freedom from responsibility."

Again, gasps from the audience.

"This guy's Looneytunes," Chug Allen whispered to Adam in one of the back rows.

The discussion turned to other matters. Shenford discoursed on such topics as the advertising business ("An industry founded on deception and half-truths"), the plague of multigenerational welfare families ("Cash incentives for voluntary sterilization of recipients could break the cycle of poverty, while stemming further erosion of America's gene pool"), the folly of the nuclear freeze movement ("Right now, there are Soviet lobbyists and spies working the halls of Congress, doing their damnedest to get that passed"). The students, in spite of themselves, roundly applauded this last comment.

Brandon was outraged. Not waiting to be recognized, he shot to his feet and in a shrill voice screamed, "What are you saying? The arms race is sheer insanity, don't you see that? Here the planet's survival is at stake, and we're playing chicken games for the benefit of the rich!"

From the audience, nervous titters. Suppressed laughs, with audible murmurs of "What?" and "Are you high?"

Shenford studied Brandon as if observing a new viral species. "The reason America must remain strong," he said, "is to deny the Soviets their aim of world conquest." The audience burst immediately into loud, enthusiastic applause.

Stubbornly, Brandon persisted. "You're trying to claim a moral superiority that doesn't exist!" he shouted over the din. "Remember something called Manifest Destiny? And what about the slaughter and displacement of American Indians over four hundred years of territorial expansion—"

"Tell it to the people of Poland!" The president cut him off with a wave of his hand. "You'll find them highly receptive, I'm sure." The crowd brayed with laughter, the applause seeming to feed on itself.

Brandon again opened his mouth to continue the exchange.

"Give it up, dude," a whispered voice said.

Slowly, unwillingly Brandon sat down. Humiliated beyond endurance, he said no more that evening.

"Shenford wiped away Brandon." Jay half-smiled at his floormates as they left the auditorium, after the president had departed to a raucous ovation. Meanwhile, Brandon worked to put his own spin on events.

"That was incredible!" he said to Evan Rovner, the sophomore who'd tried vainly to discourage his performance. "He just spent two hours telling these people what morons they are, and made them like it. Literally made them like it. It's like those pledges in *Animal House*: 'Thank you sir, may I have another?'"

Rovner shook his head in response.

"They might as well bend over and take it," he advised. "Because they're sure as hell not going to beat him."

It was a familiar scenario for the Mutants' intramural football squad. Late in the final game of another winless season, with zero points on offense. Despite the fall's infusion of new blood, the team had kept up its losing ways en route to a perfect 0-8 mark.

"At least it gets better from here." Pete Garrett turned to Wally and Troll on the Mutant sideline. Tonight the three had taken the bus from Leeds Road to Brentwood Stadium, where the Mutants trailed 31-0, to the Gnarly Dudes of Whitmarsh 5. The other floor partisans watched dutifully, awaiting the last-second charity score.

The Mutants managed to move the ball near midfield. A rush by quarterback Jay Levin produced no gain, then a bad snap sent the ball bounding back fifteen yards. Third and light-years, under one minute left and counting.

"Oh, god!" Beth Brown laughed mirthlessly in the audience. Wally gently shushed her.

"They should send Dwight in. It couldn't make things worse," she remarked softly to herself.

Wally's expression brightened. "Hey, yeah!" he said. And yelled to his ex-floormates on the field: "Hey, let the Captain take it in!

"That was an awesome idea." He leered at Beth, who looked suddenly stricken.

Wally's exhortation quickly became a rallying cry. "Yo—let the

Captain do it!" Troll screamed.

"Come on, Captain—punch it in!" Rosemary, standing beside Megan, jabbed the air with her fist. Dwight watched in silence as the players broke huddle and looked expectantly toward the sideline.

"Go for it, Captain!" Jay exhorted. Dwight exchanged glances with Megan, the layers bulging beneath his down jacket. Though it was still early November he'd bundled up against the cold, having been hospitalized with pneumonia that summer.

"Let's do this." He nodded conspiratorially to his attendant, and savored the applause when she wheeled him onto the turf.

"Late substitution, ref." Jay winked before turning and walking casually from the field. The ball was then snapped, center Dave Logan placing it securely in Dwight's lap.

"All right," Stu shouted from the backfield. "Everybody except Dwight and Megan...Wax Museum!" The Mutants froze on the line of scrimmage; their opponents, quickly catching on, followed suit. Megan smiled mischievously as she steered around right end and moved Dwight toward the end zone.

Seventy-one yards later, the chair crossed the goal line, Stu giving the okay to move again. The official's arms flashed skyward, as both sidelines erupted in applause.

"Spike it, Captain!" Troll yelled downfield.

With Megan's help, Dwight worked the ball free. And, using both hands, threw it to the turf in celebration. Bringing further applause from the audience.

It was the highlight of Dwight's athletic career. Rivaled only by his subsequent election as the team's Most Valuable Player.

Of all floor events, Sterling 4's Winter Hawaiian Party was most steeped in tradition. Each year, with elaborate precision, preparations were made in keeping with custom.

Thus at exactly three o'clock on the morning of December 10—the term's last Friday of regular instruction—the Doke Committee began making its rounds, visiting each of the floor's male residents.

"What do you guys want?" Freshman Mitch Flanders stood sullen in his doorway, wearing a ragged flannel bathrobe, roommate Nick Bernhardt snoring vigorously.

"This is your Doke Assignment for tonight's Hawaiian Party." Dave Logan handed him a folded slip of notebook paper, his voice solemn as Adam, Stu and Josh looked on. Mitch took the message disinterestedly and opened it, his eyes half-lidded.

Dear Mitchster:

Please be advised that your Doke Assignment for Hawaiian Party IV is Shelby Morgan (Room 413).

With best wishes,

The Sterling 4 Doke Committee

"What's this?" he grunted, perplexed.

"I thought 'Doke Assignment' would be fairly self-explanatory." Dave and his fellow committee members exchanged glances. Though the game was understood to be in fun, with no record of any man actually attaining his quest.

"Should you fail in this mission," Adam gravely warned, "the Committee will disavow any knowledge of you."

"Right." Mitch tucked the message into his robe pocket; a second later the door began to close.

But the committee's task was not done. Overpowering their reluctant host, the four rushed in and clicked on the room lights. And, at Nick's bedside, began a frightful, off-key rendition of *Stop in the Name of Love*.

"What's going on?" Nick sat up and rubbed his eyes, the words heavy with sleep.

Receiving his Doke Assignment, Nick tossed it on the night table without a glance and crawled back under the covers. His sacrilege spurring the Committee to more forceful action.

"Pile on!" Dave screamed, leaping atop the burly freshman resident. His companions then jumped on Nick's prostrate form, and rode him until he yelled for mercy.

Later, its mission fulfilled, the Committee disbanded *sine die*. Its members retiring to Stu and Josh's room, for another round of Spades.

That night, nearly one hundred partygoers—current and former residents and guests—jammed Sterling 4, appropriately bedecked for the occasion. The boys mostly wore island shirts; the girls sporting bright-colored muumuus, bathing suits and sundresses. All adorned with plastic leis.

In the elevator loading area, couples danced to music from Chug's stereo: Laura Branigan's *Gloria*, the Pointer Sisters' *I'm So Excited*...plus of course, the theme from *Hawaii Five-O*. For refreshments, guests chose from a variety of mixed drinks, from

Manhattans in Dave and George's room to strawberry daiquiris at Stu and Josh's.

"Hey, nice outfit." Stu greeted Bonnie Randall, who stood in the hallway with her boyfriend, a roughhewn Meldon sophomore named Rick Casey.

"Thank you." The pallid blonde freshman, seldom seen at parties, smiled back at him. Her white sleeveless sundress was thin-strapped, revealing smooth ivory shoulders.

Before she could speak further, Rick slipped a proprietary arm around Bonnie's waist, his snarl menacing. "Back off, buddy," he warned.

"Sheesh—what's your problem?" Stu walked off shaking his head.

At one end of the hall, Rosemary and Megan chatted with Dwight, Marcus standing mutely on the perimeter. The two girls by now had become close friends, having already agreed to room together next year. (Marcus, however, had seldom dared speak to Rosemary since he'd called Directory Assistance last month for her number, then hung up without a word upon recognizing the operator's voice.)

"I'm telling you, that's *not* what it says," Megan insisted with disapprobation while *Rock the Casbah* blared in the background.

Behind them, a hammered Chug Allen quietly stalked his prey. Watching Rosemary in her modest green one-piece reminded him that she was his D.A. for the evening (the photo he'd received as an added touch had shown her balancing a bottle of Rolling Rock on her head), the thought evoking a lecherous grin.

Approaching his quarry from behind, Chug planted a swat on her slim, taut rump. As Rosemary turned furiously on her assailant, Jay Levin grasped the opportunity of a lifetime.

"Wax Museum!" he promptly shouted.

Chug was delighted to abide. But this time Rosemary wouldn't play along. Forcefully she brushed his hand aside, and in his drunken unsteadiness he lurched forward, landing heavily on the green-tiled floor.

"Ah, you screwed it up." Jay shook his head, disappointed, his floormates applauding in derisive fashion. Rosemary glared at him.

Chug rose on wobbly legs, gazed about as if nothing had happened. And then yelled: "Hey, where's Brandon? I'm psyched for some good Marxist propaganda!"

"He's in Washington this weekend. Protesting the MX missile again," Marcus volunteered.

"Yo—guys who look like that in swimsuits shouldn't say nuthin'." Glancing up from Marcus's spindly legs, Chug reached under the thin shirt and tweaked one of the nipples on his concave, hairless chest. Marcus let out a yelp.

But no one heard him. Instead, all eyes turned toward the floor lounge, and the sound of another, more agonizing scream. The guests then heard a loud slap, and another cry of pain.

"You want some more, just keep on blubbering!" Rick Casey's voice was filled with drunken rage. The next sound was the shuffling of feet as the crowd surged forward and the lounge door was yanked open.

Rick and Bonnie stood alone in the room, his hands clamping her wrists as she struggled to get free. Her face contorted in anguish, the tears overflowing.

"What did I tell you—huh?" Rick shouted. "Didn't I say if you wore that dress tonight, every guy here'd be looking at you? Is that what you want—you like all these guys staring at you?"

"No, it's not true—I swear! Rick, please stop...you're hurting me—"

Rick again slapped her, knocking her to her knees on the thin aquamarine rug. Blood ran from Bonnie's nose as she knelt at his feet, wailing piteously.

Spurred into action, Rob Moreland forced his way through the crowd, then entered the lounge and in one swift motion grabbed Rick by his Dallas Cowboys football jersey and slammed him against the wall.

"What the hell are you doing?" He smelled the whiskey on Rick's breath at once. Keeping your girlfriend in line was one thing—but to Rob's mind, any man who would hit a woman represented the lowest form of life.

Rick responded in exactly the way Rob had hoped—he swung on Rob. Slipping his drunken antagonist's clumsy effort, Rob smashed home a right to the chin, forcing Rick's head into the wall with a satisfying thud. The kid from Meldon slumped to the floor on his back, unconscious.

"Say goodnight, scumbag!" Rob hissed. While off in the distance, the Go-Gos sang *We Got the Beat*.

Bonnie emitted a loud scream. Wild with rage, she turned on Rob and began pounding ineffectually at his arms and chest. Rob let her do it and stared at her until she collapsed at his feet, exhausted and in tears.

Rob waved his hands, as if to disperse the crowd. "Everything's copacetic," he advised. Then relented as the girls protectively surrounded Bonnie, the boys working to bring Rick around.

Rob did not join them, but turned and left the lounge, Cheryl close at his side.

"Why do girls go for guys like that?" Marcus nearly screamed at Brandon Monday morning over breakfast, after relating the weekend's events. "Seriously, someone explain it to me—how is it that nice girls like Bonnie *always* end up with guys like Rick? And *vice versa?*"

Wearily, Brandon shook his head. He'd returned from D.C. in the back of a van hours ago and had scarcely slept all weekend, his clothes saggy and rumpled.

"Don't you get it by now?" he explained. "Romance is a reverse meritocracy."

On December 22, the annual "Dear Parents" letter arrived at The House. The tuition increase for next year was a hefty one, bringing the total to just under ten thousand dollars. Met's basic tuition, for the first time, would surpass that of Harvard.

Though reaction to the announcement was not universally glum. The House's three seniors, unaffected by the increase, in fact celebrated with perverse glee.

"Seventeen point four percent." Pete Garrett, the aspiring law student, shook his head as they went upstairs, each with a copy of the notice in hand. "Can you believe it?"

"Why do they send these holdup notes to seniors anyway? You'd think they'd know better." Bob Spencer looked dubiously at his companions.

"No, that's why they have to keep jacking up tuition. Because they're wasteful and inefficient," Wally glibly replied.

The trio passed through Wally's room, which opened onto the second-floor sundeck. (The boys just called it a porch; "sundeck" seemed too flattering a word for the unvarnished wooden platform whose planks showed signs of rot.) Centered on one wall was Wally's "Rodney Board," an oversized cork rectangle displaying the rejection letters from his job search. THE RODNEY, he'd scrawled on each missive in black ink. THE RODERICK Q. CRAWFORD, he'd marked one especially invidious rebuff.

Bracing himself against the cold, Wally opened the door and led the others out onto the porch. Tonight's temperature was in the single digits, the boys bundled up warmly.

"Counselor, you may do the honors." Wally lifted the cover of the portable barbecue that had lain dormant since August, and handed Pete a Bic lighter. Within seconds, the three letters lay ablaze at the bottom of the pit.

While the hated messages burned, the seniors sang a carol Bob had composed for the occasion, to the tune of *O Christmas Tree*:

> O Fortin C! O Fortin C!
> How dry thou hast bled me
> O Fortin C! O Fortin C!
> How dry thou hast bled me
> I know not where the money went,
> hope for my sake it was well spent
> O Fortin C! O Fortin C!
> How dry thou hast bled me
>
> O Fortin C! O Fortin C!
> How rich we must have made thee
> O Fortin C! O Fortin C!
> How rich we must have made thee
> Five years from now, and even more
> Our gowns we'll still be paying for
> O Fortin C! O Fortin C!
> How rich we must have made thee…

When the flame had exhausted itself, Wally picked up a stick and prodded at the letters' charred remains. The ash separated into fragments, and mixed with the residue from last summer's coals. Like their parents' tuition money it was gone, irrevocably, untraceably lost.

SOPHOMORE II

"What did you get last semester?" Rob Moreland asked his now-ex-roommate at lunch.

"Three-five." Marcus smiled back, with a rare touch of boastfulness. "And now that I'm off A.P., I'm switching my major to accounting. Everyone says it's for math nerds, but I think it suits me."

Rob let this one pass. "I thought something math-related would be right up your alley," he said. Now living in Zeta House, Rob remained on the meal plan, with full cafeteria privileges.

He swallowed a forkful of rice pilaf, and then glanced at Marcus's new roommate, a polo-shirted freshman named Frank Sorenson. "This kid's good with numbers. I swear, he used to get his rocks off every month adding up the phone bills."

"I can believe it," Frank said. He was handsome in a bored way, with close-cropped hair and a bovine expression. A business major from Worcester, Mass., Frank was the son of Donovan Sorenson, founder and managing partner of the DSX Financial Group. Despite which, he'd been bunked with two other "nomads" in the sixth-floor lounge last fall, victim to an on-campus housing shortage.

"Is it true that you're living with your girlfriend at the frat house?" Stu asked Rob.

"Not officially, of course. But—seventy bucks a month rent, with no restrictions on guests? It doesn't get much better than that."

163

"I can't believe they let you do such things on campus." Megan shook her head.

Sweetly, Debbie Grafton asked, "How does Cheryl fit in over there? Doesn't she feel...you know, out of place sometimes?"

She never quits, Rob thought. Aloud he said: "Are you referring to the SES thing?"

"That's one way of putting it. I mean, she's a townie, right? A local girl, not from one of the better neighborhoods—"

"Doesn't mean shit." Rob looked at her coldly, remembering how she'd once taped a box of condoms to his door, in a less-than-subtle invitation.

"So what's your blonde-supremacist group up to lately?" Brandon intervened.

Rob ignored this anti-frat gibe. (Brandon, he thought, was a wimp and a person of no consequence.) Cheerfully he said: "We joined the city's winter park basketball league—it's a blast. Twice a week, we get to kick ass on a bunch of middle-aged losers—these blue-collar ass-wipes with menial jobs, fat wives and booger-eating kids. We get 'faced before every game to give them a chance, but they're just so pathetic. And they take it so seriously on top of everything..."

"How about you, Brandon?" Frank looked up from the morning's *Guardian* and its short piece on the newly-formed Mushroom Society, an unsanctioned, unfunded student organization devoted to nuclear disarmament. "What's this about you starting a communist junta on campus?"

"Just doing our part to save the Earth from senseless destruction. And you?" Brandon returned. A rabid social Darwinist, Frank had quickly become Brandon's main foil, often baiting him with simplistic pronouncements.

"And FYI, there's nothing communist about our organization. Communism is an ideal that can never work in practice, because human beings are greedy and selfish bastards."

His dormmates laughed nervously, for lack of a better response. Finally Jay Levin said, "Speak for yourself."

Brandon ignored him. "And why are we debating ideology anyway?" he said. "Ideology is simply a pretext for subjugation. It's not about freedom, or principles or beliefs—it's about land, money, power, greed and exploitation. The way it always has been.

"Bottom line: This is our survival we're talking about. Meaning all of mankind. We feel that this country should do its part to avoid nuclear annihilation. And if that means unilateral disarmament, then so be it."

"Unilateral disarmament?" Frank echoed, unbelieving.

Without hesitation Brandon replied, "Yes, if that's what it takes to convince the Soviets we're serious about peace."

"Convince *them*? Why should we have to convince them of anything? We're not the ones who've been invading and terrorizing our neighbors for the past forty years."

"No, we've had way more experience. Just ask the Indians. Only now you never hear anything, because it's all done behind the scenes. In the fifties, it was the CIA who returned the Shah—one of the world's most corrupt and brutal tyrants—to power in Iran. Then in Chile, we overthrew a democratically-elected government and put in a bloodthirsty puppet regime. Not to mention the right-wing death squads in Central America, killing tens of thousands of people with the full backing of the current administration.

"By the way, I missed you all at our organizational meeting." Brandon sarcastically eyed his neighbors.

Chug met his gaze evenly. "I thought absence would speak louder than words."

Frank remained silent, distracted by a pretty blonde exiting the cafeteria's back door. The girl was obviously braless, her sheer white cotton blouse further enhancing the frontal view.

165

"They look nice and ready," he quietly told Rob.

"You're sexist." Debbie whirled on him at once.

"I can't help it." Frank leered, unabashed. "I'm just a lesbian trapped in a man's body."

Deb smiled coldly—a toothy, insincere meniscus that appeared when she was challenged. "Frank...you're sexist," she repeated.

"Sexist. That sounds so...'70's," he mockingly laughed. But she would not let go.

"Well, excuse me for being normal," Frank said beneath her disapproving stare. "I'm a guy; that means I like girls. According to your standard, bi's would be the only nonsexist people around."

From there, the discussion moved to the topic of homosexuality—an exercise generating more heat than light.

"What's the big deal, anyway?" Stu looked round to his dormmates. "I mean, who cares what people do in private, as long as no one gets hurt?"

Rob had a different perspective. "You ask me, any man who would rather go to bed with another guy than a gorgeous girl has got serious problems. But some woman getting hot for Loni Anderson, I could understand."

"That's because you're a guy..." Carol James's voice trailed off.

"I liked Jan Smithers better," Marcus blurted.

Chug said with a half-smile, "My father told me if I ever turned out queer, he'd shoot me, bury me, and tell everyone I ran away."

"Thanks for sharing." Deb regarded him frostily.

All at once everyone realized something was lacking. There was an expectant pause, all eyes turning in one direction.

"Brandon, what about you?" Jay asked. "What's your position—no pun intended?"

Brandon's brief response, typically, transcended the debate.

"Straight or gay, it makes no difference," he said. "Love is a crock, period."

Graffiti on a restroom wall in Phillips Arena:

> Q – What do you get when you cross a 500-pound ape with a jockstrap?
>
> A - An athletic scholarship to Metropolitan.

Wile Brandon lectured his floormates on the folly of romantic love (which he termed "the most common of mental diseases"), Willard Ferris toasted his daughter's success.

"To the newest Assistant Director at DEM." The white-haired academic beamed proudly at his only child, holding aloft a double bourbon.

Demurely, Christina raised her water glass in return, surrounded by the predominantly male lunch crowd at the Capital Grille. The restaurant stood a half block from the State House, and was a prime venue for Bristol's movers and shakers: politicians, corporate executives, high-powered attorneys and lobbyists.

"You know, Dad, it's really not that big a deal." Christina lowered her glass, somewhat self-consciously. At twenty-seven she had her mother's dark hair and almond eyes, her oval face smooth and unblemished. "There's like, thirty A.D.'s in the whole Department."

"True. But you, at least, have earned the position." With its top-heavy hierarchical structure, the Department of Environmental Management was among the state's notorious hackeramas, its ranks filled largely through nepotism. Last week Harry Kahn, the *Telegraph*'s poison-pen political columnist, had branded the agency "a dumping ground for the idiot children of the well-connected."

"It isn't quite what I imagined. Definitely not what I pictured when I graduated from school and joined the Department four years ago. Then, I thought I could help clean up the world and get paid for it. Instead, there's all the politics and the schmoozing and red tape…"

"Welcome to the real world." Her father nodded sagely. But Ferris had encouraged his daughter's independence from the outset.

In this day and age, any woman who can't support herself is in for a royal screwing.

"Although it does keep me busy," she added, aware that they'd seen each other less often in recent months. His hair, once jet-black, appeared lifeless and unkempt, his eyes bloodshot, cheeks and jowls sagging. She retained a mental image of her father's office, knowing inwardly that it hadn't changed in years—a dark, airless cubicle, with a framed *Wire* headline in the background: NIXON RESIGNS.

Cautiously, as though treading on sensitive ground, she said: "I don't suppose you've heard from Mom lately?"

"Negative," he answered without emotion. It was late January, almost nine years since the divorce had been finalized. Like many exiles from the Shenford regime, Rhonda Ferris had found herself blacklisted, the gates of *academe* bolted shut.

"I got the usual holiday card." Christina took a sip from her water glass. "She's still in Carbondale, writing features for the *Southern Illinois Weekly*." Not adding that her mother now shared a condo with the paper's managing editor.

Ferris said sardonically, "It's nice she found a stable home."

Christina looked to close the subject. "I think we'd better order now," she said. And with the barest of smiles added: "Unless you'd rather drink your lunch."

Adhering to her diet, she chose the garden salad, her father ordering a cheeseburger with fries—and another double bourbon. Her salad arrived at once, and she picked at it while he waited for his lunch.

"Your boss is in the news again." She regretted her choice of topic at once. From her teen years, "Mr. Shenford" had been the family bogeyman—to her mind, the one responsible for her parents' divorce.

Ferris thanked the waiter as his bourbon arrived. "Not so unusual these days," he said. Last night, Channel 11 had aired footage of Shenford leaving the mayor's office after a meeting on Met's planned condominium conversions in the North Campus neighborhood. According to the usual background sources, Shenford had lectured the mayor on the economic benefits of the project, ignoring concerns over the depletion of affordable housing.

"I don't think you're interested in practical solutions," he'd told Steadham for the cameras.

"What is this guy's problem? Does he truly thrive on hatred?" Christina's words were filled with odium.

"No one truly *thrives* on hatred, Chrissie," her father explained. "But hatred cannot exist without a modicum of respect. Insane though he was, I think Caligula phrased it best: 'Let them hate, so long as they fear.'"

"But he can't fight City Hall. He must know that." She looked back at him wanly.

"Of course he knows it. He'd never admit it to anyone in a million years, but he knows it. So he'll do what he always does when confronted with higher authority. He'll agree to all kinds of concessions, then fail to keep his end of the bargain.

"All of those buildings will eventually go condo. You watch." The tired voice of a man relating what he has seen a thousand times before.

"But how does he keep getting away with it?"

Wearily, Ferris sighed.

"Frankly, that's what we'd all like to know," he replied. "We vote overwhelmingly for him to leave, and he simply ignores it. Now, when he has a dispute with someone on the board, they end up leaving, not him. In effect, he can fire his bosses.

"If I had to guess, I'd say it comes down to sheer chutzpah. That, and a complete lack of conscience."

An hour later, his meal finished, the professor reached for his wallet to pay the check. Whereupon Christina produced her American Express card.

"It's okay. I've got this one," she said brightly.

Flustered, Ferris began to protest. But his daughter was insistent.

"It's all right, Dad," she whispered, gently touching his hand.

"Rosemary...they're showing *The World According to Garp* tonight at the Union." Marcus willed himself to maintain eye contact as they stood out in the hall, her door open, her roommate listening intently. It was Friday night, his shift at the bookstore over, the words carefully rehearsed.

"Anyway, I hear that's supposed to be really good." He paused without blinking. "And I was wondering if...you'd like to go?"

Rosemary replied without hesitation.

"Actually, a bunch of us are going," she said. "Stu and Josh, Megan and Dwight, Chug and those guys...You should come with us."

Inwardly, Marcus slapped his forehead in frustration. The legendary Pullman luck strikes again, he observed. Couldn't *something* go right, just once, anything at all—?

"Uh—yeah, sure. That'd be great."

"It starts at ten o'clock," she advised. "So we'll be leaving at about twenty minutes till."

It was now just past seven-thirty. Through the window at one end of the corridor, he saw that the light snowfall which had begun earlier was intensifying.

"That'd be great," he repeated. And, hiding his disappointment, added, "I guess I'll see you then" before turning to leave.

"I take it back—you do have standards." Debbie Grafton smiled thinly when Rosemary re-entered the room.

"What do you mean?" Her eyes narrowed at the slight.

"He was asking you out on a date—!" Deb laughed, highly amused. By Marcus's fumbling approach, her roommate's unawareness.

Rosemary in fact took a casual view toward dating. Having palled around with boys when younger, she'd always felt comfortable around males, and was unsure when her first date had been. (Though if asked, she would note the time her father had taken her and Paul Fink to see *Lafayette Escadrille* at the base theater, the summer after seventh grade.)

Guys ask her out, Debbie would tell her girlfriends when discussing her roommate's social life, but it never goes anywhere. I think she's just too inexperienced to really know how to hook a man.

"Anyway, you did the right thing," she said. "You can't hang with guys like that, even out of pity. I mean, we're talking about *Marcus*. I knew he was a loser from day one, when we were playing volleyball and he was wearing *black socks* with his gym shorts…!"

What are you saying, Rosemary frowned. That doesn't make sense.

"I think he's a good person," she objected.

"I know he's a good person," Debbie replied. "Too bad he's such a total geek."

Geek, Rosemary thought. Sounds like a noise a monkey makes. Yet another aspect of Deb's reasoning eluded her.

"What's so bad about geeks anyway? It's jerks I can't stand."

Marcus returned from the Union shortly after 1 A.M., his phone ringing insistently.

"Sorry, Frank's not here right now," he told the girl on the other end, the snow melting from his down jacket. The jacket had received a liberal dusting from tonight's storm, and subsequent snowball fight in Sterling's courtyard.

It's the same thing, only different, he thought cynically while hanging up the phone. What Rob had accomplished with muscles, Frank Sorenson duplicated with his lavish spending allowance, the parade of female guests ongoing.

In time, the list came to include Debbie Grafton. The pairing was inevitable, Marcus observed, she and Frank being the two most conceited snots in the dorm. ("Marcus—I came to see you!" she once said mockingly when told that Frank wasn't in.) By mid-March their relationship had become exclusive, despite the strain on Frank's personal funds.

"You know what the difference is between prostitution and free sex?" Frank asked his roommate one night after they'd hit the sack. For once he was sleeping alone, despite having taken Debbie to Antoine's earlier that evening. Somehow they'd gotten into an argument over the prospect of a new ERA, which Frank opposed. In the end she had hissed at him to "Just pay the check, and let's go!"

Languidly, Marcus prompted, "This ought to be good."

"Free sex costs more," Frank sagely advised.

"After you, Mr. President."

Pete Garrett stood in front of the open shaft door and waved Chug onto the roof of the elevator cab, while Jay and Brandon waited anxiously inside.

"A Rookie Drinker emeritus outranks a mere President-elect," said Chug, who'd run unopposed in his bid to succeed George Hunter as head of Sterling Student Government next fall. But he scrambled quickly onto the car roof, dispensing with the protocol question.

"It's real simple. Just push the right buttons when I tell you." Pete bent down and peered into the cab, where the heads of their accomplices peeked above floor level. Even at 3:30 A.M., with the floor dead quiet, speed was of the essence.

"And whatever you do, don't close that door until I say." Clark and Levin nodded, extremely nervous, impatient for the ride to begin.

The four had returned from Fred's a half-hour ago, smashed from another weekend saturnalia. It had been Pete's idea to go 'vatorhopping, as the practice was known, "once more for old times' sake." To his disappointment the old guard had wimped out entirely, his Housemates opting instead for poker with Stu and Josh. But Chug had been just swacked enough to come along, Brandon and Jay enlisting for pilot duty.

"I'm sorry, but a future officer of the court should not be doing this." The soon-to-be Met Law student hauled himself upward, squatting beside Chug on the dark, grease-coated surface.

"Okay, this is the light." Pete turned on the exposed 40-watt bulb behind the door operator, then slid the outer door closed, plunging the shaft into hazy semidarkness. "And this orange switch here, that stops the elevator. We can start and stop it anytime we want..." Chug absorbed this briefing in silence.

"And don't touch anything else." Pete indicated the thicket of cables and wires attached to the roof. "There must be a bazillion volts going through this thing."

"Thanks for the heads-up," Chug sullenly replied.

"Remember—all you have to do is stay on for eight seconds."

"Oh, that's funny."

Using the prearranged signal, Pete knocked twice on the cab roof. The inner doors closed, and Chug's stomach hitched as the car began to descend.

The technique was simple; as a freshman Pete had acquired the basics from an issue of *Forbidden Knowledge*. First, you pried open the inner door to stop the car between floors. Then you used a mop to open the shaft door, tripping an overhead safety switch. Wriggling out onto the floor—now at around shoulder height—you then mounted the cab and reclosed the doors.

Pete tapped the emergency hatch on the car roof. "Before, people could just climb through these things," he said. Not adding that the emergency hatches had been bolted shut since 1974, when a drunken Vernon Hall freshman had slipped and fallen sixteen stories to his death.

At the building's basement level, the car came to a stop. Pete again gave the roof two quick thumps.

"Fourteen, James," he said superfluously.

"Very good, sir." Responding in kind, Jay hit the button for the top floor.

"...And we have liftoff." Pete remained sanguine; yet Chug scarcely could contain himself. Gliding by at three feet per second, the shaft's steel-gray doors were close enough to touch. To the right, beyond Pete's seated form, a series of transverse beams ran between shafts. The maize-colored brick walls matched the building's exterior, the counterweight guideposts probing the dark reaches above…

"Nice place to just chill out." Chug relaxed almost at once, attuned to the mysterious force bearing them upward. At this hour all was quiet, save for the low, gentle *swishh* of the car's motion.

"I used to do my homework in here." Pete thought back to his freshman days, to when he'd stood on a 12th-floor crossbeam to watch the elevator descend, his testicles drawing upward as the car plunged into the abyss. ("You're a sick puppy!" Wally had said in admiration.)

At around the fifth floor, the great black mass of the counterweight came into view, falling like a piledriver from the shadows. The huge block of iron appeared headed straight for them, and Chug shrank from the vision of his onrushing doom.

"It's not gonna hit you." Pete chortled, the voice of experience. Yet it was all he could do to keep still as the immense dark shape bore down on them, at the last moment disappearing harmlessly behind the cab.

Quickly regaining his composure, Chug said, "That looked like the ultimate Nautilus rack." And then changed the subject: "Think you guys were the first to do this?"

"Not close." Pete looked to the wall on the left, where the graffiti of earlier explorers whizzed by: ROACH 2/5/72… RANDY WAS HERE 1970… GIVE CHANCE A PIECE… LED ZEPPELIN RULES… LYSDEXIA… EVERYONE MUST GET STONED.

"'…And now his future will never come to pass.'" Chug read from Wally's oft-quoted limerick about Ted Kennedy, dwarfed by the huge red number 12 on the shaft door. Pete readmired his brushwork, added three years earlier, when Twelve had been Mutant Central.

"Our old floor," he said needlessly. Looking upward as they neared the top of the shaft. Through the metal grating Chug viewed the complex network of motors, pulleys, winches and hoists which powered the elevator. The enormous secondary sheave, black and wicked-looking, made a rhythmic humming sound, revolving between two support beams.

"That is so awesome..." Chug gazed with unconcealed, childlike wonderment. Fascinated, he watched the fearsome machinery for seconds, before he realized how close it was coming...

"Top floor—last stop." Pete hit the orange switch as the car came to a halt at 14.

"Let's just hang here a while...no pun intended."

"None taken," Chug replied. Thirty seconds then passed before Brandon mounted the handrail and knocked on the ceiling.

For several minutes they shuttled up and down in near-silence. Pete sang a few bars of *Fly Like an Eagle*, while Chug tossed some pennies into the void, listening for the faint *clink* at the bottom.

The car again touched basement level. Absently, Jay hit the 14th-floor button, then started suddenly as the doors opened and a passenger entered at lobby level.

"You two are up late." Hall Director Jean Cornell regarded them with a trace of reproof. She was dressed in bathrobe and curlers, obviously agitated.

Like two preteens caught smoking in the restroom, the boys paled in horror. But Cornell had other things on her mind. Awakened by a report of a possible alcohol poisoning, she silently pressed the buttons for 4 and 13.

"Shit! Cornell!" Chug hissed atop the cab roof. Through the small slit of light up front he'd watched her come aboard, her stout form filling the entrance.

"I heard you the first time. Just be cool..." Pete gazed back at him, unperturbed.

Cornell looked sullen as the elevator rose. "Your floor?" she asked when the doors opened at Four.

"I…forgot something downstairs," Jay weakly replied.

Brandon mustered his courage. "Is there a problem?" he asked.

"That's what I'm going to find out." Cornell remained tight-lipped; and as the doors opened on 13, wished the boys goodnight and stalked off.

Descending from the top floor, Brandon quickly hit the fourth-floor button before climbing onto the handrail, then rapped on the ceiling.

"Who is it?" Pete's voice became a high falsetto.

"You'd better get off!" His voice fraught with tension, Brandon warned, "If you don't, we will."

To his surprise, Pete readily acquiesced. And with a flip of the emergency switch brought them to a stop between Eight and Nine.

"Come on, quit screwing around!" Brandon again castigated him before the door opened, and a green-tiled floor appeared at chest level.

"Come on out…" Pete held the door operator in the Open position. Jay and Brandon hesitated a split second, then quickly crawled out of the cab.

Behind them, a slurry voice said, "Holy shit."

Startled, the pair leaped to their feet. And watched as three of the ninth floor's drunkest residents approached for a better look. "Holy shit," their spokesman repeated, seeing two others perched on the elevator cab. The floor was otherwise dark and silent, seemingly deserted.

"Hey—it's cool, right?" Pete said in an assured upperclassman's voice. And then vaulted from the roof, a nanosecond behind Chug.

As casually as possible, Pete turned and shut the door behind him. Then followed his fleeing companions toward the stairwell, and the safety of Sterling 4.

Anticipating Josh's right lead, Stu ducked and countered with a short jab. Seeing an opening, he then shot in a left to the other's stomach, which made him wince. Yet Josh quickly regained the advantage, using superior reach to hold off his opponent while scoring with two rights to the head.

"Time!" Jay Levin called from the judges' table, ending the second and final round. The Sterling 4 lounge reverberated with applause, Josh ruffling his roommate's hair with one glove as the weary combatants embraced. Briefly, the three judges conferred before declaring Josh the winner by unanimous decision.

The training gloves were courtesy of Frank Sorenson, who last weekend had brought them from his father's private gym. The end result was tonight's exhibition, which had packed the floor lounge. One card table served as a judges' stand, the boys officiating on a rotating basis.

"How do you guys score these fights, anyway?" Mitch Flanders asked, curious.

"I know when somebody gets his ass kicked." Chug's reply was in jest; the fights, of course, weren't supposed to get serious.

Added Dave Logan: "What do you want us to do, count punches?"

The evening's card assembled itself without plan. A series of challenges were made and accepted, the floor's male denizens goaded into the arena.

When the bouts resumed, Logan overcame George Hunter's height advantage to take a close decision. Then Frank, who'd begun boxing lessons at age nine, cruised to a unanimous win over a lethargic Adam Conway. Mitch Flanders posted the night's only TKO when roommate Nick Bernhardt retired with a nosebleed at the end of round one; and Rob Moreland, who'd eagerly crashed the event, scored the only knockdown, dropping Jay Levin with a right hook en route to a lopsided victory. Following the knockdown, the two were quickly separated, and the judges cautioned Rob about "fighting for real."

Grinning, Josh tried to lure Rosemary and Debbie into the ring. The women demurred; though Rosemary couldn't resist needling the roommate she'd wanted to punch out more than once. ("Josh—what's the matter? Don't you like Deb?")

From the judges' table, Chug scanned the room for fresh victims.

"Brandon, how about you? I don't think you've been up yet," he cajoled.

"I think I'll pass." Clark shook his head, suddenly self-conscious.

"Ah, come on," Jay taunted him. "Unless you want to be the BWOC—Big Wussy on Campus."

"Wuss! Wuss! Wuss!" the boys gleefully chanted. Ignoring his attempts to wave them off.

Expecting a snotty lecture on nonviolence, his floormates were amazed when Brandon instead opened his mouth in a vain effort to speak, glanced helplessly about the room, then turned and ran from the lounge.

"What the hell's his problem?" Chug shook his head, amused.

"Leave him alone!" Megan and Rosemary stood glaring at Chug; the others averted their eyes.

Moments later the two girls stood outside Brandon's room, tapping gently on the door. "Brandon? It's us. Can we come in?" Megan said.

"It's open," he answered in a hollow voice.

The room was completely dark, save for the small study lamp on

Brandon's desk. Brandon sat at the desk with head bowed, and they saw that he was nearly crying.

"Nobody here but us chickens," he said bitterly.

There was an awkward silence. Finally Rosemary said, "Look, it's okay. Really, it's no big deal..."

"Boxing is barbaric, anyway!" Megan interjected. Having witnessed most of the night's card since leaving Dwight with Moira Perry for the evening.

"Hey, I don't need your pity, all right?" Brandon sounded less than convincing.

"It's not pity," Megan quickly assured him. "I respect you for taking a stand. You didn't let everyone pressure you into doing something you don't believe in—that took courage."

Brandon sighed and shook his head. "No, you don't understand. That's not it at all," he confessed.

In truth, Brandon was afraid of physical confrontation. Once when he'd been in second grade, a group of boys had cornered him after school and beaten the snot out of him for no apparent reason. He'd come home with torn clothes and a bloody nose, his parents reacting as if he were at fault. ("You must have done *something* to make them angry," his mother had accused.) Since then, he'd invariably run from the threat of violence.

"It's all right." Megan put a hand gently on his shoulder. "It's nothing to be ashamed of..."

Aloud, Rosemary wondered, "Why do boys always think they have to prove they're tough anyway? It's so stupid!"

"I don't know," Brandon replied. Then with sudden, fierce determination rose and threw off his fatigue jacket. "But I'm going back in there."

"Brandon—no!" Megan looked suddenly alarmed. "You don't have to do this—"

"That's right, you don't," Rosemary quickly added. "No one will think less of you if you don't fight."

You can't believe that, Brandon mused.

"Forget them. This is something I have to do for myself." With the faintest trace of humor, he added, "Besides, you know I don't care what others think." In the end, the girls could not dissuade him.

Brandon re-entered the lounge to tense silence. The others watched as he lifted one pair of gloves from the floor, and with fastidious deliberation slipped them on. Then, picking up the second pair, sauntered to the judges' table and dropped them in Chug's lap.

"Let's party," he said, to raucous applause from his floormates.

Chug's face froze. Both were of average height; yet Chug was much more solidly built. He had at least forty pounds on Brandon.

"I can't," he said lamely.

"Oh, come on," Brandon replied. "I promise I'll take it easy on you."

A long, provocative moan rose from the audience.

"Come on," Jay said, grinning at Chug. "He's calling you!"

"I can't," Chug repeated. The crowd began to boo and razz him.

"Come to think of it, you haven't been up yet either, have you?" Brandon eyed him matter-of-factly while the audience oohed again.

Feeling himself trapped, Chug stood and began putting on the gloves.

"All right," he said grudgingly. And, palm raised in a gesture of self-absolution, added, "But remember—I did *not* ask for this fight."

The gloves were laced on, and referee George Hunter called the two to the center of the ring for their instructions.

"Okay, you guys know the rules," he began good-naturedly. "Keep your punches up, break when I tell you to, and—the most important rule of all—don't hit the referee!" he grinned.

"All right, let's git it on!" George screeched in imitation of Mills Lane. Brandon walked to his corner, knees shaking, and awaited the call of time.

Brandon came out winging. Charging from his corner at the opening bell, he began flailing wildly at Chug with both hands. Startled, Chug retreated to a corner, where Brandon launched a furious flurry to his body.

As the round dragged on, Brandon began to tire. He was feeling the weight of the sixteen-ounce gloves and was arm-weary, his shirt front soaked with sweat. Chug then began to assert himself, backing his opponent across the ring with a series of straight lefts. By the end of the round Chug was landing at will, scoring with two stiff smacks to the head as time wound down.

In the corner, Brandon was sweating profusely. His gallant effort had won the hearts of his neighbors, who yelled encouragement throughout the minute rest.

"Come on, Brandon—you can beat him!" He heard Megan's voice above the din. And, too winded to speak, raised one glove in her direction.

In the second round, Chug landed a stinging left to the liver, and Brandon felt his insides turn to liquid. "It's all right," he said, mostly to himself, backpedaling quickly out of danger.

"Let's go, Brandon!" a voice from the crowd exhorted. But his arms were like lead weights, and he couldn't lift his gloves to shield himself. Sensing his plight, Chug then eased up, scoring with a light left and backing off.

"Thirty seconds." Adam indicated the time left in the round. As if finding a second wind, Brandon gamely resumed throwing punches, but Chug slipped his weak blows, content to run out the clock.

At the final bell Brandon collapsed, panting, into his floormate's arms. To the roars of the satisfied crowd, Chug embraced his opponent as they stood in mid-ring.

Chug would take the clear-cut decision. But Brandon had won a greater victory.

Throughout spring semester, Dwight's condition had worsened.

He had lost weight steadily, and could no longer budge his handgrips at even the loosest setting. His body looked shrunken, his face pale and drawn.

There were other outward signs of regression. The suppositories had become less effective, sometimes failing to work at all. These episodes usually presaged an accident the next day, once forcing his exit from class.

Finally, one morning in late April a battered Ford van, loaded with packing crates, pulled up outside Sterling Hall. The van, a gray Econoline, belonged to Dwight's father.

"Good luck, Captain!" Debbie Grafton waved, passing outside his door. Other, similarly brief goodbyes followed.

"Will you be back?" Rosemary leaned over his chair, at once hopeful and concerned.

"Sure—you bet." But his voice lacked conviction. Gently she pecked Dwight's cheek and his returning hug lingered, belying his words.

As their embrace broke, his hand lightly brushed her breast. Certain it was an accident, she did not respond.

Stu and Josh offered to help load Dwight's things into the van. But Mr. Manning replied stoically that everything was under control. "Thank you boys all the same," he added in parting, Dwight laboriously shaking his neighbors' hands.

Through the van's rear window he watched as Megan stood outside the dorm, waving from the sidewalk while Dwight feebly reciprocated. Then the vehicle turned onto Hilton Way and she vanished from sight.

By midnight, the living room was a haze of thick smog, the beer free-flowing. The May Commencement ceremonies were hours past; at 8 Leeds Road the celebration had begun.

"Sshh—listen to this." Bob Spencer began reading from the "Teacher Comments" section of the fifth-grade report card Wally had brought down from home that weekend. The entire House was dimly lit, some fifteen guests seated in an intimate circle on the living-room floor.

Happily, Bob recited: "'Michael has become a disruptive influence in class. He often displays inappropriate levity. While academically his work is outstanding, his conduct leaves much to be desired.'"

Bob and his friends laughed heartily in response. But none more than his fellow alumnus. The Rodney Board was history now; soon Hall would begin working as an engineer at Glanbury's General Electric plant.

"Look—all N's and U's in Citizenship, but all G's in getting along with others." Bob passed the report card into the circle for viewing.

The stereo played a succession of the late quadrennium's best—from *My Sharona* to *Mr. Roboto*. Classic events were retold and embellished, milestones recalled. John Lennon's assassination, announced on Monday Night Football. Troll Philbrick singing "Bomb Iran" to the tune of *Barbara Ann* the night Reagan was elected. The time one of Wally's Outward Bound counselees, a fifteen-year-old from White Plains named

Matthew Colvin, had shown up at the dorm and spent three days before being convinced to return home.

"He hooked up with one of the girls on Five, too," Pete said, grinning. "At least, that's the story. We never did get confirmation."

The celebrants leafed through both volumes of Bob's thick scrapbook, a veritable pictorial history of Mutantdom. (A typical candid snapshot showed Wally and Troll posing with various women's unmentionables, taken from the laundry room.) Again laughing at the familiar pictures and anecdotes, agreeing that none from Sterling 4 could aspire to public office.

Pete focused intently on one image, a close-up of the memo board he and Wally had shared, the one with the cartoon bear strumming on a banjo. And printed in black, fully decipherable, the last message they'd posted during freshman year:

DURING FINALS WEEK, THE ROOM WILL BE OPEN ALL NIGHT (9 PM – 7 AM) FOR A STUDY PARTY. ASSUME AT ANY OTHER TIME THAT WE ARE SLEEPING OR SMOKING POT.

"That is just so *awesome!*" Wally howled in delight.

"Not the smartest thing we ever did," Pete said. "We ended up passing by an RCH."

"That'll be forgotten when you're a rich lawyer." Joanne Stewart smiled.

Filling their shot glasses with Smirnoff vodka, the three seniors began a round of graduation toasts. But it was Pete who captured the moment's essence.

"Today would not have been possible," he said, glass upraised, "had UPenn not given me the Rodney."

Dwight Manning was not enjoying his premature vacation. Now at home, he spent his time looking halfheartedly through computer correspondence course catalogs (which his mother patiently held up for him to read), watching a good deal of daytime television, and trying vainly to remaster his handgrips.

Contact with friends was rare. Of his former PCA's, only Megan Brunelle had kept in touch, calling perhaps once every other week. In May his cousin Bob had invited him up for Met's graduation ceremonies, but Dwight was forced to decline. Then Marcus had written him a letter from Glanbury, where he was taking summer courses to make up the credits he'd blown during freshman year. In Park Lane, the only friend he'd remained close with was Kenny Sanders, a onetime pinball-playing buddy who had gone into his father's roofing business after two stints on probation for possession of marijuana.

And as always, there were the video games.

He didn't visit the arcade as often now, maybe twice a week max when Kenny had some free time and could drive him there. (Regardless of the circumstances, having your mother take you to the video arcade simply wasn't cool.) Lately, the arrival of the new Pac-Man Plus game had presented a fresh challenge. The game varied from the original in its fruits (*e.g.* Coke cans, martinis, loaves of bread), which turned the monsters blue while doubling their point values.

Eventually, Dwight succeeded in crafting a set of patterns for the game. With some improvisation—and a fair amount of luck—he managed one day to reach the twelfth stack of pancakes before his failing hands betrayed him.

Despite adding another arcade record to his résumé, Dwight felt depressed. His final score of 336,720 was scarcely a third of what he'd tallied on the original version eight months before. Dwight could measure his rapid deterioration in the decline of his scores. And it would never get any better.

As if sensing something, he took a long wistful look around the Outer Limits before Kenny wheeled him out the door. He was wearing a hat, sweater and windbreaker, though it was the first of June.

It was his final game.

The hospital bed felt light and airy beneath his limp form, though after eight days the rubber tubing in his mouth tasted as gross as ever. So this is what it comes down to, Dwight mused. All these years of wearing jackets in June and Ma getting hysterical and locking Roger in his room every time he catches a cold, and this is what it all comes down to. A respirator doing my breathing for me, since I no longer can. Watching that rubber diaphragm expand and contract. Listening to that hissing noise and watching those needles swing back and forth on their dials, wondering what they mean. Tubes in me everywhere—nose and mouth, one in my arm where they're feeding me intravenously.

This was Dwight's third such hospital stay since age fourteen, with events following a familiar pattern. The first sneeze—a quick, muffled high-pitched sound, the way a dog (or one of Met's dainty ice princesses) might sneeze. Telling yourself that it was only a draft, or some dust in the air. The feeble attempts at sniffling when your nose began to run, then the still feebler attempts to cough, your throat closing up, your lungs too weak to expel the phlegm which is choking the life out of you.

Signaling frantically to Roger to get Mrs. Carmody next door because Ma's out buying groceries at Stop and Shop. A mad dash to the hospital that seems to last forever—for no time seems short when you're fighting for breath. Several pairs of hands converging on you in the emergency room, the voices behind them growing fainter.

And then nothing. Lots of nothing. Drifting in and out of consciousness.

Extensive bilateral pneumonia. It was extensive bilateral pneumonia this time. Not just regular bilateral pneumonia, but *extensive* bilateral pneumonia. Plus, the antibiotics aren't exactly kicking ass. I can hear you talking to Ma outside the door just fine from here, Dr. Buonanno. Just fine. There's nothing wrong with my ears. It's just everything below the neck that's gone.

Up your nose with a rubber hose. Hadn't everyone said that in seventh grade, and thought it was so cool? Well this is the real deal, my friends. And it sucks. It blows too, ha-ha. What a major crush he once had on Mrs. Kotter.

The best thing we can do now, the doctor was saying, is to keep him as comfortable as possible.

He was dying. He had been dying all his life. Doomed from the moment of conception to this hospital bed, this fate. This was what they called biting the big one, buying the farm, going permanently 10-7. The Captain lays down his blaster for the last time.

Dwight wondered what it would have been like to make love to a girl, or drive a car. Or even to get totally wasted. He would never go to Europe, or see the Green Flash when the sun rose. A million on Pac-Man Plus, now that would have been the ultimate challenge.

Random waves of memory washed over him. The time he and Kenny had played 152 games of pinball on one dime at Park Lanes, after discovering the machine always matched on 60 (it had been a simple matter of tilting accordingly). Vince Patterson chaining Dwight's wheelchair to the bathroom radiator with a bicycle lock in ninth grade, and thinking it was funny. Less imaginative souls occasionally locking the chair's brakes.

College life. Shooting the breeze with Wally and the gang during L.B. The time Josh called a Wax Museum as they were coming out of the elevator, forcing Stu to stand still while the door tried repeatedly to close on him. And of course, that wonderful night when he had stood alone atop the video-game world.

Did your life really flash before you at this point? Or was it your own last effort to convince yourself that it had been a worthwhile existence after all? Most likely, it was just something that happened when you had lots of time with nothing to do but think.

He wished they would take the tube out of his mouth, so he could tell his parents once more that he loved them.

On June 25, 1983 Dwight Manning died as his mother held his hand. He was three months short of his twentieth birthday.

The funeral took place the following Tuesday, at St. Agnes' Church in Park Lane. In all, some two hundred people attended the service, the church nearly filled to capacity.

In the front pew Dwight's immediate family sat, surrounded by grief-stricken relatives. Robert Manning, grave but composed, held a comforting arm about his wife and their surviving son. At his father's side, ten-year-old Roger sat with head bowed, eyes focused downward, away from his brother's casket.

Amid the congregation, Dwight's ex-floormates sat huddled in silence. The girls buried their noses in handkerchiefs, while the boys stared straight ahead. In the liberated eighties it was of course permissible for men to cry, but with the understanding that one must never be seen.

Upon arrival, Marcus was still seething from the fight he'd had with his parents that morning. He had taken the day off from his classes, that was no problem—yet incredibly, Mom and Dad had made an issue of his attendance.

Did someone say you should come, his mother had asked, as though he were in kindergarten.

An invitation to a funeral? Give me a break. What planet are you from, he'd lashed back fiercely.

I don't think it's a good idea for you to take the car on that long a trip anyway, his father said as if to end the discussion, noting that Marcus had never driven out of state before. Thus spake the primary male authority figure in Marcus's life, the optometrist who had custom-made every pair of his son's glasses since the boy was four. At that moment, Marcus suddenly remembered every slight his parents had ever inflicted upon him. The time a six-year-old Marcus had spent most of a Sunday afternoon copying an entire page from *Time* magazine, only to be told that his writing looked "like worms crawling on the sidewalk." His mother's dismissive "You have to be tough" when he'd mentioned the idea of playing football with the other kids. His father's disgusted "Oh, you idiot!" when he spilled his milk or lost his gloves. The way these people STILL answered for him when others asked him questions…

And then it happened. Goaded into an overpowering rage, Marcus snatched the keys to his father's Vega from the living-room table and stormed from the house. And before anyone could stop him, roared out of the driveway, bound for Connecticut. (His mother had suggested reporting the car stolen and having the police bring him home, but his father overruled her, pleased that Marcus had shown some guts at last.)

He got to the church in the nick of time, arriving at the close of the organ prelude. As inconspicuously as possible, he took a seat next to his floormates without saying a word. (He was dimly aware that Rosemary was wearing a skirt for the first time he could recall.) The somber setting drove home the fact of the funeral, and the thought that he had nearly missed it made his anger come flooding back.

Then he saw the open coffin, and remembered why he had come.

The corners of his mouth began to twitch. He found himself wondering if Wally would cry. If he did, it would be no big deal. Cool is as cool does, that was what Wally had said.

He made no sound, but wiped gently at the corner of his eye, brushing aside the tears as they came.

Only later did Marcus realize that for the first time in his life, he had stood up to his parents and made his will prevail.

In his eulogy, the minister praised Dwight's shining example of courage against adversity, while assuring his mourners that Dwight was in God's care, in a world without pain or suffering or disease. At the family's request, the service featured a sampling of Dwight's favorite hymns; selections included *I Serve a Risen Savior*, an oddly upbeat choice for the occasion.

Filing out of the church after the service, Dwight's friends from Sterling 4 offered their condolences to his family. Bob Spencer, who was among his cousin's pallbearers, numbly accepted the sympathies of his old dormmates as they passed through the front vestibule. Walking toward the door, Troll idly watched Debbie Grafton's legs, a guilty pleasure enhanced by her sheer nylon hose.

Outside, the sun was shining gauchely. The conversation was generally brief and pointless. Several floor members instinctively came over to comfort Megan Brunelle, who had been closest to Dwight.

"We're all going to miss him, but this must be especially hard on you..." Rosemary's eyes were wet with tears as the two embraced.

"He's with God now," Megan replied in a faraway, almost mechanical voice. She had not shed a tear during the service, and seemed strangely calm and unaffected.

The cars began to pull slowly out of the parking lot. Rosemary, who had taken a summer job in Glanbury as a bicycle messenger, rode back with Stu and Josh, who like Marcus were making up credits of their own. The three invited Marcus to join them for dinner back in town, and Marcus decided he could wait a bit longer to return his father's car.

Only Bob and Megan were at the Manning house that night for the ritual of the neighbors bearing casseroles. The others slipped quietly out of Park Lane, retracing their steps through hastily-scrawled directions they would not need again.

II

Of the Material
Universe

JUNIOR I

"No shit?"

"No shit, Wally. A real touchdown." Stu grabbed another Molson from Chug's refrigerator while Wally struggled to grasp the unthinkable: After four years of offensive impotence, the Mutants' intramural football team had scored against an opponent's will.

"Awe-some!" Michael Francis Hall, research and development engineer at General Electric, leaned forward in his chair, his dark suit jacket slung over the wooden back. ("He stops by on the way to work—that's dedication!" Stu had heralded Wally's 7 A.M. arrival for this, the fall's first L.B.)

"Jay works his way open and I chuck it to him—" Stu made a throwing motion with his right arm—"then he grabs it on a dead run and takes it in." Hall turned to Jay Levin, who feigned appropriate modesty. "Thirty-one yards. It was great. We did the Fun Bunch celebration and everything."

"Did you guys win?" Wally edged still closer.

"Nah, not this time." Josh smiled forlornly before adding, "But we did score in double figures." Last night the Mutants had bowed, 21-13, to Hamilton House, the string of setbacks unbroken.

"That's right." Chug sat nursing a bottle between his thighs. The newly-anointed Rookie Drinker of the Year, fresh from his award ceremony, added: "Sanjay can kick field goals."

"Sanjay—?" Wally frowned, unsure he had heard correctly.

"He's disgusting. No expression, just boots it through from 30, 35 yards out—it's incredible."

"It's an extracurricular activity. For his med school apps." Adam spat a stream of tobacco juice into an almost-full quart jar. Now rooming next door with Jay Levin, he sat across from his ex-roommate, on what had become Frank Sorenson's bed. "Still, it's good that he's getting out of his room more often."

"It's incredible," Chug reiterated. "It's the only thing he can do. He's like an athletic idiot savant."

"They play soccer in India, don't they?" Jay asked.

"I guess so." Stu shrugged, adding, "Apparently they play it everywhere else."

"He must have had a hidden talent all along," Chug said. Behind him the cinderblock wall was bare, but for the framed QUIET, PLEASE sign that once graced his hometown library.

Dave Logan studied his second brew. "Is it me, or does the floor seem different this year?" said the ex-Union Senator, now residing off campus, on Spring Hill Road.

"Seems like there's a lot of rich kids." Stu's tone was reflective.

"No surprise," Chug said. "The way they've been gouging the tuition, only rich people will be able to afford it."

"Can you believe some guys actually cared about the America's Cup?" he added. "Watching the races on TV, and they were so pissed when Australia won…"

"How can anybody watch that?" Josh shook his head, bemused. "It's like watching Astroturf grow."

But sailing races weren't the whole story. The group sensed that a seismic cultural shift had taken place, reflected in the current freshman class. The new breed was more conservative than its elders; also more worldly and materialistic. Its members viewed privilege as a birthright, with Daddy-bought BMW's and designer outfits the norm. Many admired Shenford because he kicked ass, and that was all that ever mattered in this world. Among girls straight hair was considered passé, with gender equality less pressing. The boys cut their hair shorter, while swelling ROTC enlistments in record numbers.

"You have to wear a tie every day now?" Stu asked Wally.

Hall nodded wistfully. "It still feels like a slow hanging," he remarked.

His third beer finished, Chug stood abruptly, saying, "I don't mean to be rude—but if I blow this off now, it won't get done today." From the desktop he took a deck of cards and, moving aside yesterday's socks and his copy of *Outrageously Offensive Jokes,* hit the floor for his morning workout.

"A guy back home showed me this," he said, his guests curiously looking on. "You're supposed to do it every other day…"

As Chug explained, the technique was simple. You flipped a card, did that many pushups, then moved on to the next card. Face cards counted as ten; aces fifteen; and jokers two. Chug could do the entire deck—with the two jokers, an even four hundred pushups—in under twenty minutes.

"Time me," he instructed, slipping off his watch and throwing it at Josh.

Eighteen minutes and forty seconds later, his workout completed, Chug lurched, panting, to his feet. Uncapping a fresh bottle of beer, he downed the contents in four seconds flat, his performance topped by a powerful eructation.

When the applause faded, Chug stepped outside the room and flung the empty bottle down the hall, to shatter noisily on the floor.

"I say the maids should earn their money once in a while." He'd lately made a habit of disposing of bottles in this fashion.

Jay said, "You've been hanging around Frank too long."

"Hey, where is Sorenson, anyway?" Adam said. "Don't tell me he's up and about?"

Stone-faced, Chug responded, "You might try Deb's room."

"Debbie Grafton. That spoiled, snotty bitch." Jay shook his head, then added, "She's living with Bonnie Randall now, right?"

"Yeah. But you know Bonnie. She won't say anything."

The conversation turned to other topics. Floor residents shared their impressions of new Hall director Judy Billey, a dour martinet with a face resembling a sucked lemon. At Wally's behest, the boys knelt in homage to new dorm president Chug, the fourth member of the Mutant Regime. ("How much honor can one man take?" he'd emoted in his Rookie Drinker acceptance speech at The House.)

His chew finished, Adam silently stood and left the room with jar in hand. Approaching the stairwell door, he opened it and threw the jar down onto the next landing. The jar shattered on impact, in a spray of broken glass and tobacco juice.

Adam returned and again sat down, stone-faced. "Oops," he said quietly.

"You know, Troll dropped out of school," Dave matter-of-factly reported. There were surprised looks, edged with concern.

"Was it because of money, or was it grades?" Chug asked.

"I think it was a little bit of both."

Solicitously, Stu asked, "So what's he doing now?"

"He got a job selling sporting goods at J.C. Penney's, down in Kent. He says he might start taking classes again, part-time, next semester." Privately, Logan pondered his own sketchy financial position.

"Brandon and Marcus are roommates this year, did you know that?" Chug again glanced at Wally.

"Get out—how did that happen?"

"It was like a package deal. Frank came here after Adam and Jay decided to hook up, then those two were kind of left over. But allegedly,

Brandon promised not to use the room for his commie meetings."

"I'd say Marcus gets along with Brandon as well as anyone does," Josh thoughtfully mused.

"Is he still pursuing Miss Rosemary, by chance?" Wally smiled.

"What do you mean, 'still?' 'Still' would imply that he'd taken action at some point."

At eight-fifteen, Wally stood and slipped on his jacket. "All right— I'm outta here. Time to rejoin the rat race," he said. "Gentlemen—it's been real..."

Starting for the door, he felt a slight pressure on his crown. Wally turned, and then froze as Chug set a full plastic cup of beer on his head.

"Come on, that's a suit!" Stu reminded him. Unchastened, Chug paused to admire his handiwork.

Without hesitation, Wally began walking across the room in a straight line, his headwear perfectly balanced. Opening the door with one hand, he removed the cup and drained it in three large draughts.

"That's lesson number one in modeling school." Wally bowed, acknowledging the applause from his audience. And, crumpling the empty cup in his fist, lobbed it neatly across the room, into Chug's wastebasket.

"Later on." He gave an insouciant valedictory nod. And with a satisfied belch, smoothed his tie and left for the workplace.

Since Dwight's death, Megan had been in a funk.

For weeks she'd attended classes indifferently, somnambulating through the clinicals she once yearned to begin. Her mind was a chaos of conflicting emotions: lingering shock, grief, anger at God, guilt and fear at harboring such thoughts. And for the first time, doubt about all she'd ever believed.

In her sheltered existence she had not known real grief, or experienced genuine loss. Now, suddenly, nothing in her neat and orderly world made sense anymore.

Tonight she sat alone in the floor lounge, hair unkempt, staring sightlessly at the wall. The blue-pinstriped student nurse's uniform clung tiredly to her small frame, hours after classes had adjourned.

What's the whole point of life anyway, she wondered in despair. What possible hope for humanity was there in a world filled with random, pointless suffering? And above all, how could a loving and just God allow it to happen?

In her acute distress, she did not hear the door open behind her.

"Ah—there you are." Rosemary stepped inside, her roommate unresponsive. "Just so you know—*Cheers* in Kara D'Alessio's room, fifteen minutes from now. I'm making some popcorn, in case you want to join us."

Again there was no response.

"Hey, are you all right?" Rosemary's voice was edged with concern. Megan's eyes looked blank, her body rigid, as if in a catatonic state.

With a sudden burst of strength, she stood and tipped over the wooden table. And from the depths of her anguish, emitted an agonized cry.

"Why? Why, damn it?—*It isn't fair!*" Her arms flailed hysterically. "Not fair!" Megan screamed again and again. And collapsed, sobbing, into her roommate's arms.

The lounge door again opened and Marcus stood on the threshold in silence, Jay Levin peering over his shoulder.

After a long pause Marcus quietly asked, "Is she okay?"

Rosemary ignored him. "It's all right," she told Megan in a soft voice, still gently holding her as she wept. "It's all right..."

Two days later, Megan Brunelle returned home to Allentown. Leaving school unceremoniously, the issue of further studies unaddressed.

For the onetime aspiring nurse, everything now was in limbo.

As a professor of constitutional law, Elizabeth Kerr was highly in demand. While less fiercely Socratic than some of her subordinates, the dean rated as a brilliant lecturer, who brought life to an otherwise dull subject.

This morning, one hundred and ten of her first-year students were crowded into Room 101, the largest of Kennedy Hall's classrooms. The 1L's sat in eight ascending rows, engaged in a spirited colloquium on landmark abortion cases. (While many con law profs downplayed this topic, Kerr favored open dialogue, and managed tactfully to keep the debates from becoming acrimonious.)

In the fifth row, Pete Garrett abruptly stopped scribbling on his yellow pad. From a passing car stereo, the strains of *The Logical Song* wafted through the courtyard, stirring memories of his freshman days. Pete turned toward the window, and listened intently until Supertramp faded into the distance. It was early October, his sixth week of law school, the lyrics seeming especially poignant.

From the beginning he'd felt his mind shift to another plane, out of necessity. He had experienced the self-doubts common to all first-years, along with the nagging sense that he did not belong, that he was out of his depth. And to top it off, his course grades would depend solely on the final exams at the end of each semester.

He had also moved from The House. He'd left The House because, let's face it, The House was no place for serious study. Word had it that Hall and Spencer were still partying their asses off (they would learn their lesson after showing up for work hung over once or twice), the others continuing to jerk off as usual. Pete now lived in a tiny apartment on Callender Drive, alone but for his books and the Sony three-inch black-and-white TV set that had seen him through his undergraduate years.

It's all worth it in the end, a friendly upperclasswoman named Sandy Kates had advised. You just have to keep telling yourself that.

Idly, he glanced out the window. North of the main campus there was more open space, and the courtyard looked almost suburban. The lawn was wide and green, with a single elm tree in the foreground—the perfect spot to just kick back and listen to tunes if one could…

Pete was hearkened back to the discussion by another familiar sound, more ingrained in memory than *The Logical Song*. It was the sound of his own name.

"Mr. Garrett, do you want to talk about *Akron v. Akron Center for Reproductive Health*?" Kerr asked.

Pete's mind suddenly went blank, the nightmare scenario come true. It was the first time he'd been called on this year, and he would become the first in his section to pass for lack of preparedness. Shamefaced, he stared down at his notepad, avoiding the dean's steady gaze.

"I…just read the new stuff," he said sheepishly, alluding to the material in the casebook. The *Akron* decision had been handed down over the summer, and was among several supplemental cases Kerr had "recommended" for review.

The dean was not so easily discouraged. "We can take up these cases in chronological order just as well," she said, shifting gears smoothly, eyes unwavering. "Can you explain Justice Powell's opinion in the second *Bellotti v. Baird* case?"

Pete dared to draw breath at last. *Bellotti* was in the casebook, and he had abstracted it over the weekend. Intrepidly, he reached forward and turned on the microphone before him.

"The case involved a Massachusetts statute requiring parental consent for abortions performed on minors," he began. "The Court held the statute unconstitutional..." Pete paused for a moment, while flipping pages to refresh his recollection.

"Did the statute make any other provision?" Kerr prompted.

"Yes," Pete recalled. "It said that a state judge could authorize the abortion 'for good cause shown.'"

"In addition to parental consent or in lieu of it?"

"In lieu of it," Pete echoed. "Under the statute, the woman—or rather, the girl—could get permission either from her parents or a judge."

"So, unlike the statute involved in *Planned Parenthood v. Danforth*, this one provides an alternative to parental consent. Why does the Court still strike it down?"

"The statute provides an alternative, but it still takes the decision out of the girl's hands. *Either* her parents or a judge can give consent, but not the girl herself. In essence, Powell says that pregnant minors should be given a chance to make the decision on their own."

"All pregnant minors?" Kerr nudged.

"Well, no. The opinion states that the girl should have the opportunity to go directly to the court—bypassing her parents—and convince them that she is mature enough to make the decision on her own, or that the procedure would be 'in her best interests.'"

"And where does the Massachusetts statute fail?"

"Well, in every case, the parents would have to be notified in advance. Meaning that a minor could go to a judge only after her parents refused to consent. I think the Court felt that might have a chilling effect." (Pete thought that he was picking up law school parlance quite nicely.)

"Now, Mr. Garrett," Kerr moved in, "where do you suppose this concept of the 'mature minor' comes from? Why is it that a teenager may be required to obtain parental consent, for example, to get her ears pierced, but not to obtain an abortion?"

"I guess," Pete said, reaching, "it's because there's no express constitutional right to get your ears pierced." His hopeful stab met with suppressed laughs.

"You smile, Mr. Garrett," the dean lightly returned, "but you're not so far off. You remember that in *Danforth,* the Court held that parents and spouses could not be given blanket veto power over a woman's decision to end her pregnancy, because it was within her constitutionally-protected right of privacy to make that decision.

"In other words, minors may be required to jump through hoops where a valid state interest is involved. But only to the extent that they do not unduly impinge on that right."

While the class digested this concept, Kerr looked down at her copy of the text. "What about the statute in *H.L. v. Matheson?*" she said after a short pause. "What was different about that statute so that the Court upheld it?"

Absorbed in his presentation of *Bellotti,* Pete could not readily call *Matheson* to mind. Quickly he scanned the textbook for details, amid expectant silence.

In the front row, Derek Finch lifted his hand. Pete slowly relaxed, his section mates sighing in resignation. Derek Finch, who would grade onto law review next spring, was known for his tendency to monopolize class discussions.

Derek, buddy, I owe you one. Pete listened as the ex-rugby forward from UPenn outlined the distinction between parental notice and parental consent requirements. To his mind, he had entered the arena and lived to fight another day.

"Good job, Pete," Tyler Scott said as they left class. Pete, less certain, nodded his thanks. The first-year students, as always, were a mutual support group. Absent a single mark on their transcripts, they were all on equal footing.

From the Sports section of the *Guardian*, Oct. 11, 1983:

INTRAMURAL SQUAD ENDS RECORD LOSING STREAK

By Tim Whiteside
Guardian Sports Staff

Last Thursday night, hell froze over. The Pope converted to Zoroastrianism. Bears began using Portajohns. A team from Sterling Hall's fourth floor won an intramural football game.

They really won.

After a campus-record 34 consecutive defeats, including 29 shutout losses, the Mutants of Sterling 4 really and truly won a University Intramural League contest.

At Brentwood Stadium, when sophomore team captain Josh McFadden's last-second interception iced the Mutants' 17-7 triumph over the Vernon 22 Breakers ("We beat the *top* team on campus, get it?" nonplaying floor resident Marcus Pullman joked afterward), an elated Sterling 4 squad jubilantly converged on McFadden and co-captain Stu Cabral, in celebration of the floor's first win since 1978.

"It's good to get that first one under our belt," McFadden quipped after the game. Added Cabral: "Seriously—bring on Nebraska!"

Prior to last week's contest, Sterling 4's intramural teams had been outscored 863-41 in an epic saga of futility dating to a time when the Shah ruled Iran, and

few outside central Pennsylvania were acquainted with
Three Mile Island....

Posted on Chug and Frank's message board, week of October 17, 1983:

Q – How many Glanburyites does it take to change a
light bulb?

A – Nunnaya freakin' business! Whatta you, on drugs?

"This isn't a newspaper!" Brandon Clark slammed the latest edition of the *Press* down on the cafeteria table in disgust. "It's an attempt to create a personality cult around Shenford!"

As usual, the leader's image appeared prominently on the house organ's front page. The lead article heralded the launch of Campaign 2000, a University-wide effort to raise two billion dollars by the close of the century. The campaign—its goal unprecedented in the annals of higher education—had been announced by President Shenford at a news conference, following reports that he had interviewed for the post of baseball commissioner.

"Hey, P.R. is the name of the game." Frank Sorenson swallowed a mouthful of hamburger, heedless of Deb's admonition not to talk while eating. It was bad enough, she thought, that Frank made such a pig of himself when the caf served patty melts for lunch.

Brandon ignored the interruption. "Listen to this," he began reading aloud from the article. "'While expressing "utmost confidence" in the campaign's success, the President downplayed his chances of being in office to witness its fruition. "They'll never put up with me for that long," he joked.'"

Incensed, Brandon slapped the paper down again. "Did you ever read such mindless drivel?"

"Hey, let me tell you something," Frank replied. "Shenford is the best thing that ever happened to this school. Until he came along, the place was going nowhere."

"He's a glorified principal!" Brandon sniffed. "I can't understand why he gets so much attention, even if he is a shameless publicity hound."

"Because he tells it like it is. And he knows what he's talking about." Frank looked around and addressed the others at the table. "You know, he is amazing. I remember last year, when he came to this dorm to give a talk, there were these hecklers trying to give him a hard time, and he was just *blowing them out of the water.* He just has such command of the facts…He probably knows what I had for breakfast yesterday."

"He's not God," Debbie reminded Frank. Who to her knowledge hadn't been up for breakfast once.

"Don't tell *him* that," Brandon muttered. Recalling his evisceration at the president's hands.

Characteristically, opinions on Shenford's merits ranged across the spectrum.

"It's true that he's a hard-ass authoritarian," said freshman Matt Helfand, whose mother chaired Met's Department of Economics. "He had to be, to turn this place around the way he has."

"I heard him speak last year, too," Jay said. "He's like, the most brilliant man you'll ever meet in your life…"

"But he turns people off," Debbie countered. "He's so arrogant and abrasive…"

"I thought he was just plain rude." Rosemary sipped a spoonful of vegetable soup.

Chug snickered, "He's James Watt with a brain."

"Listening to him talk," Marcus said, "I felt that between the two of us we knew all there was to know. He seemed to know everything except that he was an insufferable jerk, and I knew that."

From two seats away, Josh reached out and clapped him on the back.

"Say, that's pretty good, Marcus!"

"He can't be all that bad," Carol James objected. "I know he's done a lot for poor kids, in terms of financial aid. Percentagewise, Met gives out more need-based scholarships than any other school in the region."

Chug laughed, unimpressed. "Are you sure that wasn't his good twin?"

"I respect him," Adam somewhat grudgingly offered. "I mean, you have to respect the man. But does anyone actually like him?"

"I know that Professor Ferris guy doesn't like him." Kara D'Alessio folded a napkin on her tray.

"Ferris is a joke!" Frank laughed in disdain. "He comes across like this middle-aged Yippie, and it's so pathetic."

Jay said, "I read somewhere that Shenford might get a job in Washington, running some federal agency. You know, because he's on that government thing…"

"Yeah, that Grace Commission deal," Stu supplied.

"He could kick some ass down in Washington." Matt reflectively nodded. "Or, they think he might become an ambassador to some country…"

Chug again smirked. "It better be a country whose friendship we can afford to lose," he said.

The debate rages on. As it rages across campus, as it has raged through the years.

Until now, Bonnie Randall had enjoyed the perfect evening. Zeta Pi's Autumn Formal had been a fantasy come true, a fairy-tale moment when nothing, it seemed, could go wrong.

"Wait—what are you doing?" She inched slowly away from Bruce Dunham as they sat on her bed. Her date's tuxedo was unbuttoned, his fingers working the strap of her rented blue gown.

The tall, dark-haired junior looked puzzled. "What's wrong?" he asked in a calming voice. The couple had left the Sheraton ballroom a half-hour earlier, returning to the dorm in a Yellow Cab.

"I just think we should slow down." Bonnie's face was flushed. Remembering how she had changed rooms earlier in the semester, weary of Deb and Frank's constant rutting. ("We should start a club," Rosemary had said when Bonnie moved in, filling Megan's place.)

"Now, don't be a tease." Bruce smiled, but the humor did not touch his eyes. She recalled the night, almost a month ago, when they had met at a frat party, and her inward excitement when he'd called the next day. Worldly and charming, he'd seemed the perfect antidote to her ex-boyfriend, the hapless Rick Casey.

Softly he kissed her lips again, one hand stroking the swell of her breast.

"Stop it!" She pushed his arm aside. No longer smiling, he reached out and cupped her face in one hand.

"Hey, I know the score." The dark eyes were predatory, entirely without tenderness. "You invited me up to *your* room, what was I supposed to think?"

She stared at him in disbelief. *Of all the presumptuous, sexist—*

Roughly he forced her down, her shoulders pinned to the mattress.

"You got me hard—and I ain't gonna whack off." Bruce shed his jacket and tie, then began unbuttoning his ruffled white shirt. "That's the way it's gonna be…"

A feeble cry of distress passed her lips.

"Shut up!" He raised one hand threateningly. Her eyes squeezed shut, his lips caressing her neck and shoulders.

Bonnie suppressed a sob. "Sshh," he whispered gently, his hands working underneath, deftly unzipping her gown. Intent in his purpose, he did not hear the room door open.

"Hey, do you mind?" Bruce sat upright as Rosemary entered, keys jangling. Bonnie slipped free of his grasp and, moving toward the head of the bed, shrank back against the wall.

Rosemary perceived the situation at once. "Get out!" she told Bruce. "Get out now, or I'll call the cops!"

Bruce was unfazed. "You get out," he replied, his tone disbelieving. "Walking in on people like this—maybe you'd like to join us?" Bonnie's back was braced against the wall, her hands dug firmly into the mattress.

Rosemary tensed herself to spring at him.

Anxious to avoid any scenes, Bruce became less belligerent. "Okay, look…we didn't mean to put you out, and we're sorry." He smiled slightly, as though this were a simple misunderstanding, before turning back toward Bonnie. "But if you could just come back a bit later—"

The square heel caught him on the bridge of the nose, shattering it with a sickening crunch. The pain was immense, excruciating. Bruce howled in agony and clutched at his face, blood spurting through his fingers.

Bonnie's second kick raked the side of her assailant's head. Bruce slid down onto the floor in a kneeling position, still holding his injured nose.

"Go on—get out of here!" Rosemary hauled him upright and marched him to the door, one arm held firmly behind his back. Quickly she opened the door, and stopped short as three male figures blocked their exit.

"We heard all the noise. What's going on?" Stu said. Adam and Josh staring silently at the blood-soaked front of Bruce's shirt.

"He tried to attack Bonnie. Get him out of here!" Rosemary hurled her captive forward.

"You bet..." The three boys seized Dunham at once. Stu looked again at the fountain of blood, then at Rosemary with misplaced admiration.

"Do you want us to call the police?" Rosemary looked back at Bonnie, who managed to shake her head. Snatching Bruce's jacket and tie from the floor, Rosemary threw them after him as he was led, still moaning in pain, down the corridor.

The room door again closed. Rosemary rushed to comfort Bonnie, who returned her embrace, giving vent to her tears.

Eight students stood in a circle on the main floor of Digby Library, imbued with purpose, Brandon's associates apprehending his steady gaze. The wheels were in motion, and there was no turning back.

Until now, the Mushroom Society faithful had remained content with petition drives and protest rallies against the nuclear arms race. Yet the fall's events made clear more drastic steps were needed. Within the past month there had been the failure of the nuclear freeze resolution in Congress, and redeployment of American cruise missiles in Europe.

And—most ominously—there had been the Grenada invasion. America again had tasted blood, and remembered how it once relished the flavor. (The ultraconservative Bristol *Telegraph* had run an eight-page spread on the operation, with the jingoistic subtitle "Americans in Action.")

Aware of the security guard eying them from his booth, Brandon focused on the clock above the main entrance, the sweep of its second hand. It was Thursday, November 17, moments before 4 P.M.

Brandon watched the second hand draw nearer to the hour. "Ten!" he suddenly shouted at the top of his lungs. The guard emerged from behind the desk, moved forward, then hesitated. "Nine! Eight! Seven! Six!..."

In neighboring study carrels, books were abandoned as students flocked to the disturbance. The security guard, plainly out of his depth, returned to his kiosk and reached for the telephone.

When the countdown reached zero, the others hit the floor, assuming a fetal position on the maroon rug. Lying motionless for ninety seconds, while their leader addressed the gathering crowd.

"What you are seeing here," Brandon narrated, "is a microcosmic vision of a postnuclear world, with hundreds of millions of corpses scattered over the earth. A tragedy that looms nearer each day, now seeming all but inevitable. Unless the peace-loving majority can make its voice heard…"

Taking their cue, his followers sat upright in a half-circle and applauded. Then began chanting antiwar slogans, their handcrafted signs visible. NO NUKES. SUPPORT THE FREEZE. END THE ARMS RACE, NOT THE HUMAN RACE.

With midterm exams ongoing, the library was fully packed, and it was not long before an audience had assembled. The onlookers remained mostly silent, watching in idle curiosity.

From his knapsack Brandon took a stack of pamphlets, which he began distributing among the crowd. The pamphlet, entitled "The World After Nuclear War," detailed the aftereffects of such a conflagration. Clouds of radioactive dust, preventing sunlight from reaching Earth. A "nuclear winter" then causing a breakdown of the food chain, killing all surviving animal and plant life. Including, of course, the last remnants of humankind.

"The current administration talks about ridding the world of nuclear weapons, while overseeing the most massive arms buildup in history," Brandon warned. "Backed by their rich patrons, they have put all of humanity on a collision course with extinction. This is what we must stand together to oppose."

A sudden, tense murmur swept through the crowd as two campus cops arrived on the scene—an event the Society had anticipated with foreboding.

"I can think of more sensible ways to get your point across." The younger officer spoke calmly, without belligerence. He recognized Brandon as the group's leader, and addressed him.

The young activist responded in kind. "Sir, we're not out to make trouble, but this is something far bigger than all of us," he said. "Will the powers-that-be in Washington finally come to their senses and halt the mad race to nuclear destruction? Will American industrialists cease manufacturing these devastating weapons of war for the sake of the bottom line? And above all, will our leaders grasp that imperialism is no longer a luxury we can afford? Until then, we have no choice but to take a stand." His cohorts vigorously applauded.

"You want to take a stand, you can do it without causing a disturbance." The officer's tone hardened. "Right now, for all your noble intentions, you are committing an act of disorderly conduct. Unless you disperse at once, we will have no choice but to arrest you."

His partner, who had stood sullenly in the background, lunged forward and took Brandon by the arm. "Come on, let's go," the older man snarled. A veteran of the 1969 campus uprisings, he equated all demonstrators with those long-haired faggots hoping to keep their sorry, expendable asses out of Vietnam.

Brandon pulled free with a convulsive jerk. "You take your filthy hooves off of me!"

From the audience, a collective gasp. "Oh shit," someone moaned.

The officer's hand moved menacingly toward his nightstick. But this time Brandon held his ground, unflinching.

"Excuse me, gentlemen," a voice then intervened.

Ignoring the boos from the demonstrators, Casper Grayling approached with phlegmatic calm. The Dean of Students was tall and slope-shouldered, his thinning hair and mustache charcoal-gray.

"Okay, you folks will have to leave now." Grayling sounded as if he expected no argument. His face was pale and cadaverous; his brown eyes, behind tinted lenses, small and tired. "This is a place for quiet study, and your fellow students deserve a little consideration."

"I don't think so." Brandon again stepped forward, his voice quiet but firm. "We came to make a statement, and we're not leaving until we've had our say."

Grayling opened his mouth to respond, but Brandon beat him to the punch. For minutes he rattled on about Met's "sponsorship of the march toward nuclear oblivion," citing the school's investments in such defense giants as Westinghouse and United Technologies. The dean folded his arms and waited, unwilling to dignify this fanaticism.

"Are you quite through, son?" Grayling spoke softly as Brandon paused.

"Not—even—close." Brandon's comrades yelled their support, backed by a few members of the audience. "In fact, so far as we're concerned, this is only the beginning."

The administrator's expression clouded. "All right, then, I'll put it another way. I've been patient with you all up to now, but I've reached my limit. Either you leave the building now, or you will be arrested for trespassing and disorderly conduct. And suspended from this university."

"As I said...this is just the beginning." But Brandon had made his point, and going to jail now would serve no purpose. Grayling read him well, and stood by while Brandon gave the order to withdraw.

"You can put your guns away now—we're leaving," he taunted the cops. The senior officer flushed, but wisely did not respond. As they filed out the door, Brandon led his flock in chanting, "The people united can never be defeated."

"That was so cool, the way you stood up to the dean." Sandy Ellsworth praised him after the others had scattered in the late-fall twilight. Smiling, she cheerily added, "That took the ultimate in balls."

"If we're afraid of a mere college dean, then we cannot expect to get through to the leaders of the world." Brandon spoke with deliberate loftiness as they crossed the darkened mall between the library and Walden Chapel.

Unconcerned with the opinions of this flighty freshman, Brandon was nonetheless aware of her physical charms. (Beneath the baggy wool sweaters she favored, it was obvious Sandy had an amazing figure.) He could spurn the idiocy of romantic love; yet the biological needs remained.

"Could you walk me back to my dorm?" She looked at him shyly. "I have this thing about walking alone at night, and I'd feel a lot safer..."

Her unspoken message negated the fact that she lived in Vernon Hall, across the bridge, a half-mile out of his way.

"Sure. No problem," he said gallantly.

"I don't know what you all think you accomplished." Frank Sorenson set down his copy of the *Guardian*, with its front-page shot of Brandon fiercely confronting the dean. "Seriously, what do you expect to gain by making such asses of yourselves?"

Around the table, Brandon's floormates awaited his response. It was Friday night, and they had stopped for dinner at Fred's before trekking downtown to see *The Big Chill*.

Brandon countered sharply, "It's called standing up for what you believe in. The concept would seem self-explanatory, even if it is alien to you."

Frank smiled, unperturbed. "I hate to tell you this, but you're in the minority here. Judging by the polls, people seem to approve of the way the Reagan administration is handling things. Which is simple common sense. Not long ago, we were actually losing the arms race. We'd been pushed around for years, and it was about time we started pushing back."

"The people are sheep," Brandon said with contempt. "They have never been anything other than pawns, to be brainwashed and manipulated by those in power…and this is true regardless of what type of political system is nominally in place. Only now they're being led blindly down the path to destruction, for the enrichment of corporate America."

"Are you still on that kick?" Frank laughed.

"Think about it. Who else profits from this massive arms buildup? Not the working people who are forced to subsidize it with their taxes. Right now, we already have enough nuclear weapons to blow up the world forty times over. Someone explain that to me—was thirty-nine not enough?

"What does it matter who makes the first move? I say this country should just get rid of its entire nuclear arsenal, if that's what it takes."

Sarcastically, Frank retorted, "Congratulations. You've just made Yuri Andropov ruler of the world."

"That's right." Jay Levin nodded agreement.

"That is, if he's still alive. Nobody's seen the guy in what, like three months now?"

"Why does everyone automatically assume the Soviets want to take over the world?" Brandon challenged.

"Because that's what the ultimate goal of communism is," Frank replied. "Read your *Communist Manifesto*. It's in there."

"Suppose that's true. Does it really make a difference? I'm talking about the survival of our species. If we wound up living under communism, we'd at least be living."

Brandon eyed Frank across the table, prepared to strip the bark from his flag-waving riposte. Knowing Sorenson and his kind, with their fatuous arrogance. They were armchair patriots, holding their own worthless lives above risk.

"It wouldn't be much of a life. It would be more like slavery," Frank offered instead.

"But it would be a life, nonetheless. Which makes it preferable to the alternative."

"Would you two please stop? You're giving me a headache!" Debbie Grafton moaned plaintively, clutching at her temples.

I'm sorry if we made you think, Brandon mused.

That Sunday evening, 100 million Americans tuned in to watch *The Day After*. Seeking solace in numbers, they flocked to local libraries and school auditoriums to view the landmark drama, with its depiction of nuclear holocaust.

At nine o'clock in Sterling 408, the mood, curiously, appeared almost festive. With forced humor, Stu and Josh and Company masked their own unease, the floor's residents bantering as tensions mounted onscreen.

Yet as events progressed, the façade quickly vanished. The adversarial rhetoric between the superpowers seemed disquietingly familiar, the events presaging Armageddon frighteningly plausible.

"I knew we would start it!" Chug crowed when the U.S. fired the first nuclear warning shot. Moments after, the blinding flash of an atomic explosion filled the screen.

An hour later, the audience rose to its feet without a word. Even Brandon was quiet, while no one spared him the slightest glance.

"Less severe?" Carol James whispered hauntingly, reading from the postscript at the end of the program.

"Now everybody's all bummed out!" Chug said awkwardly, to break the trancelike silence. But no response came.

Stu and Josh turned on the room lights, then shut the door when their neighbors had gone. For once by themselves, they played two-handed draw poker and said little.

December brought another round of final exams, amid glum forecasts of another steep rise in tuition. (The *Guardian* calculated fancifully that if Met's annual increases continued at a "credible" 12 percent rate, the yearly cost would hit $2.8 million by 2034.) The holiday edition of *Forbidden Knowledge* featured the usual parody carols, including an antinuclear piece by Brandon Clark entitled "Children Roasting on an Open Fire," and a less macabre critique of Met's fiscal policies, to the tune of "O Come, All Ye Faithful":

> Hike our tuition,
> Raise it beyond Harvard's
> and at the same time cut back fi-nancial aid
> Steal from the rich and
> leave none for the poor
> That's how Met U. is buying,
> That's how Met U. is buying,
> That's how Met U. is buying up all Glan-bury...

Sterling 4 was not immune from the end-of-semester anxieties. As usual, the Mutants found ways of blowing off steam, subjecting their floormates to a pandemic of practical jokes and other off-the-wall behavior.

One night Chug cranked his stereo at full volume, for no reason beyond idle curiosity. The experiment earned Chug a noise violation, with an automatic DP, courtesy of R.A. Gordon Sylvester.

(Unchastened, Chug dumped an entire six-pack of empty Moosehead bottles from the lounge window a night later.) During finals week, Chug, Jay and Adam went on "Shower Patrol," seizing unsuspecting floormates and throwing them into the shower fully clothed. ("It took three of you," Rosemary twitted, tossing back a handful of water at her captors.)

In the small hours of Wednesday morning, after the first winter storm, Jay and Adam snuck out onto the dorm roof to build a snowman. (A snapshot of their anonymous handiwork would grace the Metro section of the next day's *Wire*.) That same evening, Sanjay Motwani returned to his room to find all his underpants stuffed in the refrigerator.

"It was a joke, Sanjay." Gordon Sylvester looked almost put-upon when the future doctor came to report the incident. To himself the R.A. added, It's not like you were robbed or anything.

"Everything here is joke..." Sanjay turned and left Gordon's room, dissatisfied.

Yet as always, the dorms emptied at the end of exam week, and all was quiet.

During the holiday, the administration announced a 7.9 percent tuition increase for the coming year, the first single-digit rise since 1978. Bringing Met's annual cost, with room and board, to the sum of $16,240, seventh-highest in the nation.

JUNIOR II

On January 16, 1984 the Grace Commission presented its final report to President Reagan. The 656-page document contained nearly 2,500 separate recommendations for reducing government waste, and warned of future deficits in the trillions, barring prompt remedial action.

Following his service on the panel, Fortin Shenford actively espoused its findings. Through essays and public lectures, he urged wholesale consolidation of federal service facilities, with curbs on the lavish health and retirement benefits of government workers.

Taking a step further, the president warned of "the overwhelming and potentially calamitous burden" faced by Social Security in decades ahead, with the growing number and unprecedented life span of elderly Americans. Actuarial projections, Shenford said, demanded that the age of entitlement be immediately raised by at least five years, with periodic adjustments for increased longevity.

Nationwide, many editorialists condemned Shenford's sacrilege. Yet others praised his remarks as long-overdue realism. That winter *Glanbury* magazine, in its annual poll, named the Met chief one of the city's ten most influential figures.

Following this honor, a profile of Fortin Shenford appeared in the pages of *Time*.

Outside, the night air was frigid, the streets covered in snow and ice. It was 1:30 A.M.; the city buses had stopped running an hour ago.

Rounding the corner at Sims Street and Alston Boulevard, Chug kicked a snow divot from the curb. The sidewalk was shin-deep in the white stuff, unfit for human passage. His companions followed wordlessly as he began walking the side of the road, four miles from campus.

"We didn't have to leave, you know," Chug muttered to his floormates, a safe distance from Met's Rugby House. Where minutes before, they'd been ignominiously ejected for chicken-fighting amid a noisy crowd of revelers. Jostling back and forth, they had tipped over a stereo speaker, smashing a bottle of Lowenbrau on the hardwood floor.

"Oh, really?" Jay and Adam turned on him at once.

"Between the three of us, we could have cleaned out the place." Chug's words dripped with masculine bravado. He looked doubtfully at Brandon and Marcus, then corrected himself: "Five of us."

Yeah. Right, Chug. But no one contradicted him aloud. Marcus thought privately that if Rob had come along, the boys would likely be headed for the emergency room now.

That is, instead of freezing our tails off trudging back to the dorm.

Still smarting, the boys sought diversions along the path. Chug and Adam tried to pull the receiver from a pay phone; and Jay kicked over a trash barrel in front of Herman's Subs. Approaching St. John's Lane, the five came upon an abandoned grocery cart and sent it clattering downhill, where it careered to the left and sideswiped a parked van.

"I guess it's true—those things never go straight," Brandon said. The great student activist, for once, having taken a weekend respite from his causes.

His wrath seemingly abated, Chug then turned and fired a fastball from out of left field.

"So Marcus, have you asked out Rosemary yet?"

Taken by surprise, Marcus paused. "None of your beeswax," he said, in a feeble effort at humor. Last month, Rosemary had been his D.A. at the annual Hawaiian Party, indicating his floormates' knowledge.

"Marcus doesn't miss and tell." Jay smiled at his companions.

"She's too big for you, Elroy," Adam said, the voice of sound logic.

"There's no such thing," Marcus indignantly replied. The newer floor members seldom used his freshman nickname.

"You people are so shallow…" Brandon muttered, before Adam tactfully changed the subject.

"Ohh, what a piss I gotta take!" Rubbing his groin for emphasis.

Chug said, "We'll stop at Rite-Aid and hang one." The pharmacy was a block away, next to Craig's Pet Emporium.

"It's gotta be closed by now." Marcus looked at him, puzzled.

Chug said scornfully, "We're not going *inside*."

Soon after, the band stood behind the drugstore in a semicircle, voiding themselves. They made their usual games of it, "writing" their initials in the snow or reciting the alphabet multiple times before finishing (three was good). To fully savor the moment, Jay called a Wax Museum toward the end.

"I micturated!" Brandon pumped his fist as they emerged from the shadows. Like Marcus he'd stopped at two beers, yet managed to hold his own.

"You'd better cut that out, before you go blind." Chug zipped up his jeans.

"Hold it!" Jay suddenly stopped, bent down and grabbed a handful of snow as a vehicle approached in the distance. He waited, then let fly as the car—a late-model Lincoln—passed. His missile sailing across the hood in a tight arc, inches from the Lincoln's windshield.

Startled, the driver slammed on his brakes, and with a ridiculously long horn blast flipped the boys the bird before moving on.

Levin shook his head, amazed. "What is it with you New Englanders, anyway?" Again, looking back at Chug: "Do you have a stick implanted in your ass at birth?"

"No such luck," Chug deadpanned.

"It's the direct result of overpopulation," Brandon said. "If you put ten rats in a small cage, they'd be nasty and short-tempered and sick of each other too."

A block further, the Nuestra Casa pub beckoned, with its promise of a respite from the cold. A promise soon dashed by the burly attendant at the door.

"Sorry guys, we're closed. It's after two o'clock," he said.

"Yer ugly!" Frustrated, Adam stalked off, ignoring any response.

"I want to snag that hood ornament..." Chug focused on a silver Mercedes parked at the curb. Approaching the vehicle, he seized the ornament in one hand, then felt Brandon's ungloved mitts over his own, tugging forward in earnest.

"Hey—leggo!" Chug yelled. The ornament then came off in his hand, victim to Brandon's assault on crass materialism.

Somewhere in the distance, a door slammed. Chug dropped the ornament and began to run, the others close on his heels. After three blocks they stopped to catch their breath, satisfied no one was in pursuit.

"Oh, we're gonna get arrested tonight. I just know it," Chug said between deep gasps.

Thirty minutes later, frozen and exhausted, the quintet reached Sterling Hall. And rode upstairs in silence, intent on a long winter's nap.

As Chug entered their room, Frank Sorenson stirred, and while his roommate undressed in the dark murmured, "So what did you guys do tonight?"

"Ah, nothing much," Chug said.

From the *Guardian*, January 24, 1984 (p. 1):

MET BOARD CHAIRMAN TO RETIRE

By Beth Brown
Staff Writer

Edward W. Poole, longtime chairman of Metropolitan's Board of Overseers, will retire from his post effective July 1, the university announced last week.

The 72-year-old Poole, managing partner of the Glanbury investment banking firm of Poole and Wingate, was first elected to the Board in 1953 and has served as its chairman since July 1970. During his tenure, Poole's staunch support of University president Fortin C. Shenford has been credited with enabling the latter to weather calls for his resignation and to implement his administration's policies, often despite vocal opposition from critics...

Chug stumbled blindly into the men's shower room, the jackhammers busily pounding inside his brain. It was nearly 5 A.M., the hangover in full spate.

Dressed in a long flannel robe, he knelt before the toilet and felt his stomach turn inside out. Still nauseous, he wiped his mouth, and then stood erect, squinting against the room's bright lights.

Maybe a hot shower will help, he thought. Surely it can't make things worse.

He gazed down at the floor, watched his feet shuffle across the cold beige tiles...and still managed to step on a wet piece of newspaper, which stuck to his right foot. Through the fog his brain registered the image of the new Soviet leader, the aged Konstantin Chernenko, who had succeeded Yuri Andropov days prior. ("The longest recorded cold in medical history," Frank had termed Andropov's final illness.)

Annoyed, Chug tried to kick off the wet scrap, then raised his leg and reached downward. He had just succeeded in shedding the Russian's pale visage when suddenly he lost his balance and pitched forward, his head striking the edge of an open shower stall door.

Yeah, that helps, he thought wildly, clutching at his bruised forehead, cursing and bellowing with pain. Enraged, he seized the door by the handle and jerked as hard as he could. The door came off in his hands, its metal hinges giving way with a loud snap.

Acting without thought, Chug lifted the door by its stainless-steel edges and reversed course. Reaching the exit door, he nudged it open with one shoulder, swung his trophy into the darkened hall...and narrowly missed hitting Gordon Sylvester in the eye. The R.A. flinched backward, his blonde crewcut receding into the shadows.

Quickly regaining his equilibrium, Gordon looked hard at Chug, who stared back at him without flinching.

"Allen," the junior poli-sci major finally said, "is that shower door yours?"

Notice on Chug and Frank's message board, afternoon of February 15, 1984:

> EVERYBODY, GUESS WHAT?
> I'M OFFICIALLY BACK ON
> PROBATION! GET
> PSYCHED!

With his privileged background, Frank Sorenson was accustomed to lavish surroundings. But the palatial splendor of the administration building exceeded expectations.

I wonder what it cost to furnish this place, Frank thought, en route to the provost's fourth-floor office, where his Aunt Cornelia worked on staff. The marble hallway's fifteen-foot ceilings were decorated with crystal chandeliers; along one wall a row of oil paintings depicted Met's founder and past presidents, overlooking elegant statuary.

"I love what they've done with this place—*trés classe*." Frank emulated his aunt's diction as they left the provost's outer office. For reasons of age and temperament the two had never been close, and her birthday invitation to lunch at Yee's had been unexpected.

"Find this impressive, do you?" Cornelia Sorenson's response was efficient, precise. At fifty-two, the former prep-school librarian wore severe horn-rimmed spectacles, her manner brisk and aloof.

"Come with me, then." Frank silently obeyed as she turned and led him down the opposite corridor, to the floor's riverfront side.

Discreetly, she showed him what her less formal colleagues termed "the power alley." The executive dining room, where in 1971 his father had been feted, with other major donors, after endowing a chair in the School of Medicine. (Sister Cornelia having joined the secretarial staff not long afterward.) The university boardroom, with its paneled mahogany double doors. The entrance to the president's office, framed by recessed marble columns, topped by a majestic entablature.

Waiting for an elevator, the pair soon heard the sound of approaching footsteps. Followed by an authoritative voice, directing them to step aside.

"No, that's fine. We'll ride down together." Fortin Shenford overruled his bodyguards as the doors opened. According to protocol, Shenford marched in the lead, and Frank recognized the university president at once.

"Excuse me, Dr. Shenford, if I may…?" he blurted as they stepped inside the cab. And quickly stopped short, aware of the two bodyguards' watchful eyes, his aunt's reproving stare.

"Dr. Shenford," he repeated more tentatively, the car beginning its descent. "I just wanted to say that I enjoyed your comments in *Time* last month on Star Wars and nuclear weapons—I agreed completely with what you said about maintaining an effective deterrent. And that thing about the Soviets wanting to take over the world was right on the money, I wish more public figures had the courage to say so…. I enjoyed it, sir. You were absolutely right."

Fortin Shenford was more patient with blathering when done in reverence. "Thank you," he smiled cordially at Frank. "Though it seems not many here would agree with you." He took Frank's name and shook his hand, inquiring briefly about his studies and aspirations.

At street level the doors again opened, and one of the bodyguards stepped smartly outside. But the great man's manner had put Frank at ease, and there was one question he yearned to ask.

"Have you ever thought about someday running for President?"

"I am the president," Shenford replied, unblinking.

"No, I mean—of the United States."

Shenford's smile broadened. "I have far greater influence here," he joked. Then he passed through the doorway and was gone.

Lunch, by comparison, seemed anticlimactic.

Since leaving Metropolitan, Megan Brunelle had remained despondent. For the past four months she'd simply hung about the house, seldom speaking a word, searching for answers that remained elusive.

Nevertheless, her mother had insisted that she make herself useful from time to time. And so it was that Megan sat parked outside St. Hippolytus' School on a Thursday afternoon, waiting in the family's ancient LTD wagon to pick up her brother Luke.

This place never changes, she mused yet again. According to the dashboard clock it was 2:45 P.M., and in five minutes school would let out for the day, as it had each afternoon since time immemorial.

The school was a battered two-story structure, its chrome-yellow façade faded and peeling. With its open walkways and rows of brown doors, the building looked like a cheap motel, an image dispelled by the flagpole in the foreground. And beyond the school, across the dusty playground with its rusting swingsets and rotting wooden seesaws, stood St. Hippolytus' Church, the towering rose-windowed edifice around which her life had centered from the beginning.

Though she rarely left home, Megan continued to attend Sunday Mass with her family. Church, her mother had said, was the best medicine for the soul. Yet her soul took no comfort in what now seemed a hollow exercise.

And to whom, Megan wondered, could she ever confess such a thought? Or, for that matter, her growing doubts about what her mother devoutly professed to be the One True Faith?

The Bible says that Christ Himself gave St. Peter the keys to heaven, Alicia Brunelle had instructed her children at a young age. And St. Peter, as we know, was the first Pope. To Mrs. Brunelle's mind, this reasoning obviated further discussion.

From far away, there came the familiar tinkling sound of a brass handbell, announcing the end of the day. Megan smiled wryly in spite of herself. For as long as she could remember, there had been talk of installing an electric bell system at the school. But like fiscal stability, it was merely a pipe dream.

The school's uniforms were likewise unchanged. In a sea of blue, five hundred students scurried toward their buses, the boys in navy dress pants and the girls in knee-length skirts. And since it was February, all wore their St. Hippolytus jackets with the school's emblem on the left breast. For the younger children, the unvarying routine had begun, and would continue until one day they too were ninth-graders and were accorded the privilege of ringing the handbell themselves. Or submitting lame written queries to Father Pickett during Friday-morning Religion class, the smart-alecks often inseparable from the merely obtuse.

Is there a Mass for Halloween? I have heard that, 'He who sings, prays twice.' Does that include songs with curse words in them? Why do we spend so much time discussing masturbation? I'm sure nobody here does it.

Each year, the entire ninth grade would be drafted for Chorus. Rehearsals for the Christmas pageant would begin in late August, with fifty students struggling to memorize "Angels from the Realms of Glory." During practice sessions, boys would pinch girls (and sometimes *vice versa*), their adolescent boredom trumping the sanctity of the choir loft.

Yesterday, today and forever, amen, Megan thought.

She spotted her brother as he approached the playground, accompanied by second-grade classmates Neil Higgins and Eddie LeFleur. At age eight, Luke was by seven years the youngest of the Brunelle children, and the last remaining at St. Hyp's. The boys walked three abreast, for the moment unaware of her presence, engaged in a rousing verse of "Glory Glory Hallelujah, Teacher Hit Me With a Ruler."

"…Meet her at the door with a loaded forty-four, and I wouldn't have a teacher no more," they finished in gleeful chorus.

I can't believe kids still sing that, Megan privately mused.

"Eww, there's your wacko sister." Neil spotted the station wagon at the curb, and looked back to his friends.

Luke's smile promptly vanished. He'd been vaguely aware of the unflattering rumors since Megan's return home. Regardless, he knew the rules: No one was allowed to cut down your family except you.

"Hey, shut up," he warned.

"You wanna make me?" Neil taunted, still smiling.

Luke did not reply. Instead, he hit Neil in the face. Neil hit him back in the stomach, and the two wrestled each other to the ground while Eddie looked on, goggle-eyed.

"Stop it! Stop it right now, both of you!" Megan was out of the car at once, racing toward the two combatants. Quickly she separated them and pulled them to their feet, holding each firmly by the elbow.

"Honestly, what's the matter with you two?" She glared at both fighters, neither resisting her grasp. "You know better than to behave like that—shame on you!"

"He called you a wacko!" Luke blurted, red-faced, stung by the unjust rebuke.

"I don't care. That's no excuse to go around hitting people," Megan responded without blinking. Neil hung his head and looked at the ground.

Abruptly Megan released him, then dusted off her brother's uniform and steered him toward the car. "I don't wanna play with Neil no more—ever!" Luke said hotly once they were inside.

"*Any* more," Megan automatically corrected. And, pulling away from the curb, began a lecture on the evils of violence.

When she finished, Luke hung his head in docile silence.

"You gonna tell Mom?" he finally asked.

Megan hadn't considered this. Yet she knew that in two days at most, the boys would be friends again, their quarrel forgotten. (With young children, forever seldom lasted very long.) And it had been sweet of Luke to defend her.

"I don't think that'll be necessary," she said, much to his surprise.

It was actually quite comical, the way Sterling Student Government president Warren "Chug" Allen wound up being expelled from the dorm.

His outwardly cavalier attitude notwithstanding, Chug had kept his stereo down since returning to probationary status. He'd cut back on his beer consumption, and watched where he threw his empties. Then, shortly after Spring Break, there had been that stupid 1 A.M. water fight with Stu and Josh when one of his salvos accidentally hit the hall's smoke detector, causing the fire alarm to go off and the entire building to be evacuated.

"I don't think there's much to talk about," Judy Billey said, stone-faced, when Chug met with her in the dorm director's office that afternoon. At the end of the meeting, Chug was ordered to leave by the following Monday, *sans* visiting privileges.

"That fully bites. You got reamed big-time." Adam voiced his sympathies as the two aimlessly patrolled the corridor. It was Saturday morning, 3 A.M., and the floor was a morgue. It was also pitch dark. That night, in tribute to their departing comrade, the floor's members had shut off the hall lights after covering the windows with black construction paper. The construction paper was now gone, the darkness little abated by the muted glow from the streetlamps outside.

"Tell me about it," Chug muttered sardonically. He was drunk, and in an ugly mood.

There was a long silence, before Adam hesitantly asked, "So where are you staying?"

"Wally and the boys will let me crash at The House for a while. Then I guess I'll have to find an apartment."

"For two months?"

"No...I needed a place for the summer anyway." Chug's fingers knotted into a fist, and he felt the urge to hit something inquisitive. Instead, he gazed toward the Exit sign near the back stairwell.

Approaching the target, he struck the unframed plastic sign a chopping blow with the heel of his fist. The sign neatly detached itself from the ceiling and went skidding across the floor, its lamp extinguished.

"Cheap," Chug said contemptuously, and blew on his knuckles.

But it wasn't enough. Suddenly it wasn't nearly enough.

Looking up again at the ceiling, he reached for the nearest light fixture. And, wedging his fingers beneath the flat, square metal frame, pulled down hard. The light—a boxlike, plastic-covered job—wrenched free of its socket, trailed by a thin black wire.

"Well, hell—these things pop right out." Chug yanked downward again, tearing the fixture from its moorings.

Adam paused beneath the next light, considered, reached upward. Soon after, the remains of every hall light on Four lay scattered at their feet.

And yet it still wasn't enough.

"They're gonna remember me," Chug vowed, a far-off look in his eye. "I'm talking something really outrageous. Something that'll go down in Sterling history..."

***

From the *Guardian*, March 20, 1984 (p. 3):

ENTIRE FLOOR ON PROBATION IN STERLING

By Allison Crane
Staff Writer

In what is believed to be an unprecedented action, the entire fourth floor of Sterling Hall has been placed on disciplinary probation for the remainder of the spring term. Hall Director Judith P. Billey, in a letter sent to each of the floor's residents last Friday, said the move was necessitated by the incidence of vandalism and excessive noise on the floor, and by "a lack of cooperation" from the floor's members in identifying those responsible.

Among recent occurrences, Billey cited the destruction and/or removal of fixtures, including hall lights and Exit signs; objects thrown from windows; and broken glass littering the hallways and stairwells. The letter further noted that Sterling 4 had been designated as a quiet floor, all residents having signed agreements to that effect.

When contacted by the Guardian, Billey declined to comment on the matter. The director also refused to confirm or deny an earlier report that unknown vandals had spray-painted the message MUTANTS RULE! In six-foot red letters along one wall of the 14-story building's elevator shaft. (Elton Brock, supervisor of Campus Elevator Maintenance, similarly declined to discuss the shaft-painting story.)

Billey's action is the latest in a series of disciplinary crackdowns which have been imposed in Sterling, and comes on the heels of last week's expulsion from the dorm of former Sterling Student Government president Warren Allen. Allen, who had also been a fourth-floor resident, is believed to be the first such student leader at Metropolitan to be evicted from his residence hall...

With Chug's fall from power, Vice-President Janet Heckhaus of Sterling 8 succeeded to the top spot, ending a five-year Mutant dynasty.

Apart from wounded floor pride and loss of presidential backing for SSG-sponsored paintball outings, it made little difference that anyone observed.

"Gentlemen. As you are aware, today's primary order of business is the election of a new Board chairman." Edward Poole's refined, aristocratic voice betrayed no emotion, his time approaching its end. The outgoing chair then admonished his fellow Overseers. "I feel we have had ample time to consider the matter, and for the sake of continuity I propose that we address this at once."

Since January, Fortin Shenford had planned for this meeting. Discreetly he'd canvassed his colleagues on the board; and with the exception of Leland Hayes, the punctilious former CEO at Channel 8, little arm-twisting had been required. For as the president inwardly exulted, he had chosen his board well.

And even Hayes, it must be said, had become malleable when confronted with the facts in the case of a young female assistant who'd left his service six years ago. The former staffer now enjoyed a leisurely existence in Orange County, with a young son closely resembling her ex-employer.

Thus far, the meeting had progressed in routine fashion. The president delivered an initial update on Campaign 2000 (running months ahead of schedule). Treasurer William Prescott, in his final report of the fiscal year, forecast a record $15.7 million surplus with the closing of the books on March 31. The opening of an admissions field office in Seattle was unanimously endorsed, to aid recruitment in the Pacific Northwest.

Hearing no objections, Poole recognized Benjamin Littleton after declaring nominations open.

"Mr. Chairman," the tall, bespectacled hotel magnate said, "I believe that our choice is a clear one, and that there exists a consensus among the members of this board..."

Around the table, murmurs of assent. Jacob Klein, again out of step with his colleagues, looked nonplussed.

"...The next Chairman of the Overseers should be the man whose visionary and courageous leadership has lifted Metropolitan into the first rank of universities nationwide..."

Klein emitted an audible gasp.

"...Mr. Chairman, I nominate our distinguished president, Dr. Fortin Shenford."

Klein leaped suddenly from his chair, his face ashen. "My god, what are you people thinking—are you all insane?" he wildly blurted.

His fellow Overseers, appalled by this breach of decorum, glared at Klein in disbelief. "Jacob, please—for heaven's sake, calm yourself," Philip Kean admonished.

Far from being silenced, Klein raved, "What hold does this man have over all of you? You pay him the highest salary of any university president in America. You ignore the legal repercussions, the community backlash, the adverse publicity from his misdeeds. You advance him interest-free loans totaling hundreds of thousands of dollars, secured by insurance policies payable upon death—gifts, for all practical purposes. And now you're prepared, in effect, to cede him complete control of this institution." He gestured with a sweep of his arm. "Do you really think that this man gives a damn about Metropolitan, other than as a vehicle for his personal aspirations?"

Several angry voices erupted at once. Shenford did not deign to address these grievances, but lifted a dubious eyebrow at Klein. The others, moved by his commanding presence, fell silent.

"Mr. Klein, you are out of order." The chairman rapped his gavel for emphasis, his tone unyielding.

"I promise you, we will all regret this." Defeated, Klein sank back into his chair, his words ignored.

"Second the nomination," Brook Miller said, as if Klein had not intervened. With no other names forthcoming, Poole suggested then that nominations be closed.

Of the thirty-two Overseers in attendance, twenty-eight endorsed Shenford's election. Jacob Klein cast the sole dissenting vote, with Ken Wasserstein, Al Gravely, and Shenford himself abstaining. Several of the president's supporters then shook his hand, offering congratulations.

Shenford's outward humility belied a supreme satisfaction. As befitting the country's most powerful university administrator, his leadership at Met unchallenged.

"Let's be reasonable, Fortin. You got what you wanted."

Leland Hayes stood before the president's desk like a small boy before his teacher, the fingers of his mottled, blue-veined hands working tremulously.

"Not quite yet." Shenford stared at him darkly, a thick brown folder in one hand.

Hayes made no reply, but glanced again at the folder, with its private investigator's report on his extramarital dalliance. The file had been periodically updated, the woman's subsequent history of drug rehabilitation duly chronicled.

Shenford opened the desk drawer without a word and handed him an envelope, which Hayes meekly accepted. Inside there was a single airline ticket.

"Your flight to New York leaves at noon, the sixteenth of next month. First class, of course. From there, I leave it to your own sound judgment." Grim-faced, the president warned, "Though I'd stay clear of

New England from now on."

Hayes's mouth opened, then closed soundlessly. The Overseer placed the envelope in his jacket pocket, then turned and left without another word.

Two weeks later, Leland Hayes resigned his seat on the board and retired to Key Biscayne. The president's office issued a statement commending the Overseer's years of meritorious service, and wishing him Godspeed.

"That was the guy from the realty company." Stu smiled excitedly after hanging up the phone. "He says the place is ours April first. All we have to do is sign the lease."

From his floormates, shouts of congratulations. Stu and Josh then exchanging high-threes with Jay and Adam, who would be sharing the new digs.

"Hey, cool, you guys found an apartment." Rosemary weighed in as Channel 61's *Twilight Zone* mini-marathon resumed. "So where is it?"

"It's in Southampton," Stu advised. "On Buxton Street. That's off South Wayland Avenue, about two miles from campus."

Frank Sorenson winced, genuinely pained. "Oh *please*, you guys— *Southampton?*" he groaned.

"What's wrong with Southampton?" Rosemary challenged.

"Nothing. If you like being surrounded by drug dealers, and having to step over bums in the street every day." Frank had never actually visited Southampton, which ranked among the city's lower-class neighborhoods. "I'm telling you, that place is a shithole."

"Well, excuse us. We're not rich like you," Josh said. The new place was not exactly a Trump Tower condo, but it was clean, unlike some of the rat-infested dumps the city's slumlords had tried to foist upon them.

"Wow, your first apartment. Congratulations—that's so awesome!" Carol James said.

"Thank you. Thank you very much." Josh grinned smugly at Frank.

Curious, Matt Helfand asked, "What's this place going to cost?"

"It's a thousand a month for rent, including water and electricity. Split four ways, that's two-fifty each." Stu recited this information matter-of-factly.

Logically, Carol concluded, "I guess you'll be moving out of the dorm, then."

"Well, yes and no." When Adam failed to elaborate, Josh explained that the four would maintain a dual residence through the end of the term.

"Seriously, you folks are getting out just in time. This campus is really turning into a police state." Brandon took a copy of the *Guardian* from Stu's desk, and held it aloft. "In case you missed it, starting next fall, students living in Met housing will be required to have their fingerprints taken."

Jay frowned at him curiously. "But why would they want to do that?"

"The usual. 'For security reasons.' 'For identification purposes.' 'For our protection.'" His neighbors rolled their eyes at this flagrant bureaucratic bullshit.

"It figures, though," Matt remarked, almost to himself. "Isn't this supposed to be the year of Big Brother and the all-intrusive, totalitarian state?"

"I think Met can take credit for having been ahead of its time," Brandon said sardonically.

The Apartmentwarming celebration was on Friday the thirteenth, with floor members past and present in attendance. By car, by bus and on foot they arrived at Buxton Street, anticipating a blowout of epic proportions.

"You sure this is it?" Pete Garrett turned to his former Housemates as they stood outside the aged three-story brick building. The street was typical of Southampton, with decaying tenements overlooking run-down commercial enterprises: liquor stores, laundromats, a corner newsstand. The block smelled of bus fumes and human misery.

"Yeah. They said 1013, this must be the place." Wally indicated the old-style brass numerals on the front door, Troll Philbrick and Bob Spencer standing quietly in the shadows. Then he scanned the row of aluminum mailboxes and soon brightened.

"Excellent!" Hall laughed. "There's your evidence, counselor." Taped on the box for Apartment 3, scarcely readable in the dim light filtering through the transom, a scrap of white paper listed the names of their comrades. Across the top in block printing it read:

STERLING 4 MUTANTS
SOUTHAMPTON POD
ALL MEMBERS WELCOME

"Only three apartments. Must be on the top floor." Bob reached forward and pressed the old-fashioned electric bell.

"Figures. When there's no elevator, it's always on the top floor." But Pete wasn't griping in earnest. Since starting law school he'd seldom enjoyed a night out, and hadn't seen his friends in months.

The buzzer sounded and Pete opened the door, followed his companions up the dark stairwell. At the third-floor landing was a short hall and a single door marked 3.

"Hey, look who's here!" Stu greeted him warmly inside. Pete shook hands with his hosts, somewhat self-consciously, while the boys were given the grand tour.

The main hall was long and narrow, terminating in the Apartment's kitchen at the rear. Its length trimmed with varnished pinewood, allowing for satisfactory Wiffle Ball drives. The four bedrooms each contained a single unframed mattress, the living room stocked with sixthhand furniture. (For the occasion, signs mandating 20 MINUTES

MAXIMUM PER COUPLE were posted on the closet doors.)

"How did you manage to get these?" Pete paused by the two beer kegs in the kitchen, near the ancient gas stove and plain Formica countertops. "It sucks now, you have to be twenty-one."

"What do you think I grew this for?" Adam fingered one end of the mustache he'd sprouted since leaving the dorm. The 'stache was thin but neatly trimmed, matching his short brown hair.

"Beats the hell out of me." Pete laughed, and he and his buds went to toss their coats on Jay's mattress, the stereo in Stu's room playing *Karma Chameleon.*

From the closet there was the faintest sound—a slight rustling noise, followed by a soft moan. Spencer's ears picked up and, having turned to leave the room, he quickly reversed direction, leering fiendishly at his companions.

"Who's in there?" Troll asked, bemused. Bob did not answer, but shut off the room light and tiptoed toward the closet door, the others following in the darkness.

Troll grabbed a flashlight from the desk, then stood to one side as Bob silently clasped the doorknob. "Ready?" Bob whispered, and at Troll's impatient nod repeated, "Ready? One...two...THREE!"

Bob yanked open the closet door. While simultaneously, Troll shone the flashlight on Frank and Deb, catching them in a most unguarded position.

"Excuse me, but could you two hurry it up a little?" he asked, with extreme politeness. "There are others who wish to doke as well." Bob then slammed the door on the couple's angry protests, the four making a hasty exit from the room.

"Hey Wally," Pete airily said, "isn't it like a really creepy thing to do, to give a guy the business for doing mushy stuff with girls?"

"Heck no, Beav!" His ex-Housemate sneered in fraternal reproof. "You know, for such a little guy, you can sure ask some dumb questions."

"Come on, Marcus—you gotta dance!" Rosemary moved in front of him without missing a beat, the voice of Cyndi Lauper stressing *Girls Just Want to Have Fun*.

She's asking *you* to dance, you dink. Surprised, he hesitated before stepping out onto the floor in Stu's room, where others gyrated to the music.

Rosemary, he thought, had an instinct for dancing. Her style, like his, largely imitative—but with her it was ballet, infused with a lissome grace he could never match. Though he felt not the least bit awkward, scarcely noticing as the song ended and *Uptown Girl* came on...

Then Stu cut in for *Footloose*. And later, when Lionel Richie's *Hello* came on, she was slow-dancing with Josh, eyes closed, her head resting lightly on his shoulder.

Envious, Marcus watched in silence. In his mind, he'd come to associate this song with her. The tentative approach, the silent yearnings—the lyrics captured it all...

Marcus stood and watched them a moment longer. And with an air of accustomed defeat, turned and left the room.

"Have you guys thought about applying for statehood yet?" George Hunter winked at Jay from the bathroom line. The hallway had by now become impassable, the Apartment filled to overflowing. Girls were groped trying to squeeze through the crowd, their anxious hosts praying the beer would last.

"Nah, they wouldn't take us." Facetiously, Jay shook his head. "They said we had to outlaw polygamy first. So we blew 'em off..."

Not surprisingly, Frank and Deb were among the first to leave. When Pete said his farewells it was just past 2 A.M., the night beginning to wind down.

"Ah, you're becoming a lightweight in your old age," Bob said. But he and his Housemates were gone within the hour.

By four-thirty, the last of the guests had departed. Leaving the neighborhood at peace.

"Oh man, we'll be lucky if we don't get evicted." Stu sighed as he and his cotenants surveyed the damage the next morning. The Apartment's floors were layered with a sticky film of spilled beer, the kitchen and hallway ankle-deep in plastic cups and assorted other debris. In the living room one window was cracked, and the chain ripped from the door to the back stairwell.

"I think we just blew our security deposit." Josh kicked aside a shard of broken glass.

By any measure, the party had been a roaring success.

Chug's separation from Sterling Hall would prove short-lived. For despite his banishment, he had not been excluded from the Spring Housing Lottery.

As an upperclassman he drew a favorable number, and without difficulty reclaimed Room 407, while pulling in Frank for good measure. (A chagrined Judy Billey tried to have the selection voided, but the Housing Department overruled her on policy grounds.)

Chug's move secured his status as a Hall legend. And set the stage for his triumphal return.

Alone at the bar, Beth Brown watched the Celtics-Knicks game with feigned interest. It was the second of May, her spring semester's classes at an end.

As usual, the Nuestra Casa pub was filled with sports fans, attention focused on the bar's two screens. Tonight's atmosphere was jubilant, the C's dominating the New Yorkers in their quarterfinal playoff tilt; while at Tiger Stadium the Red Sox handed mighty Detroit just its third loss of the young season.

Beth drained the last of her drink. This year, she had leased an apartment on nearby Gatwick Road with Kirsten and Joanne, her roommates obsessively devoted to the men in their lives. Wally Hall (still quaintly together with Joanne) commuted from the apartment on a regular basis; and Kirsten's current boyfriend—a thirtyish Maytag repairman—was around so often that Beth wondered if his name were on the lease.

From behind, an errant thigh brushed her stool in passing. Beth turned, and looked into a familiar tired face.

"Beth—good to see you!" Willard Ferris hugged her tightly to his chest, the whiskey on his breath overpowering. Beth recoiled in protest, his sloppy kiss grazing her left cheek.

"And what brings you to this den of iniquity?" Her former Introduction to Newswriting professor smiled and released his grip, his speech slurred. Last year, she had struggled through his course, her work less than outstanding.

Without missing a beat Beth replied, "It's a step up from the one I live in." She focused on his bloodshot eyes. "Don't tell me—you like the food here, right?"

Ferris tactically changed the subject. "How are your exams going, Beth?"

"Don't have any. Journalism School, remember?"

"I know it well," Ferris said idiotically, his squat form sagging onto the stool beside her. *Oh, lovely,* Beth mused.

"Your man seems to be losing momentum lately." He indicated the Gary Hart button on her white cotton sweater. In recent weeks Mondale had widened his delegate lead, all but locking up the Democratic nomination.

"It's not over yet," she said stoically. Ferris bought her a mudslide, and ordered another scotch for himself.

Surrounded by oblivious sports fans, the pair exchanged political insights. (Beth had been a Hart supporter since the New Hampshire primary, having volunteered as an exit pollster for the *Telegraph*, and witnessing firsthand the Colorado senator's upset victory.) She was aware of his small, ratlike eyes scanning her sweater as they talked…yet her revulsion abated with each passing drink.

"A lot of my students say they're voting for Reagan in November, regardless," he admitted. "Including some of the smarter ones. I'd hate to see them get sent off to Nicaragua, to fight some senseless war we can't afford."

"Do you really think that could happen?" she frowned.

"Once he gets that second term, he can do just about anything he wants."

Beth pushed the topic aside. "I liked your letter in the *Wire* about Shenford's power grab," she said truthfully.

"Oh you saw that, did you?" The letter at issue was an open one to the state's attorney general, questioning the legitimacy of one man holding Met's two top executive offices at once—an appeal that fell on deaf ears.

"My good buddy." Ferris sniggered, lifted his glass in mock toast. "Son of a bitch even ruined my marriage, did you know that?"

Beth simply shook her head. But mercifully, he did not elaborate.

"We shouldn't be sitting here together, drinking and talking like this," he said suddenly, his scotch half-finished. "It's just not right."

She met his gaze evenly. "Do you have a better place in mind?" she asked.

Nine hours later, Beth emerged from the old-fashioned claw-foot tub in his upstairs bathroom, filled with self-loathing and remorse.

God, how could this ever have happened? How could anybody be so stupid? Lately, with the threat of herpes, there had been fewer one-night stands. But this—this was inexcusable…

Ferris was downstairs in the kitchen, whistling and making his breakfast when she walked in, fully dressed, her purse slung over her right shoulder.

"Good morning." He turned to look her over, his expression leering, last night's pleasures recalled with surprising clarity. There was no hangover, nor the least semblance of remorse.

Beth stood in the doorway, anxious to get this over with. "Want some breakfast?" He turned back to the stove, and his morning repast of bacon and eggs.

"Look—this was a mistake." She ignored his invitation, intent on making this brief as possible. "And it can't happen again, ever."

Still smiling, he countered, "It didn't feel like a mistake to me."

"Professor Ferris." She invoked the title deliberately. "Last night, I was drunk off my ass…" When there was no response, she added: "I just want to leave here and forget that this ever happened."

"Is that so? You could have fooled me last night..."

Beth's deferential façade vanished. "Are you even listening—do you really not get it? You're a miserable, drunken slob—a loser, a has-been. If you ever were." She looked the older man straight in the eye. "Are you really so delusional that you think I might be attracted to you?"

Ferris responded, unflinching, with his usual candor.

"I don't give a shit," he laughed sourly. And watched, without emotion, as she fled in disgust.

Marcus's junior year had been a resounding success.

In both semesters he'd made the Dean's List, boosting his prospects for admission to Met's graduate accounting program. Between coursework and prepping for his GMAT's that summer, he had managed even to enjoy himself, reveling in the boisterous camaraderie of his floormates.

Yet curiously he felt empty.

Preparing to leave the dorm, he packed without haste, aware it was for the last time. September would find him absent from Sterling's familiar environs, in a small rowhouse on Franklin Street.

September, Marcus thought with trepidation. The beginning of the end. One year from now he would be cast from this amniotic universe, toward the terrifying abyss of the adult world. With Brandon gone, the room looked barren, empty, uninhabited—as he'd found it in the beginning…

"Hi, Marcus!" Rosemary, riding piggyback on Adam Conway, waved as they passed his open door. The Southampton Quartet having returned to the Hall for exam week.

His thoughts interrupted, Marcus waved back feebly, without asking. And, soon afterward, snapped his brown suitcase shut.

There was nothing to do now but sweep the floor and return the room-condition report to the R.A.

Slowly he went out into the hall, to get a broom from the utility closet. As usual he was among the dorm's last remaining occupants, and the hallway was quiet.

From the rear, he felt two fingers dig into his sides. Marcus jumped.

"Aha—you're ticklish!" Rosemary said playfully.

"No fair sneaking up from behind." He turned to confront his assailant, who was grinning mischievously. Marcus grinned back.

"You all done?" he said at last.

"Yep. Sure am," Rosemary replied. Exam week had ended yesterday, with the dorm slated to close at noon. "In fact, my train leaves in an hour and a half."

"I thought you were staying in town for the summer."

"I am. But my job at Friedrich's doesn't start till after Memorial Day. So I thought I'd get home to Virginia for a couple of weeks." Friedrich's was a gift shop in the downtown area, mostly catering to summer tourists.

She paused for a brief second. "So this is it—you're really leaving us?"

"I guess I figured it was time to move on." With feigned nonchalance, Marcus shrugged. "But I'll be around," he quickly added.

"At least one of us is getting out of the zoo," said Rosemary. Who after two years of uneven luck with roommates had opted for the women's single on Four.

"Hey, you have a good summer, hear?" she added with affection.

"You too, Rosemary. See you next year."

Rosemary reached down and hugged him. Stunned, Marcus froze for an instant, then hugged back, not daring to breathe, his eyes squeezed shut.

As she turned away he watched in silence, as if to remember every detail. The tousled auburn hair, her gray sweats, the plain white back of her T-shirt. He felt a dull ache in his heart—an incipient sense of regret.

At chances lost, at chances not taken, at leaving the one place where he had known something like acceptance.

But he had not severed himself entirely. His rowhouse was in Sterling's cluster, and he would continue to dine in the caf with his ex-floormates. Then there would be the usual get-togethers, at The House and at the newly-christened "Apt."

And he would still see Rosemary.

He knew now that he'd waited too long to make his move. By now she was surely beyond seeing him as anything more than a friend. But Marcus remained thankful for small favors. Every so often, he would get to see her, and then it would be all right.

Twenty minutes later, Marcus shut the door for good on Sterling 405.

Shortly before eleven-thirty, Adam and Jay emerged from their room, having taken the last of their belongings. By now the floor was completely deserted, and downstairs a rental car waited to take them back to Southampton.

"One last time," Adam whispered fondly, a half-full jar of tobacco juice in hand.

Without waiting for a response, he turned and crept silently toward the back stairwell. Then opened the door and flung the jar to the landing below.

SENIOR I

On July 1, Fortin Shenford took office as Chairman of the Overseers, while retaining his function as University president. Within days, he'd convened a special session of the board's Executive Committee, which endorsed several sweeping changes. Included were provisions for tripling the president's contingency fund, and an increase in the president's annual salary to a whopping $435,000, "in consideration of further duties assumed by the incumbent."

Excerpt from "It Has Happened Here" (*Guardian* editorial, Sept. 13, 1984):

> In the six months since he annexed the chairmanship of Metropolitan's Board of Overseers, University President-for-Life Fortin Shenford has turned back the clock. Since consolidating his power, Shenford has transported Met back to an age when absolute monarchs owned the bodies and property of their subjects, answerable only to the God who granted their limitless authority.
> Never content to reign in ceremonial fashion, Shenford has again proven himself a master in the ruthless exercise of dominion. According to a source who was present at the July 12 board meeting, the session was merely an exercise in rubber-stamp ratification of the President/Chairman's personal measures. The source, who spoke on condition of anonymity, said that Shenford required less than two hours to secure passage of twenty-nine directives previously adopted by the president and his cronies on

the Executive Committee—including authorization for the infamous 90 percent raise. (See story, page 1.) Debate on these measures was reportedly limited to three minutes apiece, dissenting voices stricken from the record. To one Overseer's complaint that the proceedings were in violation of Met's charter, Shenford is said to have replied, "There is but one charter this university will need from now on, and you're looking at him."

With absolute power comes the ability to flaunt it unchallenged. But regardless of whether or not Shenford actually made this grandiose statement, the recent actions of the Shenford-led board have made plain that his long-cherished dream of unfettered control has become reality.

On campus, the specter of one-man rule may no longer be dismissed as caricature or delusion. It is a *fait accompli.* It has happened....

His Monday classes over, Frank Sorenson returned to the Hall just as Chug emerged from the director's office.

"Hey, what's the deal? Are you already in trouble again?"

"Not yet." Chug stood poker-faced, a wooden clipboard in one hand.

Frank suddenly switched tacks. "Oh, you know what?" His face brightening, he added, "Since no one ran for president last year, they're holding a new election in the dorm. They put a notice up on the bulletin board—"

"I saw it," said Chug dryly. At present there were seven candidates—including four ambitious freshmen—in the running.

Frank continued to bait him. "Anyway, it happens next week—Wednesday the eighteenth. Just for your reference."

"Nineteenth," Chug corrected. And put out his nominating petition for his roommate's signature.

Sterling Hall's first contested presidential race in six years generated widespread interest, mainly centered on Chug's candidacy. The deposed president seemed to be running on a comedic platform, posting campaign placards with such themes as "Redemption" and "Return from Exile."

Yet there was method to his madness. For given the short campaign and a crowded field, Chug sensed that name recognition alone would allow him to emerge victorious.

And he was right.

"Before I was so rudely interrupted…" Chug crowed, to the raucous approval of his floormates in a post-election victory speech at The House. His audience was, for the moment, exclusively male. The girls had been invited to come later, unaware that the boys had hired a stripper for the occasion.

By the time the girls appeared, several of the boys had stripped to the waist and were wrestling on the living-room rug; while others performed headfirst slides down The House's thickly-carpeted stairway. (As long as you kept your back straight and your arms thrust forward, it seemed, there was nothing to it.) In their testosterone-fueled frenzy they then began tearing the furniture apart, bombarding the living room and kitchen with bits of flying wood and metal. ("We scared all the chicks away in like, twenty minutes," Troll Philbrick subsequently boasted.) In the end the police were summoned, and the party's hosts cited in Municipal Court for disturbing the peace.

For the Mutants of Sterling 4, another year had begun.

"Come on Sorenson, quit cheating." Stu sighed wearily.

They were seated at the rickety card table in The Apartment's kitchen, the four tenants and their guests waging a fierce game of Trivial Pursuit.

Frank would not budge. Pointing to the card in his hand, he insisted, "That's what it says. The jack of hearts faces right."

"No, sir!" Josh hotly disputed him. But Frank refused to relent.

"I'm telling you, it's right here on this card…"

"Let me see that!" Stu held out his hand, unconvinced.

"Forget it." Abruptly, Frank stood and thrust the card back into the pile. "If that's your attitude, you can all go screw yourselves." Then he stormed out of The Apartment and slammed the door.

Uncharacteristically, it was Adam who broke the silence: "He's pissed."

"Well, he has no right to be. Trying to cheat like that." Jay shook his head, disapproving. "I mean, that's just low."

"I can't believe he tried to fool you on a question about cards." Marcus murmured almost to himself. And with a senior's inchoate nostalgia added, "Those all-night poker games ruined many a college career."

"They ruined mine." Stu's words held a touch of regret. This semester, he and Josh were on part-time status. During the day both worked as bellhops at the Glanbury Hilton, while taking courses three nights a week.

Adam stood, smiling, as the doorbell rang. "Can you believe it— what a loser," he smirked before buzzing Frank in.

"Come on up, you low-down dirty scumbag," he said into the intercom, then opened the hall door and waited.

"Please tell Stu that I am ready." Sanjay Motwani appeared at the head of the stairs, dressed in dark polo shirt and khaki pants. Adam blinked in surprise as his ex-floormate moved past him without waiting.

"So you are ready to go now?" Sanjay entered and purposefully approached Stu, heedless of the others.

"Go where?" Marcus interjected.

"Oh shit, I forgot…" Stu thought glumly of his five-page astronomy paper, due in less than twenty-four hours.

Sanjay looked insistently at his watch. "You told me eight o'clock P.M."

"Yeah, I know." Feeling himself cornered, Stu put on a light jacket and fished for his car keys. "Okay, let's go," he announced.

"Go where?" Marcus again asked.

"We're just going driving," Stu explained. "Sanjay's taking his road test next month, and I've been helping him practice." The studious Punjabi, who'd quietly maintained a 4.0 average, had won his med school acceptance through Met's Early Decision program. Over the summer he'd taken intensive English instruction and—as a practical concession—obtained his learner's permit.

Downstairs, the boys piled into Stu's gold 1977 Chevy Malibu, he and Josh riding shotgun as Sanjay pulled onto South Wayland Avenue.

"I know no other licensed drivers here whom I can ask," he'd said candidly at the beginning. (The future M.D. had offered to pay for Stu's services, before being told this was unnecessary.)

"So Marcus, what've you been up to?" Josh smiled with genuine interest.

"Oh, the usual." Marcus, seated directly behind him, shrugged. "Still working at the bookstore, applying to grad school to get my master's…"

"How do you like that rowhouse, though? Must be a lot different than living in the dorm."

"It is—it's much quieter. More peaceful and mellow." Marcus considered, and then remarked, "Not that it's always a good thing."

Stu turned partially in his direction. "Which schools are you applying to?"

"Well, I'd like to stay here at Met—that'd be my first choice. Their graduate accounting program is supposed to be one of the best in the country. But there's nothing wrong with Reigate, either. Then I'll likely apply to Meldon too, to be on the safe side." The others noted that he'd mentioned only Glanbury schools.

"It seems a lot of people apply to grad school to put off having to face the real world." Adam said this with his usual lack of inflection.

Marcus replied, only half-joking: "Unfortunately, it's just a two-year program."

His right-turn signal flashing, Sanjay stopped for the light at the Alston Boulevard intersection. Behind them, the driver of a black Cadillac impatiently began honking his horn. But Sanjay, mindful of the NO TURN ON RED sign, stayed put. The other driver then pulled into the left lane and roared past them, again honking as he rounded the vacant intersection.

"Masshole!" Jay noted the Cadillac's Bay State plates. Glanburyites were atrocious, but Massholes were far and away the worst drivers on the road.

"What is the problem?" Sanjay looked anxious.

"No problem," Stu quickly replied. "It's just that some of these drivers here are—uh—kind of…"

"Psychotic," Jay finished.

From Charlton Avenue, Sanjay mistakenly turned right at Essex. The surrounding network of one-way streets—those narrow, tortuous Colonial cow paths that had never been planned with automobile traffic in mind—then forced him to pass through Havelock Square, the city's notorious red-light district. On Branch Street traffic slowed to a crawl, besieged by a gauntlet of hookers plying their trade, an array of neon signs advertising peep shows and LIVE NUDE GIRLS.

"Hey, how are you boys doing tonight?"

Outside the car, a woman in a black leather miniskirt approached and leaned casually over the driver's-side window. The woman's heels measured at least four inches, her hair an artificial blonde, the low-necked blouse leaving little to the imagination.

From the back seat Adam reached out and whacked her on the rump. And, opening his wallet, removed a dollar bill and handed it to their visitor, who glared at him fiercely before leaving without a word.

"Hey, where's my change?" Adam called after her.

Jay momentarily gawped in admiration, then slapped high-threes with Adam. *"That* was classic!" he exulted.

Sanjay turned back onto Charlton Ave, which ran through the heart of downtown. Past the Glanbury Mercantile Bank Building, whose glass-and-steel façade dominated the city's skyline. The 30-story Bramhall Place Condominium, where Adam had worked over the summer as a security guard, and where Debbie Grafton was currently subletting a unit. The Starcase Cinema Theater, where Rosemary and Megan had wept softly at a special screening of *The Elephant Man.*

"Hey, what's the name of the chick on the G.I. Joe cartoons?" Jay inquired while passing over Crocker Bridge, across the dark river and into the city's North End. "It's Penny, right?"

Adam shook his head. "Lady Jaye. Penny's Inspector Gadget's niece," he said with authority.

As usual, traffic was lighter on the north side. The Monadnock ran to their left, the Malibu cruising west on Callender Drive. During a lull in the conversation, Stu began whistling the theme from *Taxi*.

On the footpath, a shapely auburn-haired jogger skirted the river's edge, her teal warmup suit resplendent in the moonlight. "Doke?" Adam leaned out the car window as they approached the woman, who remained oblivious.

"No doke?" Forlornly, Adam sat down again.

"What is this 'doke'?" Sanjay frowned, confused. "You are always talking about it."

The explosion of laughter was immediate, uproarious. Finally Josh said: "Adam, you want to take that one?"

"It's when you bag a babe." Adam's tone was straightforward. "You know, when you have a woman," he advised.

Sanjay's lips pursed. "Oh," he said.

"It can also be a noun as well as a verb. It can refer to the act of bagging said babe, or to the babe so bagged."

The others regarded Adam in silence, stunned by this loquacious outburst.

"That was good." Jay nodded, sincerely impressed. "You're not as dumb as you look, talk, act, and otherwise generally seem to be."

"You're a waste product." Adam hurled an empty Busch beer can at him.

"Now I understand." Sanjay was smiling when the lights of Brentwood Stadium welcomed them to North Campus.

"And how's the old football team doing this year? Any idea?"

"Not bad, actually." Marcus at once understood that Josh meant the Mutants. "At last report they were 4-1, and Chug says they've got a shot at the intramural playoffs."

"Really? That's great." Josh smiled with a trace of envy.

Sanjay turned left onto the Dunhill Street Bridge, then onto the Boulevard, and the familiar confines of the main campus. (By tradition, the boys saluted their old dorm while passing in the distance.) Beyond Sterling Hall, then Whitehall Theater, where George McGovern had spoken in January, during his quixotic primary campaign. Passing by Umberto's, then Fred's and Jokers, the apartment Chug had rented after being kicked out of the dorm…

So many places, so many memories, Marcus thought.

Six minutes later, his practice run concluded, Sanjay pulled up to the curb on Buxton Street. Within weeks he would ace his road test, with flying colors.

"Sanjay, you're a senior—that means you're over twenty-one," Adam said as they stepped outside the car. "How about going across the street and getting us some beer?"

Motwani smiled, and without hesitation replied, "Yes, I will be happy to do so."

"Are you serious?" Adam's features brightened. "Cool—make it a case of Stroh's, then." From his wallet he took a twenty-dollar bill, which Sanjay refused.

"No, I will pay," he insisted. Edging toward the nearer of the block's two liquor stores. "This is my present to you. A token of my appreciation…"

F̲ortin Shenford was interrupted at his work one night by a call from Tom Becker, Met's chief Congressional lobbyist and Washington insider *par excellence*.

"Tom, this had better be good," he warned. The president's private number was changed frequently, its use restricted to emergency situations.

Becker did not hesitate. "I've received some information I thought would be of interest," he said. "It concerns Jim Camp—"

"Then how could it possibly be of significance?" Shenford had little regard for the state's junior Senator, whom he considered an intellectual featherweight.

"I'll let you be the judge. But here it is: My sources say the Senator has liver cancer. It's a terminal case. The doctors give him only a few months." Becker paused, then added, "This information is really hush-hush. They intend to keep it quiet to the end."

"So why are you telling me this?" But Shenford had grasped the implications.

"Don't you get it? When the seat becomes vacant, the governor will appoint a successor. Fortin, this is your opportunity! Remember, nobody up there knows about this. So you've got a jump on the competition, and if you play your cards right we could have you here in Washington where you belong."

"Tom, this sounds to me like morbid speculation." Almost imperceptibly, the president's tone softened. "And what makes you think I'd be interested in public office?"

"As you say. But you can do it, Fortin. The budget's gotten completely out of control, and voters are getting wise to the fact that they're being governed by incompetent boobs. They're going to start wanting people who can actually do the job."

"The question was, why me?" Shenford snapped.

"Well, look at Peter Ueberroth, for instance. He's been mentioned as a possible presidential candidate in 1988—"

The baseball commissioner, no less, Shenford thought wryly.

"And Lee Iacocca—some people are talking seriously about running *him* next time, and he might just go for it. These are men like you, Fortin—dynamic leaders who have revived moribund institutions. And right now, there ain't no more hurting institution than the United States government. I'm telling you, Fortin, if Eckhardt gets in you can have him begging you to take it." Richard Eckhardt was the state's lieutenant governor, and current Republican nominee for the top job. The two-term incumbent, Louis Worrell, had twice been investigated by the U.S. Attorney's office, and had chosen not to press his luck.

Shenford thanked Becker for the information and hung up the phone. His eyes bright with intrigue, the flames of aspiration kindled.

During that fall, the president's office lights burned late into the evening. After-hours guests included Judy Cochran, onetime press secretary to Governor Worrell; former Nixon delegate hunter and conservative firebrand Joseph Marchak; and William Waycross, director of Reigate's Coleman Institute for Political Science. Along with various pollsters and public relations consultants.

These secret sessions took place under cover of darkness, after the rest of the building had emptied. The president himself had ordered all other offices vacated by 8 P.M., pending further notice. His subordinates, accustomed to Shenford's whims, complied without question.

Behind closed doors, the power office was abuzz with intrigue.

"Again, good evening. I trust no one has been unduly inconvenienced by the late hour. However, under the circumstances, a measure of discretion is warranted…"

"Our research indicates that you enjoy nearly 50 percent name recognition statewide—an enviable figure for the president of a private institution. Though your comparatively high "unfavorable" rating is something we will need to address…"

"We must, in fact, be prepared for any contingency. If it comes down to a statewide campaign, we will need the resources in place to mount a full-scale effort. That means money and manpower and organization…"

"Of course, we're all realists here. We understand that public opinion is fluid and readily pliant, given the level of intelligence and sophistication of the average voter…"

"Though with the proper buildup, you should emerge as the governor's logical choice. That way, we eliminate the need for a campaign, and can focus on looking toward the future…"

In their 17th-floor suite across the river, sophomore premeds Jeff Ryan and Phil Cambria brewed a fresh pot of coffee while prepping for the next day's microbiology exam. Consigned by lottery to the chaos of Vernon Hall, the pair found occasional solace in its sweeping views of the Monadnock.

"Must be something major going down." Jeff looked out the window, toward the single speck of light from the administration building. "Every night this week, that light's been on at all hours."

Cambria seemed uninterested. "Really? Guess I wasn't paying attention.

"They're probably deciding how much to hit us up for next year," he said as an afterthought.

Still eying the solitary beacon, his roommate said, "Did you know that if you had sophisticated enough equipment, you could eavesdrop on people's conversations by monitoring vibrations in windowpanes?"

"Get outta town!" Phil scoffed.

While across the dark water, the light shone on.

"**Y**ou know, you're really milking this thing."

Kathleen Brunelle looked down at her older sister, who stared blankly at the TV screen, sprawled on the living-room couch.

"What 'thing'?" Megan's voice was listless, her attention focused on *Family Feud*.

"You know—all this lying around, acting depressed. You don't work, you don't go out, you don't do anything. It's been over a year now, in case you hadn't noticed."

"Go on, get off my back." Megan continued to stare at the screen. Tonight was a cool October evening, the house otherwise strangely calm. Darby and Christopher, the two elder sons, having gone to the movies with friends; brother Luke staying over at Eddie LaFleur's. And Kathy, a vivacious blonde of sixteen, awaiting her Friday-night date.

"Look, I know you're bummed about—losing your friend and all, but you need to get over it," she said. "It's been way too long. And whether you realize it or not, this is a selfish thing you're doing. You sit around doing nothing, and expect everybody else to pick up the slack—"

"You be quiet!" Megan turned on her sibling, suddenly aroused. "You have no idea what you're talking about, so just leave me alone!"

"Okay, fine. You want to veg out on that couch for the rest of your life, go ahead. You're only my sister, why should I give a damn—"

"Kathleen Marie Brunelle!" Their mother's voice thundered from the kitchen doorway. The girls involuntarily straightened as she entered the room, eyes blazing.

"Sorry, Mom." Kathleen glanced down at the floor, avoiding Mrs. Brunelle's steely gaze.

Outside, a car horn honked impatiently.

"Gotta go—that's Bob!" She went to the hall closet and slipped on a light-blue windbreaker, her low-necked blouse evading maternal scrutiny. *"Ciao…"*

"Your sister's right, you know," Alicia Brunelle echoed later that evening, in the sparsely-furnished third-floor loft that functioned as the girls' bedroom. "You can't go on like this forever."

"Mom, I don't know…" Evasively, Megan turned and glanced about the room.

"No, I'm serious," her mother persisted. "You know your father and I love you and we'll support you whatever you decide to do. You can go back to school or get a job, it's fine with me. What you can't do is spend your life sitting and moping around the house."

"Mom, I've been trying to get it together—really I have. But every day it just seems more hopeless. I'm trying to make sense out of this; instead I feel more lost and confused than ever."

"This? Do you mean what happened with Dwight?"

"It's not just that—it's everything," Megan confessed. "Life, the universe, whatever you want to call it. It's like nothing seems right anymore."

Alicia Brunelle sat down on the bed next to her daughter. She was a small woman with fading blonde hair, once voted Most Attractive in her sophomore class at St. Anne's.

"Well honey, we don't always understand why things happen the way they do," she said. "But God will give you the strength to endure, if you believe and trust in Him—"

"Oh, save it, Mom!" Megan returned, frustrated. "That crap doesn't cut it anymore!"

Following this outburst, deathly silence. None of Mrs. Brunelle's children had spoken to her this way before, particularly on matters of faith. Helpless before the Inquisition, Megan sat with head bowed, unable to face her judge.

But she was not yet finished. Gathering her courage, she said, "All my life, you told me that God was fair and just. Then why is there so much pain and suffering in the world? All this starvation and disease in Africa, that crazy guy shooting all those people in McDonald's....How can He let this go on? Where was He when all this happened?"

Her mother's response was entirely unexpected.

"Well, did it ever occur to you that God might be as unhappy as you are about all of this?"

Megan looked stunned. "But—how can that be? Wasn't He the One who made it happen in the first place?"

"I don't think God is like that," her mother replied, unblinking. "I can't believe that God is directly responsible for all the evil and sickness and suffering in the world."

This contradicted everything Megan had ever believed. From the beginning she'd assumed that God had His finger on all the world's buttons, and that nothing occurred which He did not will.

"Then why does it happen?" she nearly screamed in outrage. "Why are people like Dwight born with those kinds of diseases—forced to go through life unable to do the things that other people take for granted, being left out of everything, and then dying before they've had a chance to live?"

"Well, that I don't know. But I'm sure there are certain natural laws involved that we can understand, that at least make some sense. If you fall off the Grand Canyon, you know God won't reach out and catch you—it doesn't matter how good a person you are. And if someone wants to take a gun and start shooting into a crowd, He won't put out a hand to stop him."

"Then what's the point of it all?" Megan challenged. "The whole concept of faith—all this praying and going to confession and attending Sunday Mass—what good does it do?"

Mrs. Brunelle did not respond at once. Instead of reproach, her words reflected understanding.

"The truth is, I had the same doubts when I was younger."

Megan could scarcely credit what she had heard. She remained silent, waited for her mother to go on.

"When I was fifteen..." Her mother faltered, then started over. "When I was fifteen, my best friend Lucy Zimmer died of polio. This was in 1951, a few years before the Salk vaccine...but anyway, it seemed that one day we were out picking berries and giggling about boys, then the next day she was gone and I was never going to see her again."

"But how did you deal with it? Didn't you ask these same questions...?"

"Well, I never dared ask them out loud. Not in our house. When we were kids, my mother really laid down the law to us..." Alicia Brunelle again paused.

"Before the funeral," she went on, "I remember her telling me I shouldn't feel sad, because Lucy had gone to a better place. That everything happened for a reason, and that God picked only the best flowers from His garden. But that didn't change the fact that it seemed so horribly unfair."

Megan felt a sudden surge of empathy. She said, "Then I guess you never found the answers either."

"Oh, no. Not then. But later I realized it had nothing to do with any Master Plan of God's. It was a virus that caused it, and nothing else. There really was no reason, and I could search forever without finding any answers.

"Sometimes there is no justice in this world—but there is perfect justice in the next. I believe that devoutly."

"But that makes everything seem so futile!" Megan protested. "If you can't change things, then what's the purpose in trying to make them better?"

"When you were a volunteer at the hospital," her mother said—evoking Megan's three summers at Mercy General—"didn't you help care for patients who eventually died?"

"That was different..." Megan replied.

"Why was it different?" her mother asked. "Because you weren't close to them personally? Didn't every one of those patients have someone to mourn them—husbands, wives? Children, relatives, friends?"

Megan offered no response.

"My point is that pain and suffering are a part of life. Everybody's life. Maybe not everyone suffers equally, but everyone suffers." Alicia Brunelle paused to let this sink in.

"But you did make a difference in those people's lives. Especially Dwight's. By being a friend, you filled a need in his life. You gave him comfort, and made his burdens a little lighter because you cared. In the end, that's really all we can do for anyone."

Megan felt the tears begin to swim in her eyes.

"That's what doing God's work is all about," her mother concluded. "Because that's what the God I believe in stands for. Not inflicting pointless misery and suffering and sickness as the spirit moves Him."

Megan said nothing, but did what she had not done since she was ten years old. She cried in her mother's arms.

For several minutes the room was quiet, save for her muffled sobs.

"So what are you going to do now?" her mother gently whispered.

"I don't know." Megan shook her head, still softly weeping. "But I'll give it some thought. I promise..."

***

Three weeks later, the phone in Rosemary's room rang just after 8 P.M. Excusing herself, she raced down the hall from the floor lounge, where her dormmates were watching *Three's a Crowd.*

Rosemary was gone for nearly an hour. When she returned, her expression was jubilant.

"That was Megan Brunelle," she announced, her voice filled with emotion. "She says everything's all right now. She's decided to continue with nursing, and she's coming back next semester."

For Chug Allen, the advent of his junior year marked a turning point.

His undergraduate days having passed the halfway mark, Chug for once got serious. He attacked his English Lit studies with a vengeance, and discovered for the first time his own natural flair for language. Once, almost on a whim, he succeeded in crafting a 26-letter sentence including every letter of the alphabet, which was proudly displayed on his message board. ("Lynx growth jumped," fibs Zack [*q.v.*].) He cut down on drinking, this time in earnest, and became a virtual recluse, seldom leaving his room on weeknights.

His second run as Sterling's president was equally successful. Under his administration the Hall added a weight room, and began publishing a weekly newsletter in-house. For the semester he recorded a 3.8 average and—in a historic first—avoided disciplinary probation.

Yet he could not resist a parting shot at his old nemesis, dorm director Judy Billey.

In mid-December, on the eve of exam week, a pair of brightly wrapped boxes appeared outside the director's ground-floor apartment. The packages contained a jar of wrinkle cream and a copy of *The James Coco Diet*, courtesy of Chug and his floormates.

By chance, Frank Sorenson was waiting for an elevator across the hall when Billey opened the door and discovered her gifts. The director frowned suspiciously for a moment before bringing the anonymous parcels inside.

The elevator arrived and Frank stepped quickly on board, not waiting for her reaction.

The fall was a busy and eventful season for Brandon Clark.

From a dozen hard-core zealots, his organization grew to approximately forty members. And, following the October riots in South Africa, assumed leadership of Met's growing antiapartheid movement.

In an open letter to President Shenford, the Society called for Met to immediately divest itself of its shareholdings in companies doing business in that nation. Then protested the administration's refusal by occupying the Student Union courtyard, camping overnight in pup tents before being ejected by campus police.

Through renewed petition drives and public demonstrations, he continued to lead opposition to the nuclear arms race. Along with other various and sundry evils, from U.S. intervention abroad to Met's suppression of student publications.

On campus, his name was synonymous with student activism. The *Guardian* termed him "among the last of a dying breed," while praising his efforts to heighten awareness.

And yet he sensed things were headed tragically in the wrong direction.

"It's sickening how gullible people are!" Brandon pushed aside the front section of the Sunday *Wire* in disgust, surrounded by his dormmates in the cafeteria. The national elections were two days hence,

286

the polls forecasting a landslide Republican victory.

"Seriously, can you imagine another four years of this?" he huffed. Meaning government that turned its back on the poor, while bankrupting the country in preparation for nuclear holocaust.

"Hey, Reagan got the economy moving again, didn't he?" Frank Sorenson noted. "Who knew, after the disaster of the Carter years, it would *ever* bounce back?"

"I'm not a fan of Jimmy Carter, or any of them," Brandon said. "By the time they're in position to even think about the presidency, they're all supremely evil and corrupt. Fully prepared to commit war crimes on behalf of the faceless corporate entities they serve. But relatively speaking, the Carter administration outclassed this one in human decency."

"Don't give me that!" Frank scoffed. "Sure, Carter was a nice guy and all, but he was just…a total wimp. He lost Iran, he lost Nicaragua, the Russians went into Afghanistan on his watch—America's ass was being kicked all over the world. But name one country that's gone communist since Reagan took over.

"And stayed there," he added, proudly invoking Grenada.

"Hey Brandon, who're you voting for, Gus Hall?" Chug smirked from the far end of the table.

"He's as good as anybody running." (Brandon had actually written in Alan Cranston's name on his Iowa absentee ballot.) Turning back to Frank to continue the discussion, he again inveighed against the current White House occupant, calling the nation's Chief Executive "a prop," "a stooge for his rich backers," and "so out of it it's scary.

"And what about this Star Wars nonsense?" he fumed. "There's no way that's going to work, and they want to squander all that money on it… My god, you could practically eliminate poverty in America for—"

"Of course it's not gonna work. That's not the point," Frank interrupted. "The thing is, the Soviets will have to keep up, and they can't afford it. It'll destroy their economy, and their whole country will fall apart."

"And what happens to our economy," Brandon said, "after we blow a couple of trillion dollars on some senseless chicken game?"

"Some things are more important than money, you know." Frank smiled, with sanctimonious, exquisite irony. And, having for once aced his antagonist, stood and excused himself.

"I could hang with Reagan again." Freshman Greg Roth resumed the debate once Brandon had walked off, feigning loss of interest. "He seems like the first real President we've had in ages."

"I don't know..." Todd French was more skeptical, adding, "I've always had the feeling there was more style than substance there."

Chug replied sadly, "But Mondale's just...nothing."

It was an assessment that sealed the fate of the Democratic campaign.

The election returns were the most anticlimactic in memory. Four years ago, there had been complaints when the networks called the election for Reagan with the polls still open on the West Coast. Tonight, their projections seemed a needless formality.

On Frank's small color screen, the electoral map was an undivided sea of Republican blue. The state had gone for Reagan, as had the entire Northeastern seaboard. The phrase "Solid South" now meant staunchly Republican. And Mondale's home state of Minnesota was still in doubt.

"Watch him lose that too," Chug smirked. A registered Democrat, he was among legions who had crossed party lines.

"Hey, where's Brandon?" Greg suddenly brightened, eying his neighbors with sadistic glee.

"Probably in his room hanging himself. We won't be seeing him tonight, anyway."

In his living room, Fortin Shenford viewed the results with

satisfaction. The White House, for another four years, was safely in Republican hands. And on the undercard, Dick Eckhardt had been projected the winner in the governor's race, with an estimated 56 percent of the vote.

The second Reagan landslide had resoundingly returned a popular incumbent to office. While raising the question of whom the party would nominate four years hence.

In the foreign policy arena, the Republicans had established that strength was the only language adversaries understood. Yet few chose to address the mounting national debt, or the looming crisis when the red ink caught up with the economy at last. Tonight, as Republicans savored the euphoria of electoral dominance, Shenford saw a party that could prove vulnerable the next time around.

Unless they nominated a strong, fresh-faced candidate. Someone new and independent, less a politician than a capable leader. A savior for a disenchanted nation on the brink of insolvency.

From the main ballroom of the Sheraton Glanbury Hotel, Dick Eckhardt began his victory speech. Shenford half-listened, still scanning the thick dossier his investigators had compiled on the governor-elect.

"Oh, this is beautiful. Absolutely perfect!" he said aloud. And, picking up the phone, instructed his secretary to wire Eckhardt his personal congratulations.

On November 14, Shenford made it official: he named Steve Patrick his eventual successor as president, in an unprecedented unilateral edict. The announcement stated further that Patrick, as Met's current executive V.P., would assume greater oversight of its day-to-day affairs.

To some observers, the move hinted at Shenford's retirement. ("At 62, he must realize that his days on campus are numbered," penned one *Guardian* editorialist.) The Bristol *Telegraph* was closer to the mark— noting Shenford's enhanced public profile, the conservative tabloid touted him as a possible challenger to incumbent Joel Hollenbeck in the 1986 U.S. Senate race.

During the next several weeks, Shenford was ubiquitous. On the editorial page of the *Wire*, attacking Congress' "inherently inefficient" seniority system. An appearance on Channel 11's "Editorial Reply" feature, blasting federally-funded research on why inmates wanted to escape from jails. And in mid-December a critically-acclaimed piece in *National Review* entitled "Self-Worship Without Self-Respect," lamenting the paganlike hedonism of recent times. Increasing avoidance of adult responsibility, Shenford wrote, had bred an atmosphere of moral anarchy. A dystopian existence characterized by broken families, rampant drug abuse, and the callous slaughter of the unborn for reasons of personal convenience.

"It is time," he held in closing, "to acknowledge the failure of our ruinous experiment with permissiveness, and to begin the process of healing a fractured civilization."

His heightened visibility did not escape the notice of local political pundits. With growing frequency, the tea-leaf readers speculated that the Met president was positioning himself for a future electoral run.

Only Shenford and his inner circle knew the campaign was well under way.

SENIOR II

"You'll protect me from the muggers, won't you?" Uneasily, Megan smiled as she and Rosemary walked to The Apartment via South Wayland Avenue, hours after darkness had fallen.

"Sure, kid. Anytime," Rosemary replied. Like most visitors to the Buxton Street Outpost, she'd been known to pass through the neighborhood with her floormates at 3 A.M., en route back to campus.

Until Rosemary had called that afternoon to inform her of the boys' back-to-school soiree, Megan's return to Met had left her feeling lonelier than at any time in the past. The campus had seemed oddly unfamiliar, like a place long forgotten. There were seven other nursing students, all strangers, in the rowhouse she now occupied.

But now, as the pair fought their way through the bitter, howling January winds, her mind raced with questions she could never ask aloud. How would they receive her? Were they still her friends? Or had she merely become "that quiet, really religious girl who flipped out"? Or, alternatively, had they simply forgotten her?

"...And here we are." Atop the building's front doorstep, Rosemary indicated the boys' mailbox, with its welcoming sign.

"This is it?" To Megan's mind the aged brick exterior looked gloomy and forbidding.

"Yep. See there?" Rosemary nodded before ringing the bell. And when the buzzer sounded, eased open the front door.

"It's okay. I told everybody you were coming." She sensed Megan's nervousness as they approached the third-floor landing. When Megan did not respond, Rosemary knocked twice on the Apartment door.

"Come in!" Megan recognized Josh's voice at once. And with small, shuffling steps followed Rosemary inside.

Stu was the first to spot her.

"Megan!" he joyously cried. Whereupon The Apartment exploded in a roar of welcome, unlike anything she'd heard before.

Immediately, the crowd rushed forward as one. Stu and Josh hugged her, then Brandon, then Marcus (he seems more relaxed, Megan thought), then all the girls. Even Beth Brown, her ex-freshman roommate, embraced her warmly as she entered the kitchen.

"It's good to see you back," Beth said, not without sincerity.

By unspoken agreement, Megan's hosts took her to Josh's room when the hugging was done, seating her on the unframed mattress.

"How are you, ma'am?" Josh smiled tenderly, gripping her narrow shoulders.

"It's good to be back," she replied. Her voice somewhat unsteady, overcome by this outpouring of affection. "This scene reminds me of what I've been missing."

In the kitchen a quartet of first-years stood quietly by the beer keg, mystified at what they'd seen.

"My god, who *is* that girl?" Courtney Frankfurth said. "The second she walked in, the whole apartment went crazy. I've never seen anything like it…"

Megan stayed for the entire evening. She danced. She met the new floor members. She laughed upon hearing of Chug's elevator-shaft painting escapade, even Jay's aborted scheme to fill the Nursing School fountain with bubble bath for Homecoming Weekend.

Her sense of enchantment was scarcely diminished when the police broke up the affair at around 3 A.M.

Megan wound up sharing a cab with Rosemary, Marcus and Brandon. Dropping her off in front of her rowhouse, the three invited her to join her ex-floormates for the hockey game with B.C. that Thursday night.

She fell asleep not long after, her soul praising God for the drunk and disorderly people known as the Mutants of Sterling 4.

The reception was formal, its guest list exclusive. Over drinks and canapés, board members chatted with visiting dignitaries and faculty eminences; outside, a trio of campus police vehicles cordoned off access to the president's mansion.

Tonight's guest of honor was Richard T. Eckhardt, the newly inaugurated governor of the state.

"Sir, this is a distinct privilege." Fortin Shenford smiled amiably after the two had posed for pictures in the mansion's elegant dining room. Earlier, the governor had addressed a small crowd in Whitehall Theater, lecturing on the merits of public service. Though short on substance, Eckhardt's talk was well received; afterward he had taken questions informally.

"I'm honored to be here—thank you for the invitation," he responded. The governor was a trim, genial-looking man of sixty, balding and well-tanned. A career bureaucrat, he had served as administrator of the State Supreme Court before becoming Louis Worrell's reluctant understudy.

Eckhardt graciously added, "I was impressed with your students. They can really keep you on your toes with their questions."

Shenford looked pleased. "Our student body includes some of today's finest young minds. Chosen from among the best applicants worldwide."

"Well, surely you deserve credit for—"

The governor felt an elbow brush his right forearm. "Oh—I beg your pardon," a woman's voice said.

"Not at all..." Eckhardt dismissed this minor *faux pas*, before turning in her direction.

She was tall and statuesque, with blue eyes and shoulder-length, honey-blonde hair. The conservative dark suit was form-flattering, her hoseless legs lithe and supple. The governor's heart skipped a beat, and he felt a sensation of lightness he hadn't experienced in decades.

"Not at all," he repeated. And, quickly recovering himself, added: "That's quite all right."

"You're the governor, aren't you? This must be my lucky day." She offered a chastened smile, full of perfect teeth. Eckhardt smiled back, scarcely noticing as Shenford excused himself to tend to other guests.

"I guess I am," he replied. "I've got a bloated state bureaucracy that calls me boss."

The woman's laugh was short and polite. Eckhardt thought that she showed unusual poise for one so young. (An honest twenty-nine, he estimated.) "Samille Potter. A pleasure to meet you, Governor." She stuck out her hand.

"Dick Eckhardt. The pleasure is mine." Their handshake lasted but a moment longer than normal.

"And what do you do for a living, Ms. Potter?"

"I'm an attorney with Everett and Dingle in Boston. We do some of Met's legal work. And please, it's Sami. Those formal titles make me feel old."

"Dick and Sami, then," the governor said affably. He noted the absence of a wedding ring, and thought of his own unfortunate spouse. Yet he *was* still a married man...

Near the buffet table, President Shenford chatted with Overseer and Mrs. Benjamin Littleton. Between pleasantries, Gail Littleton looked over the woman with whom Eckhart was speaking—the practiced scrutiny of the social arbiter.

"Our distinguished guest seems to have found a friend," she remarked, stone-faced.

"We're all working to make his visit enjoyable." Shenford smiled enigmatically, and signaled for a waiter to refill his glass.

It was Sunday afternoon, the men of Sterling 4 assembled in the Presidential Suite (a.k.a. Chug's room), watching college hoops. Midway through the second half, the defending national champion Georgetown Hoyas led Arkansas, 42-31. The Hoya lead was down from sixteen, and the Razorbacks had cut the deficit to nine when suddenly the screen went blank.

"This is a Channel 11 News Special Report," a voice-over announced, the boys howling in protest. The station's logo flashed onscreen, followed by a harried-looking Karen Grace.

"Good afternoon." The anchorwoman perfunctorily introduced herself. "I'm Karen Grace, coming to you live from the Channel 11 newsroom in Bristol…"

"This sucks," Greg Roth impatiently murmured.

"U.S. Senator James Camp, one of the state's most prominent and powerful politicians, is dead." Grace paused to allow this to sink in. The floor's members, largely unfamiliar with the deceased, showed lukewarm interest.

"According to a statement released by the Senator's office, Camp died of liver cancer shortly after eleven o'clock this morning at Bethesda Naval Hospital, where he had been undergoing chemotherapy and radiation treatments for the past several months. The Bristol Democrat, first elected to the upper house in 1976, was known as a champion of liberal causes, and played a key role in last year's Congressional cutoff of American aid to rebel forces in Nicaragua…"

"Is this a state senator or a real one?" Todd French glanced about the room.

Frank Sorenson looked amused. "She said Congress, dummy."

"…Funeral arrangements are incomplete at this time. Once again, U.S. Senator James Camp—dead of liver cancer at forty-nine. For a live report, we take you now to Clive Connolly in Washington…"

After an appropriate interval, the boys switched to Channel 7 in Boston, where the game ran uninterrupted.

"So what happens now? How do they get someone to take his place?" Todd asked.

"Beats the hell out of me." Frank shrugged in dismissive fashion. Georgetown's lead now was back in double figures, the contest well in hand.

"They look good to repeat this year," Chug said.

From the Glanbury Wire, February 5, 1985 (p. 1):

DECISION SEEN NEAR ON CAMP SUCCESSION

By Lawrence Jacobs
Wire Staff

Governor Richard T. Eckhardt hinted yesterday that he would act quickly to fill the vacancy left by the death of U.S. Senator James Camp (D-Bristol) this past Sunday. At a State House press conference, Eckhardt praised the late senator's accomplishments, and stressed the need to fill the seat without delay.

"Clearly, Jim has left some large shoes to fill. Nonetheless, it is imperative that we find a qualified successor ASAP," the governor said, noting that Camp's death has left the state without full Senate representation at a critical juncture, one month after the opening of the 99th Congress.

Under state law, the governor must certify the vacancy within 30 days, after which he may schedule a special election or appoint a successor to serve the remainder of Camp's unexpired term, which ends Jan. 3, 1989. Administration sources say the governor is leaning toward the latter option, with state Republican Party chairman Alan Swinton and Metropolitan University president Fortin C. Shenford among the names being considered.

Political analysts also believe that the appointment

option appears more likely, as it would allow Republicans to immediately add a critical seat to their current 53-46 majority in the Senate, and to ensure that the seat would remain in the GOP column for at least the next four years...

"Mom…I'm really gonna miss my friends."

Rosemary made this frank confession over the phone, while discussing plans to leave school.

Over Christmas break, her father had received orders to Kaneohe Air Station in Hawaii, effective in June. Then Met's latest tuition increase had put the price tag further beyond her family's means, and this time her financial aid package would not close the gap.

After weighing her options, she'd decided to apply to the University of Hawaii at Manoa, in Honolulu. As a transfer student, she would not qualify for in-state tuition status; yet the bill for her senior year would be less than one-third what Met was charging.

"That's terrific, honey," her father had said when she called to relay the news. "It'll save a bundle in costs; and if you get a secondhand car you can live at home and commute to school. Honolulu's only a half-hour from the base."

"That's an idea," Rosemary noncommittally replied.

"Bill's out gallivanting with some friends. I'll tell him you said hello," William Senior added, and Rosemary grinned despite herself. The pesky kid brother whose battles she'd so often been enlisted to fight now outweighed her by a buck and change, and had won a wrestling scholarship to Iowa after leading his high-school team to the semifinal round of this year's state championship tournament.

The phone was then passed to her mother, who avidly voiced her own excitement at going to Hawaii.

"But I'll bet you're looking forward to this even more than we are," Nancy Porter said, thinking of Glanbury's brutally cold winters.

Rosemary thought that she would never miss New England's self-absorbed shallowness, nor its lack of common sense. Yet she repeated what she'd said ten years earlier, when her family had moved to Cherry Point from Camp Pendleton the summer before fifth grade.

Surprised by Rosemary's words, Mrs. Porter hesitated. Then gently reminded her that staying on at Met was not feasible. Change, she said not for the first time, was simply a fact of life, and learning to adjust was what growing up was all about.

"Remember, dear, it's for the best," her mother concluded.

Rosemary hung up the phone feeling empty inside.

Through its network of supporters and lobbyists in Bristol, the Shenford team went into full-court press. Scores of letters poured into the State House, urging his appointment to the Senate. With other, more discreet recommendations coming by word of mouth.

From his detractors, there were equal volumes of opposition. Though with the exception of Willard Ferris, none of Shenford's faculty critics would comment on record.

The president, holding true to form, would leave nothing to chance.

The governor was at a loss to explain his arrival on campus, particularly at ten in the evening. (His predecessor had famously insisted that within the state's boundaries, it was impermissible for a sitting chief executive to call on anyone.) Yet Fortin Shenford could be extremely persuasive.

Eckhardt entered the administration building alone, his state police chauffeur remaining behind in the car. The black Chevy parked discreetly at the rear of the building, dwarfed by Shenford's Cadillac stretch limousine.

Inside the ovate, rosewood-paneled fourth-floor office, the governor stopped short. From across the room, a TV with a videocassette recorder looked back at him. The president remained at his desk, like a monarch on his throne, Steve Patrick and a uniformed Met policeman at his side.

Slowly Eckhardt walked the length of the room, over the plush green carpet embroidered with the University seal.

"Good evening, sir." Shenford stood as Eckhardt approached, shook the governor's hand with a half-smile. "I'm glad you could come tonight; I only wish it were under more favorable circumstances." He motioned his guest to a chair.

Eckhardt remained standing. "What's this about, Fortin?" he demanded. "What's so urgent that you felt compelled to bring me here at this hour?"

"As I've said, the matter is quite delicate. I hardly thought it appropriate for discussion over the phone." The strange smile lingered, as Eckhardt began sweating nervously.

"I've no idea what you're talking about, Fortin." Shenford made no response, but signaled Patrick to switch on the VCR.

The governor gave a sharp gasp, and slid into a chair, his face ashen. On the screen, he and a young woman with honey-blonde hair were in a hotel bed, engaged in a vigorous romp. Eckhardt's face was recognizable at once, flush with an ecstasy he hadn't known in years, the woman moaning in feigned delight—a craft honed by long experience.

"Okay, that's enough." Shenford then stopped the tape himself. Eckhardt was speechless, the room swimming before his eyes.

With supreme effort, the governor mastered himself. "Where did you get that tape?"

"That's not important now." Shenford waved this inquiry aside, adding, "Naturally, it stays within this office, as far as I'm concerned."

"Let's not play games, Fortin. What is it you want?"

"What do I *want?*" The president looked genuinely wounded. "Governor, you misunderstand…I only have your best interests at heart.

"Your wife, Annabelle, has suffered from myasthenia gravis for the past twelve years," he recited. Eckhardt's jaw slackened further. "For the last six years, she has remained bedridden, her valetudinarian state likely precluding normal marital relations. I would think it's been rather some time since—"

"Stop it! Stop it, you slimy bastard!" Goaded beyond endurance, Eckhardt sprang from his chair, facing his tormentor across the desk.

The blue-clad officer moved toward Eckhardt, as if to restrain him. Shenford waved him off, and smiled contemptuously as the governor again sat down.

"Then again, why should voters be outraged? It's quite understandable, given the circumstances—your wife not being much fun, and you only human. Hell, these days anything goes, right?

"Of course it does." Shenford answered his own question. "But though the people forgive, they couldn't forget if they wanted to. And you'd be hard-pressed to maintain credibility, being the topic of bordello humor throughout the state."

The governor winced at Shenford's blunt words. Still shaken, he again rose and retreated a step.

"I will not have this! This meeting is over as far as I'm concerned," he rasped.

"Yes, Governor, I'm sure we're both busy men. I look forward to working with you from Washington." Shenford watched, satisfied, as Eckhardt turned and left the room.

"Gentlemen, well done," he quietly congratulated his minions.

Backstage at Hale Auditorium, Pete Garrett's troupe waited in the wings, the Law School's annual variety show under way. Their production, like most of tonight's acts, born of frivolity and revenge— payback for the sadistic grillings and hours of research endured in the second-year Moot Court process.

As usual, faculty and students had flocked to the auditorium. The crowd applauded Doug Wehrli's impression of Professor Martin's stilted Secured Transactions lectures, then laughed knowingly at the Randy McShane Four's ode to Professor Kersch, entitled "I Taught the Law (But to No One)."

"A good deal of truth is told in jest." Professor Eileen Bridge turned, unsmiling, to Dean Kerr in the front row. Amos Kersch's Criminal Law students were notorious for their chronic absenteeism, fewer than half attending class regularly.

"I know; it's a sin." Kerr smiled back faintly, resolved to speak later with Kersch.

Between acts, an "ad" for Casenote Legal Briefs ran onstage. Pete helped classmate Sean Westbrook straighten his tie, the moment of truth at hand.

The Casenote Briefs pitchman, sandwich board and all, slipped back behind the curtain. "You're up," he advised, chagrined at his reception from the audience.

Sean was first onstage, followed by his counterpart Angela Rowen. Pete and the others then watched as Elaine Sheldon, dressed in a marshal's uniform, emerged to begin the proceedings.

"Oi, vay! Oi, vay! Oi, vay!" she solemnly declared. "The Mock Supreme Let's-Pretend Court of Fantasyland is now in session. All persons having business before the Court draw near and ye shall be heard, if not heeded. God save our nation from this Court…"

Chief Justice Garrett entered and assumed the makeshift bench, flanked by Associates Brad Peale and Jane Molinari. Befitting the dignity of their lofty tribunal, the three wore loud plaid bathrobes, grim-faced as they took their seats.

"May it convince the Court." Sean stood at the lectern, impeccably attired, to open the Plaintiff's case. Thus began oral arguments in the matter of *Brown v. Van Pelt.*

Plaintiff-Appellant, Sean stated, was suing the Defendant for battery and negligent infliction of emotional distress. The case stemming from an incident in which Defendant enticed Plaintiff to place-kick a football, while promising to hold the same. Instead, counsel averred, Defendant deliberately and with malice aforethought pulled said football away, the Plaintiff's momentum then carrying him some six feet into the air, causing him to give an anguished cry of "AAUGH!" before landing on his back with a violent WUMP! ("I submit to this Court that as a practicing psychiatrist, Defendant should have been especially aware of the likelihood of emotional suffering," Sean stressed.)

The defense countered that Plaintiff was guilty of contributory negligence, and that consent could be inferred from Plaintiff's having been regularly victimized in such fashion over a thirty-year period. ("Surely none but a complete blockhead would persist in falling for the same trick on an annual basis.") There followed a masterful exchange of rebuttals and surrebuttals, citing applicable precedents: *Garratt v. Dailey, Doe v. Roe, Hogan v. Iron Sheik.*

The courtroom was then cleared for deliberation. A process that soon went from heated words to mock slaps, then nose tweaks and eye gouges, an occasional *nyuk-nyuk* sound. The audience roared its approbation.

The litigants were resummoned before the bench. Frowning, Pete said that Gee, this was a tough one, with but a single fair and equitable solution.

Pete produced a coin from the pocket of his robe. "Plaintiff, call it in the air," he instructed. Defendant quickly objecting to this travesty of justice.

"How come he gets to call it?" Angela yelled, the curtain descending to laughter and applause.

"Good job, Mr. Garrett." Sean nodded, satisfied, as they shed their costumes backstage, the performance a rousing success. "Next year, if you can't find a job, you should go on *Saturday Night Live* instead."

"It's good to have a fallback." Pete smiled, his remark not wholly in jest.

The voice on his line was one the governor knew well—arrogant, incisive and very much in command.

"Shenford speaking."

"Fortin, Dick Eckhardt." The governor switched on the speakerphone, while Attorney General Mike Molinsky and Chief of Staff Henry Wirth listened in. The two were his most trusted advisors, and had forgone judgment upon his confession.

"My guess is, he won't go public, at least not now," Molinsky had said. "By all accounts he's an extremely vindictive man—but for the moment, he has nothing to gain."

"Governor—to what do I owe the pleasure?" Behind the words, a presumption that set Eckhardt's teeth on edge.

"I'm calling in regard to the Senate vacancy. In the end, the decision wasn't a difficult one..." The governor paused for breath, then added, "I'm scheduling a special election in the fall. And I will see that Alan Swinton has the party's full support. You won't be going to the Senate, Fortin. Now or ever, as long as I have anything to say about it, *you son of a bitch!*" His fury erupted in one cathartic burst.

Shenford's reply was smooth and unctuous. "Perhaps we should discuss this further," he offered. "Say, in my private screening room?"

"Do your worst, Fortin. I should have told you to go to hell from the beginning—superfluous though that might have been. Beyond that, I

309

have nothing more to say to you."

Angrily, Eckhardt slammed the receiver into its cradle. And looked almost needfully to his aides for support.

GOVERNOR SETS SPECIAL ELECTION FOR NOV. 5, read the headline in the *Wire* the next morning. Per Eckhardt's order, party primaries were slated for August, the winner of the November final to be immediately sworn in.

In the interim, the governor had announced, the seat would be filled by a temporary caretaker. The appointee was Harry Wysznicki, a retired Superior Court justice who, it was understood, would not seek election in the fall.

From the Bristol *Telegraph*, February 28, 1985 (p. 3):

GOP GROUP: DRAFT MET U. PREXY

By Alvin Wall

A group of Republican Party activists yesterday announced the formation of a committee to draft Metropolitan University president Fortin C. Shenford to run for the U.S. Senate seat vacated earlier this month by the death of incumbent James Camp. The announcement came shortly after the committee, headed by former state representative Joseph B. Marchak (R-Bristol), had filed notice of its organization with the Federal Election Commission, and with the State Board of Elections.

"We need his leadership, pure and simple," Marchak said in a press briefing at his York Street law office. "Dr. Shenford has worked miracles at Metropolitan, and has shown a profound understanding of national and international issues. His record demonstrates the kind of leadership that has unfortunately become a rarity in public life."

The 63-year-old Shenford, who has served as Met's chief executive since 1962, yesterday disclaimed any interest in running, though he conceded that he "felt honored" by the committee's efforts, and could reconsider his position should his boosters succeed in placing him on the ballot.

"I've often fielded such inquiries in the past,"

Shenford said, "but this is the first time I've been offered such extensive organizational support." He added that, "This isn't something I'd do on my own, but should the people of this state ask me to run, I would have to consider it very carefully."

The committee faces an immediate and daunting hurdle, however, in gathering the requisite number of signatures to put their man on the Aug. 20 primary ballot. Under state law, a candidate must submit 5,000 signatures from registered Republican or independent voters to gain ballot access, and most observers believe the Mar. 12 filing deadline will present a formidable challenge.

"It can't be done," said veteran GOP consultant Skip Lantz. "Not when you're up against this time frame, starting from square one. It simply isn't feasible." Asked about the committee's chances of meeting the deadline, Marchak tersely replied, "We have people working on that."

However, committee advisor William Waycross, director of Reigate College's Coleman Institute for Political Science, was more openly optimistic, expressing confidence that the outspoken educator would be on the ballot this summer.

"Despite the current robust economy, the federal government is not a well-managed institution, and the soaring deficit cannot bode well for the long term," Waycross said. "The truth is, we need people like Fortin Shenford in Washington to help put our house in order. Voters intuitively sense this, and that's why he'll get the support he needs."

"I've never seen anything like it." Waycross exultantly briefed his client over the phone. "The lines are ringing off the hook, and the money started to pour in literally overnight. We've really struck a chord someplace."

"I expected no less," Shenford calmly replied. "The people have long hungered for genuine leadership. They perceive our strengths and abilities."

Waycross said, "Eckhardt did you a favor with that short cut-off date.

That made it clear the insiders were trying to stack the deck. So right now, you're enjoying the best of both worlds. Officially, you're not even a candidate; yet you're seen as the feisty underdog."

"Good—play up that angle. It's definitely worth some short-term mileage. Then when we beat the insiders at their own game, we'll be off and running.

"Speaking of which," Shenford asked, "how are we doing on those signatures?"

Waycross smirked. "Let's say you've made a believer of that Lantz."

On March 12, an hour before the 4 P.M. deadline, Fortin Shenford's nomination papers arrived in the office of Secretary of State Michael Egan. They contained 10,952 signatures, more than enough to ensure a place on the primary ballot. Now all Shenford had to do was formally announce his candidacy.

"Ten thousand signatures?" The governor edged forward in disbelief, perched on the edge of his leather chair.

"Yes, sir." Chief of Staff Wirth glumly nodded. "And it appears most of them are going to check out. We just got the word from the Secretary's office."

Mike Molinsky was immediately suspicious. "But how could anyone round up that many names in that short time? It doesn't seem possible. Not without an organization in place. And I mean a real organization, not some raggedy-assed volunteer brigade starting from scratch—"

"Don't you see?" Eckhardt stood and brought his fist down on the desk. "He's *had* an organization in place all along. It's the only answer. Somehow, he's had this whole operation planned from the beginning. Sonofabitch!"

Mike Molinsky had been the state's attorney general for five years, and was known as a staunch foe of public corruption. Appointed during the Worrell administration, he'd maintained prosecutorial independence, sending two of his former boss's top aides to the sneezer on graft charges.

Tall and trim at fifty-five, with a full head of curly white hair, the Brooklyn native had an imposing courtroom presence. And by reputation, had no qualms about stepping on the toes of the state's self-exalted grand high mucky-mucks.

From his earliest days as an assistant in the Criminal Division, he had been sickened by the influence-peddling which defined state politics. The system was a fetid, stinking cesspool of human sewage, its ranks dominated by greaseball lowlifes. Molinsky remembered well his first major corruption case, and the sight of then-state House Majority Leader O'Brien Quinn crying with snot running down his chin as he begged a Superior Court judge not to send him to prison for extorting a paltry twenty-five grand in kickbacks from state contractors. The topper was that the recently-paroled Quinn had sought pension credit for the time he'd served in the can—and gotten it, thanks to his cronies on the State Retirement Board.

But Molinsky reasoned that this moral vacuum had been foreordained. A democracy was only as sound as its citizens, and here integrity was an alien concept. In this state public unions bled the taxpayers for every possible dime, executives in their sixties claimed unemployment benefits as a retirement bonus, and everyone cheated his neighbor for the simple pleasure of it.

This case, however, was different. This was big.

From the moment the governor had deduced Shenford's clandestine campaign operation, Molinsky had determined to succeed where his predecessors had failed: to bring the Met president to justice at last.

Yet thus far, his investigation had been fruitless.

At the outset, his deputies had solicited the aid of several key university staffers. When nobody bit, a reward was offered: twenty thousand dollars. Still no takers, which was a measure of the fear in which the target was held. Meanwhile, the target's own web was already woven, threatening the most sordid scandal in state history.

For once, Molinsky had a foe worthy of the name. And prayed he was equal to the task.

"No way—you can't be serious!"

Chug looked across the table at Brandon in disbelief, his breakfast forgotten. It was seven-thirty A.M., the two virtually alone in the cafeteria.

"I'm completely serious. I'm going to register to vote in this state as a Republican," Brandon repeated. "To vote against Shenford in the primary," he hastened to explain.

"But...you don't live here. The dorm doesn't count, you know that."

"I'll use the guys' address at The Apartment. They won't even have to know about it. Or, I'll get a state driver's license first, whatever it takes."

"What if he doesn't even run?" Chug asked.

Brandon just stared at him.

"Okay, stupid question." Chug pondered the legal implications of

Brandon's scheme before asking: "So who *are* you gonna vote for?"

"Whoever's his strongest opponent. I don't care who it is, as long as it isn't Shenford…that's all that matters."

"You mean, you're going to all this trouble and you don't know—"

Grimly, Brandon replied, "You don't understand. This is strictly about playing keep-away."

From the sidelines Willard Ferris watched, transfixed, as the Shenford juggernaut continued to gain momentum. The candidate-in-waiting was everywhere, addressing various civic organizations, touring the state in a black Buick Regal leased by his supporters.

On editorial pages, letters appeared urging Shenford's candidacy. The evening news ran almost nightly updates on the rising groundswell of support for the Met president. And a Channel 11 news poll put Shenford in a statistical tie with Alan Swinton for the lead in a primary trial heat.

Ferris looked up from his kitchen table, where the fruits of his research lay in an open cardboard box. Five hundred copies of a small booklet, printed at his expense, slated for media release the next day. The booklet, entitled "The Truth About Fortin Shenford," followed endless hours at the City Library and the School of Journalism morgue.

As usual, the president pulled no punches. Speaking before the Bristol Rotary Club, he condemned "the ignorant barbarism and continued Crusades mentality" of the Middle East. He termed creeping overpopulation "the unaddressed root cause of environmental crisis." While deploring the inability of modern parents to instill character in children, a failure ascribed to the Baby Boomers' own moral paucity.

"Parents without core values," Shenford said, "breed children without the concept of values."

Amazingly, Shenford's audiences seemed captivated by his harsh rhetoric. Even more amazingly, the media embraced his unsparing candor. In an age of sterile public discourse, some were openly electrified at the prospect of this fiercely voluble man on the national stage.

"Fools," Ferris murmured aloud. "You blind, stupid fools." Peering into the adjoining living room, where tonight's late newscast had ended. Barring exposure, he realized, Shenford would steamroll his way into the Senate that fall. And his ambitions would not end there.

The booklet recited the evils of the Shenford administration, anecdotally documented: abuse of power, intolerance of dissent, enriching himself at the university's expense. Along with his history of provocative utterances, now curiously forgotten by the media.

In 1971, Shenford had railed against the 26th Amendment, calling America's youth "morally and intellectually unwashed, without sense of political realities." As late as 1982, he had called for the voting age to be lifted to twenty-five. And last fall he'd stated publicly that realization of the Strategic Defense Initiative would create a moral duty to free Eastern Europe and the Baltic Republics from the Soviet sphere, "on pain of a few 20-megaton lessons in continence."

Following the 1970 shootings at Kent State, Met had remained open while hundreds of schools nationwide shut down due to student unrest. "They've learned their lesson here," Shenford explained, noting past failed uprisings. He later said that the four students killed by National Guardsmen had "brought it on themselves."

From a tumbler, Ferris took a sip of Chivas Regal, the nightmare scenario unfolding in his mind. Shenford standing victorious on election night, outlining his agenda for a national audience. That oafish thug Patrick then taking over Metropolitan—but in name only, warming the power office as Shenford continued to exercise control from Washington. The next presidential campaign beginning little more than a year later,

New Hampshire's inaugural primary virtually next door...

At ten past midnight, Ferris turned off the TV and went up to bed. Though aided by the whiskey, he did not sleep for a long time.

The news conference was a dismal failure.

Despite Ferris's efforts, the event had been poorly attended, with one reporter—Channel 2's Leslie Jernigan—giving his exposé a cursory treatment on the evening news.

Alone in his office, he swallowed the last of the Chivas Regal from the flask secreted in his desk drawer. There had scarcely been enough of the whiskey left to get a decent buzz on, requiring him to finish the task at home. His car was parked on Franklin's east end, several blocks from the School of Journalism.

Ten minutes later, Ferris sagged behind the wheel of his black 1972 Impala, a pre-OPEC beast he and Rhonda had whimsically christened Vlad. The car had since logged over 200,000 miles, its neglected interior caked with dirt, the rocker panels nearly rusted through.

"Contact," Ferris said lifelessly, turning his key in the ignition. At this hour the street was calm, with light pedestrian traffic.

The engine started on the second try and he eased out onto the narrow road, his U-joints grinding in protest.

Freshman Heather Danforth clung tightly to her boyfriend's waist, neither wearing a helmet as the Suzuki 450 pulled away from the curb and sped past University Green. The boyfriend, a local welder named Ian Corey, had tuned the idle recently, and the motorbike was quite loud.

A block from her rowhouse, the blonde nursing student squealed in delight as they roared through the Bright Street intersection without stopping. The Suzuki continued to accelerate, passing rows of parked cars on either side as they headed east on Franklin.

Nudging 65 miles per hour, Corey eased off the throttle, the busier

Hilton Way intersection in sight.

The Impala approached from the opposite direction, its left-turn signal blinking erratically as the junction neared. With a fierce rebel yell, Corey opened the throttle again, determined to beat it through the crossing. With perhaps, a digital salute for the proud owner of the old pissbucket.

In an instant the car blocked his path, and Corey realized he'd misgauged his distance. Unable to stop, he veered hard to the right, instinctively seeking an escape route.

He felt Heather's nails dig into his suede jacket as she began to scream. The driver of the Impala braked hard, then floored the accelerator in a last, desperate effort to avoid the crash.

"Ohhhh, shit!" Corey wailed, a split-second before impact.

Steve Patrick answered the phone in the president's office, where the two replayed the story from the six P.M. news. His scowl deepening, the president listened as Ferris branded him "a militarist, a right-wing ideologue—an evil and dangerous man."

Patrick listened to the voice on the line, incredulous. And with an evil, exultant grin put the caller on hold.

"Sir, it's Chief Fullerton. You may want to take this," he advised.

The two young victims were rushed to Glanbury Memorial Hospital's emergency room, suffering from extensive head injuries. All efforts at resuscitation failed, and both were pronounced dead within minutes of arrival.

"Case Number C2-85-03047," the clerk of the Cheshire County District Court read in a tired drone. "State versus Willard M. Ferris."

Escorted by two sheriff's deputies, the academic stepped forward, unshaven and in handcuffs. It was Monday morning and he'd spent the weekend in the city jail, awaiting arraignment.

The three charges were read into the record. Two counts of vehicular homicide, one of driving under the influence. Aware of the cameras in the packed courtroom, Ferris stared down at the defense table, flanked by attorney Vance Needham. The former assistant city solicitor was a longtime acquaintance, who had agreed to handle today's proceeding.

"Mr. Ferris, how do you wish to plead?" Judge Oscar Ferrelli glowered from the bench, his dark eyes like lasers.

"Not guilty, Your Honor," he replied, the words scarcely audible.

Following the arguments of counsel, Judge Ferrelli set bail at $200,000 personal recognizance. And with the ritual admonition to maintain good behavior, ordered the defendant released, pending further action in Superior Court.

Outside the mob of jackals waited, with cameras and microphones poised. Ferris scarcely heard their shouted questions, or his attorney's repeated "No comments" as they left the building.

But for his crime, there could be no amends.

Shirtless and disheveled, Ferris sat on his bed—the king-size bed

Rhonda had once shared—conscious only of the one thing that mattered: His responsibility for the death of two human beings.

By some paternal instinct he reached for the bedside telephone and dialed his daughter's home number.

"Christina, honey, you've made me proud." His voice was broken. "Please always remember that I love you…and wish you the best." Mawkishly, he rambled on until the answering machine cut him off.

Gently he replaced the receiver in its cradle. And opened the drawer of the nightstand, where a bottle of sleeping pills lay on its side.

Seven hours later, Christina Ferris's red Pontiac Sunbird swept into the driveway of her father's house. Brakes screeching, she stopped in front of the garage, got out, and raced for the front door.

I knew I should never have left him alone, she thought over and over again. This morning, at his insistence, she had returned to work after staying with him the past two nights.

Using her old key, she entered the unlit dwelling and ran upstairs to her father's bedroom, where a figure lay motionless beneath the covers.

Her fingers found the light switch, then hesitated.

"Dad?" she said softly. "It's me. It's Christina. I got your message. I just figured I'd stop by. You sounded like you could use some company, so I thought I'd come over…"

She waited fifteen seconds, then turned on the lights in her father's room.

Soon after, she began to scream.

From the Metropolitan University *Press*, March 29, 1985 (p. 8):

Obituary

Willard M. Ferris, Professor of Journalism at the University since 1967, died unexpectedly at his home in Glanbury on March 20. He was 56.

Professor Ferris received his bachelor's and master's degrees in journalism from Washington and Lee University before beginning his career as a radio announcer at WGLN-AM in Glanbury. In 1960, he signed on with WDDK-TV in Bristol, where he served as Channel 11's State House correspondent prior to joining the School of Journalism faculty.

He is survived by his mother, Amanda LeClear Ferris of McLean, Va.; a daughter, Christina Ferris of Bristol; and several nieces and nephews.

From her desk Elizabeth Kerr took a blank sheet of Law School stationery, her conscience spurred by the events of recent days.

On a personal level, the dean lacked any connection with Willard Ferris. Yet his tortured history had followed a familiar pattern.

The final straw, however, had been Shenford's appearance on the morning news, praising his fallen foe. A towering figure among New England newsmen, Shenford had called him. A tireless crusader, whose tragic end could not erase the memory of his accomplishments.

Eschewing secretary and typewriter, she wrote the letter herself, in longhand:

Dear Dr. Shenford:

It is with deep regret that I hereby tender my resignation as Dean of the School of Law, effective June 1, 1985.

My regret stems not from my planned departure, but from having remained blind as long as I have, indifferent to the misery and human suffering which you have caused.

I wanted to believe that your administration had the university's best interests at heart. I sought to convince myself, against my better judgment, that you were guilty only of overzealousness in your desire to bring excellence to this institution. But there is no way of denying the truth now. I finally understand that there is no lie you will not tell, no deceit you will not propound, and no injustice you will not condone in your all-consuming thirst for power.

For years I have watched grown men and women quake in their boots, ever mindful of Caesar's wrath. I have listened to colleagues converse in meaningless circumlocution, lest they suffer reprisals. I have witnessed deserving scholars denied tenure and promotion, in some cases their very livelihood, for no reason beyond their political beliefs. Even now, faced with the ominous specter of your ambitions, we remain silent, our tongues stilled by fear of retribution. But I, for one, can remain silent no longer.

For these reasons I am unable, in good conscience, to maintain my affiliation with the university. I leave in the hope that my colleagues may find the belated courage to reclaim their freedom, and to dispel the dark cloud of repression which you have cast over our lives.

Yours truly,

Elizabeth M. Kerr

She reread the letter once, through moist eyes, and placed it in an interdepartmental envelope. Which was then given to her secretary for forwarding.

At the sound of Steve Patrick's voice on her line the next morning, the dean winced.

"Elizabeth, I'm calling in regard to your letter. We received it yesterday, and frankly we have some concerns."

"Mr. Patrick, as far as *I'm* concerned the subject is closed. The letter speaks for itself, and we've nothing further to discuss."

"I'm afraid it's not that simple. The president was really quite shocked by your belligerent and unprofessional tone. As a psychiatrist, he found this sudden, unprovoked hostility worrisome." Patrick paused before adding, "Under the circumstances, we think it best that you be placed on administrative leave, effective immediately."

Kerr stood behind the desk, her face flushed. "Exactly what are you saying?"

"You will remain on our payroll, with full benefits, through May 31st. But as of now, you are relieved of your duties."

Stunned, she made no reply as Patrick pronounced his farewell benediction.

"You have two hours to vacate your office. Or you will be escorted from Kennedy Hall."

Elizabeth Kerr's resignation caused little stir on campus. For it was soon lost in the firestorm of outrage following Ferris's death.

For once, the president's opponents were loud and demonstrative. From Walden Plaza, a massive protest culminated in a march on the administration building, where more than 1000 people shouted anti-Shenford slogans. Emboldened faculty members joined students on the front lines, others calling openly for the president's resignation.

The media, smelling blood, intensified their scrutiny of the would-be candidate. The *Telegraph* highlighted his more controversial stands, with excerpts from his writings on democracy. ("One might fairly question the moral basis for a system exalting the caprice of the ignorant many over the wisdom of the enlightened few.") His stewardship of Metropolitan was reexamined, the *Wire* chronicling his financial ties with fellow Board members.

In the face of this onslaught, Shenford's tracking polls showed him plummeting 14 points, to 16 behind Swinton. The candidate's brain trust huddled in its York Street bunker, confronted with the first crisis of a campaign in its nascent stages.

"Christ, they're killing me out there." The president fumed, a copy of the day's *Telegraph* in hand. "You'd think I was the one who stuffed those pills down that man's throat!"

"It's just a temporary, misplaced sympathetic reaction, I'm sure." Pollster Geoff Norman sought to assuage his client's wrath.

"How nicely put," Shenford said acidly.

Judy Cochran broke the silence. "We've had an interview request from *Newsmakers*," she announced. "They want to have you speak with Mitch Davenport live on NBC, tomorrow night at ten. I think we should do it—the best approach is to meet this head-on."

Her colleagues were less enthused. Since the newsmagazine's launch, in September 1983, Mitch Davenport had emerged as the most ruthless interrogator on television. Bold and unflinching, he'd once asked a startled Vice-President Bush whether his superior's "The bombing begins in five minutes" remark had not been foolish and ill-advised.

Shenford, however, agreed without hesitation: "Fine."

Precisely on the hour Mitch Davenport appeared onscreen, wearing his trademark charcoal suit. The host was impeccably groomed, with an air of authority belying his forty-one years.

"He wants to raise the voting age to twenty-five." Davenport looked into the camera at his audience. "He wants to have unwed welfare parents sterilized. And he may want to serve in the U.S. Senate. Tonight, a talk with controversial Metropolitan University president Fortin Shenford. Good evening. I'm Mitch Davenport, and this is *Newsmakers...*"

"It's about time Shenford got his..." Bob Spencer began while Davenport welcomed his guest. Tonight's show had become a media event, with Bob and his Housemates watching from their living room.

Troll Philbrick silenced him, one finger raised to his lips. "Shh. It's starting," he said.

Excerpts from Fortin Shenford's appearance on *Newsmakers*, March 25, 1985:

DAVENPORT: Well, let's begin with the recent spate of protests on campus. Dr. Shenford, after 23 years as Metropolitan's president, were you surprised by the level of opposition remaining on campus, and how much they hated you?

SHENFORD: Mitch, as you know, it's the lunatic fringe that tends to make the most noise—often encouraged by the news media, who grant them exposure out of proportion to their merits. These so-called protesters represent only a small, self-serving faction. They do not represent the university community as a whole...

D: It's estimated that Friday's rally was attended by some 1200 individuals. That would make it one of the largest protest demonstrations to take place on an American campus in recent years. Are you denying that these events reflect widespread opposition?

S: As you say, Mitch, you're talking about 1200 people. Twelve hundred people, out of more than 80,000 students, faculty and staff who have passed through Metropolitan University during my administration. That works out to an approval rating of over 98 percent—an enviable figure, in light of the changes I've had to make in order to bring quality to this institution.

D: Sir, do I understand you correctly? Do you seriously contend that 98 percent of those who have passed through the university during your tenure have supported you?

S: I just did the arithmetic for you. The numbers speak for themselves, and I'm content to stand on them.

D: The protests seem to have crystallized following the death—the suicide of Willard Ferris, who was a frequent and outspoken critic of your administration and its policies...

S: I have no comment on Professor Ferris's case. Our differences over time notwithstanding, I respected his integrity and conviction, and have no wish to add to his family's suffering.

D: In the past you have advocated, among other things, raising the voting age to 25, and conditioning welfare benefits on sterilization of unwed recipients. You have been mentioned as a possible candidate for public office—do you believe that the electorate in your state would endorse such ideas?

S: I have never advocated any such things. And whoever is feeding you this rubbish has an active imagination.

D: But these statements are a matter of public record. They have appeared in the Glanbury Wire, the Bristol Telegraph, even the New York Times. Not just in interviews, but in guest columns written by you.

S: I've never made any such pronouncements. And I believe that my recollection is more reliable than yours.

D: Your memory is not in doubt, Dr. Shenford. The question is, are you telling the truth?

S: Mitch, after airing those slanderous distortions, you are in no position to question my integrity.

D: Dr. Shenford, tell me, why would you consider a run for the U.S. Senate?

S: I think it only fitting that the most able among us should govern. At any rate, we could surely improve on our recent track record. Even now our esteemed lawmakers on Capitol Hill are again looking to pick the taxpayers' pockets, claiming they can't live on their present salary. *(Pause.)* In my view, anyone who can't make ends meet on $66,000 a year has no business passing on the federal budget.

D: Isn't that a rather simplistic statement? The cost of living in Washington, for instance, in and of itself...

S: Check the apartment listings in the Post sometime. Then tell me you need that kind of salary to get along. And keep in mind, this is in addition to the lavish benefits they receive. Free travel to and from Washington, for instance, with many legislators flying home every weekend at taxpayer expense...

D: Well they have to run for reelection, in the case of House members, every two years...

S: Nobody *has* to run for reelection. If reelection is your first priority, then you do your constituents a disservice. You're putting your own interests above the people's welfare, ahead of the public good. I can think of nothing more antithetical to democracy than this mindset.

D: Your own annual salary at Metropolitan is reportedly $435,000—more than twice that of any other university president in America. Benefits and perks—free room and board, for instance, in a mansion with servants—add approximately another $130,000 to the package. How can you then turn around and complain that members of Congress, earning less than one-eighth as much, are overpaid?

S: I am honored to have my services so highly valued. And considering our record of achievement, an impartial observer would have to conclude that the university has gotten its money's worth. Can the American taxpayer say the same for his elected representatives? I doubt it, Mitch…

"So what did you guys think?" Bob looked nervously at his companions once the interview had concluded.

There was a brief, heavy silence before Wally admitted, "I think Shenford ate his lunch." An assessment that went unchallenged.

"The overnight numbers are in, sir. All good news." Geoff Norman beamed the next morning, in the president's private study. "Statewide, slightly more than two-thirds of those surveyed responded favorably to your position, while 72 percent felt you 'won' the showdown with Davenport. Your overall standing is up seven points, with significant gains among likely primary voters."

"Excellent." The president nodded, unsmiling. This was all preliminary.

"Steve, I know you'll do a bang-up job." Shenford turned to his chosen successor, seated across the desk, the transition in his mind already begun.

"Nevertheless, I'll be sure to stay in touch. And if ever I can be of service, know that I am always accessible."

Patrick nodded silently, the message received. Though in line for Met's top job, he would remain the loyal subordinate.

Thursday, eight P.M. Seventy hours after the Davenport interview.

The president laid the evening edition of the *Wire* on his desk, pleased with his poll numbers. He was now just six points behind Swinton, and closing. On campus, the protests had visibly abated, his would-be character assassins leaderless and disorganized.

The formal announcement was scheduled for mid-April, at Bristol's Colonial Meeting House. And from there, it was on to Washington in the fall.

The intercom on his desk buzzed—a shrill, grating sound, ceasing only when he hit the button to respond.

"Yes? What is it, Gloria?"

"You—you have a visitor, sir." The receptionist stammered nervously.

Angered by his secretary's lapse, the president bridled. "What do you mean, 'a visitor?'" he snapped. "Does this person have a name—or an appointment? I don't see one on the schedule!"

From the intercom, a muffled groan, then silence. "Hello?" Shenford was standing now, hunched over the speaker. "Gloria, what the hell's going on out there?"

He waited three seconds, then started for the door, arriving just as it opened and the figure of a dark-haired young woman burst into the office, a .32-caliber revolver in hand.

"Get back!" Christina Ferris snarled, the gun pointed at his chest. Startled, Shenford complied at once, the door closing on Gloria Stiehl's recumbent form. Her forehead showing an ugly bruise, where she'd been slugged with the butt end of the weapon.

Recognizing his assailant, Shenford moved toward the desk. "Miss Ferris, put that down—don't be a fool!"

"You killed my father, you bastard!" She advanced on him, her eyes filled with rage.

Stealthily, his fingers probed the underside of the desk. "Miss Ferris—you're mistaken. Obviously you're upset now, and you're not thinking rationally. Your father's passing was a blow to us all—"

"Liar!" she shrieked. "You drove him to it—you, you did it to him! Murdering scum—!

"Wasn't it enough that you froze his salary all those years?" Christina raged. "Wasn't it enough that you destroyed his career, and made his life a living hell?" She was six feet from him now, the revolver at shoulder height, her hands trembling.

He took a calculated risk. "You are likely unaware that on my desk is a silent alarm button, which I've just activated. The building's security force is on its way now." Harsh and unrelenting, he added, "If you fire that weapon, you'll not leave this room alive.

"Not so brave now, are you, little girl?" He watched as the gun barrel dipped slowly. Her lower lip trembled and her hands dropped to her sides, the .32 angled almost straight down.

"Miss Ferris…Christina. I am not a heartless person." His voice softened as he took one step forward. "Just give me the gun, and we'll put this episode behind us. And I'll personally see that you get any…assistance you may need. It's the least we can do, in light of your father's service."

Ferris began sobbing violently. Shenford again took a step closer.

"Give me the gun," he repeated softly, hand outstretched, again having prevailed. Within the year, Capitol Hill would similarly lie at his feet. And next, the free world.

His glorious reverie was shattered by the report of the revolver, and a searing pain exploded through Shenford's body as Christina's bullet entered his left side.

On the building's front lawn, several Sterling residents had gathered, waiting out another false fire alarm. From the courtyard they had drifted across the street, the fire trucks standing parked at the curb.

"Too bad no one brought a Frisbee. We could have played some Ultimate," Rosemary remarked to her neighbors, the grass beneath her feet slightly damp. Tonight the lawn sprinklers had remained on until after dark, a sign of the coming of spring.

"Listen…did anybody else hear that?" Brandon cocked his head to the right as he stood on the building's front steps, beneath the massive iron doors that seemed strictly ornamental.

"I heard it too," Marcus Pullman volunteered. His McDonald's run on hold while he chatted with his ex-dormmates.

The others let it pass. "So what's new and exciting in your life?" Chug asked the visiting senior.

"Well...I've been accepted into Met's graduate accounting program," Marcus evenly announced. "Starting next fall. I just got the word today."

"Wow, grad school. Congratulations." Rosemary looked suitably impressed. Having recently gained her own transfer acceptance to Hawaii.

Beaming with pleasure, Marcus turned, then gave a sudden start. This time, the noise was unmistakable.

His legs heavy and unresponsive, Fortin Shenford staggered behind the desk, blood seeping through his fingers as he clutched his wounded left side.

"Have fun in hell, you cocksucker!" Ferris squeezed the trigger again. The bullet struck his right shoulder, bringing a fresh flare of agony.

As he slowly sank to the floor, a third shot grazed his neck and passed through the half-open window in the background. Then the door burst open, and the room exploded in gunfire as Shenford's University Police bodyguards stormed the office, emptying their revolvers into the would-be assassin.

"Don't tell me you didn't hear that!" Frank looked round to his floormates. But of course, everyone had. The noise of shattering glass, followed by what sounded like an indoor fireworks display.

"It came from around back. Come on, let's check it out." Chug waved the others toward the rear of the building, where the president's office lights pinpointed the location at once.

Joined by others racing across the street, they stared up at the broken windows, braced for another explosion. Instead, they heard the sound of muffled voices—and beneath the shadows, a frenzy of flurried movement. Mystified, the crowd eased slowly toward the side entrance, not knowing what to expect.

The sound of wailing sirens intensified, then took shape as an ambulance and two University Police cruisers converged on the building. The occupants of the three vehicles got out at once, merging into a single unit as they moved briskly toward the door.

"Clear the way, please," the officer in command barked without breaking stride. "Come on—make way, make way!"

Arriving at Glanbury Memorial Hospital, Fortin Shenford was immediately rushed into surgery. The bullet in the abdomen, it was discovered, had ruptured his spleen, necessitating removal of the organ.

The procedure, however, was not an extraordinary one, and the patient's constitution was strong. The surgery was an unqualified success, with full recovery anticipated.

At 12:40 A.M., Met's Public Relations office issued a statement updating the president's condition, while downplaying the fatal shooting of Christina Ferris.

"Due to the exigency of the situation, and the obvious futility of less forceful means," Chief Fullerton was quoted as saying, "it became necessary for our officers to fire on the President's assailant. And regrettably, the wounds sustained by the subject proved fatal."

There was little mention of Gloria Stiehl, the president's executive secretary, who was treated for a concussion, then kept overnight for observation and released.

By morning, the campus was a media vortex. Reporters and cameramen were everywhere, seeking the latest updates while canvassing reaction from the Met community.

Outwardly, the mood was sober and restrained. Yet apart from those mourning Christina Ferris's tragic end, there was little emotion apparent. And beneath the surface, a distinct element of black humor.

"Hey, better luck next time."

"I'm surprised nobody did it sooner."

"It wouldn't have happened to a nicer guy."

"I wish she'da said something to me," remarked one Building Maintenance worker to his colleagues at break time. "I'da got her a .44 Magnum, make sure she done the job right."

"You know, I got the weirdest phone call from Brandon Clark's mother this morning," Sterling 4 R.A. Stephanie Hayden told her med-student boyfriend over lunch at Yee's Restaurant. "I didn't get all of what she was saying, but she calls me from Iowa at seven A.M. and insists on knowing where he is—I think he was downstairs eating breakfast at the time. And then she doesn't want to leave a message, or even let him know she called—"

It was the calm after the storm. And before the storm to come.

"Sir, we're moving in." Attorney General Molinsky briefed his boss over the phone, stressing, "I've got a hunch it's now or never."

The governor appeared hesitant. "I assume you've obtained the proper warrants. And mobilized the manpower you'll need—"

"Done. I have the warrants in my hand," the AG replied. On his desk was a lengthy affidavit from Gloria Stiehl, which had put to rest the issue of probable cause. "The State Police and the State Marshal's office are on alert as we speak."

Eckhardt paused but a moment before giving the order: "Let's roll."

Within the hour, an army of uniformed officers descended on campus. From the administration building, state marshals seized boxfuls of documents and videotapes while four police vans stood guard outside. The building's workers, cowed by this display of force, watched in silence as the marshals went about their task.

On Langston Road, University Police headquarters was quickly secured, yielding additional evidence. And further north, on Raleigh Street, another cordon of state vehicles surrounded the president's mansion.

The story unfolded quickly. Citing various unnamed sources, the media laid bare the details of Molinsky's investigation, and of Shenford's illegal activities. The ill-gotten real estate profits; the campaign preparations preceding Jim Camp's demise; the existence of videotape evidence as to all counts.

On Franklin Street, chaos reigned. Steve Patrick, now acting president, worked to hold things together, without success. The Shenford machine was a wreck, his own indictment a foregone conclusion.

Outside, demonstrators gleefully waved signs, shouting "Jail to the Chief." START SINGING, FATSO read one message taped to the building's front doors.

From *Forbidden Knowledge* (Special Edition, Spring 1985), p. 4:

"YOU JUST TAKE CARE OF THAT FERRIS"

By Howard Cummings

In an irony reminiscent of the Watergate affair, Fortin Shenford's downfall stemmed from his practice of recording office conversations on videotape. Forbidden Knowledge has obtained a transcript of one such recording, allegedly from a meeting with Met U. Police chief James Fullerton and then-executive vice president Steven Patrick on the morning of March 16, following a fatal traffic accident on campus. During the meeting, the three reportedly agreed to falsify Breathalyzer test results obtained from faculty member and longtime Shenford critic Willard Ferris in connection with the accident, in order to frame the latter on vehicular homicide charges. The most damning excerpts:

CHIEF FULLERTON: Okay. Now these readings taken (from Ferris) at the scene indicate a blood-alcohol level of .07 (percent). This is not considered legally under the influence.

SHENFORD: What about a lesser charge? Is there anything else that may be viable?

F: As far as impairment goes, it's an all-or-nothing proposition. A driver is either under the influence or he isn't. Even a charge of reckless driving would be iffy, from what I can see.

S: So, in order to establish the drunk-driving element (of the offense), we would have to produce a reading of at least .10.

PATRICK: Right. That's what he's saying.

F: It could easily be done. We do it every year, for those public service presentations on drunk driving at the (Student) Union. You add alcohol to the machine beforehand, and have somebody blow in.

S: Well, that sounds simple enough. Nothing difficult about that, right?

F: No, sir.

P: Like he said, it's the only way. If we want to make this (charge) stick.

S: Then I leave it to you, gentlemen. You just take care of that nitwit Ferris…

On the afternoon of April third, Steve Patrick calmly entered his office and took a .38-caliber pistol from the desk drawer. The desk itself free of personal mementos—there was no family to be considered, and he felt no bitterness or remorse.

Without hesitation he slipped the barrel into his mouth, the steel cold and oily against his teeth.

Death before dishonor, he silently vowed. There was no fear, but a sense of pride in his years of faithful service.

Death before dishonor, Patrick repeated to himself. Then closed his eyes and squeezed the trigger.

The two men emerged from the stairwell on the hospital's third floor, where administrator Harvey Kembrick waited. Both wore dark trenchcoats, their features hidden behind sunglasses and wide-brimmed fedoras. It was exactly 1 A.M.

Wordlessly the two followed Kembrick through the sleeping corridor to Room 312, where a security guard stood watch. As they approached, the officer straightened, and without knocking opened the door to the private room. Kembrick nodded to his guests, then quickly departed, the door closing behind him.

"Good evening, General." Fortin Shenford sat up in bed, his back against the partly-elevated mattress, as Molinsky revealed himself. "Your Excellency." He invoked the governor's formal title—a relic from Colonial times—as Eckhardt shed his accoutrements, resentful of this cloak-and-dagger game.

"Have you come to make the arrest yourself?" Shenford appeared unfazed by this bizarre intrusion, though his wounds had taken their toll. To his guests he looked frail and thin, a shadow of his former self.

"No, Fortin," Molinsky carefully replied. "But this is an official investigation, and we would like a word with you."

"An official investigation? Skulking around hospital corridors in the middle of the night, hiding behind those ridiculous getups?" The president half-smiled, mocking this transparent charade. "And why are you here, Governor?"

Eckhardt looked back at him, unflinching. "We'll ask the questions, Fortin," he said stonily.

"Please do. I'll be glad to assist you if I can." Molinsky almost had to admire him.

Dispassionately, the AG reconstructed the tangled web which Shenford had woven over time. Secret Pen numbers. Hidden accounts in Zurich and Liechtenstein. Wiretap transcripts stretching back fifteen years. And the conspiracy to frame Willard Ferris.

Molinsky then threw his cards on the table. "The camera doesn't lie, Fortin."

Shenford remained poised. "Surely that statement cuts both ways, gentlemen," he said quietly. "Which brings us to why you're really here."

Forced to play along, Molinsky asked: "What are you driving at, Fortin?"

"I believe you know, sir. It seems your boss is quite the ladies' man." Shenford turned, and smiled thinly at Eckhardt. "I wouldn't have believed it myself—but as you say, the camera is an impartial witness."

The governor involuntarily flushed. "Fortin, that tape will never again see the light of day!"

"I assumed you'd find it when you burglarized my office. Though it isn't germane to your case, and has gone curiously unmentioned among the slanderous stories your surrogates have leaked to the press. Thankfully, I had the foresight to make copies."

Molinsky's gruff manner wavered for an instant. "Copies—plural?"

"Yes. All safely locked away in storage, I'm afraid." Shenford sought to force the advantage. "I forget the exact number," he said ominously.

"Forget about blackmail, Fortin." Eckhardt shook his head, unblinking. "We've had this discussion before. I will not intervene in the state's case."

Unwilling to accept defeat, Shenford gathered himself for a last stand.

"You know you could never hold me," he warned. "I'd be out on my own recognizance in a minute. And then every media outlet in New England would have a copy of that tape before you could say 'Fanny Hill.'"

"I'm afraid not, Fortin," Molinsky quickly replied. "Even bail would be out of the question. You have no family in-state. You have substantial assets hidden abroad. And you're looking at what for a man your age would effectively be a life sentence." He paused before adding, "It's obvious you have every incentive to flee."

Molinsky leaned over the bed and spoke very slowly, the words blunt and unsparing. "Read my lips, Fortin: *You lose.* It's over. You're finished."

The AG's implacable tone had its effect. Speechless for the first time in years, Shenford averted his eyes.

"You sons of bitches," he murmured at last. "To smear a man's good name, you apply all the resources of this pissant little state. This genetic waste dump, which has produced no persons of consequence..." To his visitors, it sounded quite feeble.

"The State looks forward to seeing you in court, Doctor." Molinsky brought the meeting to a close. Eckhardt stood, nodded to his subordinate, and together they left the room.

"...WGLN-650 News time is seven o'clock. (*beep*) Good morning. In Glanbury, it's clear and cool, 45 degrees. In the news at this hour, Fortin Shenford has resigned as president of Metropolitan University..."

"No way!" Frank Sorenson sat up in bed, wide-eyed, focused on Chug's clock-radio. His roommate was awake and dressed, his attention equally riveted.

"What do you mean, 'No way'? It's obvious they had him dead to rights." But Frank remained silent as the announcer went on.

"In a statement released through Met's Department of Public Affairs, Shenford said that he had been hounded from office by what he termed 'the sensationalism of a hostile media.' State Attorney General Michael Molinsky has scheduled a news conference for later this morning, when he is expected to announce Shenford's indictment on multiple charges, following a grand jury investigation. The U.S. Attorney's office in Bristol is also reportedly looking into the case…"

"That means federal charges too," Chug said.

"And—this just in—Glanbury Memorial Hospital reports that Shenford has left the facility, his present whereabouts unknown. The 63-year-old Shenford was scheduled to be released today from the hospital, where he had been recovering from gunshot wounds sustained in an assault two weeks ago. There are unconfirmed reports that the former university head has left the country…"

"No way!" both roommates simultaneously yelled.

For a minute neither of them spoke; then Frank again found his voice.

"I thought he'd have the balls to stay and fight this," he said, disappointed.

In the end, fifteen of the president's minions were indicted for their complicity in Shenford's schemes. Convicted of election law offenses, Tom Becker would forfeit his lobbyist's credentials; and Bill Waycross his position at Reigate College.

Charged with conspiracy and illegal wiretapping were two presidential staffers, along with seven current and former members of the University Police. Including Chief Fullerton, who would serve eighteen months in State Prison.

From top to bottom, the housecleaning had begun.

Elizabeth Kerr answered the phone as her live-in graduate-student daughter came running downstairs, dressed in cyclist's gear.

"If that's Eileen, tell her I said, 'What's shakin'?'" Liz paused in the front hall before heading out the door, her sunset-pink bob peering from under her helmet.

Her mother frowned at the young woman's excessive familiarity. Since leaving the dean's post, she'd in fact had no communion with her former faculty colleagues. At forty-seven, her job prospects were murky at best, with retirement no option.

"Dean Kerr?" A man's voice, nasal, high-pitched, vaguely familiar.

"Not lately," she replied.

"This is Ken Wasserstein calling." A small, dapper, round-faced man, Kerr remembered from Met functions past. And by reputation, one of the few independent-minded Overseers.

She waited for him to proceed. "As you can guess, there have been some changes on the board. As its newly-elected chairman, I speak for all of our members. It is our hope that you'll reconsider your decision to leave the university."

Kerr felt suddenly lighter, as if an oppressive weight had been shed. And yet she knew to avoid excessive eagerness.

"Mr. Wasserstein, you're very kind," she said guardedly. "Though under the circumstances, if I were to stay on as dean—"

"That actually isn't what we had in mind." The Overseer then paused.

Eyebrows arched, she replied: "I'm sorry—I don't quite understand."

"Dean Kerr, on behalf of the Overseers, I am calling to offer you the presidency of Metropolitan."

It was early evening when Elizabeth Kerr entered the administration building, accompanied by her husband, daughter and son-in-law. The party proceeded upstairs to the fourth-floor boardroom, where members of the Executive Committee waited.

Since Wasserstein's phone call, twenty-six hours had elapsed. The day had been one of intense negotiation, and discussion of her role as the new University chief. Yet the board had insisted on an immediate inaugural.

"Can we do this right away?" Wasserstein had urged. "Someone desperately needs to take charge now."

Entering the room, she approached the area where Wasserstein stood surrounded by his colleagues. In his hands were a symbolic brass key to the president's office, and a copy of Met's original charter.

There were perfunctory nods as she introduced her family to the Overseers. By fall, most of the Committee's members would be replaced, the AG's threat of a civil suit appeased only by the mass resignation of Shenford's former cronies.

The chairman quickly got down to business. "Dean Kerr, are you ready to assume the office of president?"

"I am." Privately, debating the wisdom of her acceptance. Healing Met's wounds would be at once a delicate and arduous task, with the institution's long-term viability at stake.

At 7:15 P.M., Elizabeth Kerr accepted the regalia of office as Metropolitan's sixth president. Then, silently, turned to embrace her loved ones.

"Congratulations, Madam President," Wasserstein said soberly.

From "Downfall of a Dictator" (*Time* cover story, April 19, 1985):

> For more than two decades, Fortin Shenford personified Metropolitan University. Despite a management style described by one faculty opponent as "an iron fist in a spiked cestus," most Glanburyites viewed the iconoclastic college president as the driving force behind the school's rise to preeminence. But on campus, there had always been furtive whisperings about the dark side of Shenford's ambitious leadership. For years rumors had circulated of shady financial dealings; of intimidation and harassment of faculty dissidents; and systematic abuse of power. An investigation concluded last week by a state grand jury revealed—in chilling detail—that the truth was worse than Shenford's harshest critics had speculated...

Excerpt from "Fortin the Terrible" (*Newsweek*, April 19, 1985):

> ...Elizabeth Kerr, Shenford's hastily-chosen successor and former dean of the School of Law, stressed the need for reconciliation, proclaiming an end to "the toxic culture of autocratic misrule." But overall, reaction to Shenford's exit was curiously subdued. Shenford's resignation, even his indictment and subsequent flight from the country were an emotional anticlimax to the lurid tale that had unfolded in recent weeks.
>
> "There is no satisfaction whatsoever in this," University Overseer Jacob Klein, a longtime Shenford antagonist, said. "I'd waited years for this, and there is no pleasure in it at all. When I think of the damage he's done to this institution's name, I am simply heartsick."

Liberal student activist Brandon Clark, who had clashed frequently with the Shenford administration, posted a message of deliverance in the window of his dorm room: DING DONG, THE WITCH IS DEAD. The school's student newspaper, the *Guardian*, ran a somewhat restrained editorial postmortem under the heading "Sic Semper Tyrannis."

"When I heard that he had been shot," said one instructor who requested anonymity, "my initial reaction was, I hoped that he would die. God forgive me, but I truly hoped that he would die... To me, the idea of that man vying for national office was truly frightening." Somewhat less viscerally, a colleague added: "It's true that Fortin Shenford improved Metropolitan's standing in many respects, but that is no different from acknowledging that Mussolini made the trains run on time. In the end, he has left it under a dark cloud of disgrace, from which it will only emerge over time, if at all."

Perhaps the most fitting epitaph of all, though, came from Eileen Bridge, a 12-year veteran of the Law School faculty. "When you think of Fortin Shenford, you have to mourn the tragic waste of potential," Bridge said. "He was an enormously brilliant and gifted man, with a mind that might have guided the destiny of nations. Undoubtedly he might have achieved greatness—had he not been such a wretched human being..."

For the seniors, the spring's cataclysmic events could not cloud the fact that the end was near.

At one point, it was rumored that Commencement exercises would be cancelled. A report President Kerr quickly scotched, affirming that the ceremonies would proceed as scheduled, with Secretary of Defense Caspar Weinberger to deliver the main address.

"Now more than ever, it is essential that we maintain continuity," the president stated.

Yet continuity was the furthest thing from the seniors' minds. For as they were all aware, the halcyon days of college life would soon be a memory.

Most would enter the working world, others seeking refuge in graduate studies. Yet for all, the advent of May signaled the closing of a chapter. A farewell to the boundless freedom they would never again experience.

Not the least anxious of them could be observed wandering the campus on the afternoon of May 9.

Strolling the Boulevard on that eventful summerlike day, Marcus Pullman felt neither joy nor sorrow, but a dull sense of finality. Twenty-four hours ago he'd completed his last exam, and it was all over but the waiting.

He had spent the day walking idly about, revisiting various historical markers of his undergraduate life. The Engineering School, site of his freshman academic follies. The Three Jokers Pub, where the guys had taken him last year for his twenty-first birthday. (Bowing to pressure, Marcus had consumed two Long Island iced teas, and wound up puking-drunk for what would be the second and final time in his life.) The Galaga machine on which the Captain had broken the world record in another era, now unplugged and gathering dust in a corner of the Union gameroom.

Approaching Fred's Diner, he decided to grab a late lunch. It was now mid-afternoon, the restaurant nearly deserted.

"Hey, how's it going, Chief?" Fred Sheehan smiled warmly behind the counter. Despite his genial welcoming grin, the proprietor's face looked haggard, and Marcus noticed suddenly how Sheehan's hair had grayed in the past four years.

"Oh, not too bad, I guess. How's it with you?"

"Ah, you know how it is...SSDD." Sheehan shrugged. He would retire to Orlando a year later, after banking his second million.

Marcus ordered a cheeseburger and a Mountain Dew. Seating himself at a corner booth, he did not readily perceive the familiar figure nearby.

"Hey," Adam Conway said softly, turning from the Punch-Out machine. Marcus rose, then hastened to greet his ex-dormmate. "Just in time. Grab yourself a ringside seat." Adam dropped two quarters into the slot. The screen then heralded his first opponent, a 112-pound weakling named Glass Joe.

"I can beat this guy without looking, watch." Adam turned his back to the game and felt for the controls. Seconds later, an uppercut sent Joe down for an eight-count, the right hook finishing him.

"Freakin' showoff!" Sheehan yelled over the counter. Adam smiled back at him.

Turning to face the screen, Adam fought his way up through the ranks. Dispatching four more rivals before succumbing to the champion, the fearsome Mr. Sandman, in a title bout.

"I've won the title six or eight times on this thing." Adam watched indifferently while his man was counted out. "It's the only time they show your guy's face."

"What does he look like?" Marcus asked, not really interested.

"He looks like a total lunkhead." Adam answered without elaboration. Declining a rematch, he ordered a drink and a burger for himself, joined Marcus at his booth. In the background, the soft strains of *We Are the World* began playing on the jukebox.

"This stuff blows." Adam put down his can of New Coke, dissatisfied. "They never should have changed it." But Marcus sensed something more was on his mind.

"So what's going down at The Apartment these days?"

"Ah, the usual stuff." Adam paused before adding: "Anyway, I won't be there much longer."

"What do you mean?" Marcus glanced up from his tray.

"I mean, I'm moving out the first of June. So I was thinking, if you need a place to stay this summer..."

"Yeah, I guess I do." Marcus briefly considered. "I mean, I *could* go home, but I'd rather not, if you know what I'm saying. Then I'll have to find a place for September, when grad school starts..."

"You can do both. I'm not coming back in September either. Next year, I'll be taking classes at SUNY—the Buffalo campus is just ten minutes from my house."

"Oh," Marcus answered in monosyllabic surprise. And added, somewhat awkwardly, "I'm sorry to hear that."

Adam shrugged. "What can you do? This place is just too damned expensive."

Eventually the two began to discuss terms.

"The rent's two-fifty a month," Adam said. "That includes water and electricity. But the gas is no big deal, and you won't need heat in the summertime."

"You don't have air conditioning, do you?" Marcus remembered the other tenants' gripes about Adam hogging the bathtub on hot days.

"Nope. You'll have to get your own fan."

"That's no problem. Anyhow, two-fifty a month is fine with me. I doubt I'll find anything cheaper in this town." Yet there was one nagging question on Marcus's mind.

He hesitated, then asked, "Are you sure this is okay with everyone?"

"Don't worry, it'll be cool." Adam doubted the others would mind. His dorkiness notwithstanding, Marcus could likely be counted on to pay his share of the rent on time.

"When do you have to be out of your room by?" Adam inquired.

"Well you know, graduation's a week from tomorrow. Then I have to hand in my keys at noon the next day."

"We'll let you sleep on the couch for free until the first, how does that sound?"

"Sounds good to me," Marcus advised.

"Great, then—it's a deal." Adam thrust his hand across the table. Marcus shook it, and the bargain was sealed.

"Oh, and make sure you come by Saturday night," Adam said. "We're having a going-away party for Rosemary, so don't make any plans."

A ball of lead suddenly formed in Marcus's chest. "What do you mean, 'a going-away party'?" he asked. "She's coming back next year, isn't she?"

"Nah. Her father got transferred to Hawaii, and she'll be going to school there. They're leaving Virginia next month.

"You didn't know about that?" Adam frowned, mildly surprised. But he was talking to empty space. Marcus was gone.

***

For once, Marcus had thrown caution to the wind. He'd put himself a thousand dollars in hock; yet nothing could have been further from his mind as he sprinted toward the dorm like a madman, indifferent to the stares of fellow pedestrians.

This whole idea was insane, he thought, his lungs on fire, his breath coming in short, painful stabs. And yet he knew there was no other way.

Reaching the Hilton Way intersection, he practically leaped across the road, narrowly avoiding an oncoming car. The angry horn blast followed him as he raced for Sterling's front door...and then stopped short, aware that he would have to be signed in.

He entered the vestibule, grabbed the house phone (still free, thank God for small favors) and dialed Brandon's room. No one there. Annoyed, he then tried Frank and Chug's. Again no answer.

Marcus gave a yell of frustration. Desperate, he searched his memory for names and numbers, but nothing else clicked. Except...

Punching in her number, he listened in agony as it rang six times. Of course she wasn't there, he thought bitterly. Not now, when it mattered—Oh god, what if she'd left early—?

"Hello?" answered the familiar vibrant voice. Not at all winded, though he knew she'd raced to pick up the phone.

"Rosemary, this is Marcus. I'm downstairs in the lobby. Could you sign me in? I—I need to talk to you. About something," he added nervously.

"Sure, Marcus. I'll be right down." They exchanged goodbyes.

Past the point of no return, he waited, unmoving. Peripherally surveying the lobby traffic, absurdly convinced she wouldn't show.

Rosemary waved when she saw him, before rounding the concrete partition in the front hall. She wore jeans and a red football jersey, heedlessly untucked. Marcus echoed her greeting softly, and fiddled with his fingernails as she signed him in.

Mercifully she did not act curious, making light conversation as they entered the dorm. He followed her up the stairs, heart pounding, one hand smoothing his disheveled hair.

"El-roy!" a familiar voice called as they passed the fourth-floor lounge.

Still slightly winded, Marcus turned toward the voice. Through the open door Wally Hall, seated behind a card table, smiled broadly. Joined by Troll Philbrick, in green dress shirt and salmon-pink tie; and a half-dozen others on study break, hunched over a game of Trivial Pursuit.

"We decided to call in sick at work today." Smiling, Wally explained, "You gotta do it every so often. All work and no play, you know."

"Marcus Elroy Pullman!" Troll hailed him in a carnival barker's shout: "The man!—The doking legend!..."

"I'll be back later—I gotta talk to him." Rosemary touched her guest lightly on the shoulder, to insinuating moans from her neighbors.

"Don't close that door!" Megan's light jest followed them down the hallway to the women's single.

But her door did close, and the two were alone at last.

"So what's up?" She sat down on the bed casually, facing him as he perched sideways on the desk chair.

Marcus opened his mouth to speak, faltered, then abruptly reached for her hand. "Oh," she said in surprise, not resisting.

"Rosemary," he managed. "Listen, I—I've been meaning to say…"

Within the corridor, time stopped dead. The couple's friends stood frozen in shock, a tableau of wax figures, unable—unwilling—to grasp what they had heard.

"What—? How—?" Wally's voice failed him for the first time in years.

"Marcus and I have decided to get married." Rosemary repeated this

353

in a matter-of-fact way. Her hands crossed behind her back, the diamond engagement ring hidden from view.

Standing beside her, Marcus looked away, as if he were no part of this development.

"You know, they've been in there over an hour," Hall had speculated mere moments ago, before curiosity impelled the Mutants to abandon their game. "You don't think they might be—"

"Bite your tongue—that's just sickening!" Troll said. Stealing quietly from the lounge, they'd arrived as Rosemary's door swung open.

Her neighbors, paralyzed with stupefaction, stood silent, unbelieving, before Megan broke the spell.

"*Ohhhh,* congratulations—I'm so happy for you two!" She ran to embrace the unlikely pair. As if a switch had been thrown, the others joined in, surrounding them in a flurry of hugs, kisses, handshakes and high-threes.

"*Pile on!*" Troll suddenly roared.

Marcus backed into his fiancée's room and collapsed on the bed. Troll covered him first, then Wally, Brandon and Chug. He was conscious of Philbrick's tie pressed against his nose, while the boys grunted and made mock thrusts.

"Okay, that's enough." Rosemary intervened as the body count reached ten, her bedsprings slowly sighing in relief as the Mutants unpiled themselves.

"Are you all right?" She looked down at Marcus, who sat up on the bed, then groaned softly before mustering a dry laugh.

"Never better," he sighed.

Later, the celebration at an end, the speculation and second-guessing began.

"But they never even went out…"

"Where does it say you have to date first?"

"Could it be that they've had a thing going all this time?"

"I still can't believe it. I mean, it just doesn't compute…"

Rosemary, however, had no second thoughts. The decision had been made, and there was no going back.

At first she'd thought his proposal an elaborate joke, and had playfully punched his arm in response. But the pressure on her hand tightened, and she perceived the almost-frighteningly solemn expression on his face.

I love you, he had said. I need you. Nothing in this life would have meaning without you. I promise you, you won't regret it, ever…

You're serious. You really mean it, she'd said wonderingly. A billion questions flooding her mind at once.

For an hour he poured it on, stressing how much she meant to him, how well they got along, how perfect they'd be together. Rosemary listened in a daze, her thoughts a swirling maelstrom of confusion.

Why me? Why now? she wondered. How long have you felt this way? This is nuts, he's a good friend—a dear friend, not a husband…

But she had been asked a question. Suddenly forcing a decision for which she was entirely unprepared. Okay, what *would* I want in a husband, Rosemary thought.

Well, he would have to respect me for who I am. And he would have to be somebody I could depend on. Someone sincere and thoughtful and kind. And if you're going to spend the rest of your life with someone, it should really be someone whose company you enjoy.

She looked into his eyes, into those owlish features she'd always found cute in a disarming way. She remembered the parties, the hockey games, the fun times they'd shared. She thought fleetingly how intersexual relations had lapsed into a power struggle, the notion of completely trusting another human being having largely gone by the wayside.

And suddenly there was but one possible answer.

After she had accepted, her eyes wet with tears, the newly-betrothed couple embraced for the first time.

Commencement Day—Friday, May 17, 1985—dawned clear and warm. Parents and guests began arriving early on campus, with parking space at a premium through early evening.

Precisely at 9 A.M.—two hours before the ceremony—Rob Moreland's clock-radio alarm went off. Rob moaned in protest, and with a string of curses groped for the alarm and shut it off, the sunlight flooding his upstairs room at Zeta House.

Ah, blow it off, he thought hazily, still half slumbering. But of course he wouldn't.

Ninety minutes later, the members of the senior class marched from Phillips Gym in a sea of rented green gowns and black mortarboards, Met's eleven schools and colleges represented in turn. Led by their chosen student marshals, they left the building in two columns, to begin the traditional procession down Callender Drive.

"I can't believe they charged me fifty bucks for this outfit," one Arts and Sciences graduate remarked to his neighbor, his gold-yellow tassel hung prematurely on the left side.

"More like fifty *thousand* bucks," the other retorted, unimpressed.

"Hey, look—the Duke's directing traffic." Dave Logan, completing his five-year plan, turned toward the Lott Avenue intersection, where a harried Stanley Boston waved a pair of orange signal flags. Before him Beth Brown, graduating *cum laude*, remarked that, "They must have hired him just for the day.

"Hey, Duuuke!" she shouted raucously, thinking of the night he'd spent in the Hall. The denim-jacketed vagrant nodded tenuously and returned to his task.

The seniors marched beyond Hale Auditorium and the University boathouse, to a clearing on the river's edge. A verdant expanse, roped off for the occasion, with a speaker's platform and aluminum bleachers in place. The graduates sat on metal folding chairs facing the platform, several mortarboards with messages lettered in masking tape.

THANKS MOM AND DAD, read one. FOR HIRE, another proclaimed. And from the Engineering section, that perennial favorite BEAM ME UP.

The day's ceremonies began with an invocation by Bishop William O'Toole of Glanbury, recipient of an honorary doctorate in Humane Letters. President Kerr then delivered her brief welcoming remarks, before turning over the platform to this year's student speaker.

The speaker, chosen by the Office of Academic Affairs, was Sanjay Motwani of the College of Arts and Sciences. Who in flawless English encouraged his audience to explore cross-cultural vistas, humorously citing his own experience in coming to America.

His classmates and their guests applauded warmly in response. Led by Drs. Haresh and Rashmi Motwani, who had flown seven thousand miles to witness their son's glory.

The annual Founder's Awards for Excellence in Teaching garnered polite applause. (Faculty honorees this year included Willard Ferris, recognized posthumously with a special award.) The four honorary degree recipients were then cited; joining Weinberger and Bishop O'Toole were Carol Naismith, noted New England historian; and Gloria Stiehl, retiring after twenty-seven years as executive secretary to Metropolitan's presidents.

Weinberger's address was nearly anticlimactic. To applause

unmarred by protests or catcalls, the Secretary rendered an upbeat homily on the preservation of ideals in a changing world. His remarks were delivered without notes, the audience of twelve thousand outwardly unanimous in its approval.

By tradition, the deans of the various schools rose to present their graduating classes to the president. Whereupon Kerr bade them receive their degrees, *en masse*, "with all of the rights and privileges thereof."

Following the benediction by Bishop O'Toole, a chorus of singers struck up Met's Alma Mater—a trite turn-of-the-century piece with the standard hail-to-thees and pledges of eternal troth. To the unfamiliar strains of this anthem, the graduates stood in celebration as the platform party recessed.

Marcus and his fiancée had joined his parents at Yee's Restaurant for a lunch of lo mein and fried rice. Walden and Marcia Pullman, predictably, had been floored by the news of their son's engagement, and were less than supportive; his mother in particular had disapproved of the girl's background.

Yet as they talked, Rosemary and Walden discovered their mutual fondness for football and fishing. And, wonder of wonders, Marcia was simply enamored by Rosemary's refreshingly guileless manner. Though the elder Pullmans still struggled with the concept of Marcus *getting married...*

While Rosemary charmed his parents, Marcus said little. Ashamed at his earlier design to keep the wedding plans under wraps, for fear of losing their financial support.

Diplomas were awarded in the afternoon, at separate school convocations. These ceremonies were chiefly indoor events; the Schools of Journalism and Law, each with sufficient lawn space for an outdoor gathering, were the exceptions.

Later, at day's end, the seniors left to celebrate with family and friends. By tomorrow the last of them would leave campus, launched on three thousand separate paths.

"Yo Rob, what happened to that Cheryl chick? I don't see her around lately."

Fraternity vice-president Brian Davies had joined the other members of Zeta Pi's graduating class for a last chowdown at Fred's, an order of sirloin tips on his plate. The cost of this meal, Rob Moreland noted, was still just $5.45, up slightly from freshman year.

"I dumped her," he answered evenly. "We had this huge fight. She wanted the whole church-wedding thing, and I didn't want to get married."

"Smart man." The blue-eyed coxswain nodded sagely before adding, "Sorry if you're feeling bummed."

Insouciantly, Rob shrugged. Weeks ago, Cheryl had caught him with one of the Little Sisters at Zeta House, and this time all of his charms were unable to woo her back.

But this was past history now. Come fall, he'd start a plum gig with GenDyne in Connecticut, at forty bills annually. And in between, a righteous summer of partying, surfing and jumping some serious babes.

"Life is good." Smiling, he raised his extra large Pepsi Free in toast. The others, admiring his resilience, joined in and repeated his words.

This does not look like a bride's room at all, Rosemary inwardly noted, her attendants struggling to assist with her train while music from a borrowed organ played downstairs in the living room. Not at all.

Since she'd left for college, the room hadn't changed. In fact it looked much the way her old room in Cherry Point had, when Paul Fink would come over to listen to *Boogie Fever* or do some Mad-Libs.

The walls nearest the bed were decorated with pennants—New York Knicks, Cincinnati Reds, Baltimore Colts. And on the shelves, fronting rows of Scholastic Books, pictures of football stars, mounted in plastic frames—Bob Griese, O.J., Bert Jones.

As Megan Brunelle and Cousin Felicia Porter wrestled with the bridal train, her mother adjusted Rosemary's veil, almost physically bursting with emotion. The dress was the one in which Nancy Porter herself had wed, in February of 1964. Her daughter came along ten months later, on the eve of Pearl Harbor Day.

Through the window, the late-morning sun reflected brightly from the Little League trophies atop the bookcase. Gazing upon them, Rosemary was taken back to another June Saturday, when she was twelve. Bottom of the fifth inning, one out, Jason Krause on first, her Cubs team leading by one. She could still see the 1-2 pitch coming, and hear the wholly satisfying *crack* as the metal bat connected solidly. She'd stopped at first base to make sure it was *really* going over this time, then leaped with her arms in the air as the ball cleared the right-field fence and disappeared beyond a row of shrubs. (Her brother, who was working the scoreboard, had chased it down without success while Rosemary ran merrily around the bases.) She had stroked two more in the season's final game, but nothing equaled the thrill of her first home run.

The memories came flooding back all at once. Throwing mop-handle javelins in the front yard with Allan Jenkins during the Montreal Olympics. (Scream, Rosemary had insisted. It'll make it go farther.) For a few rounds they'd tried this approach, before Mark Payne, the aptly-named class pest, rode up on his bike. The Payne kid had made some crack about mental derangement, and they'd chased him halfway down the block.

Street football. Rush on five-elephant. The 50-millimeter shell episode. Stories of old ladies living in shacks in the woods behind Seven-Eleven who would pop out with a twelve-gauge if you came too close. Taping Elton John and Kikki Dee's *Don't Go Breaking My Heart* off the Midnight Special for Paul; never understanding why Mom wouldn't let Paul stay over. Twice accompanying Allan on his paper route "'cause it's *fun* riding around at four or five o'clock in the morning."

She thought of the grief she'd caused her mother in the past, from the times Mrs. Porter had been summoned to fetch her daughter from the principal's office to the incident yesterday when Marcus walked in on his bride as she was modeling her gown, her mother darting in front of her yelling portentously about bad luck. ("Oh Mom, that's so much bull!" Rosemary had laughed.) But her mother's eyes indicated all was forgiven.

On the dresser, a vanity mirror and hair dryer were the only clues that a teenaged girl had slept here. No makeup. (The nearest thing was an ancient tube of OxyWash that had long since petrified.) And on the flat wooden surface, two faded Wacky Package stickers. The desk featured a world globe, an autographed photo of Shaun Cassidy *circa* 1978, and a kids' typewriter on which Paul had defiantly written a letter to the world champion Steelers, proclaiming MIAMI DOLPHINS IS THE BEST!

Downstairs in the living room, the familiar staccato notes of the Wedding March began.

"You're on, Rosemary," Mrs. Porter said with a final hug. Composing herself, her mother added, "You've got a fine young man. Don't keep him waiting."

The distaff side of the wedding party lined up in order. Nancy Porter then opened the room door, and discovered the tinfoil star Bill had hung on the outside.

"I'll kill him," Rosemary said, utterly without conviction. The others smiled briefly before beginning the procession downstairs.

Leaving the room, Rosemary looked back at her open closet, where an old catcher's mitt lay alongside her ABA basketball—the red-white-and-blue one her father had said would become a collector's item one day...

Postscriptum: The Last House Party
August 29, 1986

"So where will you all go?"

"Different places. Joanne and I are renting a house on Dudley Street; Logan and Garrett are getting an apartment in town; and Philbrick found a place in Kent, close to where he works…"

"Too bad everybody's moving out. I'm gonna miss this place."

"…and Kaplan's buying a frigging *house*, can you believe it?"

"Stu and Josh scored a new apartment on the West Side. Rosemary and Marcus are moving to Callender Drive for his last year of grad school, and Jay's headed to Northeastern to get his MBA. I think that about covers it…"

"Speaking of grad school, you know Chug's starting on his Master's this year…"

"Yeah, I kind of lucked out. I got a personal recommendation from Professor Yamada, the head of the English Department. Then when I interviewed with Dean McEachern, he said it was the best turnaround he'd seen so far. I finished with a 3.01 cum, but kept a 3.75 average the last two years."

"So Pete, how was the bar exam?"

"A real ballbuster. Two days, six hours each. I won't even know until October if I passed."

"Ah, I'm sure you did all right."

"Just in case, I intend to make as much as possible at Craig and Marsh between now and then."

"I hear Marcus already has a job lined up with Bradley and Stearns in Hartford when he graduates next year."

"Is that so? My, how our little Elroy has grown up..."

"Between you and me, Rosemary really knows how to relax a guy a half-hour before an interview..."

"Okay, time out. I'm not sure I want to hear this."

"Where did you guys go on your honeymoon again?"

"Well, his folks sent us on a trip to Orlando. But not right away. After the ceremony we just spent the weekend at the Days Inn, then moved into The Apartment and set up housekeeping—if you want to call it that."

"...Basically what we did was, we snuck Rosemary in as a fifth roommate. It cut everybody's rent by fifty bucks a month, so that was cool..."

"To be honest, I'm still not sure how I managed to scrape by. But living in The Apartment was a lot cheaper than paying room and board, and that was a big help..."

"Okay, I'll bite. What has feathers and glows in the dark?"

"I wouldn't advise it; it's Chicken Kiev."

"...Well no, I don't remember all the specific charges. Just a lot of mumbo-jumbo about fraud and illegal wiretapping and election law violations. And of course, income tax evasion. That's how they finally got Al Capone."

"Supposedly they think Shenford's somewhere in Europe now."

"With all those charges, he'll be in jail for life if they ever catch him."

"...And you know Beth had a job offer from Senator Swinton's office, but she turned it down. She said she'd rather be a real journalist than some P.R. flunky."

"Hey, why do they call you N.H., anyway? What does it stand for?"

"...That whole week, all the girls in my department could talk about was how ugly the Princess was. If you ask me, she's way better looking than most of them..."

"Whoa, when did *you* stop smoking pot?"

"What can I say? Nancy Reagan really opened my eyes."

"...After that, I don't remember anything until I woke up next to a tree on the Boulevard..."

"All right, one last time. Here we go, ready? One, two, three... *Wax Museuumm!*"

"Okay."

"Yeah, I read Miss Manners sometimes. She has a lot more sense than you might think."

"I'm telling you, Roger Clemens is simply amazing. This year, he seemed to come out of nowhere..."

"That was the missing ingredient for the Sox. Quality pitching is the one thing they've always lacked."

"They're going all the way this year. I can feel it."

"...Megan's actually graduating in a few weeks. She finished her courses this summer, and next month she'll be starting at Mercy General in Allentown..."

"Well, technically there won't be a ceremony; they'll just mail me my diploma. But they let me march with everybody else at Commencement in May..."

"You know Brandon also graduated this year. And Rosemary, and Debbie Grafton..."

"Did you know that college-educated women who are still single at age 25 have only a 50 percent chance of ever getting married?"

"...Then again, whoever thought we'd see the Dow break 1800? I mean, that's out of control."

"So this is it, then. No more House, no more Apartment…"

"Face it, Halley's Comet was a major disappointment this time. But of course, there's always 2061…"

"Well, we'll see you around."

"Give us a call for Homecoming weekend."

"You have my number, so whenever you're in town…"

"Hey, what do you know? This time we got out before the cops showed up."

"Seriously, stop by anytime."

"…and take care of yourself."

"Goodbye."

III

Messages from
the Real World

STATE BOARD OF BAR EXAMINERS

Supreme Court Building
1 Melville Square
Bristol, _____ 02980

October 3, 1986

Mr. Peter Edward Garrett
35 Ball St. Apt. 2
Glanbury, _____ 02967

Dear Mr. Garrett:

We are pleased to inform you that you have passed the July 1986 bar examination, and have qualified in all respects for admission to the practice of law within this jurisdiction.

Please be advised that induction ceremonies for newly-admitted attorneys have been scheduled for Friday, October 24, 1986 at 2:00 P.M., in Room 203 of the Supreme Court Building. The oath will be administered by Chief Justice William Bray. A wine and cheese reception will follow.

We congratulate you on your success, and wish you the best in your future career.

Very truly yours,

Anthony F. Griswold
Chairman

R. Spencer
10 Halsey St.
E. Lyme CT 06333

December 19, 1986

Dear Dan (a.k.a. Handless Wonder):

Wow, what a long strange trip it HAS been... But unfortunately, this is the last stop. Reality.   Meaning no more fun allowed, and your looks go into free-fall for the rest of your life.

Well, maybe it's not quite that bad. But it is amazing how quickly everything can change. Four months ago, we were all together at The House, happy and carefree. Now you're out in Denver working for Martin Marietta, while I'm (temporarily) back home with my parents, trying to gain some sense of direction. It's tough out here in the adult world.

After leaving Glanbury in September, I came home and took some career counseling—all those bullshit jobs I'd worked in the past simply didn't cut it.   And I realized that after four years of college, I still had no clue what to do with my life. But at any rate, I have to do something.

For the past six weeks, I've been working for a financial services company in New Haven called Spectrum Funds. It's an entry-level job, so the work, at least, is not terribly demanding. I commute to New Haven every day now; last month I bought a used Nissan Sentra for that purpose. It's a hike—about 40 miles each way. Suffice it to say that the last month and a half hasn't been terribly exciting, but I at least have a steady income.

Still, life has its compensations. As the Floor's official chronicler, I've kept in touch with most of the guys, who call me when they need someone's address, or just to let me know what's up with whom. So to keep you abreast...

Jay Levin's working on his MBA, wrapping up his first semester at Northeastern. For next summer, he's planning a trip to Israel—supposedly he has several acquaintances there, including an old girlfriend. Brandon Clark also moved to Beantown—he's living in a three-decker in Dorchester, while canvassing for Greenpeace. The job involves going door-to-door in various cities and towns, soliciting funds for their cause. (He admits he'll never get rich at it, but adds that unlike most people he's doing something he actually believes in.) He's also stayed active in the antiapartheid movement, and was pleased that Congress got up the sack to override the President's veto on South African sanctions.

Stu and Josh are still rooming together in Glanbury, working part-time at the Phillips Arena ticket office (Go Titans!). Both are still taking night classes, though God only knows how many more credits they need. Meanwhile, Pete Garrett seems to have vanished from the face of the earth since passing the bar and officially joining Craig and Marsh. My sources say that in between working a million hours a week and sleeping at his desk, he's soon scheduled to close on a house in the suburb of Manchester (by reputation, an emerging Yuppieville). As for you...well, what have you been up to lately, other than crafting weapons of mass destruction and not calling me?

Anyhow, work is not all life-draining drudgery. I have met some cool people here; lately a few of us have been going out every Friday night for Happy Hour. (Last week, two co-workers and I got up onstage to sing "Satisfaction.") However, even I've noticed that I tend to go on about the old days at Met. It's as if I've had a delayed reaction to graduating from college—until recently, everyone was still around, and not much seemed to change. But now that I'm away, I FINALLY realize that those carefree days are over, and I MISS THEM.

I did manage to get back to town once, though. This was in October, when Wally and Joanne threw a party at their new digs. But now it's just not the same. The floor really has a bunch of losers this year—all they ever seem to want to do is watch cable (which they have in the dorms now) and play with their cordless phones. I hate to say it, but I think the Sterling 4 tradition is dead.

Anyhow, the party happened to coincide with Game Six of the World Series—the infamous Game Six, no further description needed. Toward the end, we were all gathered around the TV in anticipation of the Sox' historic win...but you know how that turned out.

I'm still pissed about that game. By comparison, this made 1978 look like a Cinderella story. Bruce Hurst had actually been elected Series MVP, with Marty Barrett named Player of the Game. It's wrong to blame it all on Bill Buckner, though—he had plenty of help in blowing this one. Still, one strike away from a world championship...you can't get any closer than that, you literally CAN NOT...! (I'll just stop now before I wind up screaming again.)

Here's an item for your "Hell Freezes Over" file: Met actually DID NOT RAISE TUITION THIS WINTER. Do not adjust your set; you heard correctly. Of course, they denied that this was in any way related to the Shenford scandal; in fact the administration pointed out that costs would remain on par with those at Harvard and Yale. Still, how many other major colleges do you expect will freeze tuition for next year? (Hint: it's a round number.)

The trauma of my last excursion notwithstanding, I still hope to revisit Glanbury again soon, maybe sometime after the New Year. And I have faith that distance alone will not forever keep you from partying with us again. Until then, take care and stay in touch...

TH-TH-TH-THAT'S ALL, FOLKS!

Your Friend,

Bob S.

From the Glanbury *Wire*, January 17, 1987 (p. 1):

ECKHARDT WON'T SEEK REELECTION

By Betty Capri
Wire Staff

In a bombshell that rocked the state's political establishment and surprised even his closest aides, Governor Richard T. Eckhardt said yesterday that he would not run for a second term in 1988. The 62-year-old chief executive, whose career in state government has spanned nearly four decades, made the stunning announcement at what was expected to be a routine press briefing at the State House.

"I shall not be a candidate for reelection to this office. That decision is final and immutable," Eckhardt told reporters. "After much vacillation and soul-searching, I have concluded that this will be my only term as your governor. I have served this state long and, I believe, with fealty and diligence. I feel that I have earned the right to devote my golden years to my family." (For the full text of the governor's statement, see page 4.)

The announcement seemed certain to spark a political chain reaction as would-be successors jockey for position, while others in turn scramble to fill the lower offices vacated by gubernatorial aspirants. Analysts were quick to point out that Eckhardt's unusually early withdrawal will leave the governor a lame duck for fully half his term of office, during which time his political effectiveness will likely be compromised...

———

Together with their parents

Megan Elspeth Brunelle

and

Timothy James Fitzmaurice

request the honour of your presence
at their marriage
on Sunday, the sixth of September
Nineteen hundred and eighty-seven
at five o'clock in the afternoon
Saint Hippolytus' Church
1650 Habersham Street
Allentown, Pennsylvania

Reception
immediately following ceremony

The Wilkop Inn
123 Regina Avenue
Allentown, Pennsylvania

———

Oct. 12, 1987

Dear Chug:

Belated greetings from the big wedding. The enclosed snapshot was taken at the reception, with all of us toasting the bride and groom. We were all bummed that you couldn't make it, but I guess that's life in grad school.

The whole weekend was a blast—I flew in from Boston while the rest of the gang road-tripped it; then we all checked into a nearby TraveLodge. It was like old times, with everybody hanging out in Stu and Josh's room, drinking beer and playing cards.

Naturally, Rosemary and Marcus were there—she was actually matron of honor, as you may have gathered from her dress. Wally showed up at the rehearsal dinner in a new 'Vette and made his usual spectacular entrance, tearing into the Knights of Columbus Hall parking lot with Joanne screaming at him the whole time to slow down. At the reception, he lined up the guys in order of height and had us march up to the head table one by one to kiss the bride. (Marcus was the shortest, Josh the tallest. The former was reluctant to lead the charge at first—we had to convince him that we really would follow through, and not leave him hanging up there by himself.) He also said quite loudly that if Joanne got anywhere near the bridal bouquet, we would see some flagrant pass interference. He made quite an impression on the bride's family—I overheard Mrs. Brunelle saying at one point that, "This Wally's a strange one, isn't he?" (Megan's response: "Yes—isn't it wonderful?")

You know what I've said about weddings being the ultimate in bourgeois bullshit, with families competing in pointless displays of wealth and ostentation...well, this wasn't like that. Just a simple ceremony in the church both bride and groom grew up attending. Megan's husband is a social studies teacher at her old junior high school, located right behind the church; they met while serving on the executive board of the Allentown CYO. He seems like a decent guy, albeit on the conventional side.

After the reception, Megan insisted that we all go out dancing, and it was past 3 A.M. when the happy couple left for their honeymoon on the Jersey Shore. In their own car—no limo. (Nowadays, even high-school kids feel compelled to rent limos for their proms. I think it was Nancy Reagan's china that started all the trouble.) The rest of us went to HoJo's for one last chowdown, and it was nearly five o'clock when we arrived back at the motel. I made my 9:30 flight the next morning—just barely—thanks to a lift from Stu and Josh.

On another note, my career at Greenpeace has ended. I never did get along with my boss, the canvass director—a mincing, anally-retentive little man with receding blonde curls, and a lifer in the door-to-door business. Two months ago we got into an argument, near the end of which he remarked that his piles bled for me—whereupon I immediately concurred that emotions originated in the brain. Oh well, at least I won't have to endure any more of his long-winded stories about campaigning for Save the Dinosaurs. Since then, I've been temping for a company (ugh!) called the Ready Agency in Watertown, flitting from one short-term assignment to another. "Work" consists of such meaningful tasks as typing and filing, etc. I always knew learning the alphabet would come in handy sometime. (Seriously, this political-science degree isn't worth the toilet-paper tube it's wrapped in.)

Anyway, that's the story from Allentown. The girl we dubbed St. Megan is now an old married lady of five weeks. And being the devout Catholic she is, she'll likely end up with six or seven kids running around in short order. As destructive and irresponsible as that is, there is something comforting in the knowledge that there are people like her left in today's world…

Brandon

July 1, 1988

Dear Walmeister:

Greetings from Craig and Marsh, Attorneys and Counselors at Law. We make money the modern way: We cheat our heinies off.

(Seriously, check out this fancy letterhead. Between ourselves, I'd say the gold-embossed figure of Justice is overdoing it a tad. And not simply because justice in fact has so little bearing on the legal profession.)

This epistle comes to you direct from the cafeteria of the Federal Courts Building, following the latest continuance (postponement to you lay people) of a major client's tax case. If you never see the inside of a federal courtroom (knock on wood), it gets your attention the way the judge sits directly beneath the legend "In God We Trust." On the other hand, it beats having to call some state judge "Your Honor" with a straight face. (I assume by now you've read about our respected Chief Justice being impeached for consorting with 'ho's. Considering the fate of Sodom and Gomorrah, I'd say this place is living on stolen time.)

Well, today is my second anniversary with the firm, and the work still gives literal meaning to the expression "You learn something new every day." But I no longer feel guilty about charging people $200 an hour for my services. Not after watching Mike Tyson make $22 million for a minute and a half's work. That's more money per second than the President gets in a year!

I think I've finally found my niche, at least (or rather, the firm's found it for me). I'm doing tax work almost exclusively now. At times it can be tedious; at other times the deadline pressures are unreal. But it is steady work—the new Tax Code has made sure of that for some time to come. They've got me working "only" about 70 hours a week now; since May I've been spending the extra down time volunteering with the Dukakis campaign. I like what he's done in Massachusetts—he's the only candidate with experience in turning around a serious deficit, and that's exactly what we need now. (If you agree, why not stop by our local headquarters and give us a hand? We're located at 745 Charlton Ave., across from the Mercantile Bank Building.)

Not much in the way of news to pass along—as you know, I've been out of the loop for some time. I did hear that Debbie Grafton got married last month—after she and Frank broke up for the last time, she hooked up with another guy from one of his hoity-toity clubs, and the proverbial whirlwind courtship ensued. From what I hear, she quickly turned into Peg Bundy, rejecting the idea of working outside (or inside) the home, and throwing a hissy fit about how we blew off "her" wedding (which, unfortunately, was the same weekend as Dan Kirk's).

Out here in the 'burbs, life remains as serene and tranquil (i.e. boring) as ever. The local police blotters are full of people being arrested for underage drinking, outdoor urination, brawling, grabbing women's behinds…you get the picture. Good thing we never associated with such scum, eh? (I still can't believe we used to ride on top of those elevator cars; that shaft had more ways to die than "Dragon's Lair.")

Hey, gotta run now. Literally gotta run now; it's in the job description. My best to the little woman, and to any of the guys you may run into. Between work and the campaign I won't have an abundance of free time, but you must call my office one of these days and maybe we can do lunch. (Do me a favor—if I ever start talking like that for real, just shoot me, OK?)

Peter E. Garrett, Esq.
B.S., J.D.
(reduplication intended)

From the Bristol *Telegraph*, August 17, 1988 (p. 3):

AG LANDS JOB IN FLA. LAW FIRM

By Beth Brown

State Attorney General Michael B. Molinsky announced yesterday that he has accepted a position with a Florida civil litigation firm, and will not seek to be reappointed as the state's chief law enforcement officer. In an exclusive interview with the Telegraph, Molinsky expressed no regret at leaving his post, while criticizing the state's political climate in unusually harsh language.

"I've simply had it with all the crooked dealing that goes on here," Molinsky observed. "In the beginning I reasoned that it was the sick who needed a doctor, but after fifteen years I no longer assume the patient wants to be cured." The attorney general added that he was "not even tempted" when Republican Party insiders encouraged him to run for governor earlier this year.

"It's one thing to talk of instilling reform," Molinsky said. "But you cannot change the basic character of the people."

Molinsky said that he would assume full partnership in the 20-member Tampa firm of Downs, Yates and Corey effective Jan. 1, 1989. He declined to divulge his new salary.

During his eight-year tenure, Molinsky has won bipartisan praise for diligence and impartiality in the pursuit of justice. However, he has been criticized for his handling of the 1985 investigation of fugitive former Metropolitan University president Fortin Shenford, who reportedly absconded with millions of dollars in fraudulently gained real estate profits. Information leaks from Molinsky's office have been blamed for alerting Shenford to his pending indictment and allowing him to flee to Europe, where he is believed to remain at large...

11/14/1988

Sir Peter:

'Sup, Legalman? How the law biz be going? (I know, you're probably busting your hump to convince the Supreme Court of the error of its ways while trying to save innocents from frying. But if you've got a quick nanosecond...)

I have to tell you, I am heartily sorry your man lost. I'm still pissed off about the campaign—this one really hit a new low. I wonder what it says about us that Americans will back even a dirty fighter over a nonfighter. Oh well, "facts are stupid things." (Forget I said that—I'm not going to pick on an invalid.)

I still can't believe Bush made it. I remember that debate in Nashua when Reagan took his milk money; I thought that had finished him for all time. Gotta give the Bushman credit, though—the kinder and gentler thing was right on target. So far this decade, we've evolved from Leo Buscaglia to Morton Downey, Jr. If all this progress keeps up, we'll be back in the caves before we know it.

Closer to home, Joanne's between jobs right now. No, really; she starts a new gig at Raytheon the first of the month. But for now she's milking this free time, just chillin' around the house and watching a good deal of television. She loves "Roseanne" ("Finally, a show portraying the American family the way it really is"). Myself, I prefer "The Wonder Years." And sometimes, I'll watch Tracey Ullman for the cartoons—that spike-haired kid seriously cracks me up.

You will note my reticence about my own work situation. You may take it that no news is good news. (Yes, I'm still at GE, bringing good things to life, etc.) And now that that's out of the way...

So it'll be Poppy and Woody for the next four years. Should be good for a few yuks at least. (Save those "President Quayle" buttons; they'll be worth something if he ever does get in.)

Mutagenically yours,

Wally

P.S. Have you noticed how much (and how fittingly) Roger Ailes looks like Alfred Hitchcock?

From the *Encyclopædia Britannica* (1989 edition) (Micropædia, Vol. 10):

Shenford, Fortin C(harles) (b. Feb. 26, 1922, Cincinnati, Ohio – disappeared Apr. 10, 1985, Glanbury), forceful and charismatic president of Metropolitan University, Glanbury, whose transformation of the school into an institution of world renown was eclipsed by his ruthless authoritarianism, and by his criminal exploitation of his post for personal gain.

A prodigious young scholar, Shenford matriculated at the University of Louisville at the age of 16. Transferring to Harvard for his junior year, he took his medical degree in 1949, and for a decade thereafter remained as a neuropsychiatric research specialist, winning international acclaim for his studies on brain waves. He accepted an appointment as dean of Metropolitan's School of Medicine in 1961, and was named president of the university the following year.

As president, Shenford was lauded for his improvement of Metropolitan's academic programs, while drawing equally widespread criticism for his tyrannical excesses. During his administration, standards for tenure and admissions were raised, and the university's endowment fund grew from six million dollars to 185 million, while its net worth more than decupled.

Shenford's remarkable accomplishments, however, were counterpoised by his harsh autocracy. He dismissed scores of faculty critics, and froze the salaries of numerous others. He frequently kept dissidents under the surveillance of private detectives while tapping their office telephones, resorting to blackmail and intimidation when necessary to achieve his ends. In 1970, he narrowly averted dismissal, retaining the support of a sufficient faction of the university's Board of Overseers to block his removal. The subsequent resignations of many anti-Shenford members allowed his supporters to gain control of the board, and by 1984 Shenford was able to engineer his own election to the chairmanship while continuing to function as president. In this dual capacity, he attained absolute control over every aspect of university operations, unhampered by an increasingly marginalized opposition.

By early 1985, Shenford had emerged as a likely Republican candidate for the U.S. Senate, following the death of Democratic incumbent James Camp. But in March of that year, he was shot and seriously wounded in an assassination attempt by Christina Ferris, the daughter of a faculty opponent whom he had framed for vehicular homicide. A subsequent investigation of his activities by the state attorney general disclosed numerous documents and videotapes directly implicating Shenford in the framing of the elder Ferris, and in a series of fraudulent real estate transactions from which he had personally realized millions of dollars while pledging the university's credit on his own behalf. The tapes also revealed that Shenford had known of Camp's terminal illness at a time when the general public did not, and had secretly built a campaign organization in anticipation of a race for the vacant seat, in violation of election laws. Alerted through news leaks to his pending indictment by a state grand jury, Shenford fled the country and took refuge in Europe.

February 17, 1989

Dear Stu and Josh:

Great to hear from you. Especially the news that you guys got your diplomas last month; congratulations. It must be so satisfying after all those years of hard work.

Sorry, couldn't resist. In any event, you're not alone—from what I can see, colleges have just about priced themselves out of the market these days, with part-time studies the only option for many. Now, when Bluto says "Seven years of college...down the drain," it's not as funny as it used to be.

My own work situation is going well. Though at this time of year, I look forward with dread to the upcoming tax season. Last spring they had me working so many hours, I could have used an egg timer instead of an alarm clock to get up in the morning. That's what I get for taking a salaried position.

Rosemary has her own business now. Since last fall she's been working as a freelance computer consultant, with a small but growing client base. My company— excuse me, my *firm*—has her come in twice a week to help out with tech support. She remains casual as ever, not that I'm complaining—seeing her in jeans or sweats makes me look forward to coming home.

Yet not all is sunny on the professional front. The economy seems to have returned to earth of late, and there are rumors of cutbacks within the firm. We're both keeping our fingers crossed. (Seriously, you had to wonder what would happen when the bills from all that mid-80's debt began coming due. These next few years could be a bit of a letdown.)

We got a call from Adam last month, right after the holidays. No surprise. It had only been three years since the last verified Conway sighting. As you know, he dropped out of SUNY after one semester, and is now working as an assistant manager at CVS in Cheektowaga. He's engaged to an old girlfriend named Eileen Summers, but the nuptials won't take place for a while yet. ("Don't make any plans for Columbus Day weekend, 1991," he told us.) We also called Brandon in Boston recently, and spent two hours listening to his lamentations on a variety of cultural ills: the "dumbing down" of Newsweek magazine; reduction of conversation to bubbleheaded misuse of the word "like,"; and our whole dysfunctional, misanthropic society in general. (I think he's still temping over there—he really didn't say much about himself.)

On another note, I may have added public speaking to my duties at work (God forbid). Some weeks ago, I was "asked" to give a presentation before a group of clients on the double-declining balance method. (Please don't ask; I really don't feel like going through it again.) Despite preparing like mad, I was still scared spitless. On the morning of my scheduled execution, I woke up at 5 A.M. and couldn't get back to sleep. Finally, Rosemary made some Pop-Tarts and suggested I try my spiel out on her. After an hour she stopped me, pointing out that I had just delivered my 20-minute talk three times over. In the end, I emerged unscathed...not that I'm looking forward to an encore performance.

But Rosemary's really great that way. Despite kicking my behind playing Horse on a regular (read: uniform) basis, she gives me the assurance I've always lacked. For once in my life, someone believes in me and gives me unconditional support. Until she came along, I never imagined such a thing was possible.

Ah, well—time to hit the hay now. It's almost 11 (P.M.), and the egg timer beckons. Rosemary sends her congratulations and best wishes. Both of you, be well— and if you're ever in the Hartford area, give us a shout...

Sincerely,

Marcus

August 30, 1989

Dear Megan:

I just got your letter an hour ago—congratulations! I can't believe you're going to be a mom, that's such great news. You and Tim must be so excited!

Wow. No similar earth-shattering news on this end. In fact, there really isn't much to tell. Marcus is still plugging away at Bradley and Stearns, while I enjoy the freedom of working on my own. He's on track for a senior associateship next year, and word is they'll push us to join the local country club. But I don't see any impractically expensive designer clothes in this girl's future—believe it or not, some of the partners' wives will spend $1500 on a spring outfit and think it's something to brag about.

(Then again, look who's talking about fashion. Marcus says I'd still be going around barefoot if Chug and those guys hadn't kept dumping broken glass everywhere.)

Speaking of the broken-bottle bandit, we got a letter from him last month. He finished his masters in June, and will become an instructor in the English Department while working on his Ph.D. So starting this fall, it's Professor Chug (!) A sobering thought—but at the same time, I couldn't stop laughing.

Stu and Josh called the other day. They're still rooming together on the West Side, having renewed their lease for another year. They've been back at the Hilton since May, this time working in the Reservations Department. (Both are seeing stewardesses they met on the job.) There was some bad news, though: Dave Logan got laid off in March, and has been pounding the pavement since. He had a good job with the Mercantile Bank, but they ran into trouble over some bad real estate loans, and half of his department wound up being eliminated. It's scary when you think about it, a guy with a master's degree unable to find work.

My father's retiring next July. He says 27 years in the Corps is enough for anyone, and Mom likes the idea of being able to settle down somewhere. They'll be moving to Cocoa Beach, Fla. (they wanted to stay in Hawaii, but the housing costs are outrageous). Dad plans to take the civil service exam and get a job working for the state—after 10 or 15 years of that, he figures he can retire for good.

You remember my brother Bill—he graduated from Iowa in May. The skinny little runt I used to beat up the neighborhood bullies for made All-American in his last two years on the wrestling team, and had a shot at the 1992 Olympics in Barcelona, Spain before a shoulder injury ended his chances. He's now working as a security guard in Des Moines.

Belated thanks for the nice anniversary card. I can't believe it's already been four years. These days, some marriages don't even last that long—it's really sad, what we've come to. Around the office, single girls talk of "relationships" in terms of "getting the rock," or of "commitments" that don't seem to mean much. (While the men talk of prenuptial agreements as if they were the cornerstone of civilization.) I thank God for Marcus. When I come home, I know he'll be there, not just maybe be there unless he found someone more attractive today. (And it wouldn't take much.)

I almost forgot to mention this, but lately we've been talking about BUYING A HOUSE. (Marcus's firm tacitly encourages home ownership; they consider it a sign of stability.) So far we've only scanned a few listings, but it seems we're at a crossroads point in our lives, with so many big decisions ahead.

My folks say these are the best years of our lives. Yet I sometimes think what I wouldn't give to relive that wonderful year when we lived in what everyone said was the worst part of town, swinging Wiffle Ball bats indoors at all hours, sleeping on the floor, sending out for pizzas and Cokes, listening to the radio on snow days like children for our school cancellations and high-threeing my husband when our code numbers were called, having friends drop in whenever they wanted to...that was the life.

I think I understand now what has kept us all

faithfully in touch for so long. In truth we're more than just old floormates, more than just friends.

We're a family. We grew up together.

Well, I've probably bored you to death by now, so I'll close until next time. Again, hugs and congratulations to you both!

Love,

Rosemary

P.S. Have you picked out any names yet?

December 28, 1989

Greetings, Comrade Clark!

BREAKING NEWS: As of now, our Beloved Leader is officially an old man. That's right—today, Wally hits the big three-o. (He and Joanne also celebrated their 10th anniversary last month; no word on whether any marriage plans are in the works.)

Speaking of the big guy, I partied with him Thanksgiving weekend in New Hampshire, at one of his Outward Bound reunions—kick ass. He truly hasn't changed at all. Despite his impending geriatricism, he hasn't yet given up on Jell-O sucking contests, or taking leaks on the sidewalk. We also had fun making crank calls to some of those scuzzball lawyers who are always advertising on TV these days. Hanging with him and his friends, I could almost believe myself again living in an age before fax machines, when people wore Levi's instead of Guess? jeans, not everyone was in therapy, and AIDS was unknown. When J.R. Ewing was still considered a bad guy, women were still liberated, and Elvis was still dead. Before Wall Street became impervious to economic decline, war regained its glamour, and liberalism grew cynical in defeat. God love him, he is the one constant in a world that changes too fast to keep up with. I hope I hold up as well, when it comes my time to walk the plank.

I ran into Sorenson the other day, on the Cross-State Turnpike. Obviously we couldn't say much, but he seems to be prospering nicely at DaddyCo—these days, he's driving a red Porsche with a bumper sticker that says THIS IS MY OTHER CAR. His ex and her husband are also back in town, having recently bought a condo in Bramhall Place. (It may have been just sour grapes, but when Frank called me later he said, "I give it three years, tops. I never saw Deb as the marrying kind...at least not the staying-married kind." This from a guy who dated her off and on for almost five years.)

Unfortunately, however, these study breaks have become increasingly anomalous. In fact, I've sent Wally my regrets—I won't be attending his much-anticipated New Year's party, the holiday season notwithstanding. Being antisocial, it seems, is just part of the Ph.D. grind. (Some of the required seminars are so brutal that teaching my classes seems a skate by comparison.) I also have to learn—or, more accurately, master—Latin, German and Italian, don't ask me why. Just to make it harder, that's why.

To help broaden my language horizons, I've begun reading some foreign newspapers and magazines, *e.g.* France's *Le Monde* and Germany's *Der Spiegel*. While looking through these, I actually found an item or two on the Shenford affair—the European press has taken quite an interest in the case, his identity and whereabouts being frequent subjects of speculation. The latest theory, though, centers on an elderly man in Salt Lake City who committed suicide by morphine injection last winter, around the time of the Bush inauguration. According to sources, the man had lived quietly in a posh condominium for six months under the name of Frank Arthur. The body was cremated before any autopsy or investigation could be had, and his identity remains uncertain. (I mention this only in passing, since it's as close as we may ever come to learning the real story.)

Alas, already the symptoms of decline are upon me. Last call at Jokers has given way to watching only the first half of "Monday Night Football," and to save my life I couldn't name one tune on this week's Top 40. And at this stage, I probably never will know what was in those "Surprise Packages" they always advertised in comic books. Seriously, where did my youth go?

Getting back to the topic of how the world has changed lately…well, how about the way things have changed? At this writing, another dictator is poised to bite the dust in Panama—it has not been a good year for tyrants. Before Noriega, there was Stroessner in Paraguay, Khomeini in Iran, and now Ceausescu in Romania. And to top it off, THE BERLIN WALL HAS COME DOWN, and it appears Gerald Ford may be vindicated. Who knew the man was a decade ahead of his time?

On the homefront, the change has been more of a mixed bag. In recent years, people (this writer included) have gotten smarter about such things as drunk driving, drug use and (reluctantly) sex. But they have also become more cynical, paranoid and alienated, and in general one hell of a lot less likable. It's curious, the way we've become more evolved and more bestial at the same time.

Anyway, this is it for now. I won't have much time to write from here on, nor do I anticipate getting away anytime soon. But do think of me once in a while at WKRP, as I shall do likewise. And please, give my regards to your venerable host this Sunday night…

Warren W. Allen, Jr.
"Chug"

From "Remaking Metropolitan" (*Alumni Quarterly*, Vol. 1 - Winter 1990):

When Elizabeth Kerr became President of the University in the spring of 1985, she assumed a dual mandate from the Board of Overseers: to build on the institution's past successes, and to restore morale on campus following the worst scandal in its history.

Today, nearly five years later, Metropolitan is again flourishing, with 20,000 full-time students, and a stellar faculty that includes six Nobel laureates. Financially, Met appears more robust than ever, with an endowment of $337 million and a net worth which recently surpassed the billion-dollar mark.

"From an academic standpoint, the University's fundamentals were sound. Though in the beginning, our primary goal was to restore trust between faculty and administration," Kerr says while relaxing in the living room of the president's mansion on Raleigh Street. A deceptively low-key woman with auburn hair, the 52-year-old former Law School dean shares the home with her husband James, a practicing dentist in Kent; their adult daughter Liz, a Ph.D. candidate in American History; son-in-law James Harris, a psychology instructor at Reigate College; and Francis, the family's ten-year-old chocolate Labrador. ("A perpetual student," Kerr describes her only child with mock exasperation.)

"To guard against the abuses of the past, our Board of Overseers made some fundamental changes in governance, strengthening financial disclosure rules and conflict-of-interest policies, for instance," she recalls. "But mainly it was about changing the tone on campus, putting aside the antagonism that existed before."

Toward that end, Kerr met extensively with faculty members and students, engaging them in a way previous administrations rarely had. "To me, leadership is about building consensus," she explains. "And while the decisions are not made by plebiscite, the various constituencies on campus know that they will receive the courtesy of a fair hearing." This more inclusive approach, compared with what some have called the paranoia and secrecy of the prior administration, has been instrumental to the University's success in overcoming its recent past.

Among other advances, Kerr cites the doubling of Met's research grant funding, with parallel increases in foundation gifts and alumni donations; and extensive improvements to the physical plant. Recent months have witnessed groundbreaking ceremonies for a new $38 million computer center on Alston Boulevard; and the dedication of the University Science Complex, a $150 million three-building project featuring state-of-the-art physics laboratories. Yet the changed atmosphere on campus remains her administration's signature accomplishment.

"At one time, the student publications policy forbade University funding of such projects, and effectively barred them from campus," says Dean Marc Heald of the College of Arts and Sciences. "This year, we have seven active student journals, including literary magazines, critical reviews, even essay collections. Since these are published under University auspices, we have faculty advisors in place, but the students mostly set their own editorial policies." (Met's longtime student newspaper, the *Guardian*, has thus far elected to maintain its independence.) Enhanced freedom of expression has further bred an increase in activism, though Kerr cautions against "a tendency toward extremism" in the name of diversity.

"As we know, Western culture has recently come under assault on college campuses, its defenders often vilified as being racist, sexist or Eurocentric, according to the epithet *du jour*," she notes. "Here, we emphasize that artistic and intellectual expression transcend such artificial boundaries as gender or nationality. The novels of a Jane Austen, or the poetry of an Omar Khayyam, have endured because of their intrinsic excellence, rather than the identity of their authors. And ignoring merit for the sake of diversity, to me, represents the height of intellectual fraud."

Kerr feels, though, that Metropolitan is uniquely positioned to resist such trends. "Having known repression in the recent past, we understand the value of academic freedom," she says. "We will not exchange one form of tyranny for another..."

The party was over, Wally and Joanne quietly standing in the doorway of their first-floor laundry room. Where Pete Garrett slept on an air mattress, an Indian blanket covering his fetal form.

Hours ago, champagne corks had popped, and cheers filled the living room as the widescreen set flashed "1990," the crowd in Times Square crooning "Auld Lang Syne," the party's guests boozily humming along.

Tonight they had come from across town, and from across the country. They'd come alone, with spouses, with significant and quasi-significant others. Frank Sorenson had arrived in his red Porsche, the Troll in his ancient Plymouth Duster with the bumper sticker warning that IF I DON'T GET LAID SOON, SOMEONE'S GOING TO GET HURT.

While Bill Kaplan made the rounds with a rented Camcorder, wife Ellen exhibited snapshots of their ten-month-old twin boys. Megan Fitzgerald, six months pregnant, had flaunted her impending maternity for the camera. ("Leaving childhood behind forever, only to experience it again.")

As others toasted the New Year, Marcus struggled with the cork on a bottle of Dom Perignon. After a lengthy battle the cork at last popped free, flying across the room and shattering one of Wally's Christmas ornaments.

"Nice shot, Gilligan." Josh had smiled good-naturedly, one arm about the waist of his new girlfriend, a tall strawberry-blonde named Sue Ashenbrenner.

The guests then stood through a Wax Museum, the latest in a series of Last Official WM's. With the passing of midnight, a small number adjourned upstairs to smoke weed. But not many. Not anymore.

In the decade's inaugural hour, designated drivers switched to fruit punch or ginger ale, others continuing to get crocked. Those not able to drive could crash here—to his friends, Wally's Bed and Breakfast remained open. But none had passed out tonight, or even been sick. Not anymore.

Shortly after 2 A.M., the exodus began. Marcus and Rosemary left in their new Geo for the modest suburban Hartford home they'd purchased weeks before. The spare bedroom would become a nursery in late 1991, following their son's birth.

Saying his farewells, Dave Logan returned to his Ball Street apartment, to rebegin the Endless Job Search. With wistful sincerity, Brandon Clark thanked his hosts before heading back to Dorchester and further temporary employment, and weekends falling asleep to *Tales From the Darkside*.

Wally looked again at Pete's slumbering countenance, the white dome of his ex-roommate's forehead. Tonight he'd noticed a few receding hairlines among his guests, with one or two sporting a touch of gray. Now, thanks to Sy Sperling, baldness was considered a disfiguring disease, with early detection and treatment essential.

"He looks so innocent when he's sleeping." Joanne smiled as she and Wally lingered in the doorway.

"Just like an altar boy," Wally concurred. Their wedding invitations would go out two years hence, with her promotion to section manager.

After tonight, the guys and their girls would get together perhaps once or twice yearly. Between reunion weekends there would be more weddings, then children's christenings and bar mitzvahs as they entered a new millennium and were forced to confront their own mortality, a bogeyman once mocked from afar. Fleetingly, he thought of the impersonal, long-forgotten notice from the Housing Department—now tucked away in Pete's scrapbook—which had brought them together. It had all started with those small bits of paper, the random output of a callous computer a decade ago…

Wally clicked off the room light.

"Sleep tight, guy," he whispered into the darkness. And, taking Joanne's arm, accompanied her slowly upstairs.